Maid of
the Sea

Maid of the Sea

Janet Thomas

ROBERT HALE · LONDON

© Janet Thomas 2005
First published in Great Britain 2005

ISBN 0 7090 7954 0

Robert Hale Limited
Clerkenwell House
Clerkenwell Green
London EC1R 0HT

2 4 6 8 10 9 7 5 3 1

Typeset in 10/12¾pt Plantin
by Derek Doyle & Associates, Shaw Heath.
Printed in Great Britain by St Edmundsbury Press,
Bury St Edmunds, Suffolk.
Bound by Woolnough Bookbinding Ltd.

For Jemma, Amy, Jenny, Robbie and Rebecca, with love.

Chapter One

'Don't you know me, Tom?' Morwenna had been coming out of the post office when he passed her without a sign of recognition and walked on, apparently deep in thoughts of his own. As she called his name, however, he turned on his heel and looked back.

'Morwenna Pengelly!' he gasped. His mouth dropped open with such amazement that she burst out laughing.

'You could look a bit more pleased to see me!' she teased. But she was almost as amazed, for the thin, intense boy Morwenna had known when they ran carefree on the beach together as children had now become a man. Tom was wearing the red-stained moleskin trousers and coarse shirt of a working miner, and carried his 'croust'-bag and distinctive hard hat with a stub of candle attached. Hard physical work had broadened his shoulders and roughened the hand he now held out to her. She slipped her own gloved one into his palm and watched as it disappeared.

'How you've changed!' he said, still staring at her.

'I've grown up, Tom,' she murmured. 'We both have. I'm nineteen now.' With a start she realized that he must be almost twenty-one. Morwenna looked deeper into the dark eyes she remembered so well, and her heart turned over. Adult though he might be, one thing would never change. To Morwenna, Tom would always be her childhood hero.

'I've just finished being "finished".' She smiled as they fell into step and strolled down the street between the rows of granite cottages. The tiny front gardens were bright with summer annuals, and as Morwenna paused to stroke a tabby cat which was reclining full length in the sun on top of a wall, it turned over and stuck all four paws in the air. 'I only arrived back today. The school made us come back early from the continent because of all the unrest there.' Her expression was serious now as she turned towards him. 'They say there'll be a war now that the

7

Archduke Ferdinand has been murdered. Oh Tom . . .' Morwenna's face had paled. 'We were there, you know – in Sarajevo – when it happened. I actually saw the assassination. We were in the street, watching the procession—'

'You were *there?*' Tom stared at her, his face a picture of astonishment. Morwenna supposed it must seem remarkable to him that a young woman from such a remote Cornish town as St Just should have been present at the making of history in a place he had never heard of.

'I shall never forget it.' Morwenna's eyes were far away, fixed on the distant sea but seeing the remembered carnage. 'This fellow came bursting out of the crowd just as the cavalcade was drawing up in front of us and shot them point-blank – both the Archduke and the Duchess as well. Oh, the blood! Tom, it was everywhere, and the screams – I still hear them in nightmares, and see . . . it was indescribable.' She raised both hands to her face and Tom put a comforting arm around her shoulders as he had always done as a child when she was hurt.

Now she turned to cling to him in the old way and had buried her head in his chest before she caught sight of the parasol on her arm and realized with a start that they were no longer children, but man and woman grown. Morwenna tore herself away and straightened her hat, unwilling to acknowledge the way her body had reacted with a dramatic lurch to Tom's embrace. She looked into his face to see if he had felt it as well, but he was drawing away and his expression was unreadable.

To cover the moment she gave a little laugh. 'I'm still thinking of you as a big brother, Tom,' she lied. 'That's what you were to me when we were small, remember? And Jack and Chrissie too were like the siblings I never had. You must tell me how they are and what they're both doing. I've got such a lot of catching up to do. It's been almost two years since I was home last.'

She could hear herself talking too fast and was conscious of Tom's restrained and totally polite reply. 'Is it really as long as that?'

They had come to the fork in the road where their ways parted and as they paused for a moment Tom said, 'I've just come off core. I'll be going down to the cove after I've changed. Come too if you like and I'll give you all the local news then.' He looked pointedly at her cream-coloured kid boots and lace-trimmed gown.

'I'd love to,' Morwenna replied as she followed his glance. 'But I must change too, out of these travelling clothes. I haven't even unpacked yet but I can't wait to get down to the sea again – I've missed it so much. So, yes, I will.'

Tom's face lit up with the sudden grin that she remembered so well, transforming his serious features into the small boy of old, and Morwenna smiled back in relief. Maybe they had not drifted as far apart as she had feared. 'I'll meet you outside our place in an hour.' He raised a hand in acknowledgement as they parted and Morwenna made her way towards Rayle House, home of her aunt and uncle, where she had lived since the age of twelve.

Coming back here and meeting Tom so unexpectedly had brought back all her memories in such a flood of mixed feelings that she had to bite her lip to keep the tears from falling. But there was the footpath to the cove – and there was no way she could pass the turning without taking a look at the cottage. Morwenna's feet made no sound as she ran over the fields, over the springy turf, towards the sea and back into childhood. . . .

'Mor – stop it!' screamed Chrissie as another shower of salt water sprayed over her. 'I'm getting drenched!'

Morwenna giggled and ran before her friend could retaliate. Out beyond the tumble of rocks in the cove, she and the other children were playing at the edge of the waves, and she had hauled up her skirt and pinafore in both hands, the better to kick water at her shrieking companions. Her boots and black stockings had been discarded beyond the high-tide line, and her hat flew out behind her as did her hair, a thick and springing chestnut mop, rebelling against the restraint of its ribbon bow. Fleeing from the next advancing wave, Morwenna glanced up and saw a figure leaning out of the open casement window of the cottage, which was perched on a rocky shelf just above the beach.

'There's Gramp,' she called out as she raised a hand in acknowledgement. 'I've got to go.' She shook out her skirts, smoothed down her pinafore and gathered up her boots in one deft movement. On the horizon the fiery orange ball of the sun was sinking behind the Brisons, two huge rocks standing offshore like sentinels. They had claimed many an unfortunate ship, in spite of the Longships lighthouse away to their left. A bank of grey cloud was slowly draining it of brightness, but above the cloud bank the sky retained its colours, where great swathes of apricot and lemon were fanning out into infinity.

'Coming down again tomorrow, are you?' Tom asked as the four turned to head up the pebbly beach towards the slipway.

'Of course,' Morwenna replied. 'I shall always be here.'

They had stopped to tug their boots on over damp and sticky feet, and for a moment Morwenna sat motionless, then finally said as she returned to her struggle with a knotted lace, 'I was just thinking of the first time we all met. Do you remember, Tom? When I was paddling and fell in that pool?' She glanced over her shoulder. The boy grunted and reddened slightly as he turned his face away to reach for his other boot. Morwenna's own expression was sombre. 'I really thought I was going to drown that day. I went down three times, you know? And there were all these bubbles streaming around me and I couldn't breathe . .' With one boot still unlaced, her hands had stilled and she was back in the night-mare again.

'Aw, Sheep's Pool isn't *that* deep,' Tom replied. 'You'd have been all right.'

'If it's deep enough for a sheep to drown in, then so I could have done,' Morwenna retorted, her eyes on the boy's dark curly head as she recalled the lean, lithe shape which had come diving from the rocks above and effortlessly cut a swathe through the water. Then seizing a fistful of her clothes he had dragged her back towards the edge of the pool, then out of it, when they had both collapsed together on a warm, flat rock.

That had been her first meeting with Tom, whom she had hero-worshipped ever since. He had taken her on as a kind of surrogate sister and treated her as he did his own siblings, keeping an eye on them all at school and just happening to be around at the first sign of any trouble in the playground.

Now Tom nodded as he skimmed a last couple of pebbles with expert ease and watched them bounce and skip over the crests of the waves. 'We'll be by the cave, same as today.'

'I can't come tomorrow,' Chrissie put in. She was as fair as her brother was dark, with bubbly curls and round blue eyes. 'I've got dancing prac-tice after school. You know – Miss Barnes is drilling us for the pageant next week. It's to do with the new king – King George V, and the corona-tion. Did you know she's given Mor a speaking part. . .?'

Lost in her dreams, the grown Morwenna could hear their childish voices still, echoing out of the past as the little ghosts of their former selves scrambled heedlessly over the boulders. . . .

As they came to the top of the slip, Chrissie, gazing up at the white-washed cottage tucked in a nook of the cliff, remarked, 'Your Grampa Eli's some clever, Mor, isn't he? Building your house up there like that, I mean.'

'That's because he was in the navy – the merchant navy. Sailors are always handy. They have to be, to look after themselves on board ship, see?' Morwenna reached for her straggling hair ribbon and dragged it back into place.

Chrissie scuffed a toe and said with her head lowered, 'Don't you ever mind not having a proper family, Mor – you know, like other people?' Looking up, she turned her wide blue gaze on Morwenna. One of the most disconcerting things about Chrissie was the way she said exactly what she was thinking, outright and with total honesty, and expected everyone else to do the same. There was no place in her mind for subtlety, and the concept of tact was completely unknown to her.

'Shut it, Chrissie, and mind your own business,' Tom growled, stuffing his hands deep in his pockets as he reddened with embarrassment.

'It's all right,' Morwenna replied. 'You can't miss what you've never had. Gramp and I get along fine as we are. And there are always Aunt Phoebe and the cousins up at Rayle House.' She pulled a face and shrugged. 'If we want company.'

'It was some funny when we first heard in the village that you were coming, though,' went on the irrepressible Chrissie. 'Five years ago, it must have been, because I know I was only six then, same as you, and I remember thinking that you would have brown skin because Ma said you came from India. I felt let down when you turned out to be the same as us.'

Morwenna giggled. 'Of course I am. Only we had to go to India because Papa was a soldier. . . .' Her face fell and a hard lump rose in her throat as she tried to remember their faces, Papa and Mama, but it was all too long ago. 'They died . . . when I was two. They had fever. But my ayah took me to her home up in the hills and saved me.'

Morwenna paused. A fragment of memory had come to her, like a door which had been opened just enough to catch a glimpse of the room beyond. She heard the slap of sandals on a wooden floor, saw the embroidered hem of a brilliant pink sari sweeping alongside. And she was looking up into a round, dark face which was always smiling. . . .

'But they called me "Morwenna" because in Cornish it means "sea-maiden". So I'm as Cornish as you are, see?' She skipped ahead for a few steps.

'What's an ayah?' asked Jack, hands thrust in his pockets as he caught her up.

'It's a nursemaid,' Morwenna replied. 'An Indian nursemaid. Like a nanny.'

Jack whistled through his teeth. 'Coo, you must have had some money to have a nanny,' he said, round-eyed.

'Aren't you lucky to live nearly on the beach, though?' Chrissie said with feeling, her eyes on the steep climb home which faced the rest of them. The children dawdled their way between the coloured boats drawn up on the slip and were dragging their feet as they began to climb the hill.

'Come us on, Chrissie, you know what a fuss Ma'll make if we're late back,' Tom urged as he looked back and jerked his head at his sister. Jack, as quiet as his sister was garrulous, had gone racing on ahead to the top and through the clitter of old mine workings, from where he turned to wave an arm to hurry them up. Morwenna raised a hand and climbed slowly up the meandering path to the cottage.

Two-storeyed, it was built low, hunched beneath the overhang of the cliff with its roof of grey slate pulled well down over the eaves like a tea-cosy over the pot, and its chimneys were on a level with the top road. The windows were small, the glass thick enough to withstand the winter gales that screamed in from the Atlantic with scourging, salt-laden breath.

But the spring weather was soft and balmy at the moment and the door was standing open as Morwenna reached it. In winter, however, the thick cob walls absorbed the noise of wind and sea, and the interior was always warm from the Cornish range which burned day and night.

'I'm home, Gramp,' Morwenna called as she stepped inside the narrow, slate-flagged passage which continued into the kitchen.

'All right, my handsome,' Eli replied, lighting his pipe from the range as Morwenna put her glowing face around the door.

'I'm hungry,' Morwenna announced, tossing her hat on to a chair. 'We had some fun down on the beach. Tom said he'll teach me how to dive in the holidays.'

'Aye. Well, there's plenty of bread and cheese in the cupboard. As you should know,' he said, smiling. 'You can bake a loaf as good as anybody now.'

'You must have taught me well, Gramp.' She skipped across the room. 'Do you want a cup of tea?'

'Yes, I will, maid, thanks.' Eli puffed at the pipe. 'Come over here and sit beside me while we have it,' he said, moving to the settle beside the fire and patting the space next to him. Morwenna slid into it and he encircled her with one big, warm arm.

'I've been thinking how much you're getting to look like your mama now that you're growing up,' said the old man, lifting Morwenna's chin with a finger and looking into her face. 'She was my little girl once, my Annabel, and you and she are as alike as two peas.' Morwenna smiled and cuddled closer to his side. 'And I've got something here what did used to belong to her.' He felt in a pocket with his free hand and drew forth a small box. 'I reckon you're old enough to have this now.' He placed it in Morwenna's hand. 'Here, you open it, maid.'

The child carefully lifted the lid and her eyes widened as she gave a gasp of delight. A silver pendant and chain, intricately fashioned with a scrollwork design of delicate leaves and flowers, nestled among cotton-wool padding in the velvet-lined box.

'That's what your papa gave to her just before they got married. A love token, like. He had it specially made by a craftsman in India. She always wore it after that – can't remember her ever taking it off. It's a locket, see, but the catch and the hinges are so hidden in the making of it that you'd never know you can open it up. It do have their pictures inside, take a look.'

Morwenna did so and gazed in fascination at the tiny photographs, then raised her face and kissed the old man's wrinkled cheek. 'Ooh, it's *lovely*, Gramp – thank you,' she said with a smile like sunshine. 'I'll take great care of it. Can I put it on?'

'Don't see why not, my handsome – here, I'll fasten it up for you.' His thick fingers fumbled with the tiny clasp but at last it was done. Morwenna smoothed it down over her pinafore and hardly heard what Gramp went on to say.

'Yes, well.' He cleared his throat. 'Now then, I've been talking to your Aunt Phoebe, maid. She came to see me one day when you were at school.'

Morwenna looked trustingly up into his tanned and crinkled face and stroked his bushy beard with a small hand. 'And?'

'She and I had a chat about your future. You see, maid, you're fast grow-ing up. Nearly twelve now, aren't you?' Morwenna nodded as she felt a stab of foreboding deep down inside her. 'And she thinks . . . er . . . and I think as well, of course, that it's time you was learning all the things that young ladies should know, at a school that would teach you those things, see.'

Morwenna frowned. 'But I go to school *now*, Gramp.'

The old man cleared his throat which seemed to be constricted again, and added gently, 'But this would be a . . . um . . . boarding school. The one what your cousins do go to.' He opened the door of the range to throw a billet of wood on to the fire. 'Oh, I know that your Aunt Phoebe do put on a few airs and graces. Ever since she married Arthur and went up in the world she've looked down on we a bit. But her heart's in the right place and she's only thinking of what's best for you.'

He turned back to meet Morwenna's stony stare and went on, 'The school would not only teach you lessons, but things like manners and how to behave in company, how to mix with other people and ... um ... be a lady.' With a child's acute perception Morwenna could tell that the old man was feeling uncomfortable as he looked away and twisted his hands together in his lap. 'You see, my handsome, I've taught you all I can, and we've been as happy as sand-boys together, haven't us? But you have to think about growing up now, and there's ... womanly things that are better learned from other women. And as you haven't got no Mama, nor no sister either, to instruct you. . . .'

Morwenna jumped up and looked accusingly at him. 'You want to send me away, you mean, don't you?' she shouted, stamping a foot, her face reddening and the tears rising to her eyes.

Eli's voice cracked as he answered softly, 'Oh, child, I don't want to. Never, never think that for one minute—'

But Morwenna hardly heard him, so great was her pain. 'Well, if *you* don't want to and *I* don't want to . . .' She gulped back her tears as she spread pleading hands out to her grandfather.

'It's what's best for you, maid,' said Eli dully. 'For your future. After I'm ... when I ... well, I'm an old man and I shan't be here for ever, see, maid. . . .'

'Oh Gramp – *no*, don't talk like that!' Morwenna sank to her knees on the hearth rug and flung herself into his arms. 'And another thing – if I'm away at school, who's going to look after *you*?' she sobbed.

Eli stroked her hair and looked stolidly into the fire. 'It'll only be for the term-time, my handsome – you'll be home again for the holidays. Time'll fly, you'll be so busy, you'll see. And when you come back, we shall be just like we was before,' he said.

And only with hindsight had Morwenna discovered the truth. What Eli had known then, and how he had been trying to save her from worse pain. For two weeks later he was dead.

With tears pouring down her face, Morwenna rose to her feet and surveyed the ruin of her fashionable kid boots. Scuffed from the stones of the rough track and stained with green from the grassy clifftop, they would never be the same again. She blew her nose, turned her back to the sea and tried to banish the past as she continued her interrupted journey up the steep slope and homeward.

The solid, grey and granite-built town of St Just served a thriving community whose prosperity was due to the huge tin and copper mining industry of the region. Between it and the coast stood Rayle House. And below the house on the winding road which sloped to the sea stood Praze Cottages, the modest row where the Edwards family lived.

After Gramp's death, Aunt Phoebe had taken over Morwenna's life, and the upheaval had been total. Eli's cottage, the only home she could remember, had been briskly stripped of its contents, which were to go into store, and was being held in trust for her until she came of age. This was a small crumb of comfort, but nothing could fill the aching void which had been left by the destruction of her childhood.

Her aunt, in her own words had 'taken Morwenna in hand', and apparently there was much to learn. Privately the young girl wondered how she had managed to survive so happily for all of her twelve years while knowing nothing of such essential subjects as etiquette, deportment and table manners. Her three cousins tolerated her but apart from being basically polite were not friendly and did nothing to make Morwenna feel any better. She saw herself as unloved, unwanted and nothing more than a burden to her aunt and uncle. Morwenna realized with the sharpness of all children that her aunt had taken her in chiefly out of a sense of duty, and had not been surprised to be packed off to boarding school with her cousins as soon as possible.

School had been as bad as Morwenna had anticipated, and to begin with an ache of homesickness for her old life, and for the sea which she missed like a personal friend, had enveloped her in a cloud of misery. Torn between the values of her old, simple life among her friends in the village and the middle-class standards of the company into which she had been tossed, Morwenna felt that she belonged to neither.

But that had been five years ago, and as time had passed and she had done her growing up, she had cultivated a freedom of spirit and an individuality that was all her own. The young woman now making her way up the road had an air of confidence and style about her, outwardly at least. No one but she, however, knew that deep inside, the orphan child was still crying out for the security and love that she had lost.

The detached house, formerly a large farm and still possessing several rambling outbuildings, was set back from a bend in the road, as befitted the home of a prosperous professional man. Arthur Rayle ran an expensive school of impeccable credentials in Penzance, for the sons of the middle classes. His home was solid and imposing, double fronted and built of local stone, which gave it the impression of having grown there of its own accord.

Morwenna had stopped to look back towards the sea and was enjoying the serenity until it was shattered by her eldest cousin James, who came clattering towards her on horseback from the back of the house, accompanied by a couple of noisy springer spaniels.

'I say, Mor, you'd better buck up,' he called out as he drew level and turned his mount's head towards the road. 'Mama's been looking for you – and she's not best pleased, by the sound of it.' Good-looking in an insipid kind of way, with a weak chin and pale eyes and hair, James was his mother's favourite and in her eyes could do no wrong.

'When is she ever?' Morwenna retorted, and sighed. She seemed to bring out the worst in her aunt through no fault of her own. Her independent spirit always seemed to clash with her aunt's ideas of propriety and what a lady should or should not do. But I'm an adult now, she thought, raising her head high. I can stand up to her.

She ran lightly up the steps to the front door and pushed it open. Her aunt was just descending the stairs, and when she paused on the third step and looked disapprovingly down at Morwenna, the girl knew that her face must still be flushed from her recent tears and was conscious that her unruly mass of hair had freed itself from its pins and was curling about her shoulders.

'Oh, here you are at last – and looking like a hoyden as usual.' Phoebe pursed her thin lips and glared down at her niece with eyes like gimlets. 'Why can't you keep yourself *tidy*, for goodness sake, and behave like a young lady?' She was impeccably dressed in a stiff skirt of bottle-green moiré and a spotless white blouse with a pie-frill collar. Tall and thin, she rested one hand on the banister rail and continued to look Morwenna up and down. 'Didn't you learn anything from the seminary after all the time you spent there?' She shook her head and tut-tutted her way down another step. 'I wish you'd take a leaf out of Sophie's book and follow her example.'

Trying not to laugh, Morwenna glimpsed her cousin standing in her mother's shadow and mimicking her gestures from behind her back. As Morwenna answered demurely, 'I went for a walk, Aunt Phoebe, and it's very warm today. I took my hat off and, well, my hair just fell down.' She did her best to hide her boots in the folds of her skirt as Sophie raised her eyes to the ceiling and grinned. Always clean and tidy, no matter what mischief she had been up to, Sophie had gradually, towards the end of their schooldays, become friends with Morwenna. While they were younger she had been under Tamsin's thumb and had followed her sister in everything, but after Tamsin had left school, the cousins had grown closer.

Now Tamsin at twenty was the image of her mother and looked down her long nose at them with the same haughty expression. She had become rather a remote figure since she had married Donald Miller, a solicitor's clerk, with, apparently, 'expectations', and had gone to live in a gloomy villa overlooking the town square.

'Your room is in a disgraceful state, miss,' Phoebe continued relentlessly. 'Nothing put away yet – and Sophie finished *her* unpacking an hour ago. Wherever have you been all this time?'

'I went out to post some letters, Aunt, then I met . . . a friend and we started chatting – but I'll see to it right away now.' Morwenna headed for the staircase but her aunt had not yet finished.

'That reminds me, Morwenna. I hope you don't mean to renew your friendship with that common Edwards family that you used to play with when your grandfather was alive. He let you run wild with the most unsuitable children. I warned him how you would turn out, but he took no notice, and now look at you.' She sniffed, and ramrod straight, descended the last few steps.

Morwenna felt something suddenly snap inside her. She drew herself up to her full height, met her aunt's eyes on a level with her and retorted, 'Aunt Phoebe, you have already pointed out that I am a young lady and no longer a child. Therefore, as an adult, surely I'm entitled to choose my own company?' Her chin in the air, Morwenna looked steadily at the older woman and went on, 'And if I want to see my oldest and best friends, I shall do so whenever I wish, regardless of whether you think they are "suitable" or not.' She felt her face flame as, shaking with fury, she stared her aunt down.

Phoebe's voice would have cut glass as she replied, 'I see.' She glared at Morwenna until she felt like something which had crawled out from the woodwork and added, 'Then it only goes to prove the point I was making, does it not? It's obvious that you'll never be a lady in spite of all my teaching, and if that's the way you feel, then I wash my hands of you here and now. If you won't listen to advice then you'll have to learn the hard way. So don't say in the future that I didn't warn you,' she said with venom as she swept past her niece into the drawing room.

'Phew, Mor – you told her *off*!' said Sophie with something like awe, as the two girls climbed the stairs together.

'I didn't enjoy it,' Morwenna admitted. 'In fact, I'm still shaking, but I can't stand her nagging any longer. I'm sorry, Soph, I know she's your mama, but I can't take it. Since we came back I seem to be seeing everything in a new light, do you know what I mean?'

Her cousin's fair curls danced as she nodded in agreement and her eyes were sombre. 'Yes, I do. I never realized myself how bossy she really is, but you're right.'

'The only thing is,' Morwenna said as she stopped by the door of her room, 'I feel so guilty standing up to her because, after all, she did take me in and look after me when Gramp died – I should be grateful to her.'

Sophie laid a hand on her shoulder, her eyes full of sympathy. 'There's no need to feel anything of the kind – we were the only family you had left.' With a newly dawning adult awareness, she added, 'Mor, no child should ever be made to feel it's a burden – childhood should be a carefree and happy time.'

Morwenna looked at her scatty cousin with a new respect and her eyes widened as she said, 'Sophie, I've never heard you talk like that before. That's exactly the way I feel. Do you know?' – she laid a confiding hand over that of the other girl – 'after Gramp died and I was sent away to school, I used to cry myself to sleep every night, and one day I made a vow that when I was grown up I would buy a house and take in as many abandoned, orphaned and unloved children as it would hold. Then I would fill it with warmth and love and security and give them all the happy childhood they should have – just like you were saying.' Morwenna's eyes were far away. 'I've never told anyone that before,' she confessed.

'I think it's a wonderful idea,' Sophie replied, and a small silence fell before Morwenna suddenly shook herself back to the present.

'But not for a few years,' she laughed. 'I've got to sort myself out first.' Sophie followed her into the room and sat down on the bed while Morwenna bustled about, emptying suitcases and stuffing the contents into drawers and cupboards.

'What *are* you going to do now, Mor? Now that we've left school, I mean?'

'I'll have to get myself a job of work,' replied her cousin with determination. 'I can't expect your parents to keep me any more.' She snapped shut an empty case and pushed it under the bed. 'Although I suppose the rent from the cottage would be enough to live on, I can't sit around and do nothing with my life. Maybe I could find work in an office somewhere.'

'I can't see Mama letting me go out to work,' said Sophie. 'It wouldn't fit her image of a "lady". I can see myself condemned to making endless

18

social calls and doing good works until she finds me a "suitable" husband.' They both burst out laughing and the serious moment passed.

Sophie took herself off to her own room and Morwenna, mindful of her promise to Tom, glanced at the clock on the mantelpiece and began to strip off her finery. She flung on a dark-blue cotton skirt and a fitted blouse of paler blue, tied her hair back with a ribbon and perched her old straw hat on top of it. She exchanged her battered kid boots for a pair of stout leather ones and ran down the stairs and out of the house before her aunt reappeared.

Chapter Two

Tom had similarly changed out of his working clothes and was now wearing a striped collarless shirt with a spotted neckerchief. His trousers were held up with a pair of red braces and on his curly head he wore a flat leather cap with a peak. His tall figure was propped against a granite field gatepost near the cottages, and his thin features lit up with a smile as Morwenna appeared.

'I'm taking the dog for a run down in the cove,' he said, and as Morwenna nodded they took the sloping track which ended at the small rocky beach of Priest's Cove. Spreading out to sea like the back of a slumbering beast, the promontory Cape Cornwall, the only true cape in England, dozed in the sunshine, crowned at its peak by the distinctive chimney stack of an abandoned mine.

The couple reached a low shelf of flat rocks, and the dog twined itself around their ankles, begging Tom to throw the stick he was holding tantalizingly just out of reach. 'This is Bess,' Tom added as Morwenna patted the border collie's bony head.

Gulls were squabbling as they foraged along the tideline, until the dog sent them screeching into the air, and as the pair scrambled over the boulders together, Morwenna said, 'How are things over at the mine nowadays, Tom? I heard that tin prices are on the rise.'

'Seem to be,' he said, nodding, 'and they're having the new electric compressors put in so they must think it's going to last. But you never know – the old men down the public last night were saying that if Great Britain gets involved in this war they're talking about, it'll affect all the industries, mining included.' He turned solemn eyes to the girl at his side.

'But it's Germany that's declared war – against Russia,' she replied. 'It's got nothing to do with this country, surely?'

'But since then they've come out against France as well – didn't you hear that? And now Pa says if they invade Belgium in spite of the warnings Great Britain has given them, then we *shall* be involved ourselves.'

Morwenna shivered as a cold knot of apprehension tightened her stomach. She had no knowledge of what war would mean to them personally, but the picture of a frenetic madman with a gun was still vivid in her memory. If one man could cause such mayhem and bloodshed, bringing death in seconds on a peaceful sunny afternoon, what would whole armies be capable of?

They had rounded the edge of the cove now and a sheer rocky cliff face reared over their heads. This was home to the gulls and fulmars which perched on tiny ledges far above their heads, or wheeled screeching through the middle air. Tom bent to pick up a couple of pebbles and sent them skimming deftly over the waves, while Bess sprang barking after them and almost disappeared under the water. Morwenna changed the subject for something less disturbing. 'What do you do down the mine, Tom?' she asked.

'I started off tramming – pushing the trucks of ore back to the shaft for the whim to raise them,' he replied, 'but now I'm working in a pare – that's a team – with Pa and two others, and they've been teaching me how to set the fuses. Some tricky old job, 'tis too – got to tamp them in just right and light them so there's time to get away before they blow.' His face was glowing with pride and as a small silence fell between them, Morwenna realized just how far apart from each other their different paths had taken them since they had played here as children. 'Penny for them.' Tom grinned.

Morwenna started, not really wanting to share her thoughts. She glanced back towards the cottage perched high on a ledge above the shore and swallowed the lump in her throat.

Following her gaze, Tom said softly, 'I remember Eli well. He could whittle the most amazing things out of driftwood, couldn't he?' Morwenna nodded and smiled. 'He used to try and teach me,' Tom went on, 'and I still do it in my spare time – but I shall never be as good as he was.'

'He was always clever with his hands,' said Morwenna. 'You know he made all the furniture we had in the cottage, don't you?'

Tom nodded and whistled to the dog who was barking madly at a couple of gulls and trying to scramble up the cliff face after them. The birds soared effortlessly away with a last mocking call and she gave up the attempt.

'When Gramp retired he couldn't bear to be away from the sea, so he had the house built as close to it as he could,' Morwenna went on, nimbly hopping from stone to stone. 'And one day I shall live there again, I know it.' She looked longingly over her shoulder. 'Love of the sea must run in our blood, I think,' she added, watching the great breakers rolling shorewards with plumes of foam streaming from their crests.

They walked on in silence for a few moments before Morwenna jerked out of her reverie and asked briskly, 'What are Jack and Chrissie doing now? I have such a lot of catching up to do – I must come round and see them soon.'

'Oh, Jack's nineteen now and working on Alf Rule's farm over to Ludgvan. Living in, he is – comes home at weekends. They grow broccoli and potatoes and stuff, and daffodils for Covent Garden market in the spring. Happy as a lark, he is.'

'He always did like getting his hands dirty and grubbing about in the soil, didn't he?' Morwenna remarked. 'And Chrissie?'

'She's working over to Penzance, in a drapery shop – you know Branwell's Emporium in Market Jew Street?' Morwenna nodded vigorously. 'She's happy enough – you know Chrissie, never stops talking.' He grinned. 'She gets on well with the other girls, I think.'

'She gets on well with everyone, does Chrissie, she always did,' Morwenna remarked, picturing her friend's round blue eyes, bouncing curls and wide smile.

They had walked as far as they could now and were turning to come back. Among the tumble of rocks lurked translucent pools full of fronds of coloured weed and studded with the delicate tentacles of sea anemones. Morwenna paused to dabble a hand in the water and one of the creatures closed itself over her fingertip, hoping to find it edible. 'Hard luck,' she murmured and withdrew.

'What did you say?' Tom asked.

'Nothing. Are you ready to go?'

Climbing back up the steep incline put paid to further conversation until they both reached the top together and flung themselves down on the turf, panting for breath. Here great crags of rock overlooked the cove, their hoary sides brightened with brilliant lichens and housing a myriad tiny plants which sheltered in the crevices and managed to survive in this most exposed of places.

Morwenna lay on her stomach peering over the edge while Tom leaned on his elbows at her side. Not normally given to deep thinking – there was never much time or opportunity in his life for reflection – he was suddenly struck by the beauty of this place, which he had known all his life and had always taken for granted. Now as he looked at the young woman beside him, her bright hair lifting in the breeze off the sea, a smile on her face as she met his eyes, and the whole picture caught in a loop of sunlight, he found it astonishingly touching and knew he would remember this moment for the rest of his life.

In order to break this spell which had stirred up emotions that he had never felt before, Tom reached for a stone and hurled it forcefully over the edge. As he watched it drop he cleared his throat and said gruffly, 'I say, Mor, I've been thinking. The Amateur Dramatic Society and the Philharmonic are putting on a show in Penzance in three weeks' time – at St John's Hall.' He glanced up at her as she straightened up and settled herself comfortably on a springy cushion of thrift. 'You know how good they always are, don't you?' She nodded and nibbled at a grass stem. 'Well, they're doing *HMS Pinafore*, and I'd like to go. Only . . .' He paused and kicked a foot against a stone. 'The thing is, Chrissie and her young man asked me to go with them see, but I said no, I wasn't going to play no gooseberry. But now I was wondering . . .' He raised his head and looked at her. 'You wouldn't like to come too, would you?'

Morwenna did not hesitate. 'I'd love to,' she replied with enthusiasm. 'I haven't been out for an evening in ages. It'll be fun – real light-hearted fun.' She tossed away the grass and sprang to her feet.

Tom's face cleared and broke into a huge grin as he followed her. 'That's fine then,' he said. 'I'll go ahead and book some tickets. I expect it'll be a sell-out.'

'Who's Chrissie walking out with? Anyone I know?' asked Morwenna as they fell into step. 'She used to be really keen on Walter Rule when we were at school, didn't she?'

'She still is,' replied her brother. 'She's never looked at anyone else but Walter.'

'Oh, that's really *romantic*,' Morwenna said with feeling.

'Walter's head groom up to Trengwainton now,' Tom went on, and Morwenna raised her eyebrows in surprise. 'Done very well for himself, he has. Started up there as a stable boy, then when old Ted retired, he got his job. The Bolitho family think the world of him, apparently – according to Chrissie, that is.' He smiled, and his deep-set eyes of a brown so dark they were almost black, crinkled up at the corners. As Morwenna returned the smile, she was thinking that there was no place on earth that she would rather be than here, where she belonged, with her oldest friend at her side.

The evening of the show had come round and Tom and Morwenna were strolling along the promenade before climbing the steep street to the concert hall. Fairy lights strung between the lamp-posts were twinkling in the gathering dusk and a quiet sea lapped softly below the railings. To their left, out in the bay, the silhouette of St Michael's Mount reared against the darkening sky, both dramatic and mysterious. It was an evening just made for romance.

Morwenna glanced up at the tall figure at her side, so smart in the dark suit and stiff collar and tie which he only wore on special occasions, his black hair slicked back with pomade. The scent of it was in her nostrils as she glanced up to meet his eyes. He was looking down at her with such tenderness that her heart gave a great leap, and for a moment time stood still. Their pace slowed as their eyes locked and held and she leaned a little closer.

'Morwenna!' came a squeal of delight behind her. They both leapt startled out of the dream and Morwenna whirled around to see Chrissie running towards them, one hand clutching her flower-bedecked hat, the other holding her skirt out of the way. Behind her Walter followed at a more steady pace, wearing a Norfolk jacket and tweed breeches.

'How lovely to see you! After all this time.'

The two friends embraced. 'You too – we were early so we came down here for a stroll first. . . .'

'So did we. . . .'

The two girls were soon deep in talk of their own. Tom raised an eyebrow and jerked his head to Walter as they fell in behind and left them to it.

The presentation of *HMS Pinafore* was lively and amusing and lived up to all their expectations. Several times during the show, however, Tom's eyes left the stage, drawn to the figure of the girl at his side. His devoted little slave of childhood days had blossomed into the most attractive girl he had ever seen. Her heavy auburn hair was piled neatly on top of her head tonight, secured beneath a trim little feathered hat, the weight of it seeming too much for the long, slim curve of her neck. Her eyes, as blue as the sea after which she had been named, were sparkling now with mirth at the comedy being played out on stage, but Tom had glimpsed in quieter moments a hint of vulnerability in their depths which had touched his heart and brought out a protective streak in his own nature that he had not known he possessed.

Then, as Morwenna laughed out loud at the antics of the characters, she turned to him and placed one hand on his arm. 'Oh, Tom,' she said breathlessly, 'I'm enjoying this so much, aren't you?'

And looking down into her small, glowing face, he covered the hand and squeezed it with his own as he replied fervently, 'Oh yes, I certainly am.'

As the clapping died away and the tasselled velvet curtains swung closed for the last time, a corporate sigh of satisfaction arose from the audience and with a wave of small rustlings they hurried to gather up their belongings before standing for the National Anthem. But surprisingly there was no sound from the orchestra. Instead, the compere reappeared at the front of the stage, a flustered look about him. In the hand which he raised for silence, he was clutching a piece of paper.

'Ladies and gentlemen,' he called, 'I have a special announcement to make. I have just received this telegram containing intelligence that the German army has crossed the Belgian frontier on to French soil and is marching towards Paris. This act has violated the terms of the Triple Entente peace agreement between nations and has made hostilities inevitable. Therefore it is my solemn duty to inform you that as from midnight tonight Great Britain will be at war with Germany. God save the King.'

A huge cheer erupted spontaneously from the audience and hats went flying through the air as the orchestra struck up the stirring first notes of 'Rule Britannia'. The cheers died away only to be replaced by a full-throated chorus of joyful voices as the audience joined in the singing with patriotic fervour. For of course, Great Britain and her allies were invincible – they would soon have the Kaiser on the run and our soldiers would return home in a blaze of glory after teaching him a lesson he would never forget. It would be all over in a few months – probably by Christmas.

'It'll all be over by Christmas,' said Sophie confidently a few weeks later. 'Everybody says so.'

She was perched on Morwenna's bed, black stocking-clad legs swinging as she watched her cousin arranging the books she had brought back with her on the shelves in a corner of the room.

'Mmm,' said Morwenna abstractedly, sitting back on her heels with a copy of *Pride and Prejudice* poised in one hand. 'I don't suppose it'll make much difference to us, then.'

'Mama says that all the big shops in Penzance have put up window displays with flags and decorations of red, white and blue crêpe paper, and photographs of the king and queen. And the band was playing patriotic tunes in the park on Saturday. It sounds quite fun.' Sophie jumped off the bed and skipped lightly across the room.

'Sophie,' said Morwenna, obviously not having listened to a word of her cousin's chatter, 'I want your advice on something.' Her cousin's eyes widened and she came back to Morwenna's side. 'I just can't make up my mind what to do about this.' She drew out a newspaper cutting from inside the book she was holding and waved it at the other girl. 'I've got to tell someone or I'll burst.'

'What?' Sophie took the piece of paper, which had been folded open at the 'Situations Vacant' column where a notice had been marked, and read it aloud as she paced up and down the room. 'Wanted – an educated young lady for the position of receptionist in small private hotel. Must be neat in appearance and of impeccable character. Apply with references to Mrs Matthews, "Sea-Winds", Penzance.'

Sophie finished the passage and raised sparkling eyes to Morwenna. 'Ooh, are you going to try for it, Mor?'

Her cousin nodded. 'Shall I? I'm not sure – but it does sound all right for me, doesn't it? What do you think?' She looked anxiously at Sophie, who had flopped down on the bed again.

'Of *course* you must!' Sophie squeezed her hand. 'It's ideal for you. Oh, Mor, how exciting!' She bounced up and down a couple of times, adding, 'You must write a letter straight away.'

Morwenna's face had brightened at this encouragement and she nodded firmly. 'I will, then. Oh, thanks Sophie, you've really helped me make up my mind. 'I thought – if I'm lucky enough to get it, that is – it would mean I'll be out of your mother's way during the day and when I've saved enough, I might even be able to get a room of my own somewhere.' Morwenna's eyes were far away and her hands were clasped under her chin as she lost herself in dreams of an independent future.

'All the best of luck, then,' Sophie said, getting to her feet. 'I'd better go and show myself before Mama comes looking for me. I'm supposed to be helping her with the flowers for the table tonight. You haven't forgotten the dinner party, have you?' she prompted over her shoulder as she paused at the open door.

Morwenna came back to earth with a start and clapped a hand to her mouth as she sprang up. 'Oh Sophie – I *had*! I shall have to wash and change. What time is it?' She brushed some flecks of dust from her skirt and her expression darkened. 'What a bore! Who did you say is coming?'

'Well, apart from all of us . . .' Sophie counted on her fingers. 'There's Tamsin and Donald, and James's Cynthia, plus the vicar and his wife. Ten altogether and we "children" will have to be on our best behaviour. You know how Mama makes up to the vicar.' She grinned and rolled her eyes heavenwards, just as her mother's level tread could be heard coming up the stairs. Sophie vanished and Phoebe arrived outside the room before Morwenna had a chance to close the door.

'Not changed yet, Morwenna?' The sharp black eyes looked her niece up and down. 'I do hope you're not going to be late for dinner again.' Phoebe was at her most imperious in plum-coloured silk with a fitted waist and tucked bodice, enlivened by a row of tiny pearl buttons and a touch of lace at the throat.

Once, I've only been late once since we got back, thought Morwenna through clenched teeth, and that was only because you kept me so long helping you with odd jobs that could well have waited until afterwards.

'I'm just about to do so, Aunt Phoebe,' she replied and stared the older woman down.

'What do you intend to wear?' inquired her aunt suspiciously, with a narrowing of her eyes. 'This is a special occasion as you'll discover later on.' Morwenna's own eyes widened as she wondered what this might be. 'I don't want you making an exhibition of yourself by turning up in some ghastly aesthetic creation, which would be just like you – goodness only knows what you brought back from the Continent.' She sighed and half turned away as she added over her shoulder, 'As if any lady worthy of the name would be seen in public without a corset! I don't know what the modern world is coming to.'

'I thought my turquoise poplin with the crochet trim,' Morwenna replied demurely, stifling a smile at what the reaction would be if she turned up in the cycling breeches and tweed jacket on which she had recently spent the last of her allowance. Her bicycle was a closely guarded secret. It was an outgrown one of Jack's, which was kept at the Edwards' house for the occasions when she could sneak out unobserved and go for a spin round the lanes in blissful freedom with him, Tom or Chrissie.

'Hmm, very well, and don't forget to give your hair a thorough brushing, will you? It's looking like a bird's nest again.' And with this parting sally, Phoebe walked on. Morwenna made a face as the door closed behind her. Life at Rayle House was not getting any easier.

But then her eyes sparkled and her heart gave a little skip as her head filled with her plans once more. Morwenna reached for her writing slope, opened the lid and drew out pen and ink. She would get that letter written without delay.

Consequently, Morwenna arrived downstairs to find the company already assembled in the dining room, and tried to slip in unnoticed behind the maid who was bringing in the soup. Unsuccessfully, however, as Aunt

Phoebe shot her a look to kill as she took her seat and opened her napkin, and Morwenna knew she had not heard the last of it.

The dinner party went exactly as she had expected. Arthur, her uncle, as rotund and jovial as Phoebe was thin and sharp, beamed on the assembled company from the head of the table and monopolized the small and birdlike wife of the vicar at his side, totally ignoring Morwenna to his right. On her other side her cousin James's attention was totally devoted to Cynthia, his 'intended'. Abandoned as she was between the two cold shoulders, Morwenna kept her eyes on her plate and let her thoughts wander.

A voice from the opposite side of the table brought her out of her reverie and she looked up with a start at the kindly eyes and white whiskers of the Rev. Symonds.

'Welcome back, Morwenna, it's been a long time since we saw you and Sophie at home.' She smiled and nodded as she thanked him. 'You've blossomed into a pair of very becoming young ladies, if I may say so,' he added. 'Soon be turning the heads of all our local youths, I shouldn't wonder.' His shoulders lifted as he laughed at his own roguishness. 'Seriously, though, we shall be glad of your help with parish affairs, you know. If you could spare a few hours for Sunday-school teaching or flower arranging – we can never have too many on the rota—'

Morwenna interrupted the flow and said briskly, 'I'm sorry but I doubt that, Reverend. You forget that unlike Sophie and her family, I have to find some means of earning my own living.' His eyebrows shot upwards in surprise. 'But my dear young lady—'

Morwenna ignored him. 'I feel I've been a burden on my aunt and uncle for long enough. When I was a child I had no choice, but I cannot continue to live on their charity.' She lowered her voice and glanced around the table, but her aunt was deep in conversation with Mrs Symonds and had raised her voice to carry across the table. With sudden inspiration, Morwenna made the most of the opportunity and went on, 'I intend soon to apply for a position . . .' She paused and looked him in the eye. 'And I should be very grateful if you would be kind enough to supply me with a reference.' She held her chin high and as the minister looked her intently up and down, Morwenna saw something like respect dawning on his face.

At last his expression softened and he replied, 'Gladly, gladly, my dear. I knew your grandfather well – had a great respect for him – he was a man of very strong principles.' He tapped the bowl of his spoon idly on the table, his mind in the past. 'Not that we always saw eye to eye, mind you, but he did a good job of raising you, Morwenna.' He smiled. With difficulty, Morwenna swallowed a lump in her throat and forced herself to smile back. 'Now tell me the nature of the position you are going to look for, my dear.' Morwenna explained and he nodded several times. 'Very commendable. Come and see me tomorrow afternoon and I'll have something ready for you.'

Morwenna concealed her delight with a mouthful of dessert. She would approach her uncle later, explain her plan to him and ask him for a second reference. Her stomach gave a flip of excitement and she turned her attention to the conversation around her.

'I see the British Expeditionary Force is having a tough time in France,' Donald remarked to James, a spoonful of apple pie and clotted cream poised partway to his mouth.

'At this place, um . . . Mons. Yes. Heavy casualties, they say.' James carefully speared a piece of cheese and balanced it on a cream cracker. 'Unfortunate. But of course it's only a temporary setback. With our highly trained men we're naturally in a far superior position in the long run. To be quite honest, old boy, I wouldn't mind seeing a bit of action myself.' The morsel vanished into his mouth and he leaned back, patting his blond moustache with a napkin.

'Can't say I share your enthusiasm,' Donald replied. 'I've got plenty of things to keep me at home. I've never been more busy in the office, and of course there's Tamsin to think of now,' he said smugly, giving his wife a secret smile. 'But if you're that keen to take the king's shilling you'd best make your mind up soon, else it'll be all over.'

'Oh, James,' Cynthia broke in, her high-pitched voice rising above the general hum of conversation, 'you would look so handsome as a cavalry officer. I'd be so proud of you.' She placed a dainty hand in its lace-trimmed cuff on his arm and looked adoringly into his eyes. 'I think,' she went on primly, returning to her meal, 'that it's every young man's duty to defend his country. In London, women are handing out white feathers, you know, to those who are not in uniform.' She sniffed and tossed her head.

'They'd be better occupied doing something useful with their time,' remarked Morwenna drily, infuriated by the woman's shallowness. 'Women are working everywhere now, you know, doing all the jobs the absent men used to. They're in factories filling shells, on the railways working the signals – as well as looking after their homes and families.' She glowered across the table and added, 'Apart from the nurses, of course, who have gone to the front to care for the wounded in the casualty clearing stations. Really hard, dedicated work.' She put down her spoon and dabbed her mouth with her napkin.

Cynthia turned to her with a haughty glare. 'Well, *I've* joined the Knitters' Circle at church, and we're making warm clothing to send out to the troops – socks, gloves and scarves – so no one can say I'm not doing my share in the war effort.'

'Very commendable, my dear,' murmured the vicar, and Cynthia gave him a dazzling smile, followed by a smug, sidelong look at Morwenna.

Morwenna was just about to reply when she became aware that her uncle had risen to his feet and was calling for silence by clinking his knife on a wine glass in front of him. Surprised, Morwenna realized that Fanny the maid was placing similar glasses at each of their places and that a couple of bottles of champagne had silently materialized at the table.

Arthur's round face was even pinker than usual with the effects of good food and excitement, and his gold watch-chain was stretched to its limit over his portly figure. He paused and surveyed the company in the same way, Morwenna imagined, as he did his boys at morning assembly, unhurried, slightly pompous and aiming to impress.

'Ladies and gentlemen, friends and family,' he began, rocking back on his heels, thumbs hooked in his waistcoat, 'I have some good news to announce this evening. I know one piece of it will not come as a complete surprise, as we have been half expecting and hoping for just such an occurrence for a long time.' He paused for effect and cleared his throat. 'I have to tell you that Donald has been promoted to junior partner in the business. And that's not all.' He held up a hand to still the hum of congratulations. 'He has also confided that he and Tamsin are going to give us our first grandchild in the spring, and of course Phoebe and I are absolutely delighted. Will you raise your glasses, please, and join me now in a toast to Tamsin and Donald?'

'Tamsin and Donald. . . .' came the echo amid a babble of chatter and applause. Morwenna glanced at her cousin's flushed and happy face and half envied her the secure and predictable life which lay ahead. But would she, Morwenna, be as content to settle for a routine which consisted solely of home, husband and children? Or would she miss the challenge and the satisfaction that she felt would come with independence and the earning of her own living? Only time would tell, she decided, as she followed Phoebe and the other ladies into the parlour, leaving the gentlemen to their port and cigars.

The talk then was all of babies and child-rearing, the room was stiflingly hot and Morwenna had soon had enough. She stayed to give the couple her personal congratulations then excused herself and left.

'Not so fast, young lady.' Her aunt had followed her out and closed the door behind her, her back to it and her hand still on the knob. She faced Morwenna in the passage, her colour high and her eyes glittering. 'I want an explanation of your rudeness – I suppose it's too much to expect an apology.' She drew herself up to her full height and pursed her lips, her chest heaving as she struggled to contain her anger.

'Aunt Phoebe, I—' Morwenna began, but was silenced by an imperious hand.

'Obviously your common background is coming out more and more as you grow older, just as I expected.' She looked over the beak of her nose and glared at her niece.

Until that moment, Morwenna had been perfectly prepared to apologize and had only been waiting for a break to come in all the small-talk to do so. But there had seemed to be no end to it and she had decided to postpone her apologies until later and was going outside for a breath of fresh air in the meantime.

Now however, she was furious at being denied the chance to explain herself, and quelled the tears of rage at the injustice of it, which were threatening to choke her. She would rather die than apologize to the woman after this. Without pausing to think, Morwenna snapped, 'In that case, I'm sure you'd rather I removed myself from this house altogether and spared you any further embarrassment, wouldn't you?'

For once lost for words, Phoebe's eyes nearly popped out of her head, as defiantly Morwenna spat, 'So I will, then.' Her head was up and she looked her aunt squarely in the face. 'You've always resented me being here – I know you only took me in on sufferance because you had to for appearances' sake.'

Phoebe raised a hand to her face and for a moment Morwenna thought she was going to strike her. But her aunt only placed it on her forehead as she said theatrically, 'You ungrateful little wretch! After all I've done for you – taken you in, fed and clothed you and treated you like one of my own family. . . .'

'That is precisely what never happened,' Morwenna retorted. 'Yes, you did the bare minimum you could get away with, as I said, for the sake of appearances and your own public reputation. But I was *always* made to feel an outsider – a cuckoo in the nest – and as for supporting me, I know that the rent from the cottage contributed to that, as my grandfather intended it should.'

Phoebe's shoulders slumped, and Morwenna knew that every word she had hurled at her aunt was true. But far from making her feel better in any way, the confrontation had left her with a churning stomach and a nasty taste in her mouth. And feeling more of an outsider than ever.

'So,' she finished quietly, 'I'll go and stay with my "common" friends where I'm always welcome, and who genuinely care about me, even if they don't use finger-bowls and table-napkins when they sit down to dinner!'

Blinded now by the tears which were flooding her face, Morwenna ran to the front door and wrenched it open. She was halfway down the steps before Phoebe had sufficiently recovered her breath and her composure to call after her. Ignoring her, Morwenna flew over the lawn like a small pale moth and through the garden to a side gate leading out into the lane and the cliffs beyond.

It was a rough walk down to the coast, through rutted tracks studded with great boulders where the bedrock pierced the thin soil and shouldered its way to the surface. The rough stones pierced through her thin slippers but Morwenna did not feel them. By the time she arrived at the cliff edge and sank down to draw her breath and think about what she had done, the light was already changing with the onset of night.

Seabirds wheeled and screamed in the chasm below and the Brisons caught the last rays of the blood-red sun in a frame of fretted black, while at their foot the restless sea shone like beaten silver. This place had always been her solace in times of trouble, as near the sea as she could be, and at this moment it was awe-inspiring, its angry swell exactly reflecting her own turbulent emotions.

This had been the place where she and Tom had sat a few days ago, soaking up the sunshine, but now it could hardly have been more different. In the darkness the hunched figure of the promontory was less like a sleeping beast and more of a brooding monster, the chimney stack having assumed the look of a sharp and menacing horn.

Settling herself on a tussock of thrift, Morwenna wrapped her arms around her knees. She knew she had cast herself adrift from her only security, and the realization filled her with excitement and apprehension in equal measure. At that moment she felt like a straw blowing in the wind, unsettled and belonging nowhere. Her former life had reached a point of no return and an uncertain future beckoned. And not only was a great change about to take place in her own life, but she suspected that this war was going to have a more far-reaching effect on them all than Sophie had so lightly predicted.

But the sun had disappeared now, and angry purple clouds were bruising the sky on the horizon, their swollen bodies threatening rain.

Morwenna shook herself out of her reverie and rose to her feet, wrapping her arms around herself as the wind began to freshen and whip her skirt about her ankles. She turned her face towards the friendly lights of Praze Cottages and the Edwards family's home.

Chapter Three

'**M**ORWENNA!' The door was opened by Maria Edwards, letting out a waft of warm air and the scent of freshly baked pasties. 'My dear maid, what are you doing out in this gale?' She glanced up at the sky and added, 'Rain on the way too, shouldn't wonder.' She closed the door and hugged Morwenna to her plump little figure, as round as one of her own saffron buns, as she looked her up and down. 'In they thin clothes too. You must be half-frozen. Come on in.'

'I went for a walk down on the cliffs and stayed out longer than I meant to. I didn't expect it to come in like this,' replied Morwenna with a shiver. The real explanation could wait a little longer.

Maria preceded the girl down the passage to the kitchen, her knot of dark hair threaded with grey bobbing as she went. 'Gone some cold, though, hasn't it? Reckon we're in for a storm.' She opened the fire door of the gleaming black-leaded range and poked up the coals. Wiping her hands in her apron as she laid down the poker she added, 'Sit down and have a warm-up, maid.' She pushed a chair close to the glowing embers and plumped up the cushion.

Morwenna rested her feet on the shining brass fender and thankfully held out her hands to the fire. 'Look who's here, Tom,' Maria said, adding over her shoulder to Morwenna, 'He's just come off core, see. Having a late supper we are. Father's still out in the scullery, having his wash.'

Tom was sitting at the table in his shirt-sleeves, where two places were laid on the bright oilcloth cover, eating a large pasty. At the sight of his beloved face and the unconditional welcome she had received here, Morwenna's already tense nerves almost cracked and reduced her to tears again. She swallowed hard as he looked up in surprise and said, 'Mor! What are you doing out so late?'

'I got caught by the weather and I knew I'd never get back to Rayle before the rain,' she replied, hedging around the actual truth. 'I could see it coming out at sea.' She cocked an ear. 'Listen. It's starting now.'

'You're looking some smart for a walk on the cliffs,' he remarked, pushing a lock of wavy dark hair out of his eyes, then took another mouthful.

'Cup of tea, my handsome?' interrupted Maria, pulling the kettle over to the hob.

'Please.' Morwenna nodded, managing a smile before turning back to Tom. 'We had a dinner party at home,' she explained. 'Donald's been promoted to junior partner at Clemo and Hobbs, and Tamsin's expecting.'

'Really?' Maria's rosy face was alight with interest. 'Well, that's nice for them, I'm sure. But there's something about they Millers – I could never take to none of them myself.' She thoughtfully twitched at her black skirt and smoothed out an imaginary crease as she went on, 'I don't know so much about the lad, but his father always struck me as a bit of a shifty creature, and I'm not the only one to think so. Doctor or no, I know people who stopped going into Penzance surgery when he took over, because they didn't take to him neither.' She pursed her lips and busily started to rattle teacups. 'Course, they're not from round here, that family – don't know where they do come from. They don't tell you nothing about themselves. Think they're too grand for the likes of we, I suppose.' Maria's black eyes snapped and Morwenna, knowing her fondness for gossip, could not help smiling.

Maria bustled off to the scullery where she could be heard telling her husband to get a move on or his pasty wouldn't be fit to eat. Tom raised an eyebrow and grinned. Morwenna's smile broadened. Warmed by their company as much as the tea and the heat from the fire, she said fondly, 'She never changes, your ma, does she? There's no need to ask where Chrissie gets it from!'

Tom pushed back his plate. 'You feeling all right, are you, maid?' he asked, looking intently at her. 'Looking some whisht, you are.'

Morwenna nodded. The old Cornish word described exactly how she felt – limp and washed out. She lowered her head and twisted her fingers in her lap.

Then she picked up her teacup again and wrapped her hands around its warmth as Tom rose to his feet, brushed some crumbs from his cord waistcoat, and went to the door to look out. 'Rain's stopped again already,' he remarked. 'Must only have been a heavy shower, after all. Wind's died down too.' He came back in and added, 'I'll walk you home when you're ready, Mor, before the next shower. There's something I want to tell you.'

'But I must tell you this first, Tom.' She met his eyes, which were dark and serious, then saw his face soften with concern as he must have realized there was something badly wrong. 'I don't know quite how to put it, but I was wondering if . . . if I could possibly stay for the night?' She could not prevent her voice from wavering as she went on, 'There was a big row at home and . . . and I . . .' She bit her lip as she tried in vain to stop the tears from coming and he stepped forward to put a comforting arm around her shaking shoulders.

Maria bustled into the room at that moment and took in the scene with a quizzical look. 'Morwenna's staying the night, Ma, all right?' said Tom briefly, stepping away.

'Of course,' she replied, for once asking no questions. 'You can have Jack's room, my handsome – he don't come home until the weekend. Come on up and bring your things.' She stepped out into the passage and turned towards the stairs.

'Er . .' Morwenna began, her thumbnail between her teeth.

'She hasn't brought nothing with her, Ma,' Tom called up the stairs. 'She can borrow something of Chrissie's, can't she?' And Morwenna blessed him for his sensitivity.

His mother's reply was inaudible, but Tom nodded and lifted a beckoning finger. 'Come into the parlour where we can talk,' he said. 'Pa'll be here in a minute.'

In the parlour which was Maria's pride and joy and which was used only on Sundays and important occasions, they sat on the plush-covered chaise-longue beneath a painting of 'The Monarch of the Glen' while Morwenna opened her heart and told Tom everything. He listened in silence, holding her hand until she had finished, and when she could restrain the tears no longer, slipping his warm arm around her shoulders again. She laid her head upon his chest, which felt absolutely the right place to be, and sighed. She had grown up in this man's shadow but was only now becoming aware of what his lean, strong figure and never-failing understanding and support really meant to her.

But as Morwenna nestled closer, she felt Tom stiffen and gently withdraw, to clasp both her hands in his as he said, 'I'm going away, Morwenna.'

The shock was like being thrust out into the storm again and Morwenna sat up with a start. 'Away?' she repeated, her lips almost too stiff to frame the word. 'Where. . . ? Why. . . ?'

Tom's eyes were sombre as he fixed them on her face and replied, 'I've enlisted.'

'*Enlisted*?' Morwenna repeated, as her brain struggled to take in the horror of this simple statement and all its implications. 'You mean you're joining up – to – to – go and *fight*?'

Morwenna felt all the colour draining from her face. Her heart was hammering and her head reeled at the conflicting messages that her brain was sending now. One part of her was unutterably proud of Tom that he should have volunteered, the other terrified at the thought of what was happening on the Western Front, and what his fate might be.

'Yes,' said Tom simply. There was a pause as he twisted his hands in his lap and looked down at them before continuing. 'You remember seeing Lord Lonsdale's recruiting posters all over the place when we went to Penzance, don't you? "Your country needs YOU", they said, and "Are you a Man or are you a Mouse?" Well, I want to prove I'm not a mouse, Mor. I have to go and do my duty to my country. I'm just old enough to qualify – you've got to be between nineteen and thirty – and my conscience won't let me rest easy while others are getting killed and wounded for my sake.' He raised his head and their eyes met.

Morwenna wrapped her arms around herself to still her shaking body. 'Oh, Tom, I'm so proud of you,' she said, her voice cracking with emotion, 'but so afraid too.'

Tom leaned forward and gently wiped away a tear with the tip of one finger. And when she looked at him again he was actually smiling, with a thrill in his eyes that made her blood run cold. He stood up and began to pace the room, unable to keep still for the excitement of it all. 'It'll be the most tremendous adventure, Mor. Just think. I've never been out of Cornwall in my life, and now I'm going overseas with hundreds of others, to defend our king and country.' He turned on his heel to face her again and his outspread hands said it all. 'It's a chance to *do* something, to leave my mark upon the world – even if it's only on a battlefield in Flanders.'

Morwenna shivered and gazed white-faced into his glowing eyes. She knew then that she had lost him. Soon he would be a soldier in an alien world, one which held no place for her. She covered her mouth with a hand to blanket her sobs and tried to return the smile.

Sea-Winds was a double-fronted, granite-faced house situated like several others in a street just off the sea-front in Penzance. The magical castle of St Michael's Mount floated alluringly in the bay, where turquoise water fringed with a scalloped lace edging of creamy-white flaunted its beauty to the sky.

Morwenna, however, had no eyes for anything but the house in front of her. She took note of the spotless net curtains at the bay windows and the tubs of bright geraniums flanking the steps to the front door. Nervously she patted the bag at her side to reassure herself that she had not forgotten the vital references.

It had not been easy going back to Rayle to seek out her uncle, but she had chosen a time when she knew Phoebe would be at one of her committee meetings, and had discovered to her surprise that Arthur knew nothing of the confrontation she had had with her aunt. Either Phoebe had decided that Morwenna wasn't serious about her intentions, or she had deliberately not told her husband for fear of losing face. Either way, it made no difference at this moment. Morwenna drew in a deep breath and seized the highly polished brass knocker in the form of a lion's head, letting it fall with a resounding thud.

The door was opened by a pert little maid, hardly more than a child. Morwenna stated her errand and waited in the hall while the girl went in search of her employer. There was no one at the reception desk, and Morwenna looked it over with interest. It was a large affair of solid mahogany on which stood a silver bell, a blotter and ink-stand, various ledgers, and a brass-handled telephone on a stand. Hanging on the wall above was a wooden board holding rows of numbered keys.

'Miss Pengelly.' At the sound of a voice, Morwenna turned to find a pleasant-looking middle-aged woman standing behind her. Dressed in simple black and white, her grey hair swept up into two wings at each side of her head, she was regarding Morwenna with warm toffee-brown eyes behind a pair of horn-rimmed spectacles. 'I'm Clara Matthews,' she said and held out a slim hand. 'Come through here, please,' she added, leading the way down a passage to the side of the reception desk and into a small sitting room. After asking Morwenna details about her background, to which the girl had already prepared the answers, she spent some time studying the references and finally looked up with a smile.

'Well, I think you will suit us very well,' she said. 'If, after I've shown you around and explained the terms of your employment, you feel the same way, of course.'

Morwenna's face lit up with delight. 'Oh, thank you,' she said with enthusiasm. 'I'm sure I shall.'

'Our previous receptionist has just retired – Miss Rule. She was with us for many years and I was sorry to see her go,' Clara Matthews went on as she rose to her feet, 'but she left the books in apple-pie order for you to take over. I think you will find everything fairly easy to follow. Come with me, I'll show you around.'

She led the way down a passage floored with mosaic tiles and indicated sitting-rooms to the right and left of it. Both were empty of people. 'The majority of our guests come here for holidays,' she said, 'and spend most of the time out-of-doors. We get walkers and cyclists, bird-watchers, artists and photographers who all come for the scenery – and the magnet of the famous Land's End, of course. At the moment we have five rooms occupied.'

They proceeded up the stairs, where Morwenna was shown the neat bedrooms and the gleaming bathroom furnished with the most up-to-date designs in prettily decorated ceramic-ware and brass fittings. 'Some come for the shooting and occasionally we get businessmen down from London as well – those who have shares in the mines come to see for themselves where their money is going – and there are sales representatives and so forth,' Clara went on. 'There's a local omnibus, as I'm sure you know, which runs a daily service from Penzance to Land's End, St Just and neighbouring places. It meets the Cornish Riviera Express from Paddington, so it's very convenient for visitors.'

Morwenna's eyes had widened in surprise at the comparative luxury around her, quite unlike what she had expected to find in a small hotel. Clara, possibly guessing at her thoughts, turned to her as they made their way down again and said, 'I'm a widow now and my husband left me comfortably off.' She paused and twitched a curtain at the landing window as they passed. 'Rather than sit around looking forward to a lonely old age, I decided to become a businesswoman. So I took over Sea Winds and modernized it. I enjoy the company, you see, and constantly meeting new people.'

Morwenna felt a dawning admiration for her new employer, who sounded like someone after her own heart, adapting to her circumstances with courage and enterprise. 'I employ a stable-hand, Jim, who also does any heavy work and lives in a converted outbuilding behind the house, plus two housemaids and a cook, who come in daily. And now a new receptionist.' She turned to Morwenna with a smile and laid a friendly hand on her arm.

There followed half an hour of instruction for Morwenna as to the running of the hotel and her part in it, before they arranged the date when she would start, and she found herself at the front door again.

'One thing more I almost forgot to mention,' said Clara as they stood on the top step, 'but you probably won't need it. Miss Rule used to live here – she was alone in the world, you see, and liked the feeling of company around her. So there is a small room at the back on the top floor which you could take over if you wish – but I'm sure you would rather remain with your family and come in daily, wouldn't you?'

A room! Morwenna could hardly believe what she was hearing. Trying rapidly to collect her thoughts, she stammered, 'But actually, I would love to live in – if I could afford the rent out of my salary, that is.'

'You would?' Clara's eyes widened, as did her smile. 'That would be wonderful. It's not a suitable room for a guest as it is a little out of the way on the third floor, and a fair way from the bathroom. But it would be ideal for you – and yes, you could well afford it. I shall make sure of that,' she chuckled, 'as it will be lovely to have someone living in the house again – I was not looking forward to losing Miss Rule's company and I would prefer the room to be put to good use. And besides, you'll have no excuse for being late for work if you live on the premises!'

With her new employer's laughter following her down the steps, Morwenna turned at the bottom to raise a hand in farewell and had to restrain an urge to skip all the way down the road. She had a job! And somewhere to live! And how lucky she had been to come across such a nice person as Clara to work for. They would get on very well, she was sure. From now on she was a working girl and a dependant no longer. And if it hadn't been for the thought of Tom's imminent departure, which was always there at the back of her mind, Morwenna thought wistfully that she would have been perfectly happy.

Morwenna was not looking forward to going back to Rayle House to pack her belongings and tell her aunt and uncle of her new post, but it had to be faced. When she arrived, however, early the following morning, she found that they had news of their own which was far more important to them both than the affairs of their errant niece.

Arthur had already left for his school but when Morwenna slipped in the back way she found her aunt uncharacteristically still in her dressing robe, sitting at the kitchen table with her hair loose down her back and a letter clutched in her hand.

So deep in thought was she that she seemed scarcely to register Morwenna's presence and the girl looked at her in concern. 'Is something the matter, Aunt Phoebe?' she asked, coming closer.

'Oh, it's you,' she said with asperity as she raised her head. 'I don't suppose you're interested, but yes, there is.' She held up the crumpled sheet of paper and went on, '*This* is a letter from the War Office. Telling me that Rayle House, if you please, has been requisitioned by the military.' Morwenna saw confusion and apprehension in her aunt's eyes as they widened and she fixed her gaze on the trees beyond the window, lost in thought.

'By the military?' Morwenna repeated in bewilderment. 'What do *they* want it for?'

Phoebe jerked herself out of her reverie. 'They want to use it for a convalescent home for wounded soldiers.'

Morwenna's own eyes widened. She could imagine the upheaval this would cause and in spite of everything, could not help but feel sorry for her aunt, who hated change of any sort and was the soul of neatness and order. She sat down and looked searchingly at the woman beside her. Phoebe seemed to have crumpled, as if all the stuffing had been knocked out of her.

'What will you and Uncle Arthur do? Will you stay here or do you have to move out?' she asked with unaccustomed gentleness.

'Arthur's talking about us moving into the farm cottage – it's been empty since Mrs Richards died – and he says it'll be big enough. Because we shall only be the two of us and Sophie, you see. With you gone, Tamsin married, and J-James in the army. . . .'

'James has enlisted?' Morwenna said in surprise.

Phoebe nodded and reached up her sleeve for a handkerchief. 'He's leaving for an officers' training camp next week.' She turned a bleak face towards her niece. 'Morwenna, the world I know is falling to pieces around me. I don't know if I can cope with it all. And now having to pack up and move.'

Then to her horror, Phoebe began to weep, something that Morwenna had never seen her do before. Fat tears were rolling unchecked down her face and as she leaned one hand on her bent elbow, which was propped on the table, she suddenly looked elderly and defeated.

Morwenna awkwardly patted her shoulder and tried in vain to think of some words of comfort. 'But at least you'll still have Sophie to help you,' she said encouragingly. 'Where is she now?'

'She's sleeping late. She went to a party last night – she doesn't know about this yet.' Phoebe indicated the letter. 'Arthur's delighted in a way that we'll be doing something for the war effort, but he has no idea how I . . . how I . . .' Her voice tailed off. 'Anyway, what are you doing here?' she suddenly asked with a hint of her old spirit. Morwenna told her.

'I see,' Phoebe replied thoughtfully. She sniffed and put the handkerchief away. 'Morwenna . . . um . . . about some of the things I said to you. . . .' She lowered her eyes and sketched a pattern on the tablecloth with a fingernail. 'I spoke in the heat of the moment, as I think you did too, and maybe . . . maybe I was a little harsh. . . . You're not a bad girl, and well, I shall miss you, that's all.'

Morwenna could hardly believe her ears. Her autocratic aunt was apologizing? To *her*? Mortified at the thought of what she had said and thought about her, Morwenna's generous heart was quick to forgive. 'Well, thank you, Aunt Phoebe,' she said softly, 'I'm truly sorry for what I said to you as well.'

'But you were right, child, up to a point,' she said surprisingly, raising her eyes. 'At first I did resent having to take you in, and perhaps I was a little over-strict with you – but I was so conscious of the responsibility I had for someone else's child, you see. I thought then that you were a stubborn and wilful girl, but I've since realized that it was only high spirits that made you such a handful, and the effect of losing your parents at such an early age.' She paused for breath and Morwenna was about to speak when Phoebe added, 'I still say that Eli was at fault in letting you run wild with the village children, but by giving you company of your own age he meant to do the best he could for you, I know. As I did, believe me. I only ever had your best interests at heart.' She looked with damp eyes into her niece's face.

'I do believe you, Aunt,' said Morwenna with sincerity. For looking at the pathetic figure beside her now, who could doubt that she spoke the truth?'

All too soon came the moment that Morwenna had been dreading, when Tom would also depart for his training camp, and out of her life for the foreseeable future. News that Jack had decided to go with him changed nothing, except to fill her with pity for Maria, who would be waving off not one son but two. The pride of placing a white card in her window to say that this home had sent two sons to the front would hardly compensate for the heartbreak of seeing them leave.

She called round to say her goodbyes on the eve of their departure and found the house in chaos. Maria was scuttling about the kitchen chivvying her two sons like a mother hen her chicks, alternately giving orders and dabbing her cheeks with a sodden handkerchief. Heaps of clothing and possessions lay everywhere – on chairs, the table and in corners of the room. Chrissie was checking and passing the neatly folded clothing to her brothers, who were stuffing their suitcases under their mother's direction, and when her friend looked up and saw Morwenna her face broke into a smile of welcome.

'Oh hello, Mor, I'm some glad to see you – it's like a madhouse in here, as you can see.' She rose from her knees and smoothed down her skirt, her usually merry face pale and drawn.

'I thought you'd all be busy,' Morwenna replied. 'I won't hinder you – I just came round to say goodbye.'

'We're nearly through now,' Tom added and turned to her with a heart-stopping grin on his face. His eyes were bright with excitement and Jack was whistling cheerfully as he hefted his case and carried it out of the room.

'Ma and me have been up since dawn, washing and ironing this lot and baking pasties for the boys to take on the train,' said Chrissie wearily, running a hand through her dishevelled curls. 'Pa's gone up to the public for an hour, out of the way.'

'Shall I make us all a cup of tea while you finish off?' Morwenna offered, as Maria sank into a chair and eased off her shoes.

'Oh, yes,' she said gratefully, 'that'd be lovely. Thank you, my hand-some.'

Morwenna suddenly realized just how exhausted Maria was, for under normal circumstances she would have jumped up herself and put the kettle on before any visitor was as much as over the doorstep.

An uneasy silence fell for a moment as they all slumped in various atti-tudes of weariness or contemplation and sipped their tea, before Chrissie turned a pale face to Morwenna and said, 'Walter's going too, did you know?'

Morwenna gasped. 'No, I didn't. Tomorrow, you mean – on the same train?' Her head reeled. How many more of these local young men were leaving their home town, she wondered? This exodus of boys who had been known to her since childhood had suddenly turned the small word 'war' into a ravening monster which seemed to be set on gobbling them all up. At this rate there would soon be no young men left in the district. Newspapers were all saying the same thing. Up and down the land, in towns, in villages and in the most remote of rural areas, sons, brothers and cousins were all flocking to the recruiting stations in droves. And sweet-hearts, too, she thought sadly. Chrissie and I are in the same boat there.

Her friend met her eyes and Morwenna had an idea that their thoughts were the same. Chrissie nodded. 'I've just been round to say goodbye, although I'm going to the station to see them off too. Oh, Mor—' Her eyes began to fill with tears – 'they've taken all the horses from the estate – it fair broke Walter's heart to see them go. You know how he do love them all; like a family to him they are. He's hoping that if he goes too, he can maybe look out for them, but of course they'll be separated sooner or later.'

'So he's joined the Duke of Cornwall's Light Infantry like us,' said

Tom, draining his cup. 'First Battalion – so we'll start off all together anyhow.' He jerked his head to Morwenna and went on, 'Go for a stroll, shall us? Now all the work's done I could do with a bit of fresh air.'

It was a cold night, clear with a hint of frost to come, and the sky was ablaze with stars. A sliver of new moon was hanging aloft in the immensity of a cloudless sky, with one tiny silver star swinging beneath it as if held by an invisible thread. After the warmth of the cottage the air hit them like a slap in the face and Morwenna gave an involuntary shiver. Tom placed a comforting arm around her shoulders and she cuddled into its warmth.

They followed their usual route to the cliffs and looked over the edge at the darkening sea below, where reflected starlight gleamed on the restlessly fretting water which nudged and slapped at the cruel black pinnacles of rock near the shore.

'Tom, you will write to me, won't you?' Morwenna's eyes were on the invisible horizon and her expression was unreadable.

'Of course I will – but don't get upset, Mor.' He turned her to face him. 'I'll be home again in a few months, and then. . . .' He cleared his throat and said awkwardly, 'Well, what I mean is . . . wait for me, will you, maid?'

Morwenna's heart turned over and was thumping so loudly she was sure he could hear it. There was so much that she wanted to say, but how could she mention the unmentionable – that she was terrified that he might never come home at all, that this might be the last time they would ever stand here in this familiar and beloved place? And that even if he did, common sense told her, his experiences would have changed him – changed them both, in fact – as much as the world itself was even now being transformed by the carnage he was about to face so blithely.

The next day he was gone.

From that day, Morwenna read every scrap of news that she could lay her hands on, avidly skimming the newspaper every morning and running her eyes with dread down the lists of casualties which seemed to grow longer with every day that passed. In fact, the news filtering back from the front, giving reports of freezing mud, barbed wire and death, was beginning to cast doubts upon the whole campaign which had at first been presented as such a noble undertaking.

'Oh dear, oh dear,' Clara Matthews sighed as she looked over the top of her spectacles at Morwenna and indicated the newspaper article she was reading, 'I'm so dreadfully afraid that this will all get much worse before it gets better.' She was leaning on the corner of the reception desk at Sea

Winds where Morwenna was filing letters in the bookings drawer and drinking a cup of tea as she worked.

Clara passed over the paper. 'Look, it says that Zeppelin airships have started attacking London now. You remember when the east-coast towns were bombed by those Zepps a few months ago, don't you? Buildings were flattened but there wasn't much loss of life then. But now – oh my goodness, just read it.' Clara passed over the paper and glanced out of the window at the bright spring morning. Daffodils were nodding their buttery heads in the border beside the front entrance and in the hawthorn hedge a pair of blackbirds were busily feeding a growing family of chicks. Sea and sky were almost the same shade of powder blue, the dividing line hardly discernible in the sunlight, and the Mount floated between the two, the turrets on the castle roof caught in a golden web.

'Poor things,' she added. 'It makes one feel blessed to be living in this remote corner of the country, doesn't it?'

'I don't think you can say that anywhere is completely safe any more,' replied Morwenna with a shiver. She raised wide eyes from the newspaper and handed it back. 'Think of the sea that's all around us.' She waved an expressive hand towards the view outside. 'And how open to naval attack we could be. And bombs can drop anywhere, even just by accident.'

Clara nodded, her face serious. 'I suppose so,' she replied. 'It just doesn't bear thinking about. Now, I must get on.' She straightened her skirt of navy poplin and added, 'You know where I am, Morwenna, if you need me. Don't hesitate to ring my bell if there is anything at all that you don't understand or can't cope with.' She tucked the paper under her arm and went off towards her private sitting room.

Morwenna was distracted at that moment by the sound of the front door being opened as a young man entered at the tail end of their conversation. He advanced towards the desk, pulling off his flat cap to reveal a head of springing black curls. Dressed in a Norfolk jacket and knicker-bockers with long stockings over, his jaunty air spoke of abundant self-confidence, and his twinkling black eyes of humour. He smiled and the ends of his small moustache curled attractively upwards.

'Good morning,' he said, adding in an instantly recognizable Irish accent, 'would you be after having a spare room at all, if you please, miss?'

Returning his greeting with a smile, Morwenna reached for the register. 'Yes indeed, sir, I can offer you a single room at the front of the house, with a sea view.' She gave him all the details and tilted her head curiously as he signed the register. So his name was Kieran Doyle then. Morwenna pressed the bell and while they were waiting for the maid to come and take his bag upstairs, he remarked, 'I wonder if you could be telling me where I can find Rayle House at all?'

Morwenna's jaw dropped. 'Rayle House?' she repeated in surprise. 'Why, yes, I certainly can.' Her smile broadened as she explained. 'It's my aunt and uncle's home – and I lived there myself for several years.'

'Well, there's a thing!' The bright eyes twinkled merrily and a broad grin turned his neat features into those of a mischievous leprechaun. 'I've been sent down here to look it over and report back to the Red Cross with a view to using it for a convalescent home – for wounded soldiers, you know?'

'I had heard that,' Morwenna replied, 'and as my aunt and uncle have already moved out, you'll find nothing to stand in your way. If you call at the cottage nearby when you get there, I'm sure someone will give you a key. I'll write down the directions for you, shall I?' She was just handing over the piece of paper when the maid arrived, and their new guest departed upstairs, thanking her profusely as he went.

It was a quiet morning after that and Morwenna, after attending to the books, checking the board of keys behind her and tidying the great desk, decided to take a break. From her skirt pocket she drew out the already well-read letter which she had received from Tom a day or two ago, and looked for the hundredth time at the beloved face in the photograph which he had enclosed. Here was Tom in uniform, newly pressed, immaculate, every button gleaming. How *young* he looks! had been her first reaction, drinking in the sensitive mouth, the eager expression, the eyes full of suppressed excitement and the head held proudly high. And how vulnerable. Now her own eyes brimmed with tears as she read his message again.

Dearest Mor,

We leave for Southampton today, to embark for an unknown destination in France. Our spirits are high and all are looking forward to seeing some real action at last, after the boring and endless drill of the past weeks.

I'll let you know the address where you can write to me as soon as I know it myself.

Meanwhile, think of me when you look out to sea from our own special place on the cliffs, which is where I always imagine you are, and where we'll soon be together again. With fondest love,

Your Tom

'Fondest love', he had written. In the same way that he would have ended a message to any one of his family. Morwenna realized with a pang that Tom had never, in all their times together, actually said that he loved her. 'Wait for me' had been the closest he had ever come to it. Was his love implicit in that remark? Tom had never been one to show his feelings; he had always been 'a deep one', as the village gossips would have put it. But her own love for him was profound and steadfast and she would wait for him as he had asked her for as long it took, for years if need be.

Chapter Four

A clattering of footsteps on the stairs made Morwenna hastily replace photo and letter in her pocket, and she looked up to see Kieran reappearing, holding a brown leather briefcase under his arm. He raised a friendly hand to her as he crossed the tiled hall and left the building, whistling cheerfully as he went.

Morwenna watched him skimming down the steps, and as he reached the bottom he almost bumped into someone coming round the corner. A female, for she could just see him raising his hat, presumably with an apology. No sooner had he disappeared from sight than the door opened again and there was Sophie standing on the threshold.

'Hello, Mor.' She bustled forward, removing her gloves and placing them with her basket and parasol on a convenient chair.

'Sophie – how lovely to see you!' Morwenna came out from behind the desk and they embraced. 'And what a surprise,' she added, joining her cousin on the button-backed sofa beneath the window.

'I had to come into Penzance for some shopping for Mama, and had an hour before the omnibus leaves, so I thought I'd call in and see how you're getting on.' She looked Morwenna up and down, obviously taking in the businesslike black dress with its neat white collar and cuffs, and the demure upswept hairstyle. 'How capable you look,' she said in admiration.

'I'm really enjoying the work, Sophie – and the independence even more.' Morwenna half-turned to meet her cousin's eyes. 'I can't tell you the difference it's made to my life. I really feel like an adult at last.'

Sophie regarded her critically with her head on one side. 'It's funny, but you're actually *looking* older, Mor,' she said.

'It must be all this awesome responsibility,' Morwenna replied with a smile, indicating the reception area with a wave of her hand. 'But listen, the strangest thing happened. Did you notice that young man who was leaving here just as you arrived?'

'I should say so – he came hurtling down the steps and nearly knocked me over. But I didn't mind.' Sophie clasped her hands and raised her eyes to the ceiling as she said dreamily, 'He was ever so good-looking. Do you know who he is?'

'I'll say I do. His name's Kieran Doyle and he's Irish. Now, prepare yourself for a surprise, Soph.' Morwenna paused for maximum effect and added, 'He was only looking for Rayle House!' Her eyes sparkled as she waited for Sophie's reaction, and she was not disappointed. The other girl clutched her arm as various expressions ranging from amazement to disbelief and finally excitement flitted across her face, as she squealed, 'Mor – *why?*'

Morwenna told her the whole story then and they stayed chatting for a while until Sophie caught sight of the time by the long-case clock nearby and jumped up to leave. Morwenna saw her to the door. 'Come again when you're in town, Sophie, and bring me all the news.'

They had paused at the top of the steps. Sophie pressed her hand and replied, 'I'll do that, Mor. I do miss having you around to talk to, you know. Mama's like a lost soul since we moved and she hardly lets me out of her sight these days because she misses the others so much.' Her face fell as she went on, 'I feel quite suffocated sometimes, cooped up in that tiny little cottage with her. I'm only too glad to do the errands so that I can get away for an hour or two.' She turned away, adding, 'Must go now, though. I'll never hear the end of it if I miss that bus. See you again soon, Mor. Bye.'

She ran lightly down the steps in a flurry of cherry-red skirts and waved as she turned the corner at the bottom, leaving Morwenna looking thoughtfully after her.

'It'll be an ideal place, so it will – just what they're looking for, I'd say.' Kieran pushed open the inner glass door, talking as he closed it behind him, greeted Morwenna with a smile like sunshine and sank down in a brown leather armchair to open his briefcase.

'Oh, hello, Mr Doyle.' Morwenna returned the smile and looked up from the register she had been studying.

'It's Kieran, so it is – to my friends,' he quipped, looking her straight in the eyes. 'And you are. . . ?'

Feeling that she had no choice – to stand on ceremony would make her seem prim and stand-offish in the face of his friendly charm – Morwenna told him her first name, then to emphasize the fact that she was on duty, she opened a drawer and took out a stack of receipts which she proceeded to check.

'I'm off back to London in the morning to file this report and set things in motion for the change-over,' he went on, making a note on a sheet of paper and not a bit put out by her air of busyness.

Curiosity overcame Morwenna's scruples over his forwardness and she raised her head. 'How long will it be before it can be occupied, do you think?'

'No longer than it'll take to get the equipment requisitioned and fixed up. The sooner the better – they're getting desperate for places to send the convalescents. At the moment they're taking up hospital space which is badly needed for urgent cases.' Kieran put away his papers and fastened the strap on his briefcase.

Morwenna nodded and bit her lip. 'I suppose more of the wounded are coming in all the time. I heard that our forces were hit quite badly at that place called Ypres.'

Kieran's eyes were serious for once as he looked at her innocent face and he answered shortly, 'Yes.' For how could he – how could anyone – even begin to describe the reality of the carnage taking place on the western front, to a girl like this? How to tell of the hospital ships that he had been meeting, full of men who had lost limbs, eyes, and worse. Some with only half a face – the remainder blown away with the blast of an exploding shell. Some witless, shaking and gibbering as a result of indescribable experiences which had robbed them of their senses. He tucked his briefcase under one arm and rose to his feet, pasting the smile back on his face as he took his leave and made for the stairs.

Morwenna was sending up a silent prayer for Tom. Where was he? *How* was he? The worst part of all was not knowing. He had vanished into a void where she could not follow him in her thoughts, for try as she might she was unable to imagine the conditions under which he was living, and she felt more distant from him than ever before.

Morwenna was going through the morning's postal delivery at Sea Winds. Bookings were down at the moment but it was winter time after all, apart from the fact that bookings had fallen dramatically since the onset of the war. But as Clara did not seem unduly worried by it, neither did she. Then her heart did a flip as, tucked between the business envelopes, she came across one addressed to her personally. In Tom's handwriting! Morwenna seized it with excitement and ripped it open immediately.

Dear Mor,

We have landed in France and are billeted in a small village not far from the front line. The farmer and his wife that I am staying with along with three others, are very friendly and even speak a few words of English. It puts me to shame and I am trying to understand and learn a little of their language. It was all hustle and bustle when we arrived. We were sent first of all to a big training camp at a place called Etaples. It was on a river estuary with sand dunes a bit like Hayle is at home. But now all we seem to do is tedious drill, and practise manoeuvres. We are longing to see some action! But it surely can't be long now.

Show this to Pa and Ma will you – no time to write more. Will be in touch again when I can. Tom.

Morwenna clasped the letter to her. Just 'Tom', then. Her mouth drooped. No 'fondest love' this time? Then her face brightened. But of course – she was going to have to show this to his parents – naturally he wouldn't have expressed his feelings in writing. And he had written to her, hadn't he? Not the other way round. Morwenna's spirits lifted and she hummed a little tune under her breath as she filed away the morning's correspondence for the guest-house.

The crisp and frosty weather which Tom had been enjoying in England before he left, bright with all the colours of autumn, had turned bitterly cold with relentlessly pouring rain since he had arrived in France. There was no colour in this benighted landscape but grey. Tom was sitting in the bottom of a trench, his back against the sandbag wall, and his boots sunk to the ankles in slimy mud. It had stopped raining at last, which it had been doing off and on for the last three days and nights, and the water draining from above had carried down with it the flotsam from the upper lip of the trench. Shreds of clothing, small pieces of jagged metal and several torn and bloody fragments of human flesh had filtered in and still lay in the puddle at his feet, for there had been some fierce fighting the previous evening. Now the puddle was slowly turning to ice as the temperature dropped, and raising his head Tom saw that it had started to snow. He turned his coat collar up as far as it would go and went back to what he was doing.

Tom was writing in his diary. The diary was one of his most precious possessions and he kept it wrapped in a scrap of oilskin in a pocket of his greatcoat, next to his heart. Half a lifetime ago his unit had arrived at the front along with hundreds of others in, of all things, a fleet of red London buses, singing songs of patriotic fervour all the way. But the time for singing was long gone.

First had come the exhausting task of digging and equipping mile after mile of the trenches in which they were to eat, sleep and dwell for the next weeks. Tom was no stranger to tough and demanding working conditions – as a miner he was well used to physical labour and fared better than many of his comrades – but even his strong back and arms ached so much from the effort of lifting the heavy soil shoulder high and out of the trench that he could have sometimes screamed with the pain of it.

Then, in complete contrast, when they were sufficiently well 'dug in', came a mind-numbingly boring period of time while they sat about with very little to do except wait for orders. But nothing in all those weeks had prepared them for the reality of trench warfare once it actually began.

In the diary Tom was trying to record the horrific details of the hell that was all around them, because writing it down, pencil marks on orderly lines in a bound notebook, was the only way in which he could even attempt to rationalize the enormity of it all: the filth, the futility, the utter and tragic waste of human lives. And the only way to keep himself sane. It was only when he raised the pencil to write in the date that he realized what day it was. 24 December 1915. Christmas Eve! Tom rasped a hand across his stubbled chin and gave a sardonic snort.

The first Christmas had come and gone unremarkably, with no sign of cessation of hostilities as had been confidently predicted. It was unbelievable that another year had passed with so little having been achieved.

The countryside, he wrote, *is an endless waste of thick, gluey mud pockmarked with shell-holes full of deep brown water. Trees completely stripped of their leaves wave bare boughs to the leaden sky like skeletons in some macabre dance. In this trench where I am sitting, waiting for and dreading the next order to go 'over the top', fat rats flourish and run up and down between our feet with no sign of fear. We are all lice-ridden and filthy. So much for all the longing to see some 'action' – I've now seen horror beyond description and scenes that I only wish I could forget. So much for all the jingoism as well – to think how we left home with stars in our eyes, singing songs of glory – we knew nothing of this hell that was about to swallow us up.*

The conditions under which we live and fight are degrading beyond imagination. Trench foot is a commonplace occurrence caused by mud seeping through our boots. When you can't take them off for a fortnight the flesh swells, then turns rotten and gangrenous. We have lost many men from that alone. I do the best I can for myself by rubbing my rum ration on my feet to keep them warm. This helps and so far they are all right. But I stink, as we all do, not being able to wash properly or change our clothes, and with diarrhoea being another problem. I . . .

'Got a fag, mate?' Private Joe Harris, the same age as Tom, lowered himself down beside him and tipped his tin hat to the back of his head. Tom hastily put away his diary, for it was too personal to be shared, tossed him a packet of Woodbines and shuffled towards a marginally drier spot. 'Light one for me too,' he grunted, fishing deeper in his greatcoat pocket for a lucifer. Tom had never smoked before joining up, but now it was a comfort he had come to rely upon. A cigarette in your mouth steadied your nerves and also it made you one of the lads. For in this hell-hole everybody smoked, from the highest ranking officers down to the lowly privates like themselves.

'Old Fritz's been quiet for a long time,' Joe remarked, inhaling deeply and blowing a thin trail of fragrant smoke skywards. The words were hardly out of his mouth when the terrific *crump* of an exploding shell knocked the cigarette out of his hand as he jerked sideways. It was followed by another, and a third in quick succession.

'Spoke too soon, mate,' replied Tom, grim-faced. 'The fun's starting up again.' They sat tensed, their ears singing from the blast as they waited for the next explosion. And waited, as the time dragged out and their ears began to feel stretched and aching from the strain of listening. But none came.

Then out of the eerie silence came, from the direction of the German dug-outs, a thin, wavering thread of sound. The sound of a human voice. Singing! Floating on the cold, clear air came the unmistakable notes of *Stille nacht, heilige nacht . . .'*

'Blimey! I must be dead and gone to heaven,' said Joe, his eyes wide. 'Tell me I'm not dreaming this, will you, mate?'

'You're not,' Tom replied with a grin. 'Listen – they're all joining in now.'

'And there go our boys too, with a bit of 'Good King Wenceslas!' Joe slapped his knee and laughed as they both began to join in the fun.

On the next morning – Christmas Day – there was more communication between the opposing sides, with shouts and whistles ringing out over the frosty ground. A light dusting of snow had fallen, covering the worst of the bomb damage and slightly softening the blighted landscape.

Tom followed a group of men who were climbing the parapet and cautiously peered over the top. 'Bloody hell – they're raising a white flag!' called a voice as someone produced a less than clean white handkerchief and stuck it on the end of his bayonet in return.

Soon men from both sides were pouring out of the trenches into no-man's land as shouts of 'Hello Tommy', 'Hello Fritz', 'Happy Christmas', and '*Fröhliche Weihnachten*' rang out. When a football was produced from somewhere and both sides started kicking it about, Tom stood on the sidelines and watched with amazement. It was surreal. Yesterday these men had been blowing each other to bits. Presumably tomorrow hostilities would be resumed and they would carry on blowing each other to bits.

But for these few brief hours as they fraternized with each other, exchanging cigarettes and shaking hands, they had seen their 'enemies' face to face and recognized them for what they were – young, homesick lads exactly like themselves, forced into fighting a war they did not want, for a cause they had long ago forgotten.

Morwenna, busy with her clerical work at Sea Winds, tossed the last of that day's outgoing letters into the tray for posting and leaned her elbows on the desk in front of her, supporting her chin in her hands, and sighed. There had been very few letters from Tom since he had been on the front line and most of them had been of the 'hope you are well' variety, which told her nothing of himself and left her yearning for some personal news with which she could identify. How was he really? What was he doing? Thinking? Was he in good health?

Today I am facing such a bout of homesickness that the only comfort I have is to write it all down. Tom was deep in his diary in his billet where, for two blessed weeks, they could get clean and warm, sleep in a proper bed and eat food that was not either covered in mud or cold and tasteless. *Worse even than when I was in the trenches. At least there we were kept so much on the alert that there was no time to brood. But here, away from the lines, there is still a degree of civilization and normality. The fields are green, a colour I had almost forgotten existed.*

And oh, how I long for the sea – I miss it more than I could ever have thought possible. The beach, the cliffs, the cove – and Morwenna. Morwenna, laughing, her lovely hair blowing in the breeze, fresh, clean, untouched by all this filth. I wish I could write to her properly, but to tell her the truth would be to taint her as I am tainted. Better that she should know only the lies that I dream up to protect her. Thinking of her keeps me going like the light at the end of this grim, dark tunnel, and sometimes I have to pinch myself to remember that she is real, and not some hallucination that I've dreamed up.

★

Morwenna had written to Tom every one of the long weeks since he had left, struggling to keep her letters cheerful and to find enough in the trivia of her daily life to fill each one, while inside herself she felt as if a light had been switched off and she had been plunged into a semi-permanent fog.

Absently, she picked up the daily paper which Clara left around for the benefit of her guests when she had finished it, and shook it open. It was unbelievable to think that the end of the war still seemed as far away as it had done twelve months ago.

The British Expeditionary Force, Morwenna read, *has expanded to thirty-seven divisions and progressively larger allied assaults are being launched, with unfortunately little ground being gained. In fact we have to report many casualties, the most recent of which were two British reserve divisions with the loss of eight thousand men. This is said to have hastened the end of Sir John French's career and he is to be replaced as Commander of the British Army by Field-Marshall Sir Douglas Haig.*

So many. Wide-eyed, Morwenna let the paper fall to her lap and cupped her face in her hands again. Every single one of those thousands of men was someone's husband, brother, son – or sweetheart. Oh Tom! she thought.

'You're looking as if you'd lost a pound note and found a tanner, so you are. Is something the matter at all?' Kieran Doyle's cheery voice startled Morwenna out of her reverie. 'Oh, I didn't hear you come in,' she replied, rising to reach down the key of his room. 'I was just reading the paper. This awful war – when will it ever end?'

'Ah, yes indeed, who can tell? Only the powers above can give you the answer to that one.'

He and Morwenna had established a friendly relationship during the months that Kieran had been coming and going. Always cheerful, or seemingly so, Morwenna found that he brightened the tedium of her daily life with his lively chatter and opened her mind to the wider world where he spent much of his time.

Over the past year and under Kieran's direction, Rayle House had been scrubbed, polished and cleaned from top to bottom by a squad of women from the village, smartened with fresh paint inside and out, and furnished with all the equipment necessary to convert it into the convalescent home. The first trickle of men had begun to arrive, so Kieran had told her, and Morwenna was awaiting an opportunity to go over and see for herself how it was functioning.

Kieran leaned on the counter as she handed over the key, and his black eyes held hers as he gazed closely into her face and said, 'I'd say you could do with a bit of cheering up, by the look of it.' He paused and went on, 'I'll tell you a thing now – I just saw a poster for the cinema as I came up the road and Charlie Chaplin is on in *The Tramp* this week. Would you like to go at all? Shall we? What do you say?' His black eyes twinkled and the corners of his mouth lifted in a beguiling grin.

Morwenna's brows lifted as she stared back at him, her thoughts in turmoil. Should she? Would it be disloyal to Tom? But it would only be one evening; a bit of harmless fun. It was so long since she had had fun of any kind. And she hadn't been out for an evening since she and Tom had seen *HMS Pinafore* together. That seemed like half a lifetime ago.

It took only an instant for Morwenna to make up her mind. 'Oh, well ... thank you, um ... Kieran. I'd like to – very much.' She smiled back and nodded.

'Good!' He straightened up, twirling the key in his fingers. 'Tomorrow night all right? I'll meet you here when you finish work, then we can have something to eat first.'

Kieran went bounding up the stairs before Morwenna could reply, leaving her staring at his retreating back. A meal out as well? She hadn't bargained for that. But it would be nice. She was startled out of her thoughts, however, when Kieran stopped part way up the flight to bury his face in a handkerchief as he was seized with a sudden tremendous fit of coughing.

'That's some cough you've got there,' said Morwenna with concern as she left her seat and went to the foot of the stairs to look up at him. Kieran paused for a moment and clutched at the banister rail for support, then as he recovered he replied, 'Ah, I had diphtheria as a child once, and nearly died, so I did.' He gave a forced smile. 'It left me with a damaged lung.' He paused and took a deep breath. 'The cough comes and goes. Sometimes hurrying will bring it on, like then as I was running up the stairs. It's something I just have to live with.' He wiped his damp eyes and stowed away the handkerchief in a pocket.

'Have you got anything to take for it?' Morwenna's eyes were wide and sympathetic. 'Can I get you a glass of water or something?'

Kieran raised a hand and shook his head. 'No, thank you, you're very kind but I'm over it now. Doctor Miller has offered to make me up a linctus for it, so he has. He heard me coughing when he was doing his rounds at Rayle House the other day,' he said as he took another step.

'Oh good, I certainly hope that'll soothe it,' Morwenna said as she turned back to the desk.

'Maybe a touch of the London fog got in me pipes as well while I was up there,' Kieran added as he continued up the stairs. 'Don't forget our date now, will you?' he called over his shoulder as he disappeared around the bend.

As they walked down the street together the following evening the air was crisp and cold with a stiff breeze blowing in from the sea. Morwenna pulled down the brim of her felt hat and snuggled her chin into the fur collar of her navy-blue coat. Beside her Kieran was wearing his tweed overcoat unbuttoned over a pin-stripe suit and waistcoat, and glancing at his profile Morwenna thought what an air of sophistication there was about him. He was so obviously a city person and man of the world that no one glancing at him would ever have mistaken him for a local. Kieran walked straight-backed with a confident stride and in one hand he carried a silver-topped cane.

'Here we are,' he said, bringing Morwenna back to earth again as he halted outside one of the larger hotels on the sea-front, and she realized with a shock that this must be where they were going to dine. Kieran took her elbow and guided her as they turned to walk up a flight of steps where a doorman stood waiting to usher them into the foyer. Morwenna suppressed a smile as she recalled Phoebe's lessons in etiquette and table manners, and those of the ladies' seminary as well – she could put them to good use in an establishment like this. And as she removed her coat, she breathed a sigh of relief that she had worn her best pleated skirt of bottle-green and her new cream satin blouse with the lace collar.

Her feet sinking into the crimson pile of the thick carpet, Morwenna looked around her. Heavy drapes also of crimson framed the windows but were left open to give diners a view of the starlit sea. A hint of lights at the castle windows was all that could be seen of St Michael's Mount, which was only an indistinct hump of deeper black against the dark water of the bay. An elaborate Christmas tree stood in a corner, and tasteful decorations hung around the walls.

As the waiters glided silently in and out of the dining room, bringing wafts of appetizing aromas from the kitchen, Morwenna suddenly realized how hungry she was. 'So what's it to be?' Kieran enquired after they were settled at a table overlooking the bay. He passed her the elaborate menu card. 'Dover sole? Roast turkey with chestnut stuffing? Beef Wellington?' His eyes slid down the list.

'Oh, they all sound so delicious I can't choose,' she said with a shake of her head.

'Shall I order for both of us then?' Kieran raised his head and his sharp black eyes met her own.

'Oh – no,' Morwenna replied, returning to the menu. 'I only meant I might take a little while to make up my mind, that's all.' Privately she was wondering how much he was prepared to spend and whether she should choose one of the less expensive dishes.

As if he was reading her mind, however, Kieran said, 'Have what you like. Don't worry about the expense – I can afford it. Besides, tonight is a special occasion – it's almost Christmas.' He looked her fully in the face. 'Plus it's our first date,' he said, then added after a significant pause, 'but not the last, I hope.' Morwenna lowered her eyes to the menu card and ignored the last remark. Looking at the sumptuous array, she wondered with a pang what Tom would be eating for his Christmas dinner.

While they waited for their meal to be served, Kieran met her eyes across the table again and said, 'Tell me about yourself, Morwenna. I know nothing except that you are employed as a receptionist and have your own live-in apartment at Sea Winds.'

It was not simple to give an account of a lifetime in a few polite sentences, but Morwenna gave him a brief resumé of her early years and how she had come to leave Rayle House. 'It was the right decision and came at the right time, considering the upheaval there which came soon afterwards,' she remarked, spooning Brown Windsor soup. 'There would be no place for me there now even if I'd wished it – my aunt and uncle and Sophie are living in very cramped conditions in the cottage.'

Kieran nodded. 'And this friend of yours – Tom – you sound as if you were very close.' He quirked an eyebrow and his black eyes bored into hers. Morwenna lowered her gaze to her spoon and took another mouthful. He's fishing, she thought, but she was not willing to share her private feelings on such a short acquaintance. 'He was always my childhood hero,' she said, raising her head.

'And now?' Kieran broke a bread roll and carried a piece to his mouth while still keeping his eyes on her face. He's not going to let it drop, Morwenna thought, as she broke the eye contact and gave an evasive reply. 'Now he's fighting for his country on the western front, like hundreds of others,' she said. And why aren't you? she wondered as the thought suddenly struck her. But Kieran had a damaged lung, he'd said. Maybe that was it.

'Still the hero then.' There was a sardonic note to the remark.

Does he feel jealous, perhaps, frustrated because he is unable to fight himself? Morwenna wondered again.

'I would have loved to join in the action myself, but . .' He spread his hands palms upward and shrugged, answering her unspoken question. 'But you care very much for him,' he added. 'I can tell from your tone of voice and the expression in your eyes when you mention his name.'

Morwenna started. He was more perceptive than she had thought. She swiftly changed the subject. 'And what about you?' she asked. 'I know next to nothing about your background either, apart from the fact that you're Irish. What brought you over here and how long have you lived in London?'

Kieran gave her a long look and intuition told Morwenna that he was perfectly aware of her tactics. He spooned up the last of his soup and pushed the plate aside. 'I come from Armagh,' he began, carefully wiping his moustache with a napkin. 'I'm the second youngest of four brothers and two sisters – and I wanted to spread my wings. The nest was a bit crowded.' He smiled and shrugged. He paused and sat back while the waiter removed their soup plates, then added, 'I served an apprenticeship and qualified as a carpenter and joiner. Da always drummed into us boys how important it is to have a proper trade, because he never did – he always worked for other people. Gentry. He's a stableman on a large estate. They breed and train racing horses there.'

The waiter arrived with their beef and Kieran reached for the mustard, dabbing a generous swab on the side of his plate. 'As a matter of fact, he hasn't much time for the English, my da.' Morwenna looked up at him, her brows lifting. Kieran grinned. 'Like a lot of Irishmen he's hated them ever since the potato famine!' He loaded his fork and carried it to his mouth.

'And you?' Morwenna enquired, spearing a carrot.

'I found plenty of work over here – I've got the independence that I wanted and I live in a small flat in Blackheath where I can look out over the grass. I've got friends. I shall spend Christmas with them. I'm OK.' It was not the answer to the question she had asked, but it was impossible to tell whether or not this was a deliberate misunderstanding on his part.

After a portion of fruit trifle piled high with clotted cream followed by strong, sweet coffee, Morwenna gave a sigh of repletion and said, 'That was a marvellous meal, Kieran, thank you. I've eaten so much I shall probably fall asleep during the film.'

He chuckled and replied, 'Well, that would be a crying shame, so it would.' He rose to his feet and signalled an attendant to bring their coats. 'So we'll take a little walk along the prom before we go in, shall we?' As Morwenna stretched and stood up, he slipped her coat around her shoulders.

Once outside, the cold air hit Morwenna in the face like iced water and she was instantly shaken out of her lethargy. A pale half-moon had emerged from a bank of cloud now and its light played fitfully upon the lapping water below the harbour wall, dusting each ripple with gold. Kieran courteously extended a bent elbow as they began to walk and she had no choice but to put her hand through it, although she would have preferred not to be quite so close. As they strolled up the street she glanced at the shadowy figure at her side, smiled at some remark he had made and wished with all her heart that he was someone else. Oh Tom, my dearest love, where are you?

Chapter Five

'IT'S a long way to Tipper-ary, it's a long way to go . . .' Tom's unit was on the march. Trudging weary miles through the flat and featureless countryside of north-western France, towards the next engagement. Too true it was, he thought – they'd had no respite for three hours and the seventy pounds of his backpack had begun to feel more like a ton. 'It's a long way to Tipper–ary, to the sweetest girl I know. . . .'

But his sweetest girl had never been anywhere near Tipperary. He could not imagine her anywhere but in his beloved Cornwall beside the sea where she belonged. His sea maiden. Tom slipped a hand into his pocket and drew out the photograph that he always kept within reach.

It had been taken when they were children and was the only one he had of Morwenna, for he had been too inhibited to ask her for a more recent one. This had been taken by one of a party of amateur photographers who had been on a walking tour of Land's End, taking snapshots of local places of interest, and had stopped in St Just. While they were setting up their tripods in the square, Maria had plied them with cups of tea and her home-made saffron buns, and by way of thanks they had sent her a couple of the prints afterwards.

The innocent faces of the four children looked back at him, saucer-eyed with the importance of the occasion, the little girls in frilled holland pinafores and himself and Jack in caps, waistcoats and breeches. Faces from another lifetime. Grim-faced, he shoved it back in its place.

Why the hell couldn't he bring himself to write to Morwenna and tell her how much he loved her? Even a simple thing like asking her for a photograph of herself was beyond him. Tom gritted his teeth and admitted to himself at last that deep down it was fear. It was fear of rejection which led to this damn reticence of his. For Morwenna had moved on from those childhood days – she had travelled, seen something of the world, had moved up a notch on the social scale. She could do better for herself than a common miner like him.

And now she was doing so, according to her last letter, which had been full of some fellow called 'Kieran'. Stupid fancy name for a stupid bloody Irishman. She'd gone out to dinner with him apparently, followed by a film. And he was staying at the boarding house – so presumably she would be seeing him every day! You could read what you wanted to in that, couldn't you? A surge of pure jealousy gripped him, and Tom turned aside and spat savagely into the mud as bile rose to his throat.

But he had been away for so long, was it reasonable to expect her to wait for him as he had asked her? She had her own life to lead, after all, and was obviously doing so. And by the time this bloody war was over he would have become a different person from the one she known before it began. War changed people – the hideous things he had seen and done were indescribable, and no one who hadn't shared them could be expected to understand, for there were no words to tell them.

And if he couldn't even write a truthful letter to Morwenna, how was he ever going to be able to talk normally to her when they did at last meet again? No, better that she should think he didn't care for her any more. She would be better off without him. He brushed a hand across his eyes and snarled with venom at the man beside him, who had lurched into Tom through sheer exhaustion. Hating himself and all the world, he hefted his pack and plodded on, somehow forcing his aching and blistered feet to keep going.

Pathetic bands of refugees were passing them, going the other way, mostly women with babies and children, and the elderly. They pulled or pushed perambulators, wheelbarrows and farm trucks piled high with all they now owned in the world, some dragging a few wretched cattle and goats alongside. Pitiful survivors of the massive bombardment of Verdun, which had lasted for five months, terror was etched on the faces of the young and a kind of hopeless resignation on those of the aged. The sight of their suffering did nothing to cheer Tom's spirits as he marched on, shrouded in his own personal gloom.

After another couple of hours they came within sight of an abandoned village and were ordered to halt while scouts went on ahead to make sure there were no snipers lying in wait for them. The village lay in ruins, the walls that still stood were scarred and pitted, the rest a mass of jagged broken masonry, the whole area dotted with massive crater holes full of water in which unspeakable things floated. Scattered about lay pitiful remnants of their shattered lives that had been dropped by the villagers as they fled from the advancing army. Discarded clothing, a child's doll, a couple of tattered books all ground into the mud beneath the wheel tracks, told their own story.

When the order came to fall out, the weary men dropped where they were, instantly easing off packs and boots and drinking deeply from their water bottles. Soon someone found a pump that was still blessedly working and they took turns at dousing themselves beneath the icy, exhilarating stream, before replenishing their canteens and catching a few hours' sleep where they could. When Tom found a corner in a cellar along with a dozen others, he stretched out as well as he was able, propped himself on his knapsack and was asleep as soon as his head hit his makeshift pillow.

The ancient fortress of Verdun controlled a vital route leading to Paris and was fondly looked upon by the French people as being a symbol of their former greatness. The German generals, well aware of this, had launched a huge offensive there which had opened with a massive artillery bombardment, during which in one day as many as a hundred thousand gas shells rained down on the French forces.

Despite all their efforts, however, the gallant French held on and after several months the Germans were forced to attend to their defences elsewhere, for the allies had opened an enormous offensive on the Somme. And this was where Tom and his unit were headed.

As soon as she had some free time, Morwenna boarded the lumbering omnibus for St Just in order to call on the Edwards family, putting off for a little longer her visit to Rayle House. This was more important. For one thing, it was a long time since she had managed to get away, and for another, maybe Maria would have had news of Tom by now.

But as the door opened to her knock and Maria appeared, Morwenna could see from her face that something had happened. A cold fist clutched at her heart and an even colder shiver of anxiety feathered down her spine.

'Oh, it's you, Mor – come on in, my handsome.' A subdued Maria, her normally rosy face looking pinched and drawn, led the way down the passage without any of her usual bustle, and the girl's heart sank further.

In the kitchen she turned and faced Morwenna across the scrubbed deal tabletop as she said without preamble, 'Annie Rule had a telegram this morning – Chrissie's Walter have been killed in action.' And a tear coursed down one of the newly etched lines on her familiar face.

'*Walter?* Oh, Maria – how awful!' Morwenna exclaimed as her hand flew to her mouth. But even as she strove to still it, deep inside her selfish heart a voice was singing, 'Not Tom, oh – not Tom!'

She instantly smothered this rush of relief with a stab of compassion for her friend, as she crossed to the other side of the table and clutched at Maria's arm. 'Where's Chrissie now? How is she? Can I see her?'

Maria dabbed at her eyes. 'She's shut herself up in her room and won't come out. Go upstairs, maid, and see if she'll talk to you.'

Morwenna climbed the stairs slowly, her head bowed as she digested this terrible news. Her hands balled into fists, she was filled with impotent fury. Gentle Walter, who had never harmed a living thing in his life, snuffed out like a candle flame. It brought home the total horror of this hell on earth more than all the daily casualty lists could ever do. Poor, decent Walter had never been a great thinker but, as obedient and reliable as one of his horses, had followed the path of duty and paid for it with his life.

Morwenna swallowed down the lump in her throat and tapped on the bedroom door. 'Chrissie,' she called, 'it's me – Mor. Can I come in?' She pushed the door open a crack as she spoke and peered round it. A huddled figure was lying face down on the bed and Morwenna crossed the room and laid a hand on her shoulder. Chrissie half-turned and raised a puffy face, eyes red and swollen with weeping. Clutching Morwenna's hand, she struggled into a sitting position and slumped against the brass bars of the bedhead.

'I knew he was dead before the telegram came,' she said dully. 'I knew it inside myself.' She hugged herself and rocked to and fro as if in physical pain. 'Oh, Mor, Walter wouldn't have hurt a fly, you know he wouldn't. He hated rows and fights of any sort . . . and then to die in that . . . bloodbath. . . .' She put a hand to her face as the tears began to flow again.

Morwenna placed an arm around the shaking shoulders. 'Listen, Chrissie, I'm sure he wouldn't have known anything about it – he wouldn't have suffered, it would have been so quick.' She lied in an attempt to make the horror a little less horrific.

Chrissie clutched at her hand and raised huge tear-filled blue eyes to her friend's face. She was gripping something in her other fist, and she thrust it at Morwenna as she gulped, 'They sent his things back to his mother and this was in them.' Morwenna took the grubby piece of card and turned it over. It was a battered studio photograph which had obviously been taken professionally. Against the formal background of a potted palm, Chrissie posed with one hand resting on a cane table. On her other shoulder lay a disembodied hand, and the rest of the picture had been cut away.

'We had this taken before Walter went away,' she sobbed. 'After he'd asked . . . asked . . . me to marry him.' She broke into another fit of weeping. 'We weren't going to t-t-tell anybody until he came b-back!' She pressed a sodden handkerchief to her face.

'Oh, Chrissie, darling,' Morwenna stroked the limp curls away from the damp forehead, and there was a small silence during which Morwenna's taut nerves could hear the ticking of the clock pounding in her head like a steam-hammer. It was a round metal clock with two alarm bells above, and was standing on a white crocheted mat atop a small chest of drawers beside the bed. Morwenna concentrated on its normality and tried to think of some words of comfort. Bleakly she realized that there were none.

Had she been of a religious nature she supposed there might be, but Morwenna had long ago decided that any so-called God of love who could deprive a small and stricken child of both her parents was not worthy of her veneration. And the present world situation had done nothing to make her change her mind. She tossed her head and raised her eyes heavenwards. God, if he existed at all, had turned his face away from his people and abandoned them to their fate.

She was roused from her reverie by a movement from Chrissie, who now sat up straighter in the bed, reached under the pillow for another handkerchief and blew her nose. Then she dragged herself to the edge of the bed and looked at Morwenna, who saw with pity that her friend's eyes, until now so frequently dancing with merriment, were huge and sunken in her pinched, white face.

But there was an expression in those eyes that Morwenna had never seen before, a hint of hardness, certainly of determination, as Chrissie lifted her chin and said at last, 'I've come to a decision, Mor. I've been thinking about this ever since the telegram arrived.' She padded across the room to gaze out of the window and her eyes were a long way away. Her back to Morwenna now, she went on, 'I'm going to *do* something in this bloody war. I can't go back to the shop as if nothing's changed.' She paused. 'I loved Walter totally, you see.' She rubbed at the glass pane as if something was misting it. 'There was never anyone else for either of us, right from schooldays. But you know that, don't you?' Morwenna nodded, and a small silence fell, broken only by Chrissie's sniffing.

'But what were you going to say, Chris?' Morwenna asked in a gentle voice, 'about doing something?'

'Oh, I know it sounds stupid,' Chrissie said, turning back with a sigh, 'but I thought if I go and do something useful, maybe it will help to keep Tom and Jack safe. Laugh if you like' – she glared defensively under

65

lowered brows at Morwenna, who was doing no such thing – 'but that's the way I think. I know life is never fair but if I can believe that I'm sort of . . . making up the balance a bit, it'll make me feel better.' Her eyes were far away for a moment while silence stretched between the two of them. Then Chrissie came back from the place where her thoughts had led her and said abruptly, 'I'm going to London, Mor – to train as an ambulance driver.'

'*What?*' Morwenna's jaw dropped. '*You?* But—'

'But what?' Chrissie snapped. 'Other women do.'

How could Morwenna put into words the fact that her childhood friend had never been east of Truro in her life and that she had no idea of what she was taking on by going to the nation's war-torn capital, or that she had never, as far as Morwenna knew, even sat behind the wheel of a motor vehicle, let alone contemplated driving one as enormous as an ambulance? She looked with concern at the small, determined figure before her and knew that she could never say any of this. Chrissie, for all her bubbly good nature, had a streak of stubbornness in her which had got her into much hot water as a child; now it would probably stand her in good stead.

'But where will you live? Have you anywhere to stay when you get there? Chrissie, you have to be practical about this.' Morwenna's forehead puckered with concern.

Chrissie's chin came up and she met her friend's eyes. 'Surprising as it may seem, I have thought it all out. It's not a sudden decision, Mor. I was in two minds before Walter . . . well, before.' Her hands linked behind her back, she took a few steps across the room.

'Ma's got a cousin, Beth, who lives in Lewisham. She married a travelling salesman and moved away from Cornwall. We always called her "auntie" when we was small, although she isn't really. I used to like her a lot and I knew she would have me. So I wrote to her weeks ago, secretly like, and she's agreeable.' Chrissie took a turn and came back to where Morwenna was standing. 'It would only be until I could get a room of my own – I wouldn't stay there permanently, I'd feel I was taking advantage.' She met Morwenna's eyes and added, 'Ma doesn't know yet so don't mention it. I'll tell her when the time's right.'

Morwenna put her arms around her friend and hugged her closely. 'Chrissie,' she said, 'I'm really proud of you and I admire you tremendously. You're the bravest person I know, and I wish you all the luck in the world.'

★

'Sophie! Hello. How efficient you look!' Morwenna arrived at Rayle House to find her cousin swathed in a long white apron, bustling about in the communal sitting room.

'Morwenna! It's lovely to see you.' Sophie was carrying a china ewer and a bucket and was engaged in changing the water and freshening up the flowers in the several vases and jugs which stood on the windowsills. The bunches of early daffodils and narcissus brought a homely touch to what had formerly been the Rayle's dining room.

Morwenna looked about her in amazement. This was the first time she had been here since the dinner party which had ended in such drama, when she had stormed out into the night and fled to the Edwards' cottage and Tom.

Now it sparkled with new paint and fresh curtains, which were looped back to give a view over the distant fields to the sea. Sitting about in easy chairs, in various stages of recovery, were half a dozen men, all neatly clad in the government-issue blue suits and red ties. Morwenna nodded a general 'hello' in their direction.

One man, who was gazing into space with a glazed expression, ignored her completely. Another, who was attempting to fit a child's wooden jigsaw puzzle together with hands that were shaking so much he could hardly grasp the pieces, looked up and gave her a weak smile which did not reach his eyes. Of the rest, one raised his head from the newspaper he was reading and grunted a reply, while another gave her a fixed stare and afterwards followed her every movement as if he had never seen a girl before.

With a pang of compassion Morwenna thought that maybe she reminded him of someone he loved, and resigned herself to the stare. She sighed. All these damaged lives – what these men must have seen and done to have become like this. And how would they manage to adjust to normal life again, whenever it should come? Would Tom be like one of these when she saw him next: maimed, crippled, blinded or, worse, brain damaged? Morwenna put a hand to her mouth as her stomach contracted, then jumped as Sophie spoke to her.

'It's been ages since I saw you. Where've you been?' Sophie stopped work and hugged her cousin. Morwenna removed her coat and unwound the scarf from around her neck. Mentally detaching herself from the pathos around her she replied, 'Well, I spent Christmas with the Edwards family.' She draped her coat across the back of a chair. 'You know both their sons are away at the front, don't you?' She perched on the edge of the round, polished table which stood in the centre of the room, as Sophie nodded and dropped into a vacant chair beside her. 'Well, now Chrissie's talking about going up to London to help with the war effort.' Morwenna lowered her voice and added, 'I suppose you know that her Walter was killed in action?'

'Oh yes.' Sophie's face was sombre. 'Mrs Rule's been working for Mother and Father since they moved into the lodge. She comes in every day to help out with the rough jobs – well, she did until this happened.'

'Maria begged me to stay there for Christmas – she's changed a lot and obviously worries about Tom and Jack all the time. She's always looked upon me as a daughter by proxy, and I'm really fond of her, so now I think she'll cling to me more and more when Chrissie goes.'

'And she's going to *London?*' Sophie looked at her, amazed. 'To do what?'

'She's applied to join the Ambulance Corps,' Morwenna replied. 'She wants to do something useful, she says. And also get away from here, where everything reminds her of what she's lost, you see.'

'Poor Chrissie. I don't really know her, of course – I don't know any working-class girls – but she must be really tough.'

'For goodness' sake, Sophie, don't give me that "class" thing – you sound just like your mother!' Morwenna exclaimed, as colour rose to her face. Her eyes flashing in anger, she added, 'Everybody's in this thing together – war doesn't distinguish between *classes*, you know.'

Realizing that she was becoming more heated than the occasion really warranted, Morwenna fell silent. It was only her personal feelings which had made her lash out at Sophie like that – as far as class went, she'd never felt she'd been one thing or the other. A lump rose to her throat as she thought of Eli and the halcyon days of her childhood when the word 'class' meant where she sat in school. She straightened up and said, 'But I'm keeping you from your work, Soph. Is there anything I can do to help?'

'You could give Pru a hand in the kitchen,' Sophie replied, picking up her jug again. 'She's making tea. There are sandwiches to cut and cakes to put out. She'll tell you where everything is. I'll come with you – I need some more water.'

'What are the arrangements now with all the rooms? Everything looks so strange I can hardly recognize the house,' said Morwenna, looking about her in bewilderment as Sophie followed her out into the corridor.

'Well, Matron's taken over what used to be Father's study for her own use, and the nursing staff have the old breakfast room. More WCs and wash basins have been added out the back. We can take twelve men at a time and we're always full.'

Morwenna glanced out of the window as they moved towards the kitchen. It was a soft, mild day with a gleam of pale sunshine hinting that spring was on its way. Snowdrops grew in sheltered nooks and the grass had been newly cut. A couple of patients were sitting in the conservatory and another on the stone bench below, smoking a cigarette. A nurse was pushing another in a wheelchair around the path. The man's folded-up, empty trouser-leg said it all.

Later, having helped pass round the tea and cleared up after it, Morwenna went to find Sophie and see if there was anything else she could do.

'Oh yes, bless you – come and help me change the beds,' her cousin replied and they climbed the stairs together.

'How are Tamsin and Donald, and little ... um ... Rachel, is she called?' Morwenna enquired as Sophie passed her a pile of sheets from the linen cupboard on the landing.

'They're fine. Oh, Mor, Rachel's adorable. She's nearly two now. Dark-haired like Donald, with black eyes always sparkling with mischief. He absolutely dotes on her.' She led the way into one of the bedrooms for three and began to strip off the sheets.

'And it's done Mother such a lot of good to have a little one to think about. It takes her mind off James, you see. He's still at the front line, as far as we know.'

'It seems strange that Donald hasn't joined up as well,' Morwenna said thoughtfully, taking the other end of the clean sheet that Sophie was holding, and shaking it out. 'Is there any reason why he hasn't?'

Sophie frowned. 'No,' she said sharply. She tucked the sheet under the mattress, then straightened up as she went on, 'Do you know, Mor, some woman thrust a white feather at him in the street one day, and he just walked on and pretended not to notice? I was with them and I felt so ashamed, but Tamsin's that loyal she didn't say a word.'

'Well, I've heard that the government's going to bring in conscription soon,' Morwenna said, 'so then he'll jolly well have to go.'

'Good thing, too,' retorted Sophie, thumping a pillow as if it were her brother-in-law's head. 'Why shouldn't he, when everyone else's men are out there in the thick of it?' She stopped, clasping another pillow to her chest as a thought struck her. 'Although you know, don't you, that only single men are to be conscripted at the moment, so he could still wriggle out of it for a bit longer – and I'm sure he will,' she added with a scowl.

Morwenna watched the bustling figure as they bundled up the dirty washing together and said, 'And you, Soph? Isn't there anyone you fancy? It's ages since we had a really good chat.'

'Me?' Her cousin looked up, wide-eyed. 'No', she said, a trifle wistfully. 'Footloose and fancy-free, that's me. I keep so busy I don't really think about it. What with looking after Ma and Pa – they've become so dependent since all this upheaval, you wouldn't believe. And this place too . . . But if there *was* anyone,' she added practically, 'I'd be worried stiff if he was out there fighting, so maybe it's a good thing.'

Morwenna nodded. There was some sense in that. A small silence fell while they tucked the white cotton bedspreads neatly over the whole. Then as she straightened up and anchored a stray lock of her upswept hair, Sophie gazed out of the window and remarked, 'Kieran was here earlier.'

'Oh?' Morwenna raised an eyebrow, astonished to see a faint wash of colour creeping up her cousin's face. Well, well, could that be the way the land lies? she thought with amusement. Generously she wished her cousin well if it was.

'Yes.' Sophie's eyes were still far away. 'I was in Matron's office, dusting, when they both came in. I would have left but she raised a hand and told me to carry on. Kieran had come to say that some new patients would be arriving next week. Some of the men we have here now are well enough to go back to their units, you see.'

She came back to earth and picked up a bundle of dirty linen. Morwenna reached for the other and they dropped them in the corridor while they started work in the next bedroom.

'Then Matron went out and Kieran helped me to stack a pile of heavy files into that high cupboard where she keeps them. I couldn't reach and I was just going to drag the stepladder over, when he took them from me. He's ever so tall, isn't he? And strong.' Sophie's face was dreamy again. 'And I like that moustache he wears. It suits him, don't you think?'

Morwenna smiled at her cousin's transparency but kept her thoughts to herself. They worked companionably on until Morwenna glanced at the clock on the landing and said, 'Well, I must go now, Sophie, but I'll come again whenever I can.'

'There's always plenty to do,' replied her cousin, 'as you know. And thanks for all your help today, Mor. See you soon.' Sophie waved from the top of the stairs as Morwenna went down to retrieve her coat. She was soon on her way with plenty to occupy her mind.

A few weeks later, Morwenna caught the bus into St Just and turned from the square on to the road towards Cape Cornwall that would take her to the Edwards' cottage. She had arranged to meet Chrissie today in order to say her goodbyes. Morwenna was not looking forward to the parting: she knew that she was going to miss her friend terribly. Chrissie and her parents were the only link that Morwenna had with Tom and this, tenuous though it was, meant that she could at least talk about him to someone who understood. But not for much longer.

'Go for a walk, shall we?' said Chrissie after Morwenna had had the customary cup of tea and chat with her parents in the Edwards' kitchen. 'There's some things I must get before the shops close, and Ma wants a loaf of bread. Then we can have a stroll down towards Tregeseal – if this weather don't get any worse.' She peered out of the window at the bank of cloud that was hovering out at sea.

Morwenna nodded. 'Yes, fine,' she replied absently. She was reading a letter from Tom to his mother, which Maria had shown her. In it he thanked his mother for the food parcel she had sent him for Christmas, but apart from that, so many words had been blacked out by the censor that it made a nonsense of the whole thing. It told them absolutely nothing of his whereabouts or what he was actually doing and feeling.

'But at least he's still able to write, so he can't be too bad,' Maria said, folding up the letter as Morwenna handed it back. Then she glanced at Chrissie's haunted face and put a hand over her mouth as if she wished the words unspoken. 'Although we haven't heard a word from Jack for ages. Tom says he spends a lot of time behind the lines looking after the horses. He'd like that, wouldn't he, Mor?' She looked towards the girls for reassurance.

Morwenna nodded and reached for her coat, wondering if Tom was being strictly truthful in what he was writing or was doctoring it for his mother's sake. If so, together with the compulsory censorship which they were subjected to, the only news they held was the fact that he was still actually alive. But that means everything, she told herself – I can get by on just knowing that he's safe. If I'm strong.

'Chrissie,' Morwenna said as they strolled up the road, 'do you . . . um . . . I mean . . .' Head down, she fiddled with the ends of her scarf, then jerked her head up and blurted, 'Do you really think Tom loves me? Be honest now.'

As she met her friend's eyes, Chrissie's face was a picture of astonishment. 'Of course he does, you idiot. How can you possibly doubt it? There was never anyone but you, always. Just like . . . me and Walter.' Her mouth trembled.

'Only he's never actually said so,' Morwenna replied in a small voice. 'He said "wait for me" when he went away, and before that we'd kissed and cuddled a few times, and oh, I love him from the bottom of my heart, but . . . I wondered, you see.'

'Right, just you listen to me.' Now she had been temporarily shaken out of her own concerns, Chrissie sounded almost like her old self. 'Tom's never been the sort to wear his heart on his sleeve. He's a deep one, but he's looked out for you ever since we was children, hasn't he?' Morwenna nodded dumbly. 'And all the time you was away at school he never walked out with anyone else. Truth is, I think when you come back with all this education and stuff he was a bit afraid you'd gone all posh and wouldn't want to know him no more. . . . Oh, I know it wasn't like that,' she added hastily, and held up a hand as Morwenna opened her mouth to protest. 'But I'll tell you something if you must have proof.' Chrissie waved a finger under her friend's nose. 'Ma had a letter last week and there was a note inside for me. Tom asked me to send him a photograph of you.'

Morwenna's eyes widened. 'Of me?' she echoed as her lips involuntarily curved in a smile.

'Yes. Well, I only had that one of us all together – when they photographers came to the village that summer and took ages setting up their stuff in the square. They was there nearly all day. Remember, do you?' Morwenna nodded. 'I bet Tom was too shy to ask you for a more recent one of yourself on your own,' Chrissie went on. 'That's why he wrote to me.' She gave her friend a penetrating look. 'The trouble with you, you know, is that you're always so unsure of yourself, you can never believe people do actually care about you. Add that to Tom's awkwardness and no wonder you don't know how you feel about each other. You both need a good shaking if you ask me.'

Morwenna's spirits had lifted significantly during this exchange and she had to forcibly restrain herself from laughing through sheer exhilaration. A small silence fell. It was soon broken, however, by the unexpected sound of an approaching engine, which made them jump smartly into the hedge.

It was April now and the biting winds of winter had softened with the onset of spring. Moist mild air had been blowing in from the south-west for several days, and now it was bringing with it the soft drizzle which they had seen coming out at sea. It had begun to coat their hair and clothing with pearly drops of dampness and was rapidly reducing visibility to a few hundred yards.

The girls looked up in surprise and peered through the mist, wondering what on earth was coming. When the imperious sound of a horn made them both jump for a second time, they flattened themselves even further into the hedge and watched in amazement as a motor car loomed out of the fog, drew level with them and slowed to a halt.

Chapter Six

HIGH, black and boxy, beneath the sprinkling of dampness on its bonnet and roof the vehicle positively gleamed with new paint and polish.

'Hello there!' A figure in a peaked cap and leather jacket jumped down and hailed them. 'Morwenna! I'm so glad I found you.' With a sweep of his hand and a theatrical flourish he indicated the car. 'What do you think of this, then?' he asked with a grin.

'*Kieran!*' Morwenna's brows disappeared into her hairline as Chrissie goggled beside her. 'It's *you*. I'd no idea you had a car—'

'Just bought her. What a beauty, isn't she?' He lovingly patted the bonnet. 'Model T Ford. Coupé.' He tipped his cap to the back of his head and smiled. 'Hop in, both of you. I'll take you for a spin.'

The girls looked at each other. 'How do you mean, you found me?' asked Morwenna, puzzled, as they stepped nearer. Kieran reached out and opened the passenger door. 'Oh, Clara told me you'd gone to St Just. The rest was just luck.' He looked closely into Morwenna's face and said with feeling, 'I wanted you to be the first person to ride in my new motor, so I did.'

'Oh, I see.' Morwenna broke the eye contact. 'All right then, I'd love a ride.' She put a foot tentatively on the running board. Kieran took her elbow and as she was about to climb into the back, he laid a hand on her arm. 'I want you to sit beside me,' he said, as he turned to help Chrissie up.

'This is my friend Chrissie Edwards,' Morwenna said, introducing them, 'and Chrissie, this is Kieran Doyle, who's staying at Sea Winds.'

As the girls settled themselves on the shiny black leather upholstery, Kieran jumped into the driver's seat, released the handbrake, for he had left the engine ticking over, and they were on their way. 'I feel like royalty sitting up here,' Morwenna said, laughing, and Chrissie gave a squeal as

74

they turned a sharp corner and she lurched sideways.

'Anywhere you'd like to go?' Kieran called back over his shoulder as they left the town and turned on to the coast road.

'Not really. We were only going to the shops, and for a walk,' Morwenna replied. 'Chrissie's leaving home tomorrow. She's going up to London to train as an ambulance driver.'

'Is that so now?' Kieran looked surprised. 'And have you ever sat behind a wheel before at all, Chrissie?' he asked, his eyes meeting hers in the mirror.

'Well, I've had a couple of lessons from Arthur Penrose who keeps the garage up the road,' Chrissie replied, 'but I'm nowhere near ready to take the certificate yet.'

'Have you?' Morwenna said, her eyes widening. 'You didn't tell me that.'

'No,' Chrissie said, 'I was keeping it to myself to surprise you later on.' She looked longingly round the shiny car. 'I've been watching you, though, Kieran – and it looks so much easier in a new motor. The one Arthur lets me drive rattles like an old tin can.' She paused and then said in a rush, 'It's awful cheek, I know, but I don't suppose you'd let me have a go with this one, would you?'

Kieran looked taken aback for a moment. 'Well,' he said at last, 'it's not as easy as it looks, you know. But I'll tell you a thing. If you promise to do exactly as I say, I'll let you have a turn when we come to a straight bit of road. Then you'll see what I mean.'

'Ooh, can I really?' Chrissie's face lit up and for a moment she looked almost like her old self. 'Thanks, Kieran, I'd love to.'

'You too, Morwenna, if you like,' Kieran added, looking towards her with a smile. 'I'd be happy to teach you.' There was a slight inflection in his voice on the word 'you', and when Morwenna shook her head his face fell.

'Another time, perhaps, Kieran. Thanks all the same. It's more important to Chrissie at the moment.'

'Oh. Right.' Kieran drew up and he and Chrissie changed places, then he hung over the back of the driving seat and began to issue instructions. 'But, as I said, take it easy now – if you scratch her paintwork I'll never forgive you.' The remark was casual, but in the mirror Morwenna could see that his face was like granite.

Biting her lip with concentration, Chrissie proved to be surprisingly competent at handling the controls. 'Not a bad job at all – for a beginner,' was Kieran's condescending comment as Chrissie scrambled into the back and he took hold of the wheel again, 'but you'll need a lot of practice, of course, before you can call yourself a really competent driver at all.'

He turned the car around in order to return the way they had come and called over his shoulder, 'I'll drop you back home, Chrissie.' He turned to Morwenna with a smile. 'I'll give you a lift back to Penzance, shall I?'

'Well, that would have been nice, Kieran, but not this time, thanks,' Morwenna replied. 'I came over to say goodbye to Chrissie and we haven't had a chance to chat yet because you came along just as I'd arrived. So I'll make my own way back. I can get the bus almost door to door. See you later on.' She stepped down from the car and the two girls waved as Kieran drove away without another word.

'He didn't look very pleased about that,' remarked Chrissie sagely, turning to Morwenna. 'Did you see how his face dropped when you said you weren't going back with him? I think he came out here thinking he was all set for a cosy twosome with you this afternoon. A trip out in the motor, perhaps a cup of tea somewhere. He didn't bargain for me tagging along too.' She looked her friend in the eye and added, 'He fancies you, Mor, I can tell.'

'Oh, Chris, of course he doesn't!' Morwenna laughed at the very idea. 'He's just a bit lonely when he comes down here – all the people he mixes with are in London, you see.' She shrugged. 'We're just friends.'

Chrissie gave a snort of disbelief and rounded on her. Wagging a finger under Morwenna's nose, she said with conviction, 'There is no such thing as only *friendship* between a man and a woman, Morwenna Pengelly. It just doesn't happen that way. One or the other always wants to take it further and it's usually the man.'

'Oh, come on, Chrissie – you're making a mountain out of a molehill.' Morwenna's laughter had turned to annoyance. 'You know how much I love Tom – do you really think I'm shallow enough to get involved with another man as soon as he's out of sight?'

Chrissie looked contrite. 'Sorry, Mor, I did fly off the handle a bit. But I can't take to that Kieran somehow.' Morwenna's eyebrows rose. 'There's . . . just something about him.' Chrissie wrinkled her nose. 'Oh, I know it was good of him to let me have a go at driving, but . . .' her shoulders lifted in a sigh. 'I think he's a charmer, Mor. All charm and smarm. Out for what he can get. Flashing his new motor around to impress. Looking for the main chance, you know?'

'You're wrong, Chrissie, I'm sure you are!' Morwenna retorted. 'Kieran's good fun and he cheers me up. He's been very good to me.'

But her friend's observations had sown a tiny seed of doubt in Morwenna's mind. How well *did* she actually know Kieran? she asked herself. Added to which, she had been idly wondering before then how he could afford such a brand new car.

'That's what I mean,' Chrissie said with feeling. She took a step or two and looked back over her shoulder, pulling down her tam o' shanter against the rain, which had started in earnest now. 'I'm a pretty good judge of people through working in the shop, Mor, and I've seen his sort before. Too cocky by half, you know what I mean?'

'Kieran's not like that!' Morwenna jumped to his defence as she raised her umbrella. She snapped it open, narrowly missing Chrissie's nose. 'Like I said, he's good company ... amusing ... generous. ...'

'Well, just watch your step, that's all,' Chrissie muttered, lowering her voice as they reached the cottage.

'I won't come in again – I must go if I'm to catch that bus.' Morwenna paused, put a hand on her friend's arm and gave it an affectionate squeeze. 'So this is goodbye, Chrissie.' She met the other girl's eyes and saw that the tears in her own were mirrored there. Wordlessly they embraced and let the tears fall. 'Write to me ... promise ... take care of yourself.'

'You too ... all the luck in the world ... I'll be thinking of you . .' Morwenna tore herself away at last and ran for the bus stop without looking back.

Kieran, on his way back to Penzance alone, was seething. His grand surprise had been spoiled, nothing had worked out the way he had planned, and now the weather was against him as well. It would take all the polish off the bodywork, after he had spent all morning buffing it up. Kieran swore savagely and peered through the driving rain at the dismal countryside. Even the swish of the windscreen wipers was getting on his taut and frayed nerves.

What rotten luck that Morwenna should have had her friend with her. It had never entered his head that she would not be alone. Clara had said she had gone visiting in St Just and he of course had taken it for granted that she meant at Rayle House.

Kieran came at a blind bend too fast and lurched dangerously round it, cursing under his breath. He slowed down and drew a deep breath, admitting to himself at last that it was not the trivial annoyances of the afternoon which had him worked up into such a lather. It was the news from Ireland that had reached him a few days ago.

*

Back in his room at Sea Winds, Kieran kicked off his boots, lay full length on the bed and picked up the envelope which had arrived from home. He pulled out the newspaper clipping which it contained and read it through again, although he knew it almost off by heart.

'Irish patriots stage uprising at Easter'

'An Irish republican leader, Michael Pearse, waited politely in a queue for stamps in the General Post Office in Dublin, before telling the startled counter clerk that an Irish republic had been declared.

Within hours Dublin was ablaze, as well-armed British troops – many of them veterans from the war in France – blasted republican strong-points, including the post office, with heavy artillery. Fifteen of the leaders of this revolt are to be executed.'

Across the bottom his father had written, *'Declan was standing on the street watching, and got caught up in the crossfire. He was hit in the arm and very shaken up. Nothing serious, but enough to keep him off work for a few weeks.'*

Kieran sat up, crumpled the scrap of paper into a ball and hurled it savagely across the room. Bloody English! And trust Dec to be there in the thick of it. Watching? Kieran snorted. His youngest brother would not have been satisfied with watching – he'd have been throwing stones or some such thing, for he had no more time for the English than the rest of his family.

For nothing had changed since 1914, thought Kieran, when Ulster had risen in protest against their plans for Home Rule. The war had put all that temporarily on ice, but by all accounts his outraged countrymen were obviously not prepared to wait indefinitely for the pussy-footing Asquith and his parliament at Westminster to act. Good for them.

Kieran clenched his fists, stood up and caught sight of his glowering face in the mirror which hung on the wardrobe door, shrugged his shoulders and stalked out of the room.

Morwenna awoke one morning in early June to the bitter-sweet realization that it was her twenty-first birthday. It was a momentous occasion in one respect, to have achieved adulthood at last, but what difference was it going to make to her life as it was now? The only birthday present she longed for was the one thing – or rather person – that was denied her.

She slipped out of bed and pulled back the curtains. It was going to be a perfect summer day. A golden light was already shimmering over the bay, the Mount floated on a sea of turquoise, and puffy clouds like stiffly whipped meringue hung in the powder-blue sky. Cheered, Morwenna quickly washed and dressed and went downstairs. No one could be down-hearted for long on a day like this.

Clara was just finishing her breakfast as Morwenna entered the kitchen and looked up with a smile from the folded newspaper beside her plate. 'Good morning, Morwenna,' she said with a smile. 'Happy birth-day!'

Morwenna's eyes widened in surprise.

'How did you know?' she asked in amazement. Clara rose and touched her mouth with a napkin. 'You forget that your date of birth was on your application for the position when I took you on here,' she replied, approaching Morwenna with a small package in her hand.

'And you remembered all this time!' Morwenna, touched, looked at Clara with fondness as her employer pressed something into her hand. She and Clara had developed a very good working relationship, and occa-sionally also spent comfortable evenings together in Clara's sitting room where they would sew or read together. During one of these, Morwenna, glancing at Clara's bent head, the grey hair swept tastefully up above her round, sweet face, thought wistfully that had her mother lived she would have liked her to look just like this.

'Just a little gift with all my good wishes for your twenty-first,' she said, and Morwenna murmured her thanks as she found two exquisitely embroidered handkerchiefs and a bottle of cologne inside the wrapping.

'That's really kind of you, Clara,' she said with sincerity and leaned forward to place a kiss on the other woman's cheek.

'And take the day off, my dear. Go out and enjoy yourself. I can manage perfectly well here without you for once.'

'Oh, Clara, are you sure? How lovely! Thank you very much, and thanks again for these, too.' Morwenna indicated the hankies. 'My first birthday present,' she added with a smile. 'But not the last, I hope.' Clara squeezed her arm and returned the kiss.

'It certainly isn't,' came a voice from the doorway, and Kieran strode into the room, his arms full of flowers.

Morwenna's jaw dropped. 'Kieran! You knew as well?' She glanced at Clara and saw from the twinkle in her eyes where the information had come from. 'Oh, thank you so much.'

She buried her nose in the bouquet. Lilies, scented ones, their great shining white trumpets dusted with gold, and little pink button roses set among trails of emerald-green fern. 'These are absolutely beautiful.' She looked up to meet Kieran's smile and at the same time noticed that Clara had slipped quietly out of the room.

'Happy birthday, Morwenna', he said, his eyes locking into hers, 'and congratulations on reaching such a ripe old age.'

She laughed and wondered idly how old he was. A lot more than twenty-one, she guessed.

'I reached that milestone five years ago,' Kieran said, as if answering her unspoken question. 'And I had a right old razzle to remember it by. What would you like to do to celebrate yours?'

'Celebrate? Oh . . . I hadn't thought, I've no idea . . . I never dreamt. . . .' Morwenna stammered, her head reeling.

'I've got a few days' leave before I go back up to London for a while,' Kieran went on. 'How about a drive somewhere? It's a glorious day, so it is, and perhaps a picnic lunch? Or would you rather do something else? Did you have any plans of your own at all?'

Morwenna was doing some rapid thinking. How *was* she going to spend her birthday? She hadn't the faintest idea – she'd imagined until now that it would be just an ordinary day. But since Clara had been generous enough to give her the day off, and now that Kieran was offering to take her out, it really would seem churlish to refuse their kindness. An outing *would* be nice. Since Walter had died, thoughts of Tom and what might be happening to him were always on her mind, as a backdrop of worry which impinged on her everyday life no matter how much she tried not to let it. She drew in a long breath and her face brightened.

'No, I hadn't. But a drive and perhaps a walk somewhere? That would be lovely. Do you like walking, Kieran?' It had been one of Morwenna's favourite pursuits during the awkward years of her adolescence, when summer holidays at Rayle House had been uncomfortable and seemingly endless. She and Tom had slipped away many a time to roam the spectacular coast and moors of West Penwith.

'Sure and I've never done much of it myself,' Kieran replied with a grin. 'But if that's what you'd like, it just so happens that I have a sturdy pair of boots with me, so I do.'

'Good.' Morwenna smiled back, liking his honest, open face and the way his eyes crinkled up at the corners when he smiled. 'Maybe we could go along the coast road and I could show you some of my favourite places.'

'I'll look forward to that.' Kieran glanced at his watch. 'Shall we say, be ready to leave in an hour? That'll give me time to get a few things together and collect the car from the garage.'

'Right.' Morwenna nodded, and turned to go upstairs. 'I'll see you here again in an hour, then.'

From Penzance, Morwenna directed Kieran on to the high road which wound upwards above Mount's Bay towards St Ives, but skirted the town as they turned left and headed out towards the wild and windy beauty of the moors beyond.

Here, the bare bones of the ancient land lay exposed to the elements. Huge granite boulders reared out of the ground, shaking off the thin covering of soil as a snake shrugs off its skin. Towering crags swept upwards to the skyline, where large rocks had been piled on top of smaller ones in spectacular formations, seemingly ready to topple at any moment. It was primeval, timeless and awe-inspiring.

'Wow, will you be looking at that now!' Kieran gave a whistle as he peered from side to side as much as he could, while still keeping his eyes on the roller-coaster sweeps and hairpin bends of the narrow road.

'I thought you'd be impressed,' said Morwenna. 'We turn left at the next fork. There, look,' she added, indicating an even narrower road as Kieran changed gear and swung the car into the bend. Soon Morwenna was pointing again. 'Now, pull in on the left beside the next field gate – that's where we're going to stop,' she told him.

Kieran did as she asked and the car came to a halt. They both climbed out, he wearing knickerbockers and a cord waistcoat over his white shirt, she in a shirtwaist of leaf-green poplin and a simple straw boater. The two stood looking around them for a moment, drinking in the pure air and sniffing the scents of summer – honeysuckle in the field hedge, heather and thyme drifting on the breeze, all overlaid with the faint tang of the sea, which shone in a band of purest blue in the distance.

'And that's the way we're going to walk,' Morwenna said, nodding towards a track which led inland. 'There's something up there that I want you to see.'

They fell into step for a few yards but were soon forced to walk in single file as the path narrowed. Morwenna led the way until they came to a granite stile on their right, and she scrambled over it and out on to the moor proper. 'Over here, look,' she said coming to a halt. 'Have you ever seen anything like this before?'

Ahead of them and standing about waist-high was a grey granite boulder with a circular hole cut through the middle of it, making it look like a doughnut placed on its rim. Flanking it were two upright stones of about the same height.

'This is the Men-an-Tol,' Morwenna announced, with a smile at the expression on Kieran's face. He pushed his flat cap to the back of his head and scratched his curly head in bewilderment.

'The what – and shall we be having that again, if you please?' he said blankly.

'The Men-an-Tol,' Morwenna repeated. 'It literally means "stone with a hole" in the old Cornish language.'

Kieran's forehead creased in a frown. 'Cornish language? I didn't know there was one.' He stepped forward and paced around the stones.

'Oh, there was at one time,' Morwenna replied, 'but it died out. Sometime in the eighteenth century I think it was.'

'So what was it for, this stone of yours?' He placed a hand on its rim.

'No one is quite sure, but all sorts of folk tales sprang up around it over the years. People used to pass their children through the hole supposedly to cure them of rickets.' Kieran raised an eyebrow. 'This area is full of ancient standing stones – quoits, barrows, circles,' Morwenna went on, waving a hand which took in the whole sweep of the land as far as the thrusting chimney of a mine engine house which stood like a sentinel on the skyline. 'Just up the lane from here is the Men Scryfa – that means "the inscribed stone" – and there are lots of others within walking distance.'

'You seem to know the district very well,' Kieran remarked.

'Oh, yes.' Morwenna's eyes were far away. 'I used to come here a lot in the holidays, with my friends.'

'With Tom, you mean?' Kieran's eyes were on her face as she turned towards him and Morwenna flushed under his scrutiny.

'Yes,' she said, dropping her gaze and scuffing at a stone in the path with the toe of her boot. 'And his brother and sister,' she added. 'We used to cycle over and bring a picnic – make a day of it.' She raised her eyes. 'Just like we're doing now, in fact.'

Kieran kept his eyes on the slim figure long after Morwenna had turned away, her attention distracted by some moorland ponies who were looking over the nearby hedge. She was grubbing up handfuls of the sweet grass which grew below the bank and holding it to their soft, snuffling mouths in delight. Her hat had fallen off and was swinging by its elastic from the back of her neck. With her hair streaming in the wind – for it had come unpinned again and was tumbling to her shoulders – and her simple cotton gown, he was thinking that she looked about twelve years old.

Kieran had had his share of encounters with the sophisticated young women whom he met when he was in London. He was an attractive man and knew it, playing on it to his advantage when he wanted to, and had never been short of partners. But this fresh young girl with the country bloom on her cheeks and the sea in her eyes had stirred his heart as it had never been stirred before.

He pulled himself together. The last thing he needed at this time was to fall for a woman: he had no time for such complications in his life. But as Morwenna turned and called over her shoulder, 'Oh, Kieran, aren't they adorable? Their noses are so soft, you wouldn't believe,' and smiled her captivating smile, he felt something turn over inside himself and knew that convenient or not, he was fast falling for her and there was not a thing he could do to prevent it.

They walked the moors until they could walk no more, while larks sang in the blue infinity above them, far out of sight but sending down a cascade of liquid notes like a shower of golden rain. When they had rested and eaten and were almost falling asleep, lulled by the warmth and the gentle swaying of the grasses around them, Morwenna remarked, her hands behind her head and her back resting against a comfortable rock, 'I had a letter and a birthday card from Chrissie the other day.'

'Oh yes?' said Kieran lazily, stretched out full length on his back beside her, his cap tipped over his eyes against the sun.

'Apparently she's had enough of living with her relation and has gone to stay in a Y.W.C.A. hostel.' She paused, then added, 'Where did you say you live, Kieran?'

'Blackheath.' He lay back and stared into the blue nothingness above him. 'Black because it's where they buried the victims of the Black Death, you see,' he murmured. 'There's a church there.'

'Oh? I didn't know that.' Morwenna shifted her position and her finger traced one of the speckles of vivid orange lichen which decorated the rock. 'But then I don't know much about London at all. I've only passed through it a few times. Anyway, Chrissie seems to be enjoying the company in the hostel. She says she meets all sorts of girls, has made some friends and is kept so busy that she never has time to brood.'

'That's good,' Kieran said, and a silence fell.

Morwenna idly plucked a grass stem and nibbled it between her front teeth as she said softly, 'I've been thinking lately that I'd like to do something more positive than just helping out at Rayle House when I get the time.'

'You?' Kieran sat up abruptly. 'What sort of thing do you mean?'

'Oh, I don't know, it's only a vague thought – but I really admire Chrissie for uprooting herself and going off like she did.'

'But she comes from a different background, of course, from you. You were brought up to be a young lady, after all, and Chrissie—'

'Is working *class*, was that what you were going to say, Kieran?' He looked on in astonishment as Morwenna leapt to her feet and put her hands on her hips.

'Well . . . yes, if you want to put it like that,' he replied, rising and brushing off bits of grass from his legs.

'I'll have you know' – Morwenna pointed a finger – 'that when I was growing up I received more affection and friendship from the so-called "working classes" than I ever had from my relations. They believed that everyone had been given their proper place in life and should be content to stay there.' She shrugged her shoulders and extended her hands. 'Naturally, their own position was at the top of the heap.'

Kieran seized both Morwenna's hands in his own and held her captive as he retorted, 'And what is so wrong with that at all? Sure and it's the way the world is.'

'But it shouldn't be like that!' Morwenna snapped. 'It really upsets me the way that people with money think that it makes them somehow *better* than those who have less.'

As she glowered up at him with stormy eyes, her hair blowing in strands across her face and her small, determined chin raised in defiance, Kieran knew that he was lost. It was all he could do not to wrap his arms around her there and then and tell her how he felt. But instead he dropped her hands and turned away, lest she should read in his face what he could never tell her, as long as Tom's shadow stood between them.

A few days later Morwenna was surprised to receive an official-looking letter in the post and slit it open to find that it was headed Clemo and Hobbs, Solicitors, at an address in Penzance. Her stomach did a little flip of excitement as she scanned the contents. . . . *should be pleased if you would call at your earliest convenience . . . discuss a matter of importance. . . .* And it was signed by Donald Miller.

Morwenna made a face. She would rather not have her cousin-by-marriage knowing all her business but it could hardly be helped. She would call round there in her lunch break. The office was not far away, in St Mary's Street.

'Ah, Morwenna!' Donald rose from behind his massive mahogany desk and took her hand. She looked into his narrow, pasty face, its black eyes cold as pebbles, and gave a polite smile. 'Please sit down.' He indicated a small button-back chair covered in brown leather.

'Hello, Donald.' Morwenna sat and smoothed down the skirt of her dress. Striped cotton in shades of lilac and cream, it toned well with her new straw hat trimmed with lilac flowers. A few pleasantries about the family followed, before Donald cleared his throat and picked up a sheaf of papers, removing the pink tape with which they were tied.

'I'm sure you know why we have asked you to call,' he said, placing a pair of wire-framed spectacles on his nose and looking over the top of them. Morwenna nodded and waited for him to go on. 'Of course, your grandfather placed the deeds of his cottage with us until you gained your majority.' He indicated one envelope and placed it beside him while he took up another. 'Now this' – he picked up the next document in the package – 'is a personal letter to you.' He handed it across the desk, seemingly with reluctance, the seal unbroken. Morwenna took it with thanks and buried it in her handbag. There was no way she would give Donald the satisfaction of knowing what Gramp had written to her. Donald paused, watching her, then seeing that she was not going to be forthcoming, picked up another document.

'This is your grandfather's last will and testament,' he said with gravity, 'which was dealt with at the time, of course, leaving out his bequests to you, which will now come into effect.'

He paused and ran a hand over his straight black hair, which was sleek with macassar-oil, then withdrew the stiff vellum sheets and prepared to read the document aloud. Morwenna was not expecting any surprises in it, nothing that she did not already know. Why can't he just *give* it to me? she thought with irritation as Donald pompously began to hold forth. She realized then that he was revelling in the sense of power it gave him. Oh, the self-importance of the man! she thought.

Donald came to the end at last, folded the document and steepled his fingers as he met Morwenna's eyes. 'And now,' he went on, 'we come to the business of the rents. Rents from the cottage, which has been let continuously since your grandfather's death. We have now received the figures from the agency which has been dealing with it under our direction and I think you will be very pleased at the amount which has accrued, with the accompanying interest, over the years. Even after having deducted the cost of maintenance of the place, and your own allowance, it has returned a net sum of...' Morwenna nearly fell off her seat at the amount he quoted. '... which has been placed in your bank account to date from your coming of age.'

Donald laid the paper down in front of him. 'So, it would appear that you are a wealthy young woman, Morwenna. Congratulations.' He gave a thin smile. 'You'll be able to be quite independent now.'

'Donald,' Morwenna retorted with annoyance, 'you're forgetting something, aren't you?' His head jerked up and he looked at her with surprise. 'I've been independent for almost three years now.' Her eyes bored into his. 'And I've been supporting myself very adequately ever since I left Rayle House.'

'Ah yes.' His voice and smile were full of condescension as he replied. 'But my meaning was that you won't have to *work* for your living any longer.' He rubbed his hands together and simpered. 'Like one of the lower orders, you know. You'll be able to rise in society – take a step up – mix with a better class of people.'

Class again, thought Morwenna, fuming as she glared back at him. 'Perhaps this is something that you are unable to understand, Donald,' she retorted, flushed with annoyance, 'but I do actually *enjoy* my work, you know. And I've no intention of giving it up because of my change of circumstances. Strange as it may seem, I have no desire whatsoever to move in any of these higher circles which seem to be so important to you.'

Donald's eyebrows lifted. 'You always were too headstrong for your own good,' he replied coldly. 'Tamsin was right.' His mouth was set in a thin line. 'I heard all about the way you treated Phoebe, you know, and after she'd been so good to you as well. And now you're proving to be even more foolish and self-centred than I thought.' He shrugged and spread his palms. 'But if you won't take good advice when it's given, then you must go your own way – and don't expect any sympathy from any of us if you get into trouble.' He snapped his mouth shut like a trap and ripped his spectacles from his face as two spots of red stained his pale cheeks.

'I certainly won't,' said Morwenna with asperity, jumping to her feet. 'So, as I think we have nothing left to say to each other, Donald, I'll take those papers, thank you.' She reached across the desk and he handed them to her, stony-faced. 'I'll be on my way.'

He rose, tight-lipped, and inclined his head in a mocking little bow as he opened the door for her. Morwenna swept out with her chin in the air

– and a cold place in her heart, which was aching for understanding, sympathy and support.

Morwenna opened Gramp's letter as soon as she was back in her own room and not likely to be disturbed.

To my beloved granddaughter,

By the time you read this you will be woman grown, with maybe a husband, possibly even little ones of your own. I hope so. To find someone to love and be loved by in equal measure is the greatest treasure in this life.

If that treasure has not yet come your way, then I hope that you have found happiness in whatever walk of life you have chosen. How I should love to have seen you grow up, but it was not to be. I have been told that I have not much longer to live, which is why I am arranging my affairs as best I can for the future. Especially for your future.

I have been privileged to have had you to myself for so long, Morwenna my dear. I want you to know that you have been the light of my declining years, and that you never caused me a minute's trouble while I was raising you.

The lump in her throat which had been growing steadily bigger by the minute, now spilled over into tears and Morwenna with impatience dashed a hand across her wet eyes in order to read the rest of the letter.

Our home and all its contents are to be held in waiting for you. Of course you will have to go and live at Rayle after my demise, but I should like to think that sometime during the years to come, you will want to return here, and perhaps remember all the happy times we had together.

Tears were streaming unchecked down her face as Morwenna heard the echo of her grandfather's voice and saw in her mind the craggy face and wise, kindly eyes of the old man. Subconsciously she fingered her mother's locket, which she always wore close to her heart, and so deep in the past was she that she had failed to notice that there was something else in the envelope. But as she sniffed and wiped her eyes again, her fingers came into contact with a bulky package.

Banknotes! Morwenna's mouth dropped open as she riffled through them and realized the size of the sum she was holding. She reached for the letter again.

With this letter you will find a sum of money that nobody but the two of us knows about. Not the lawyers nor the trustees, who will have to see to all the other stuff. This is a present from me to you with no strings attached. I am sure that you will use it wisely, my dear, and if it can sweeten your journey through life, then it will have achieved its purpose. You have a sensible head on your young shoulders now, and I cannot imagine that this will change much in the future.

So Morwenna, my little sea maiden, I hope you will think of me sometimes and perhaps remember with fondness your old,

Gramp

Morwenna put her hands over her face as sobs threatened to choke her, and it was a long while before she could get her feelings under control. When she eventually did so, however, she realized that wisely invested, Gramp's legacy meant that she need never worry about money again.

Chapter Seven

'OH Kieran, hello! I didn't expect to see you here today.' Morwenna, entering Rayle House by the back door one afternoon in early June, came across him sitting deep in conversation with one of the patients.

'Hello, Morwenna.' A smile lit up his face as he rose to his feet. 'Isn't it a lovely day? You're looking quite warm.'

Morwenna smiled. 'I am. I've been working in the garden for an hour, pulling up weeds in the rose beds.' She fanned her hot face with the hat she had just taken off. 'It's glorious out there – so sheltered below the conservatory that there's hardly a breeze. And that doesn't happen here very often.' On the exposed promontory where St Just was situated, the wind was usually blowing from one direction or another.

'That sounds like hard work for a summer day,' Kieran remarked. Morwenna shook her head and tossed her hat on to a chair. 'Oh no, I enjoyed it. It's nice to be outside after working indoors most of the time.' She tried to tidy her hair with her fingers, but too many pins had been lost in the flowerbed, so she shrugged and gave up the struggle.

'I've been having a chat with Captain Adams over there.' Kieran indicated with his head the man Morwenna had seen previously being pushed around the grounds in a wheelchair. 'Doctor Miller was here earlier too,' he went on as they both wandered out into the conservatory and sat down on a couple of cane chairs. 'I told him I was going away,' Kieran said, leaning back with his hands behind his head, his long legs resting on a plant pot in which a climbing jasmine was growing, filling the air with scent. 'He gave me another supply of cough medicine to take with me.' He paused for a moment, then added, 'He's a good chap, Miller, so he is.'

'I don't really know him, except that I did help him to change some dressings the other day and he said how neat my bandages were, so I have to agree with you, don't I?' Morwenna chuckled.

Kieran looked over his shoulder and lowered his voice as he said, 'That chap Adams is one of the lucky ones – he lost a leg at Verdun, you know.'

Morwenna blinked. 'Lucky?' She frowned and wrinkled her nose in bewilderment.

'He won't be going back,' Kieran said. 'He got himself a "Blighty one", as they call it.' Morwenna's face cleared as she understood. He paused, then added, 'How old do you think he is, Mor? Have a guess.'

'How old?' Morwenna repeated, as she glanced across at the man's haggard face and shaking hands. She shrugged. 'About forty?'

'He's twenty-two,' replied Kieran. Morwenna felt her face drop. 'Twenty-*two?*' she repeated again as she struggled to take it in. 'That's not much older than me! Poor fellow!'

'Yes.' Kieran's face was grave. 'He saw his commanding officer blown to bits in front of him,' he went on. 'And as the only officer left in his squad he had to take over. The responsibility aged him overnight, as you can see.'

Morwenna swallowed and blinked. Terrible things were going on out there of which she knew nothing, and could only imagine when it was brought home to her like this. Oh, my Tom! she thought. 'Oh, the poor man,' she said aloud, as she rose to her feet and turned away with a heavy heart. As she turned to go back into the main room, she almost collided with Sophie, who was just coming in bearing a laden tea-tray.

'Oops,' said her cousin with a giggle, neatly side-stepping.

'Oh – sorry, Sophie,' said Morwenna, 'I was daydreaming.'

'I'd better take that while it's still in one piece, so I had.' Kieran had followed Morwenna inside and now relieved Sophie of the tray and set it down on a corner table. Only her cousin noticed the flush that rose to Sophie's cheeks as she smiled back and thanked him. 'I'll help you pass the cups round,' Morwenna said.

'Have some yourselves, will you?' Sophie asked, hefting an enormous teapot.

'Well—' Morwenna began, and at the same time Kieran said, 'No thanks. I was after thinking that as I have to leave in a few days' time, you might like to come out to tea with me as a sort of goodbye treat—' Sophie beamed at him and drew in a breath to reply, but a small frown creased Kieran's brow as he glanced at her and away. 'Um ... Morwenna,' he finished. Morwenna watched the expectant smile slide from Sophie's face and felt a stab of compassion for her cousin, but Kieran seemed oblivious.

'Lovely,' she said. 'But first I must just go and wash my hands and tidy myself up. Shan't be a minute.'

★

'I thought The Copper Kettle, perhaps,' said Kieran as they strolled back to the town square.

'Fine,' Morwenna replied. 'They're well known for their gorgeous cakes.'

Later, after they had finished a plate of dainty sandwiches and were trying to choose from a cake stand piled high with eclairs, macaroons, fruit tartlets and other delicacies, Morwenna said lightly, 'Kieran, I don't know whether you've noticed this, but I have.' She looked across the table and met his eyes as he helped himself to a cream horn and picked up a pastry fork. 'Sophie's sweet on you,' she announced, choosing a meringue for herself.

Kieran's eyes widened. '*What?*' he spluttered into a mouthful of tea. After he had replaced the cup on to its saucer and dabbed his moustache with his napkin, he repeated, 'What? *Sophie?* Oh, no, you must be mistaken.' He gazed at Morwenna in disbelief.

'I'm not,' she replied through a mouthful, and shook her head. 'I've seen the way she looks at you and how her expression changes when she mentions your name.' Morwenna lifted her cup and took a sip of tea. 'And just now she was really disappointed because she thought you were asking both of us out for tea, and not just me.' She met Kieran's astonished face and shrugged her shoulders.

'Really?' Kieran said. 'Oh, hang it, I didn't mean to hurt her at all but I hadn't the slightest idea. . . .' He gazed at Morwenna in consternation. 'What am I going to do, Mor? I don't have any feelings for her whatsoever.' He fell silent for a moment. Then, 'In fact . . .' Morwenna's free hand was lying on the table and he placed his own warm one over it as he added softly, 'Morwenna, you must know by now how I feel about you, don't you?'

Morwenna jumped as if she had been stung, and stared back at him wide-eyed. 'N-no,' she stammered. 'I didn't . . .' Then she remembered what Chrissie had said, as she saw her friend's face again and heard the echo of her voice in her ears. 'He fancies you, Mor, I can tell. . . .' So Chrissie had been right all along and she hadn't believed her. Oh dear, this was awful. Morwenna swallowed and took a deep breath as she wondered how best to express herself.

'Kieran,' she said gently, 'I don't want to hurt you – that's the last thing I would do – and I'm genuinely fond of you as a friend, but you must know how much I love Tom, don't you? And that I could never look at anyone else.'

'I rather thought that's what you would say,' Kieran replied, downcast, his dark eyes losing their sparkle. 'Well, this Tom of yours is a lucky man, that's all I know, and I hope he realizes it, to be sure I do.'

Morwenna bent her head, removed her hand, and a small silence fell as they continued with their meal. Oh, why does everything have to be so *complicated?* she wondered. The delicious cake turned to dust and ashes in her mouth.

'Morwenna, have you heard the latest news?' Clara came bustling into Sea Winds a few days later, shaking out her umbrella – for she had been caught in a sudden shower on her way back from the shops – and letting the door swing to with a bang.

Morwenna looked up in surprise from her work at the counter. Her employer was not usually so animated. 'No.' She shook her head. 'What news?' Clara crossed the hall as she removed her hat and pushed its pearl-ended pin into the crown.

'It's all over the town,' she said, twisting up a loose lock of hair. She lowered her head and met Morwenna's eyes. 'Somebody threw a brick through the window of Doctor Miller's surgery during the night and scrawled anti-German slogans on the walls. How about that, then?' Clara pursed her lips and gave a nod as she waited for the girl's reaction.

'Doctor *Miller?*' Morwenna's eyebrows rose to her hairline. 'But Clara, why?' She frowned as she tried to take it all in. 'I know that people are ridiculously jumpy and see Germans everywhere these days, but I just don't understand that at all,' she said, nibbling a thumbnail.

'Well,' Clara replied, straightening up and pulling off her gloves finger by finger, 'rumour has it that apparently John Miller's family *are* of German origin.' She flicked a glove for emphasis and went on, 'Now how anybody discovered this is beyond me, but the story goes that their real name is "Muller" – he's actually "Jan" – and that they very wisely angli-cized it just before the war began.' She withdrew the second glove and tossed it on to a chair along with the hat.

'Good gracious, what a horrible thing to happen.' Morwenna stared up at her employer. She leaned her elbows on the desk and cupped her chin. 'I know it's been happening in other places, this persecution of anyone with German connections – you read about it in the papers all the time – but when it's this near to home it makes you shiver, doesn't it?'

'It does.' Clara nodded and her face was solemn. 'I wonder how this will affect his practice too?'

'Quite a lot, I should say,' Morwenna replied. 'And of course . . .' Her eyes widened. 'I've just had another thought.' She pointed a finger. 'Clara, there's Rayle House too. He's the doctor in attendance there. Now that could be very awkward, couldn't it – with him treating the wounded soldiers.'

'Oh yes.' Clara said, meeting her eyes. She shrugged. 'If there's any truth in the rumour, of course,' she added, picking up her hat and gloves. 'But you can't help thinking that there's no smoke without fire, can you?' she said over her shoulder as she turned to leave the room.

Morwenna sat on in a daydream. What about *Donald* Miller too, she was thinking. And Tamsin and little Rachel. If the story were true, the ramifications would be endless, especially in the light of what Sophie had said the other day about Donald being reluctant to join up and fight.

Morwenna shook herself and came back to earth. It was probably all conjecture, nothing more, for there were rumours flying about all the time – some being more far-fetched than others. There were even those who swore that they knew somebody who knew somebody who had seen enemy soldiers marching south from Scotland with snow on their boots! And only last week a tramp who had been sleeping rough under a hedge had been apprehended as a suspected spy and hauled up before the special constable. And she had work to do.

But Morwenna was interrupted for a second time, by the clattering of feet coming down the stairs, and Kieran appeared, a raincoat over his arm, carrying his hat and briefcase in one hand and a large suitcase in the other. She looked at him in surprise – dark suit, starched collar, smart tie. 'Hello, Kieran, you're in some hurry, aren't you? What's all this then?' she asked, indicating the luggage.

'Ah, Morwenna.' He stopped beside the desk and put down his suitcase. 'You remember I told you I had to go back to London soon, don't you?'

'Oh, yes. But I didn't realize you meant this soon!' She looked up at him, wide-eyed. He had a preoccupied air about him and was tapping one foot as if he couldn't wait to be off.

'I'm afraid so. Something's come up, so I'm catching the 10.15.' Kieran drew a watch on a chain from his waistcoat pocket and glanced at it. He picked up the suitcase again. 'I've left the key in the door of my room, by the way,' he said over his shoulder as he turned to leave.

'When will we be seeing you again?' Morwenna voice was anxious. She had come to rely on him always being around, and was going to miss his cheerful company.

'I can't be sure, but not for quite a while. There are more and more wounded pouring in on the hospital trains apparently, with all these latest casualties, and I'm needed there. But I'll write and keep in touch. Shall I?'

He looked doubtful as to what her reaction would be.

But Morwenna nodded. 'I'd like that,' she said, and meant it.

'Goodbye for the time, then.' Kieran gazed back at her intently for a moment as if he was trying to memorize her face.

'Goodbye, Kieran,' she replied and he shook her hand like a stranger.

As he crossed the hall and turned at the outside door to raise a hand, the postman was coming up the steps and tipped his cap as Kieran held the door for him. 'Morning, miss.' He handed Morwenna a pile of envelopes.

'Morning, Sid. Thanks,' she said absently, her eyes on Kieran's retreating figure as he hurried down the street.

When at last she turned her attention to the letters, Morwenna's face lit up as she found a personal one addressed to her. But it fell again as quickly when she realized it was not the handwriting that she longed to see. She heaved a sigh. This one was from Chrissie, though, and it would be lovely to hear from her, of course. She slit the envelope and removed the couple of sheets inside.

Dear Mor,

Well, here I am and with so much news that I don't know what to tell you first. The hostel is very comfortable although there is not much privacy. We have sleeping cubicles and you can hear every word through, the partitions are so thin. I felt very lonely and homesick at first, and sometimes I still do, but I've met some really nice people – from all sorts of different backgrounds – and made a few friends. They tease me about my Cornish accent – some of them are a bit posh – but it's all in fun.

I've just finished a First Aid course and came through that all right. I've also learnt a lot about the ambulances. At the moment I go out with a girl called Angela who drives, but I shall soon be driving myself. We have a Siddeley-Deasy vehicle and our main function is to deal with street accidents. But during the air raids of course we shall be vitally needed. Do you know that the Ambulance Corps is run entirely by women? I didn't until I got here. And we're expected to do everything that the men used to do – like clean the vehicles and scrub down the yard, which is really hard work because of all the grease and oil. But I do feel I'm doing something useful, and we're paid at the same rate as the men, so that's good.

I must tell you about the uniform we wear – you've never seen me looking so smart! Blue serge Norfolk jackets and skirts, with gloves and a lovely warm overcoat for the winter – also oilskins and leather gaiters with buttons. And a natty little cap like the V.A.D.s wear, but with a light-blue band instead, and a badge on the front. I wish you could see me in it, you'd never recognize me!

We work about twelve hours a day, but there are long periods when there's not much to do, so we sit about and chat and read, sew, etc. and write letters! But the worst thing is night driving – I dread the time when I shall be doing that – because of course all the lighting is reduced everywhere and the ambulances have only very dim headlamps. Add to that the unfamiliar streets and you can realize why I don't relish that part of it. One girl said that when it was foggy in the winter she had to cross Blackheath at a snail's pace with her partner walking ahead to keep in touch with the side of the road. Imagine trying to hurry to the scene of an accident in those conditions!

Well, I'd better close now and get this in the post. Write soon and tell me all the news from home.

Love, Chrissie.

Morwenna dropped the letter on to the desk and sat with her face cupped in her hands for a few minutes, her thoughts miles away. Since Kieran had left she had been seized with a vague restlessness which she could not identify. The letter from Chrissie had left her feeling even more unsettled. In the face of her friend's busy, active and rewarding new life, of Kieran's purposeful work for the injured, and of Tom and Jack selflessly fighting the Hun in appalling conditions that she could only imagine, Morwenna was feeling bereft, cut off from the real world and next to useless.

Clara, with her usual perception, must have noticed the change in her young employee, for she remarked upon it one evening as they were sitting together in her parlour. One each side of the unlit grate, which was disguised in summertime with a pleated paper fan, Clara was busily knitting baby garments for a niece's expected child and Morwenna, ostensibly darning a hole in the toe of her stocking, was actually spending more time gazing out of the window with a faraway expression on her face.

'I can see that something's bothering you, Morwenna,' said Clara in her forthright way. 'Would you like to talk about it, or is it a private matter?'

Morwenna looked back at her, sighed and gave up all pretence at darning. Stabbing her needle into the stocking, she tossed it to one side and said, 'Oh, Clara, I don't know where to begin. But I've been thinking and thinking about this and well, I feel that I must *do* something. To help the war effort, I mean.'

Clara lifted an eyebrow and waited for her to go on. Morwenna rose to her feet and paced across the room, talking as she went. 'All the young people I know are doing something useful,' she said, opening her hands to emphasize the point. 'Taking risks – facing danger – getting killed, even – and here am I, sitting safely and comfortably behind my desk all day long.' She shrugged. 'My sole contribution is putting in a few hours at Rayle every week, playing at nursing, arranging flowers, pottering in the garden, fetching and carrying.' She turned on her heel. 'It's not enough, Clara.'

'I see,' replied her employer. 'Well, I can understand your point of view.' She nodded. 'If I were your age I expect I would feel the same.' Clara looked up and smiled as she turned a row and changed needles. 'And I imagine that after all this thinking you've been doing, you've come up with an idea.'

'Yes.' Morwenna said briefly. She leaned an elbow on the mantelpiece and fingered a china dog, absently stroking its painted head. 'Well?' Clara prompted as the silence lengthened.

Morwenna met her eyes and held them. 'I've decided to follow Chrissie up to London and join the Voluntary Aid Detachment,' she blurted.

Clara's brows rose. 'The V.A.D.s?' She nodded approvingly. 'Well, I admire your spirit, my dear, I really do. It takes courage to pull up your roots and journey into the unknown. Isn't there a detachment nearer home that you could join?'

'I don't know, I haven't enquired,' Morwenna replied. 'I want to get right away, Clara, to be in the thick of things. I need to feel that I'm making a difference, however small. And as London's getting most of the air raids, I'm sure that I shall be needed there.' She nibbled a thumb and looked towards Clara for reassurance. 'So you don't think it's a stupid idea?'

Morwenna had been desperate to share her secret with someone, but to confide in Sophie would have her thinking that her cousin was only going to London because Kieran was there, and there was no one else left to talk to.

'Far from it. I think it's an excellent idea,' Clara said. 'I shall miss you terribly but you know how business has fallen off lately. I can manage quite well on my own as far as the clerical work goes.' She fell silent for a moment, then laid down her work in her lap and drew in a breath. 'In fact, this may be just the catalyst I was needing to further some plans of my own.' She paused again while Morwenna waited for her to go on. She raised her eyes and her expression was serious. 'You see, for some time now I've been toying with the idea of retiring – putting Sea Winds on the market and getting myself a little cottage somewhere. I don't really need to work and I'm not getting any younger. But recently I had a letter from an old friend of mine who's been very ill and is unable to live on her own any longer. She needs a live-in companion and doesn't fancy sharing her home with a stranger.' Clara drummed her fingers on the arm of her chair and Morwenna guessed what was coming. 'So you see, Violet asked in a roundabout way how would I feel about moving in with her. She lives in Brighton, so I should still be near the sea.' She smiled. 'I should never be happy living in a city. But it was the thought of you, my dear, and the other staff that made me hesitate. Particularly you, as of course you would lose your home here.' Clara paused, rolled up her work, stuffed it into the basket at her feet and looked at Morwenna. 'But all I'm saying is, if you *do* decide to go, then don't feel you would be letting me down in any way.'

Morwenna was too perceptive not to detect the note of relief in Clara's voice, unintentional though it was, she was sure, and this forced her at last into making a final decision. The world here was changing all about her; soon there would be nothing left of her old life. She would leave it all behind and set out to make a new one.

With a flash of hindsight, Morwenna recalled the conversation she had had with Phoebe, more than two years ago now, when her aunt was in very much the same position as this. 'The world I know is falling to pieces around me,' she had said. Morwenna knew exactly how she'd felt.

Then Clara brought her back to earth as, looking over the top of her spectacles, her eyes twinkling with merriment, she said, 'I'm quite fond of that china dog, by the way. I hope it survives long enough to come with me when I move!' And the seriousness of the moment dissolved, as Morwenna knew Clara meant it to, with a burst of shared laughter.

Chrissie's reply to Morwenna's letter to her had arrived by return of post.

Dearest Mor,
    I can't tell you how thrilled I am to hear that you're coming up here and that it won't be very long before I shall actually see you, and talk to you, and oh – what fun we shall have!

Morwenna smiled: Chrissie seemed to have recovered some of her former bounce, which had taken such a knock after Walter's death. She was sounding far different now from the pinched and sad-eyed waif she had been when they had parted a few months ago.

Of course I'll get you a room in the hostel – as close to mine as I can – can't wait to see you!

Now, some news – how's this for coincidence? We were having a cup of tea in one of the ABC places, Angela and me. They're not the smartest, but they're cheap and we were in our working clothes, when who should walk in but Kieran! He'd been to Charing Cross station meeting the troop trains and was taking a break with a couple of friends. So of course as he had his company and I had mine, we didn't talk a lot, but he asked where I was staying and how I liked the work and so on, although this was before your letter arrived so I didn't mention you at all.

Anyway, when we came out, Angela said that the chaps Kieran was with are both Sinn Feiners, because she knew them slightly. I didn't know he was one of them, did you? But then, I don't know a lot about him at all, come to that. Maybe you do though.

I'm driving my own ambulance now – how about that! And I've got a young probationer, Jenny, with me who's having to learn the ropes just like I did not so long ago. It makes me feel like quite an old hand. We get on well; she's a plucky person and not afraid of hard work. We've put our names down for air-raid duty. They wanted volunteers and we felt it would be a good thing to do. Besides which, there are not always that many street accidents or sick people to be rushed into hospital, and sometimes we are kicking our heels with little to occupy our time.

Write again soon and let me know what your arrangements are and when to expect you. So looking forward to seeing you!

Love, Chrissie.

'Chrissie!' Morwenna waved at the familiar figure hurrying down the station platform.

'Mor – at last!'

The two women fell into each other's arms as Morwenna stepped off the train at Paddington.

'We'll take a taxicab. Let me help you with some of those things – we don't need a porter.' Chrissie turned her back on the hovering uniform and peaked cap, picked up a couple of bags and led the way, while Morwenna followed with her portmanteau and hatbox.

'I'm so glad you were here to meet me,' Morwenna said as the car crossed Sussex Gardens and went rattling down through Edgware Road to Marble Arch. 'I'd forgotten quite how noisy and crowded London is – it's a bit overwhelming at first.'

'I know, I felt just the same,' Chrissie replied. 'It's bewildering, isn't it?

Of course, I'd never been up here before. It seemed so vast and everyone so busy and in such a hurry that it almost took my breath away.' She lurched sideways as the vehicle took a sharp turn around Hyde Park.

Morwenna squeezed her friend's hand with her gloved one and looked her in the face. 'How are you, Chrissie?' she asked. 'Really, I mean. Are you getting over Walter, is what I'm trying to say?'

Chrissie patted the hand. 'Yes I am, a bit. There are times of course when it all comes back to me and I feel churned up, but mostly I'm kept so busy that the time flies, and I'm so dead tired at the end of the day that I sleep too soundly even to dream about him.'

The driver turned off into a side street and drew up outside a row of tall buildings. 'Here we are,' Chrissie added, as they prepared to scramble out. 'This is the hostel.' There were iron railings around a basement area and a flight of steps up to a cheerful red door with a fanlight over it.

'My room's just down the corridor,' Chrissie said after she had shown Morwenna upstairs to hers. 'Third on the left, right next to the kitchen.' She grinned. 'I'll meet you there in half an hour and we can have a real good chat. I'm not on duty until eight. It's night patrol this week.'

Soon they were seated companionably in the communal rest room, drinking tea and munching the sticky Bath buns which Chrissie had produced from a paper bag. A few other young women were sitting around, relaxing with sewing or reading, a couple of whom spoke or looked up and smiled as they passed.

'I popped out for these while you were unpacking,' Chrissie said, biting into her bun. 'I thought you'd probably be starving.'

'Mm.' Morwenna nodded through a mouthful, and licked the sugar from her fingertips, 'Lovely, thanks.' She leaned back and picked up her cup. 'Chrissie, have you heard from Tom lately?' she asked.

'No, not for a month or so.' Chrissie shook her head. 'Have you?'

Morwenna shrugged. 'I wrote to tell him that I was coming here, but it crossed with a letter from him which arrived just before I left. It told me absolutely nothing, really – except the most important thing of all – that he is still alive,' she replied.

'I know what you mean,' Chrissie said, nodding, and put down her empty cup. 'Well, Mor,' she said, raising her wide blue eyes to her friend's face, 'what are your plans now that you're actually here?'

'First of all I've got to report to the Kent V.A.D. headquarters, which is in Bromley,' she replied. 'That's where the Chief of Staff Dr Yolland is, although all the detachments are ultimately under the Red Cross.'

Morwenna replaced her cup on its saucer. 'I shall go down there tomorrow. Then it's not so much what are my plans, as what plans they'll have for me. I'll tell you all about it when I get back.'

'But I'll be asleep all morning, remember.' Chrissie glanced at her with a grin. 'In fact, don't call me – I'll come and find you. My shift doesn't finish until eight, so I shan't be around much before lunchtime.'

The girls parted company and after Chrissie had introduced her to her friends, Morwenna went back to her room to unpack and settle in. She felt exhausted already.

Next morning, Morwenna travelled down to Bromley and found her destination without any trouble. She was shown into an office where a neat, middle-aged woman with a pleasant face and spectacles was seated behind a desk.

'Ah, Miss Pengelly,' she said, rising to extend a hand. 'Do sit down.' She gestured towards a chair nearby.

'Good morning,' Morwenna said with a smile, as she settled herself and drew off her white cotton gloves. She had dressed to give an impression of neatness and capability and had chosen a navy-blue cotton skirt and a frill-necked blouse of a paler blue which matched her eyes. Over it she wore a long cardigan, also in navy, as the day was overcast.

'Good morning. I'm Annie Cartwright.' She looked shrewdly at Morwenna as she said, 'You've come a long way from your home.' Morwenna smiled. 'You do know I suppose, that what you are undertaking will involve a great deal of hard work, some of it unpleasant and all of it demanding?'

Morwenna nodded. 'Yes, ma'am, I do realize that.'

'There will be times,' the woman went on, 'when you'll feel like giving up and running back to Cornwall for good.' She smiled. 'But on the other hand it is rewarding work and can be very satisfying.' She gestured with her hands as she went on, 'To have helped even one wounded soldier, not so much by tending his wounds, but by being there for him and perhaps just listening to what he wants to say before he dies, can make it all worthwhile.' She paused and looked intently at Morwenna. 'And knowing all that, are you still sure that this is what you want to do?'

Morwenna lifted her chin and returned the level gaze. 'Quite sure,' she said firmly. 'I need to feel that I'm doing something useful, you see, as so many other women are. I'm strong and healthy and willing to work anywhere you choose to send me.'

'Good.' Annie Cartwright nodded her approval. 'Now, I've been reading your letter again and I see that you have already had some experience of working in a convalescent home, so I assume you have some knowledge of First Aid, have you?'

'Only the very basic points,' Morwenna replied.

'Mm. In that case you will have to undergo training up to certificate standard before you will be allowed on the wards.' The other woman tapped her pen on the blotter as she thought for a moment, then consulted a large, leather-bound register. After a moment or two she pushed back her chair and crossed one leg over the other as she leaned back and said, 'I'm sending you down to Woolwich, Miss Pengelly, which is one of the three military hospitals we have in Kent. It's larger by far than the others – in fact, with over six hundred beds it's the largest in the country – and they can use all the extra help they can get.'

Morwenna nodded as a flip of excitement and apprehension clenched her stomach in a knot, and she only half-heard what the other woman was saying. '. . . a letter for you to take to your superintendent . . . I will inform her when to expect you. . . .' She rose and Morwenna scrambling to her feet as well, realizing that the interview was at an end.

'Thank you for joining us,' Annie Cartwright said as she extended a hand, 'and I wish you well.'

'Thank you very much, ma'am,' Morwenna said, returning the handshake, and left the room with a thankful sigh that the interview was over.

'So I've been posted to the hospital at Woolwich,' Morwenna finished, after telling Chrissie the events of the morning over their evening meal. 'I'm to report there on Monday.'

'I might even see you sometimes then – we quite often get cases to take down there,' Chrissie replied, laying down her knife and fork on her empty plate. 'Oh, Mor, what a long way we've come from St Just!'

Morwenna nodded. 'It's made so much difference having you here, Chrissie,' she said. 'It would have been awful having to face all this on my own.'

'Oh, gus on with 'ee!' said Chrissie in broad Cornish dialect, lightening the seriousness of the moment, and they both burst out laughing.

'Does Kieran know you're in London?' asked Chrissie as they took their coffee into the rest room.

'I wrote and told him I was joining the V.A.D., but not when I was actually coming up,' Morwenna replied. 'I've got his address – I'll contact him once I'm settled.'

'Well, I must go,' said Chrissie rising. 'Duty calls.' She drained her cup.

'But tomorrow's Saturday and I've got a day off, praise be. I'll probably spend it all in bed.'

But Chrissie's plan for a quiet day were to be thrown to the winds. A small boy came to the door while she was still asleep and left a message with Morwenna to say that her brother was in London and would be coming over to see her that afternoon.

'Which brother?' she almost shouted at the child, who blinked and took a step backwards.

'Dunno, miss.' He sniffed and wiped a sleeve across his nose, leaving a silvery snail-track on the material. 'Her bruvver was all the man said. On the station he was, just got off the train. He gimme a tanner and sent me over here.'

Morwenna's stomach was turning somersaults as she closed the door. Tom? Could it possibly be Tom? Hardly allowing herself to hope, a small smile lifted the corners of her mouth as she climbed the stairs to find Chrissie.

Chapter Eight

'OH, Chrissie – there you are! I looked everywhere for you when you weren't in your room.' Morwenna came panting down the stairs and bumped into her friend in the corridor.

'You're looking in some state,' Chrissie observed with her usual forthrightness. 'What's up?'

Morwenna put her hands to her hot cheeks, which must have been betraying her inner excitement. She laid a hand on Chrissie's arm. 'A message came for you while you were in bed,' she said, pausing to catch her breath. 'A boy came to the door. He said to tell you that your brother is coming round this afternoon!'

Chrissie's eyes widened. 'My *brother*?' Well, which one, you idiot?' she said with a grin and nudged Morwenna with her elbow.

'I—' Morwenna began, just as a voice from behind her made her jump and swing around.

'*This* one!' called a male voice as Jack strode down the corridor waving his cap in the air, and lifted Chrissie off her feet in a huge bear hug. 'Jack!' she squealed. 'Put me *down*. Oh, how lovely to *see* you!' She planted a kiss on his cheek and as he placed her back on her feet, Jack caught sight of Morwenna standing in the shadows. Her hopes in tatters, she forced herself to paste a smile on to her face.

'Morwenna!' he exclaimed. 'What on earth are *you* doing here? Come up to visit Chrissie, have you?' His face a picture of astonishment, he ran a hand through his thick blond hair, making it stand on end.

'Hello, Jack.' She clasped his outstretched hands, then reached up and gave him a peck on the cheek. Still as thickset and burly as she remembered, life in the trenches had left its mark on Jack – the familiar face was no longer the round and boyish one she had known and behind the superficial grin, his eyes spoke of unforgettable horrors.

'Come in here where we can sit down and talk,' Chrissie said, ushering him into the rest room, where the three of them talked themselves almost hoarse before they had covered all there was to say.

'So Tom and me, we've been in rest camp for a couple of weeks and managed to wangle a thirty-six-hour pass,' Jack said, leaning back in his chair and propping one ankle on his knee.

Morwenna gave a start and her mouth dropped open. She drew breath to speak, but Jack was oblivious as he went on talking. 'Old Tom insisted on going home,' he said, pulling out a cigarette case from his pocket. 'All the way down to Cornwall.'

Morwenna's eyes widened and her stomach lurched. Jack selected a cigarette and lit up, blowing a plume of smoke towards the ceiling. 'He caught the early train, but I said I'm not wasting such a short leave travelling all that way – I'm going to stay up here and enjoy myself. Give the parents my love, I said and . . .'

Jack went rattling on as Morwenna tore her gaze away and met Chrissie's sympathetic look. Stricken, she lowered her head as the blood sang in her ears. She felt sick, physically sick, with the anguish of it. No disappointment in the whole of her life seemed as great as this. If only her letter had reached him before. . . . A hard lump in her throat was threatening to choke her, so she excused herself and left the brother and sister together.

Up in her room, Morwenna pushed up the bottom half of the sash window and leaned out. The June afternoon was oppressively sultry and the plane trees along the edge of the street drooped their tired and dusty leaves. The patches of sky which showed between their branches was white and hazy with heat, and a few scrawny pigeons were squabbling over a crust in the gutter far below.

Tom would have looked for her in Penzance when he came off the train. Now he might be walking the cliffs at St Just, hoping to find her there. Cool breezes would be wafting in over the cornflower-blue sea, blowing his hair into his eyes, and he would run a hand through it in the impatient gesture she knew so well. In the shallows near the shore, the water would be that indescribable shade of turquoise, and Bess would be chasing seagulls in the cove, sending them tossing into the air like scraps of torn paper, their mournful cries echoing as they skimmed the edge of the land. And the waves would be surging around the Brisons, smashing themselves against their bony shoulders and tossing clouds of spray high into the glittering air.

Hot tears were trickling down her cheeks now and her shoulders began to heave. Sunk in misery, Morwenna ignored the tap on her door, until

Chrissie's insistent voice forced her to wipe her eyes, cross the room and let her in.

'I know, I know,' she said, taking in Morwenna's stricken face and damp eyes as she gave her friend a hug. She pulled her down to sit on the edge of the bed and perched beside her, clasping her hand. 'Now listen. Jack's gone back now. He's staying at the Union Jack Club in Waterloo – you know, the servicemen's place?' Morwenna nodded dumbly. 'But he's coming back later and taking us out to tea – yes, you too.' Morwenna shook her head and made to draw away. 'It won't do you any good to shut yourself away and mope,' said practical Chrissie. 'You're going to come with us. It'll take your mind off Tom for an hour or two.'

Morwenna sniffed. 'Oh, all right, Chrissie, I'll come. It's nice of you and I know what you say is sensible – really.'

'Good,' said her friend briskly, patting the limp hand. 'And I thought of something else too.' She looked Morwenna in the eye. 'Why don't we ask Jack what train they're going back on? Then we could go to the station, and you and Tom might have at least a few minutes together before we see them off. How about that? Better than nothing, isn't it?'

Morwenna felt her spirits lift a little, knowing that anything would be better than nothing. She nodded and squeezed Chrissie's hand as she felt a smile hovering at the corners of her mouth. 'Well done, Chris, that's a brilliant idea.'

'Good. That's better,' said her friend as she turned to leave. 'Be ready by five o'clock and come down to my room to make sure that I am too.'

'We're only going to the ABC round the corner,' Chrissie announced as they met outside her door. 'I told Jack we haven't got time to go up the West End to eat as well, if we're going to a show afterwards.'

'A show? Are we?' Morwenna turned round eyes in her direction.

'That's what he said.' Chrissie had turned to have a last look in the mirror and was primping her hair. 'Well, he called it a revue,' she added. 'George Robey's in it. He's well known, Jack says, but I don't know – I've never been anywhere.' She grinned at Morwenna. 'Apart from *The Pirates of Penzance* that time down home. Remember, do you?'

Morwenna winced. She remembered it only too well. Chrissie was saying, 'This is called *The Bing Boys are Here*.' She was wearing a wide hat with a feather curling up one side of her face, and was carrying the jacket of her russet linen suit over her arm. 'It's too hot to put this on now but I'll need it later.'

As they moved towards the outside door she glanced at Morwenna's dress of shot blue and turquoise, cut low at the neckline both front and back, and remarked, 'I like that – greeny-blue always suits you better than anything. It comes of having eyes that colour.' Morwenna smiled and followed her down the steps, tossing her wrap around her shoulders as she went.

The ABC chain of eating houses were plain and functional, with no frills attached to either the décor or the food, but they gave good value for money and were very popular. Jack and the two girls had to search for a table but eventually pushed through to the back and found one which had just been vacated, inside a window embrasure.

'I don't *believe* it!' came a male voice nearby. Morwenna had just settled herself and was picking up the menu card. '*Morwenna!*' She whirled round, startled, and met a pair of bright black eyes and a familiar face smiling down at her.

'*Kieran!*' It was her turn to be amazed. But with a flash of recall she remembered that Chrissie in her letter had mentioned meeting him here once before. 'Oh, how lovely to see you,' she said as she rose to her feet again. As he wrapped both arms around her in a warm hug and dropped a light kiss on her cheek, Morwenna was acutely conscious of Chrissie's observant stare, and did not prolong the moment.

'But what are you *doing* here?' he asked. 'Sure and I never dreamt for one minute that you meant what you said in that letter. I couldn't imagine you would really be after throwing up your job and everything to come to London.'

'Come and join us,' Morwenna replied, indicating the spare fourth chair. 'I'm sure the others won't mind, will you?' she said to a general shaking of heads.

'Hello, Chrissie,' Kieran said. 'So we meet here once again!' He looked inquiringly at the man sitting beside her.

'This is my brother, Jack. He's on a short leave.' Chrissie did the introductions as Kieran squeezed himself in beside them.

'I've been waiting for a friend of mine,' Kieran said, glancing up at the clock on the wall, 'but I don't think he's going to turn up now.'

The talk turned to generalities as they ordered their meal. 'Chicken casserole's about the most attractive item on the menu,' Jack remarked. A little waitress in a lacy cap and apron appeared at their table and he gave his order. 'I'll have that, followed by tapioca pudding,' he told her. They all followed suit, but Morwenna added as she wrinkled her nose, 'No tapioca for me – I can't stand the sight of it. It always reminds me of frog spawn.'

'Well, in these days of austerity I suppose we're lucky to have that,' said Kieran philosophically. 'Sure, with the German submarines after blowing up so many of our merchantmen, the shortages are only going to get worse, so they are.' He sat back as the waitress returned and handed around cutlery and cruet.

'I heard that they may be escorted by convoys soon,' Jack added, as the girl returned with their orders. 'That's the new idea. Whether it'll work or not has yet to be seen.'

'Is that so?' said Kieran thoughtfully. With his fork poised he looked closely at Jack's face. He paused and swallowed a mouthful before going on, 'What are things like at the front line now, Jack? We get told very little by the newspapers, but I'm after seeing the increasing number of casualties listed in them – it's up to about four thousand a day now.' He dabbed his moustache with a napkin as he went on, 'Every day I see this great double line of women, well, mostly women, waiting at Charing Cross station for the disembarking troop trains that we meet.'

'It's pretty grim.' Jack's face darkened. 'We've been told to be ready to mount a major offensive soon, probably in two or three weeks' time.'

'Oh?' Kieran looked up quickly. 'Whereabouts would that be, then? Along the Somme, is it?'

'Yes, I believe so.' Jack gave the other man a quizzical look, as if wondering how he would know. 'Somewhere around that area.' He rasped a hand across his jaw. 'But we don't get told much.' The smile had left his face and his voice had a bitter edge to it. 'After all, we're only killing machines.' As a small silence fell around the table, Kieran excused himself and strolled off in the direction of the gentlemen's cloakroom.

'One thing I did hear, though,' Jack said, his fork poised halfway to his mouth.

'Mm?' Morwenna raised her eyes as he spoke. 'What's that?'

'That Cornish miners are going to be in demand soon – well, along with any men with mining experience,' Jack replied.

'Miners?' Chrissie looked up from her plate and raised an eyebrow. 'Whatever for?'

Jack lowered his voice. 'I'm not really supposed to talk about it, but I know you'll keep it to yourselves. A Major Plumer has come up with a plan to dig a maze of tunnels right out under the German lines and lay landmines in them.' He carried the fork to his mouth and chewed. 'At a place called Messines Ridge. They started a while back but they need more men. Men with experience of working underground, see? We're to get a briefing when I get back.'

107

'That's a good idea – but some dangerous, I should think,' Morwenna put in.

Jack nodded and there was a look of pride about him. 'I know I haven't done much mining down home, but I did go down Geevor for a spell right after I left school, didn't I, Chrissie?'

His sister nodded. 'Before you decided that you'd rather be up on top in the fresh air, even though the pay wasn't so good,' she said with a smile. 'What about Tom?' she added. 'Will he go down as well?'

'Not him,' replied Jack, as he pushed his empty plate to one side. 'I told him it would be safer underground, but he said he'd rather take his chance up on top.' He shrugged and glanced up as Kieran returned to his seat opposite Morwenna.

The conversation turned to generalities once more and after a while Kieran cleared his throat and enquired, 'And what are you all doing this evening?' The question was an open one, but as he spoke his eyes were on Morwenna's bent head. She had stabbed her spoon into a portion of rather tasteless trifle and was stirring it aimlessly around the dish. Jack's remark about being killing machines had made her think of what the two brothers were going back to, and swallowing had become a major problem. As if she had felt Kieran's eyes on her, she jerked her head up and said, 'Jack's taking us to that revue that's been advertised so much.'

'I see.' Kieran nodded. 'I was thinking of going on to the Savoy for a drink. My favourite orchestra is playing there tonight, but my company seems to have deserted me. Have you ever been to the Savoy hotel at all, Morwenna?' Wide-eyed, she shook her head. 'Well, as it looks as if I'm after being on my own, I wonder if you'd like to come?' He raised an eyebrow. 'We could leave Chrissie and Jack to their private chat then. I expect they have a lot to talk about. How about it?'

Until then, the idea that the other two might prefer to have some time on their own had not occurred to Morwenna. Now warmth flooded her face as Kieran's remark had instantly made her feel 'de trop'.

His eyes looked warmly into hers as Morwenna, in a quandary, stammered, 'Oh – but I'm not dressed . . . for . . .' and bit her bottom lip. She had been so intent on Kieran's face since he came in and so surprised to see him, that it was only now that she realized how smartly dressed he actually was, in a dark suit with a stiff shirt and bow-tie.

'Sure and you're looking just beautiful, so you are,' he said gently, taking her arm and persuading her out of her seat.

'Don't forget that we're going to be at the station to see the boys off on that night train,' said Chrissie as they turned to leave. 'It's 11.30 from

Victoria. Tom should be able to get across from Paddington in time to have a few minutes with us before that.'

'I won't,' Morwenna said as Kieran ushered her out. Soon they were in a taxi and bowling along the Strand in the evening sunshine, where the hurrying crowds jostling each other on the pavements told their own story. There was a group of sober nurses in stiff white aprons and caps hurrying towards Charing Cross Hospital; there were servicemen in various uniforms gathered in knots on street corners, or with girls hanging on to their arms, looking in shop windows as they walked. There were a couple of civilians above the age of forty-five, too old to fight for their country, moving uncertainly through the throng with bemusement on their faces, as if the world they knew was in danger of slipping away beneath their feet.

The painted faces of the women, too, their high-pitched laughter and the chain-smoking of the men, all contributed to the underlying atmosphere of frenetic gaiety about the capital. The message was that life was fragile, the moment fleeting. Seize that moment for there may not be another. Morwenna shivered and turned away from the cab window.

'Not cold, are you?' Kieran asked and she shook her head.

'I guess someone just walked over my grave,' she said with a smile, then thought how stupid that old expression was, given the present circumstances.

As the cab lurched sideways to avoid a brewer's dray, Morwenna remarked, 'Where's your car now, Kieran? You don't drive in London, do you?'

Kieran shook his head. 'No, I've had to lay it up,' he replied with a scowl. 'Can't get the petroleum now, you see.'

They were turning a corner into the hotel entrance and Morwenna's attention was distracted by the bright posters adorning the front of the Savoy theatre next door. Glancing over her shoulder, she noticed with a pang that the D'Oyly Carte Opera company was performing *The Pirates of Penzance.*

The Savoy hotel was as opulent as she had anticipated, seeming untouched by the cold fingers of wartime austerity. A thick pile carpet muted the murmur of voices, lamps in fluted pink shades glowed on every table despite the light summer evening, and on a dais behind a screen of potted palms a small orchestra was discreetly playing the more popular of the classics.

Kieran guided her towards the lounge area, where the elegant clientele sat about in little knots drinking and smoking, the women in low-backed, slimly draped gowns, the men in evening dress like Kieran. Delectable aromas were floating over from the dining room, and as Morwenna sat down with her back to the wall on a plush sofa in one corner, she thought that nothing could be more of a contrast between this and the ABC. It was like two different worlds. Kieran had gone up to the bar and now came back with something cool and bubbly in a delicate long-stemmed glass.

'Champagne,' he said in answer to her look of enquiry. As Morwenna's eyes widened, he slipped into the seat at her side and raised his drink aloft. 'To success and happiness in your new life as a V.A.D.,' he said. His dark eyes looked deeply into hers as he added, 'You know how I've always felt about you, Morwenna, right from the first time we met. . . .' With a start she looked away and lowered her eyes. 'But I want to tell you as well how much I admire you for what you've decided to do. I know the sort of work they do and it's not always easy at all.'

One of Kieran's hands reached out to cover hers as it lay on the small table in front of them, and lulled by the atmosphere and the wine, Morwenna did not pull away. 'And I also want you to know that I am always around if you ever need someone to – well, to lean on,' he said in a low voice as he gave the hand a gentle squeeze. 'Woolwich is not that far from where I live, and you know my address. You can call around at any time, you know.'

Morwenna looked up then into the face so close to her own, and her stomach did a little flip. In the stark black and white of his evening dress, with his melting dark eyes and curly head, he was a most attractive man. She took a sip of her drink and coughed. 'Thank you, Kieran, I'll remember that,' she said demurely, while her heart beat a trifle faster and she assured herself it was only because of the warmth of the room.

'So, here you are, old man! Sorry I missed you earlier – got held up. Duty called, don't you know?' The hearty male voice behind Morwenna startled her out of her thoughts, and Kieran rose to his feet to greet the newcomer. They shook hands and he turned to introduce them. 'Morwenna, this is a friend of mine. Graham Leigh-Hunter – Morwenna Pengelly.'

'Call me Gray – everyone does, haw, haw, haw!' Morwenna took the proffered hand and looked up into a pair of tawny eyes. The sharp chin and hooked nose reminded her instantly of a bird of prey, as did the thin smile as he bent over her hand.

'How do you do,' she murmured, as the newcomer drew up a chair and joined them. Everything about him spoke of wealth and privilege – from the impeccable evening dress and heavy gold signet ring to the air of absolute self-confidence and his public-school accent.

'Pengelly – Cornish name, eh?' The eyes bored into hers as Morwenna opened her mouth to reply, but he went on, 'Not related to the Hon. Jeremy Pengelly, are you? Their seat's somewhere near Torpoint, I believe. Sound fellow, Jerry – we were at Eton together.'

Morwenna shook her head. 'Not me. I come from a small town near Penzance.'

'Oh. Yes, quite so.' He pulled out a large handkerchief and trumpeted into it as he sat down.

After a few pleasantries and an obviously forced attempt to include her in their conversation, the two men soon became absorbed in talk of their own and Morwenna's thoughts wandered as she caught only snatches of the chit-chat being bandied about her.

Her eyes were watching but not seeing the couples who had left their seats to dance. The orchestra had switched to a selection of music from *The Merry Widow* and they were now drifting about the floor to the haunting strains of 'Vilia'. Morwenna, following the words in her head, thought with a pang how appropriate they were to her own situation. '... the night is romantic and I am alone ... lonely with only a song ...' For although she was surrounded by people, her own love was far out of reach and likely to remain so.

She was jerked out of her reverie as she realized that Kieran was talking directly to her. 'I was saying to Gray that you come from a Cornish mining district, Mor, so I was,' he said. 'He's got shares in the Gwennap mines, so he tells me.'

Morwenna forced herself back to the present moment and attempted to concentrate on polite conversation. Personally she would have been pleased to see the back of Gray Leigh-Hunter, and resented the way he had spoilt the cosy twosome which she and Kieran had previously been.

'Oh yes.' She pasted a smile on her face. 'Gwennap's about thirty miles from where I live. It's a big mining area.' Racking her brains for something intelligent to say, as the two men seemed to be waiting for her to continue, she recalled what Jack had been telling them all earlier. 'I hear that Cornish miners are being recruited now for a tunnel-digging operation in France,' she said brightly, picking up her glass and taking a sip. 'It should be a piece of cake to them after hacking away at the Cornish granite in the awful conditions they work in at home.' She was gazing across the room as she spoke and missed the quick glance that passed between the two men.

'Oh yes?' remarked Gray suavely, reaching for the wine bottle which had appeared on the table, and topping up her glass. 'Why are they doing that, I wonder? I should imagine they've got all the trenches they need by now, haw, haw, haw!'

'Oh, not trenches,' Morwenna corrected him. 'Tunnels. Under the German lines, you know?' She was feeling delightfully relaxed now as a deep feeling of well-being permeated all through her. Gray wasn't such a bad chap really; he was seeming quite interested in her now, beaming over the top of his gold-rimmed spectacles and focusing all his attention on what she was saying.

'Really? How very intriguing.' He leaned back, pulled out a pocket watch and glanced at it. 'Well, old man, I think I'd better be off now,' he said to Kieran. 'I'll see you at the usual place, usual time,' he added, rising from his seat. 'Miss Pengelly.' He took her hand and gave a slight bow as he bent over it. 'A pleasure to have met you.' And picking up his hat, he turned and sauntered out of the room.

Kieran made his farewells, then put down his empty glass and rose to his feet. 'Let's dance, shall we, Mor?' he asked in a brisk tone of voice, as he put a hand beneath her arm and drew her to her feet. Morwenna, feeling that all her willpower had been sapped by the combination of champagne and the seductive atmosphere of this place, allowed herself to be drawn on to the dance floor. And once there, she drifted along to the music, her feet automatically following Kieran's lead without any conscious volition of her own.

'I didn't know that about the Cornish miners,' he said, his face very close to hers. 'Who told you?' Morwenna looked into his deep, dark eyes and swayed to the lazy rhythm of the music. 'Oh, Jack mentioned it earlier,' she replied. 'He's been drafted in to join them. He was talking about some place called, um, Messines, I think it was. Isn't this a lovely tune? One of my absolute favourites.' And she hummed along to it for a few bars.

Time lost all meaning as one dance followed another, and the windows which earlier had been filled with the summer sky slowly darkened. It was only when Morwenna felt her head drooping towards Kieran's shoulder that she realized how tired she was.

Absently she glanced at the wall clock, then as warning bells began to ring deep down inside her, with a shock she came totally awake and gasped in horror. She stiffened, one hand flying to her mouth as she gripped Kieran's arm and dragged him to a halt in the middle of the dance floor. 'Kieran, look at the time!' she exclaimed. 'It's 11.15. I promised to be at the station – to see Tom! We must go!'

But Kieran's face darkened. 'We'll never do it at all, so we won't. It's no good to be after rushing. It's far too late.'

'But we must!' Morwenna shook his arm. 'Oh, Kieran, *please*,' she said, almost sobbing as she tried to urge him into action. 'We can just about make it if we get a cab. Come *on*. Quickly!' And as Kieran continued to drag his feet, she looked towards the exit, dropped his arm, then sped across the room as she called back over her shoulder, 'I'm going, I tell you. And if you won't come with me, I shall go on my own.'

Kieran muttered an oath under his breath and followed her. Once outside he hailed a cab and sat beside Morwenna in silence as she perched on the edge of her seat biting a thumbnail and muttering under her breath as she urged the driver on. Once they reached Victoria, she leaped out of the car and was off, running into the station as she left Kieran to pay the fare.

On the platform, the train was in and steaming up, sending great plumes of smoke towards the roof. Through the milling crowds, Morwenna caught sight of Chrissie at one of the open doors, talking to someone inside, while Jack stood beside her with his bag, waiting to board.

'Chrissie!' Morwenna screamed. 'Jack!' Her voice was lost in the general hubbub as she ran towards them. She reached them just as Chrissie withdrew her head and stood back to let Jack on. 'Morwenna! At last! Where've you *been*, for goodness' sake?'

But Morwenna did not answer, could not answer, for there in the doorway stood Tom. As Jack boarded and slammed the door shut, his brother pushed him out of the way and stuck his head through the window. Tom grabbed the hands that Morwenna reached up and clasped them to him like a drowning man.

'Mor, I thought you'd never come,' he said hoarsely. His face was drawn, hollow with lack of sleep, thinner than she remembered, his eyes hungry as they bored into her own. All the eager enthusiasm of the boy she had waved off to war had vanished, leaving behind this gaunt man whom she felt she hardly knew. Tom brought her hands up to his face and his breath was hot on her skin, as he fiercely drew them to his lips in a kiss that turned her legs to jelly.

'Oh Tom, I'm so *sorry*,' she said, as tears streamed down her face. She was sorry for everything – the mix-up, her lateness. How *could* I have forgotten the time so? Morwenna thought, hating herself. And as Tom looked away and beyond her, she knew from his expression that Kieran was standing behind her.

Tom dropped her hands as the guard blew his whistle. The train was beginning to move. Swiftly she reached behind her neck and tore off her precious locket, then standing on tiptoe, she pressed it into his hand. 'Here, Tom – take this,' she called up to him, as the train was gathering speed. He gave her other hand a tight squeeze before their fingers were finally dragged apart. Over the noise of the engine and the clanking wheels, she shouted, 'I love you – so much,' but he was getting further and further away and Morwenna began to run. Had Tom heard her or not? He was mouthing something she could not catch, his voice a shadowy echo as it was carried high into the vaulted roof and lost. He was waving his hat now and getting smaller and smaller as the train pulled away. 'Remember me,' Morwenna whispered, as his beloved figure vanished around the corner in a cloud of steam.

Chapter Nine

For days afterwards Morwenna flayed herself with anguish at having been late in getting to the station. No matter how many times she told herself that she would only have had a few minutes with Tom at most, and that in a crowd, it was the thought that she could have been so easily distracted – and by the company of another man. For Tom's expression of hurt when he had seen her with Kieran was burned into her memory still, and she knew what he must be thinking. She was going to have to write a very difficult letter to him and try to explain. Morwenna threw herself into her work at the hospital to try and forget the incident, and was kept so busy that it was not difficult to put it to the back of her mind. It was when she was alone in her room that the memories came flooding back.

She had taken lodgings with a Mrs Pope in a pleasant street within walking distance of the hospital. From her window she could get a glimpse of the river and occasionally a few seagulls flying over it, their screaming bringing a poignant reminder of home. Her landlady was small and wiry with a no-nonsense air about her. She wore her hair skewered into a tight knot at the back of her neck and peered through her horn-rimmed spectacles with a pair of sharp blue eyes which missed nothing. But she was an excellent cook and the room was clean and comfortable, so Morwenna felt that she could have fared a lot worse.

Now she was sitting at a small table in the window, writing to Tom. Rather than dwelling on the fiasco at the station, she had mentioned it briefly and apologized again, then changed the tone to a more positive one and was describing her new surroundings and job. Morwenna nibbled thoughtfully at the end of her pen as she looked back to her first day at the hospital, then dipped it in the ink and tried to put her experiences into words. . . .

'Miss Pengelly, Miss Stewart, Miss Harrison, good morning. I'm Emmeline Davies, commandant of this detachment. How do you do.' It was Morwenna's first day and she was glad to find that she was not the only girl just starting. She took the proffered hand and looked up – for this woman was tall – into a pair of appraising blue eyes which made her feel like an insect skewered on a pin. But they were kindly too, and she had the impression that Miss Davies would be a firm but fair person to work under.

'Sit down, all of you, while I go through a few things you will need to know.' They sat on some upright wooden chairs which were ranged around the walls of the office and she picked up some papers from the desk.

'This detachment has twenty women in it, four of whom are trained cooks, working under a lady superintendent, Miss Jessop, whom you will meet shortly.' She paused and came to stand in front of the desk, facing them. 'I don't know how much you already know about the V.A.D.,' she went on, 'but our motto is "Willing to do Anything".' Her gaze swept over them as if mentally assessing how suitable they were for this ambitious statement.

'This can include cleaning, cooking, elementary nursing, driving, porterage and mechanical repairs. The last three, however, are usually left to the male detachments.' Miss Davies took a few steps with hands clasped behind her back, and went on, 'Ours is essentially a supportive role, assisting trained staff and keeping hospitals and ambulance services operating.'

She returned to the desk and picked up another sheaf of papers, handing them out as she was speaking. 'This is a letter of rules which is given to all new members – you may at first think them tedious but I assure you that there is a good reason for each of them, although at the time you may not fully understand what it is.'

Morwenna glanced quickly down the long list and her eyebrows rose. *You are expected to be at all times, courteous, kind, useful. . . . Whatever duty you undertake is to be done faithfully, loyally and to the best of your ability. . . . Rules and regulations . . . comply without grumbling . . . sacrifice will be asked of you . . . remember you are giving because your country needs your help. . . .* She looked up as the commandant began speaking again.

'This leaflet is to be kept in your pocket book, which will be issued to you with your uniform when you leave this office,' Miss Davies finished, then gave them a warm smile as she added, 'And thank you all for joining us. Your help is most welcome. Now I'll get someone to take you around and show you the ropes. Good morning ladies.' And they all filed out.

It's the sheer SIZE of this place that amazes me, Morwenna wrote in her letter.

*At the end of a shift I just sink down into a chair in the nurses' rest room and ease
my aching feet out of my shoes. I don't think I shall ever get really used to it.*

She refrained, however, from describing to Tom the dreadful sights that
she was faced with every day, and had kept the letter as light as possible
by giving humorous descriptions of the people she worked with and the
work she was doing.

Morwenna had been at the hospital now for almost six weeks. To begin
with she had been assigned the more menial duties of emptying and
scrubbing out bedpans, of fetching and carrying for the doctors, and
taking messages down the long clattering corridors and endless staircases.
Gradually during this time she had become used to the stomach-churning
sights of blood-soaked bandages and mangled flesh, and the stench of
gangrenous limbs and the all-pervading antiseptic.

Soon, however, because she was able to keep a steady hand and could
face these horrors without fainting away as some of the other young
women did, Morwenna found herself assisting in the changing of dressings, ministering to the patients who could not help themselves with
feeding, or moving them to another position without flinching – as this
meant coming into close contact with their appalling injuries.

Not that she was released entirely from menial duties, however. There
were still floors to be scrubbed on hands and knees, and baths, bowls and
basins to be scoured, until her hands became chapped and raw and her
back one permanent ache.

'I feel as if I shall never be able to stand up straight again,' Morwenna
said as she limped into the nurses' rest room with a hand to the small of
her back and fell into a cane chair at the end of a particularly gruelling
shift.

'I know.' Laura Harrison tucked a stray lock of auburn hair back under
her cap and picked up a bandage from the basket beside her. There was a
never-ending stack of them always waiting to be rolled, and idle hands
were frowned upon by Matron. The three girls who had started together
had since become friends, simply because they were all in the same position, and had helped each other out until they had become accustomed to
this new life, which was so different from all they had known.

Laura's highly starched apron crackled as she moved. Worn over a long
blue dress, it had the Red Cross emblem on the bib and was worn with an
equally highly starched head-dress. It had felt like a suit of armour to
Morwenna when she had put it on for the first time.

'I didn't expect the hospital to be so huge,' Laura added, echoing
Morwenna's own thoughts, 'or the wards to be so enormous either. I imag-

ined they would be divided up into smaller rooms. I bet we walk miles during a shift, don't you, Mor? I say – wouldn't it be good if someone could invent a gadget that would measure just how far we *do* walk,' she added with a giggle.

'Perhaps it's better that we don't know,' Morwenna replied with a smile and reached for a bandage.

Laura finished rolling her own bandage, neatly tucked in the end, then picked up another one. 'Don't you think that with all the patients herded in together it makes it very impersonal, too?' She looked earnestly at Morwenna. 'I like to try to talk to each one if I can, and remember their names for the next time.'

'Goodness, with the turnover we get, that's almost impossible,' Morwenna replied. 'You're too kind-hearted, Laura.' She smiled at the other girl. 'I shouldn't worry about it.' Morwenna had found herself getting on well with Laura who, despite her upper-class background, was a sensible and practical girl, highly intelligent and willing to turn her hand to anything.

Being a voluntary movement, most of the V.A.D.s came from wealthy families as they had to support themselves. Camilla Stewart was no exception, but in character was as different from Laura as she could be. Fluffy and ineffectual, she was more of a liability than an asset and inevitably made mistakes which others had to rectify. Having been brought up on a large Scottish estate with a houseful of servants, even the most simple of tasks were outside her experience, but her sweet nature and eagerness to please endeared her to everybody. Small and plump, with a round face and large brown eyes, she reminded Morwenna of an engaging puppy. Many times she found herself shielding Camilla from the worst of Matron's caustic remarks by doing her work for her, or at least covering up some of the girl's most obvious gaffes, and earning her everlasting gratitude.

So the three had propped each other up, laughed off the humiliations of their initial mistakes, and brewed tea together during their time off while they grumbled over Matron's strictures and the ruination of their fingernails.

Mrs Pope was hovering in the hallway as Morwenna came back from shopping one morning. She had a whole day off and it was a glorious Saturday in August, with enough of a breeze blowing in from the river to keep it pleasantly cool. She thought of the sweltering heat in the city she had left behind and entered the house with a spring in her step.

'Oh, Miss Pengelly,' said her landlady without preamble, 'this letter have come for you. Forwarded on it was.' She delved into her apron pocket and drew forth an official-looking brown envelope.

Clemo and Hobbs – I wonder what they want? Morwenna thought as she glanced at the envelope, and thanked the woman on her way upstairs.

She took off her hat, tossed her bag on to a chair and sat down on the bed to open the letter.

Dear Miss Pengelly,

   As an esteemed client, we have pleasure in bringing to your attention certain facts concerning your property, known as Cove Cottage, St Just, in the county of Cornwall. One of these facts being that as the tenancy of this property has recently expired, we await your instructions as to how you wish us to proceed.

   Also, it has been reported to us and it is therefore our duty to bring to your notice, that major repairs are required to the outside of the property. The section of cliff on which the cottage stands has become undermined over the years by the action of the sea which has rendered it unstable, leading to the partial collapse of the shoring beneath the building. Now urgent measures need to be taken to strengthen this before the cottage suffers permanent damage.

   It seems eminently suitable that these repairs be undertaken while the property is vacant. Accordingly, we strongly advise that you call on us at your earliest convenience in order to discuss these matters, as we shall of course need your written permission and signature on the relevant docu-ments authorizing us to act on your behalf.

   Meanwhile, madam, we remain yours etc.

Clemo and Hobbs. Solicitors.

'So I shall have to go down there and see about it.' Morwenna and Kieran were strolling down the road from Woolwich on the Sunday afternoon, and she was telling him of the letter she had received from the solicitors. 'I shan't stay long – they need every pair of hands there is at the hospital – but maybe a long weekend will do it.'

Kieran nodded. He had called at her lodgings earlier when she had been out and Mrs Pope had taken great delight in meeting her on the doorstep on her return.

'Oh, Miss Pengelly – a young man have called to see you – ever so nice he was. I put him in the parlour to wait. I said I thought you wouldn't be long, you'd only gone up the road to post a letter.' How on earth the woman knew that was beyond Morwenna, unless her landlady had second sight, which would not have surprised her.

'Thank you, Mrs Pope,' she replied, sweeping indoors and into the parlour.

'Hello, Kieran – you found the place without any trouble, then?' He rose as she walked in and put aside the newspaper he had been reading. 'Sure and it was no problem,' he replied. He met Morwenna's eyes and spoke quite normally, but she noticed the absence of his usual jaunty smile, and his face was set in an expression that she could not place. She glanced at the newspaper he was still holding and remarked, 'Is something the matter? Bad news, is there?'

'Ah, well – yes.' Kieran frowned and held the paper out to show her a headline. 'Sure and they've executed Casement after all, so they have.' His eyes were flashing sparks of anger, and he muttered something else that Morwenna did not quite catch as she was intent on reading the article, but which could have been, 'Damn them.'

Sir Roger David Casement . . . hanged at Pentonville on August the third, 1916 . . . Morwenna read. Raising enquiring eyes to Kieran's face, she said, 'Oh. Yes, I've heard the name, of course, but I can't say I know much about the case. What did he do?'

Kieran thrust his hands behind his back and began to pace the room. 'Sure and he is – was, that is – a great fighter for an independent Ireland.' He swung round and the black eyes bored into her face. 'You must have heard about the Easter uprising, didn't you?'

Morwenna, taken aback by his forcefulness, murmured, 'Yes, yes, of course I did, but I didn't realize you felt so strongly—'

'Declan, my younger brother, was wounded in that – shot in the arm for just being there. Sure and they all were mowed down, so they were. Most of them were executed and the demonstration was ruthlessly suppressed,' he hissed with contained fury. 'And is it any wonder at all that I should feel strongly about what's happening in my own country?' As he thrust his face into hers and glared at her, pointing a finger under her nose, Morwenna flinched and took a step back in alarm. An echo of what Chrissie had told her once came back to her. 'He's one of those Sinn Feiners,' she had said in one of her letters, or something like that.

Then Kieran suddenly relaxed, as if he had just realized where he was, and looked at her in consternation. 'Oh, Mor, I'm so *sorry*,' he said, backing off. 'I never meant to frighten you like that. Sure and it's this temper of mine, so it is.' He thumped his fist into his palm and his shoulders slumped. 'Please forgive me – when I get heated I forget where I am, and I just let fly.'

Shaken, Morwenna nodded. 'Of course,' she said, then turned to leave the room. 'I'll just go upstairs and tidy myself. I'll only be a minute. Smoke if you like,' Morwenna called back over her shoulder, 'Mrs P. doesn't mind,' she added with a smile, in an attempt to bring the situation back to normal. 'I think she has a secret one herself sometimes.'

Kieran shook his head. 'I'm not after smoking – because of the chest, to be sure.' He thumped it graphically.

'Oh, yes,' Morwenna said, 'I just forgot for a moment.'

She left the room, but soon returned, having changed into a slim gown of powder-pink sprigged cotton, and with a straw hat with pink roses on the brim perched on top of her upswept hair.

As Morwenna entered the room she saw that Kieran was looking at her with such an intense expression that she had to glance away. Intuition told her what he was thinking, and she felt herself flush with self-consciousness, even more so when he said softly, 'Sure and those flowers exactly match the roses in your cheeks, so they do.' He took a step closer and held out both hands. 'Morwenna, I'm so sorry that I yelled at you just now – you know I would never in my right mind do anything to hurt you at all. You are so lovely. I—'

She bent her head and made a pretence of not noticing the spread hands, delving into her bag as she neatly side-stepped out of his reach, then hung it on her arm and picked up her parasol. 'So, where are we going on this lovely day?' she said brightly and crossed the room to the door.

She noticed Kieran's face fall and his lips tighten, and felt a stab of guilt at having disappointed him, for he was after all a most agreeable companion. But why wouldn't he leave it at that companionship? she wondered. She heard Chrissie's voice as clearly as if she had been in the room with them: 'There is no such thing as *friendship* between a man and a woman. . . .'

Morwenna sighed, but Kieran answered pleasantly enough, saying, 'What I thought we might do is this. Have you ever been through the tunnel under the river and over to the Isle of Dogs at all?'

Morwenna shook her head. 'No. What tunnel?'

'Ah, right. Then we'll catch a bus down to Greenwich Pier and I'll be after showing you. If you're sure you're ready now?' Morwenna looked up sharply at the hint of sarcasm in his voice, but his expression was pleasantly bland. As a concession, she placed a hand in the crook of his extended arm as they began to walk down the road.

★

The bus dropped them near the pier and they strolled down a side street towards the river, then Kieran took Morwenna's elbow as they followed a slope up towards a large rotunda. 'Here we are,' he said. 'Now we go down in the lift.'

'Down where?' said Morwenna, puzzled.

'Down to the water,' replied Kieran with a smile, 'then we walk along underneath the river.'

'Oh, I see,' she said with a smile. They alighted in a long tiled passage-way which stretched as far as the eye could see, and their voices and footsteps echoed eerily around them as they began to walk along it. 'Imagine the weight of all that water over our heads,' Morwenna said as she glanced up at the arched roof. 'It reminds me of the mines back home that run right out under the sea.'

With her eyes on the roof, Morwenna was not looking where she was walking and, catching her foot on a loose stone in the rough floor, she would have fallen if Kieran had not grabbed her arm in time.

'That was a close one, so it was,' he remarked and tucked the arm in his own. Morwenna, shaken, let it lie there until they were entering the lift at the other end, for she had turned her ankle and was glad of someone to lean on. Wistfully she was thinking that it seemed such a long time since she had been physically close to another person, and the warmth of the contact was very soothing. It was so difficult, she sighed, knowing how he felt about her, to explain all this to Kieran. Too difficult even to attempt. She gave a shrug and they walked on.

'So this is the Isle of Dogs, is it?' Morwenna remarked, emerging into the sunlight again and squinting against the glare coming off the water. 'What lovely gardens,' she added, as they sat down on a bench to admire the view across the water, where the impressive building of the Royal Naval College spread its elegant façade. 'But what have dogs got to do with it?' She raised her eyebrows as she turned to Kieran with the question. He had stretched out his long legs and put his hands behind his head, raising his face towards the sun as he tipped his straw boater over his eyes.

'It's not known for certain,' he replied lazily. 'Some say it's a corruption of "Isle of Ducks". Another version says that Edward III kept his hunting dogs over here when the court was at Greenwich.'

'It's difficult to imagine that now,' Morwenna remarked, looking towards the hive of activity round the docks further inland, and Kieran nodded.

'So it is, to be sure.'

A small silence fell as they both followed their own thoughts, until after a while Kieran sat up and straightened the hat on top of his curly head. 'Sure, and how about a drink in the tea-room over there?' he said rising to his feet. 'My throat's as dry as dust, so it is.'

'Mm, lovely.' Morwenna closed up her parasol and followed him down the narrow path between some overhanging laurel bushes to a small kiosk with seating and tables arranged outside it.

Perched on a curly wrought-iron chair, Kieran had his eyes fixed steadily on Morwenna's bent head, as across the marble-topped table she neatly spooned strawberry ice-cream and watched some children playing with hoops and balls beneath the trees nearby. Why did he keep up this hopeless liaison, he asked himself, when she had told him so clearly that he stood no chance against the saintly Tom?

Kieran sighed, glancing at the slender, straight-backed little figure. Beneath the upswept hair, in the nape of her neck, feathery tendrils were floating like the down of a baby bird, and it required all Kieran's willpower not to lean over and stroke them. He clenched his hands into fists and kept them down on his knees. Oh no, he could no more give up seeing Morwenna than cut off one of his own limbs. And of course, Kieran mused, losing himself in the realms of fantasy, if by chance Tom ever did . . . for he was fighting on the front line, after all . . . then maybe she might turn to him. . . .

Appalled at the road down which his thoughts were taking him, Kieran came back with a start to the present moment and grasped his teacup, raising it to his lips with a kind of desperation as normality returned.

'So when are you thinking of going down to Cornwall at all?' he enquired in order to break the silence that had fallen between them.

Morwenna licked her spoon and placed it on the empty dish. 'Next weekend, probably,' she replied, meeting his eyes with a smile that made his heart turn over and his stomach clench. Kieran rose abruptly from his seat and went across to pay the bill.

Probability turned to fact, and on the following Thursday Morwenna left Paddington station with a little lift of her heart at the thought of going home to Cornwall. Although where her 'home' actually was now, she thought with a pang, it was difficult to say. The train was packed full of troops, jostling and bantering, standing in the corridors and smoking, the air thick and reeking of tobacco. But Morwenna managed to find a seat in a Ladies Only compartment without much trouble and settled herself with her own thoughts and a magazine for company.

She had decided to stay a night or two in bed and breakfast accommodation in St Just, go to the solicitors in the morning, collect the keys and then look over the cottage. She would visit Rayle House while she was there, call in on the Edwards family, and return to London on the following Monday.

'I'd like to see Mr Miller,' Morwenna announced as she entered the office of Clemo and Hobbs next morning. 'Please tell him that Miss Morwenna Pengelly is here.'

'Oh, miss, I'm so sorry.' The receptionist's eyes widened and she shook her head. 'Mr Donald isn't here no more. Joined up, he did, you see, a few months ago.'

'Oh, of course. Yes, he would have done.' When conscription came in and he had no choice, thought Morwenna. 'That was silly of me.'

'Mr Hobbs will see you, miss, if that's all right? He's free at the moment.' The woman rose and went to the door of a side office. Morwenna nodded and began to peel off her gloves. 'Certainly,' she said with a smile, and was soon ushered into the room where an elderly man with white side whiskers rose at her approach and held out a hand.

'Miss Pengelly. Please take a seat.' He waved her to a chair and resumed his seat at the desk. 'Thank you for coming so promptly.' He rummaged in a drawer and drew out a sheaf of papers. 'I have your correspondence here.' They pored over the papers together and arranged for the necessary building repairs to be started the following week, completed the business and after an hour Morwenna was outside again with the keys to the cottage in her bag.

Stepping inside the door was like hurtling back down a long tunnel into childhood. Morwenna stood in the middle of the kitchen with tears pouring down her face and felt the old walls reach out like comforting arms and wrap themselves around her. Here, without any shadow of doubt, was her home – where she really and truly belonged and always would. And now it was entirely hers.

It was unfurnished, of course. The previous tenants had supplied their own and the original furniture was still in store where it had been since the old man had died. All that remained in the kitchen was the range, and the settle beside it which had been built into a niche in the wall. Morwenna sat down on it, the wood polished smooth by years of use, and could almost feel Gramp sitting beside her childish self, both of them holding out their hands to the comforting blaze, while the winter gales howled outside and the waves pounded in the cove below the house.

Morwenna rose after a while, wiped her eyes and began a leisurely inspection of the rest of the cottage. It didn't take long. Coming out of the little parlour, she had taken the creaking wooden stairs to the two small bedrooms above, and that was it. Ablutions had been taken at the kitchen sink, and the privy out at the back had supplied the rest of their needs.

Morwenna paused for a moment on the threshold of her own former bedroom, then slowly pushed open the door. She crossed the room and tears began to flow again as she leaned both elbows on the deep window-sill and looked out through the tiny panes at the achingly familiar view. There they were, the Brisons, standing sentinel over the cove, shoulder to shoulder as they had done since time began. White foam was spraying high over their dark flanks, tossed by the stiff onshore breeze, and the sea of forget-me-not blue glittered and winked in the sunshine. Morwenna let out a trembling breath and rubbed at the misted glass, seeing in her mind's eye a quartet of laughing children dancing in and out of the waves, and hearing their shrieks of delight echoing on the wind.

She made her mind up there and then. She would stay on an extra day or two, get the furniture out of store and bring the house back to life. Morwenna nibbled a thumbnail in thought. With care, she could manage without the rent money. This was more important. It was all-important. The knowledge that Cove Cottage was going to be here waiting for her whenever she was able to return would provide the security she longed for: it would be her bolt-hole, her haven. She ran down the stairs, exhilarated now, and started back up the hill towards the town.

It was only when she was at the top and had stopped to catch her breath and look back at the view that Morwenna realized that she had completely forgotten to inspect the crumbling cliff, which was the reason for her being here at all. But she only laughed aloud as the wind whisked her hat away and tumbled her hair about her shoulders. For she had come home at last, and whatever life might throw at her in the future, her spirit would return to this glorious place and her soul be nurtured by it.

'Morwenna! My dear life, where did you spring from? How lovely to see you, my handsome.' Maria Edwards straightened up at the sound of the girl's voice, and put a hand to the small of her back as she leaned over the garden wall.

'Hello, Maria, I was just coming to see you.' Morwenna looked with affection at the familiar dumpy little figure.

'Well, come in, come in.' Maria greeted her with a hug and urged her up the path. 'Pulling up a few weeds, I was. They dandelions do have roots on them like parsnips, some job to get them out 'tis.' She wiped her hands in her apron as she led the way indoors.

'What you doing home, then? Come to stay, have you?' She was poking up the range and putting the kettle on to boil as she spoke.

'I had to go down to the cottage,' Morwenna replied, seating herself with her elbows on the bright oilcloth which covered the table in the middle of the room. 'They sent for me because it's empty now and needs some outside repairs. Thanks.' She smiled as Maria placed a steaming cup in front of her and drew up a chair for herself.

'Going to let it again then, I suppose, are you?' Maria's black eyes met her own as she wrapped her hands around her cup and blew on her tea to cool it.

'No, I'm not,' Morwenna replied, and Maria's eyebrows shot up. 'I'm going to get the furniture out of store and keep it for myself, Maria.' She placed her cup carefully on its saucer and went on. 'And that's one reason why I wanted to see you.' She smiled at the woman's wide-eyed expression. 'I was wondering, you see, if you would be willing to take the key and go down there to keep an eye on it from time to time. Keep it aired, maybe light the fire in the winter when it's damp weather, that sort of thing?' Self-consciously she added, 'You'd be paid a small sum for your time, of course – I'd make sure the solicitors saw to that.'

Maria leaned across and squeezed her hand. 'Of course I will, maid, and don't worry about no money – I'll willingly do it for you for nothing.'

Morwenna returned the squeeze. 'Thanks, but I'd feel happier if it was a business arrangement, you see.'

Maria gave a soft chuckle and looked at her with affection in her eyes. 'Always some independent you was, and you aren't going to change, are you, maid?'

Morwenna smiled back and changed the subject. 'What's the latest news in St Just, then?' she enquired, sipping her tea.

Maria leaned back in her chair and drew in a long breath. 'Well, now, you won't have heard this – it only happened last week. Do you remember ages ago that someone broke a window of Dr Miller's surgery in Penzance and wrote anti-German stuff on the walls?'

Morwenna nodded.' Yes, I do. Clara told me about it when I was working at Sea Winds.'

'Well, he and his wife have packed up and gone, no one don't know where – not even his family. But people do reckon now that he was a spy all along, see? And Bert do say there's spies everywhere – especially since Lord Kitchener got drowned. Everyone do think that his ship was scuppered on purpose, you know.'

Morwenna nodded. 'Yes, I've heard that, but I think that with him being so popular, there was such national feeling that it's boiled up into all this conspiracy idea. I don't think there's anything in it myself.'

'But the Millers, with all the rumours going around, I suppose they just took off anyway. I always did say there was something funny about they,' Maria muttered darkly, then fixed Morwenna with a look. 'Didn't their son marry some relation of yours?' she added, her forehead wrinkling in a frown of concentration.

'That's right. Tamsin's my cousin, but we're not close. Well,' Morwenna said, pausing to take it all in. 'So maybe there was some truth in it after all. Clara thought there was.' A small silence had fallen, broken only by the crackling of the fire and the singing of the kettle on the hob.

Then, as she glanced at the photographs on the dresser which stood against the far wall, Morwenna's eyes were drawn to Tom's beloved face. It was the same picture of him that she had received when he first went away, the fresh-faced, innocent boy of their childhood. She thought of the haggard man she had seen so briefly at the station and flinched. 'Have you heard from T— That is, from the boys at all lately?'

'Not since Tom went back,' his mother replied. 'Pity you weren't down here then, wasn't it?'

Morwenna gulped a mouthful of tea and coughed. 'Yes,' she said briefly.

Maria's eyes were on the photographs now. 'I do miss them all something dreadful,' she said softly. 'I don't have nobody left, see, and 'tis so quiet here with just the two of us, and Bert down the mine all hours, I sometimes think I'll go mad with it. I haven't got nothing to do to fill the days now, and I do get that lonely, Mor, I can't tell you.'

Morwenna, looking at her with sympathy, understood just how much the removal of her noisy and chattering offspring had affected Maria. She looked around the immaculate room, which had formerly been the hub of family life, and could see the change for herself. No more muddy boots slung into corners, belongings piled high on the chairs where they had been dumped, doors slamming and voices echoing up and down the stairs, dog barking. . . . She started and noticed that the dog basket which had always lain beside the range had gone.

'Where's Bess?' she said with concern, meeting Maria's eyes.

'Oh, Mor, my handsome, she died.' Her face crumpled. 'Passed away in her sleep, she did. I come down one morning and I could see. . . .' She swallowed and dabbed her eyes with the corner of her apron. 'The vet said it were a heart attack, but 'tis my belief she pined so much with missing them all, that she just gave up.'

Tom's dog. Morwenna, her own eyes filling, pictured them together. Bess running carefree on the beach, Tom laughing at her antics, for Bess never did learn that seagulls could fly.

It was too much. She stood up, enfolded Maria in a warm embrace, and took her leave.

There had been no time after all to visit Rayle and see Sophie as she had planned. Morwenna shrugged. She would have to write her a letter and explain, for surely someone would tell Sophie that she had been down, and Morwenna did not want her cousin to feel hurt or slighted.

Before she left for London again, the workmen had begun making safe the foundations of Cove Cottage, and the familiar furniture had been replaced where it had always stood. It was almost as if she had never been away, Morwenna thought, as she looked around for the last time before locking up. 'I'll be back,' she whispered to the silent rooms as she turned and walked away.

Chapter Ten

TOM had been on night watch for several hours and, perched on the fire-step, his tired mind was drifting away, deep in his own thoughts in spite of the sporadic firing coming over from the German lines, and the occasional burst of shelling.

When he had returned from leave with Morwenna's pendant tucked into his breast pocket, he had done some serious thinking. So she did still love him. She must do – he was certain of it now. It had been in her face, in her eyes, as she gripped his hands and waved him off when the train wrenched them apart. In spite of that bloody Irishman that she seemed to share her life with.

So he had written her a proper letter at last. She deserved something better than the drivel he had been sending back over the months. In this one he had opened his heart and told her truly how much she meant to him, how he had always loved her and her alone. How when he came back he would make up for all the wasted time he had spent in this blasted stinking wilderness of slime and filth. The letter was in his tunic pocket waiting to be sent. He had taken a long time over the writing of it, wanting to get it absolutely right, and it was still in his head as he squinted through the sights of his rifle . . .

Darling Morwenna,

At last I have screwed up enough courage to tell you how much you mean to me. Forgive me for taking this long, but as you know, I have never found it easy to express my feelings. But today, in this place of desolation which is like anyone's worst vision of hell, where we share these muddy holes we live in with the rats and the lice, and I am waiting for the order to be sent 'over the top' again, I know I must tell you how much I love you, have always loved you, before it is too late.

Right from the time when you first came into my life – like a half-drowned kitten that I fished out of that pool – I felt bound to you. It was as

*if by saving your life we somehow belonged together. I think I loved you
from that moment.*

*Oh, my sea maiden! If I come through this we shall never be parted
again. I think of you as the one reality in this unreal world, a shining
beacon of hope which keeps me going when I would quite happily lie down
in the mud and let it swallow me up like so many who have perished there
already.*

Think of me sometimes,
Yours for ever, Tom.

He looked out over the bleak stretch of no man's land which lay within
his range of vision. Beyond the tangle of barbed wire, the landscape did
indeed resemble the medieval artists' visions of hell. A timid moon
gleamed fitfully on the blue-white water in the shell-holes, and caught the
moving shadows of rats as they slithered over the corpses floating in them.
Rats were good swimmers and they could sniff out a body and get to work
on it even before the victim had actually breathed his last. This place was
unspeakable, godless, hopeless.

Tom had taken out Morwenna's pendant earlier when he had been
thinking of her. The solid feel of it brought her closer to him. He liked to
think that the warmth of her hand still lingered on its surface, and he had
wound it tightly around his fingers to give him a grip on reality. He
clutched it hard, making the metal dig painfully into the palm of his hand
to keep himself from falling asleep.

'Roses ... are blooming ... in Picardy....' The strains of Jim
O'Reilly's mouth organ, drifting up from the trench where the men lay
patiently waiting for orders, made him jump and stiffen up. 'Put a sock in
it, mate, for God's sake,' came an irate voice and the melody was cut off in
mid-breath.

At that moment the British bombardment, which had been sporadic up
until now, intensified and immediately the air was split apart by noise.
Shells burst in fiery arcs, their brilliance obliterating the feeble moon, and
the signal whistle shrilled for 'over the top'. The stream of waiting men
now began to scramble up the sides of the trench under the covering shell-
fire, rifles at the ready with bayonets fixed, clawing their way up over the
rim and spreading out over no man's land, as a hail of shots and fragments
of shattered metal began to rain down upon them.

—Run! Keep your head down, you bloody fool. Wriggle through a hole
in the wire now, steady – not too fast, carefully, carefully. Men had been
caught in its grasp and had died there unable to free themselves, hanging

targets for enemy fire. Over the stretch of no man's land – into the German lines and onward. No retreat allowed – to retreat was a court-martialling offence. Take your pick – death by firing squad or dice with death in action.

Tom was charging forward with the rest, gasping for breath, machine-gun fire rattling all around them, shells still exploding in blinding flashes on all sides. He had reached the German trenches and was leaping over the rim, sliding, slithering down to the bottom. Now he was barging into other bodies head-on in hand-to-hand fighting. Bayonet *in*, grunt, *out*, grunt. Bayonet *in*. . . . They're not human beings, they're only bags of straw on a pole, he had to tell himself.

Surely their own shell-fire would stop – must stop – soon? The thought was hardly out of Tom's head when the next shell exploded directly above him on the rim of the trench. Damn and blast it, was his last conscious thought, it must be a bloody freak one gone off-course – then there was a moment of blinding white light which lit up the scene for miles around, and he could see trees in the distance, a farm and a village. For the merest fraction of a second all the noise cut out, then Tom was flung high into the air, feeling the clothes being ripped from his body as he was left poised on the brink of something momentous.

Coloured stars danced in this void, making patterns of immense beauty on the velvet background of the night sky. Then with an enormous rush of air he was hurtling down, from darkness into darkness, the wind whistling in his ears as, half-naked, he was hurled deep into the putrid mud. All the breath in his body left him on impact, and Tom knew no more.

'Oh, Tom, *why* don't you answer my letter?' Morwenna, alone in her room, on her return from Cornwall, sat with her elbows on the desk at her window, nibbling her thumb. Because he saw you with Kieran at the station, of course, she thought. And with him wearing evening dress, obviously you'd both been out together enjoying yourselves somewhere, while Tom had gone all the way down to Cornwall looking for you, on a wild goose chase. He must think that you're living it up in London, having a whale of a time, while he's . . . he's going back to live like a rat in a filthy hole in the ground. Tears filled her eyes as Morwenna flayed herself with guilt and self-punishment.

'I'll see you at the hospital in the morning – I have to come down to Woolwich to organize the next batch of convalescents.' Kieran had called on Morwenna and persuaded her to go out for a walk. Not knowing the underlying reason for her low spirits, he had told her that she was spending too much time indoors, and jokingly asked whether she was trying to avoid him. Morwenna supposed that subconsciously that was just what she had been doing. And now, after a brisk walk across the park, she admitted to herself that he was right on both counts. It was the first taste of fresh air she had had for some time and she was feeling better for it, although summer had given way to autumn now and there was a chilly nip in the easterly wind.

'Although goodness knows where we can send them, to be sure,' Kieran went on. 'Everywhere is full to overflowing as it is.' He ran a hand through his hair in agitation and Morwenna thought how tired he was looking.

But no more tired than she herself was feeling. Her days were full of the sick and wounded, the sights, smells and sounds of hospital life, and when she came off duty she was too exhausted to do much more than eat and sleep, before it all began again.

They were passing the high walls of the munitions factory in Woolwich just as the gate opened and a bunch of women came pouring out at the end of a shift. 'Look how yellow their skin is, poor things,' Morwenna remarked. 'I shouldn't like to be doing their job, however good the money is.'

'No. It's the picric acid, you know, which gets into their pores, so it does, with filling the shells all day. Deadly stuff,' Kieran explained. Morwenna nodded and looked at them with sympathy. It was another reminder of this never-ending war which constantly impinged on all their lives.

She shuddered and thrust both hands into the pockets of her long cardigan. Hunched against the wind coming up the river as they turned a corner, she turned her face up to Kieran's. 'I know just what you mean about the overcrowding in the hospitals. When I came back from Cornwall I was really shocked.' She sighed. 'There never seems to be enough time for anything these days. Our hospital is flooded with casualties like everywhere else – every bed is occupied and some are lying on stretchers in the corridors. All the doctors and nurses are working flat out every hour of the day and night, and the wounded still keep pouring in.'

'Sure and it's this heavy fighting along the Somme, so it is,' said Kieran. 'The allies are suffering enormous losses, you know.' And Morwenna, looking up at him then and nodding in agreement, was struck by the bland expression on Kieran's face which did not really reflect the solemnity of his remark. She shrugged, for who could ever tell what was going on in another person's mind? And Kieran, she had discovered, for all that he was such a dear friend and an engaging companion, had another side to him which he kept very much to himself.

'I must tell you this – a strange thing happened in the hospital the other evening,' Morwenna said as Kieran took her elbow to guide her over the road.

He looked at her with interest and replied, 'Oh yes?' as he waited for her to go on.

Morwenna gestured with her hands as they walked. 'Well, I was on my way upstairs on an errand, taking a carbolic spray up to the ward that had asked for it – you know, they use them to cut down infection – when I found myself following behind one of the doctors. He was a few yards ahead of me and it struck me that there was something familiar about him – the way he walked and so on. Fifty-ish, on the short side, thickset, with dark hair going grey. Who does that remind you of?' She turned to him with an expectant look, but Kieran merely shrugged and looked blankly back at her. 'It was John Miller, Donald's father, you know?' Morwenna spelt it out to Kieran. 'Your friend the doctor from Penzance who mixed up your cough syrup for you,' she added with irritation at his slowness.

'Ah, was it now?' he replied at last. 'Well, well.'

Morwenna glanced curiously at him, for he had not actually sounded very surprised. 'Yes. I worked with him at Rayle House and he complimented me once for my neat bandaging – it seems ages ago now. Maria told me he'd left Cornwall – but this is the strange thing.' She frowned and pointed a finger for emphasis. 'I know he saw me because when he turned the corner of the landing our eyes met and I waved and called out to him, but he ignored me and pretended that he hadn't. Why should he have done that?' Morwenna went on, looking up at Kieran in bafflement. 'It felt like a slap in the face.' She shrugged. 'Then a bunch of nurses came hurrying past and he disappeared in the crowd.'

'I shouldn't worry about it,' said Kieran smoothly. 'As we said before, doctors are under so much pressure these days, that there could have been all sorts of reasons, so there could. He must have had his mind on something else at the time.'

Morwenna sighed and they walked on in silence for a while as her thoughts wandered. Then she said reflectively, 'I was talking to one of the wounded men this morning and he was saying that our side are going to bring in these new machines called "tanks" very soon. You know what I mean? They're a kind of mobile armoured car with a gun attached to it.'

'Really?' Kieran looked intently at her. 'Yes, I've heard of them. That's interesting.'

'This soldier was saying that he thinks it'll make a great deal of difference to us because for one thing they can flatten the barbed wire defences which can't be done by shell-fire alone.'

'Sure and you seem to know a lot about it, so you do,' Kieran said, turning to her with a grin.

Morwenna's face was solemn as she replied. 'Oh, I spent some time with him over several days. He was a nice chap and he had dreadful internal wounds. We talked a lot. He told me there's going to be a big push soon. He overheard one of the officers talking about it. If they can capture Messines Ridge – do you remember Jack telling me about that?' she said brightly, looking up at him, and Kieran nodded. 'Then they're going to use those tanks in force at a place called . . . um . . . Arras, I think it was.'

Then Morwenna paused and her face crumpled. 'Kieran, I was with him when he died. I was holding his hand and he – he just gave a sigh and a sort of gurgle, then he was gone.' Morwenna could not control a sob and Kieran slipped a comforting arm around her waist. 'I don't think I shall ever be able to distance myself from it all like some do,' she sniffed against his shoulder. 'Even after all the months I've been working in the hospital I still see each man as a person, not just a case. Which is exactly what I used to tell Laura not to do.' She gave a watery smile and wiped her eyes.

Kieran nodded and squeezed her hand. 'You must realize that the medics have got to see them as cases and not get personally involved, else they would crack under the strain, so they would.'

'Yes, I'm sure you're right,' Morwenna said and straightened up as they reached her lodgings. 'Thank you, Kieran, for being so . . . understanding,' she added.

He squeezed her hand again and his eyes softened as he said with feeling, 'I'll always be here for you, Mor, if you need me. You know that, don't you?'

And Morwenna, looking up into his gentle face, thought not for the first time how lucky she was to have him for a friend.

'Coo-ee, Chrissie!' Morwenna waved and called across Trafalgar Square as she spotted her friend sitting on a bench waiting for her. Morwenna had shaken herself out of her self-absorption at last, for life had to go on, and had thrust her guilt to the back of her mind at least, although it was not forgotten. She and Chrissie had arranged to meet for a shopping trip and a chat, on an afternoon when their shifts coincided.

But Chrissie was looking in the other direction and obviously had not heard her. Morwenna smiled as she picked her way between the crowds, scattering pigeons as she went. She was really looking forward to this break. She had not seen Chrissie for some weeks and they would have a lot to catch up on. The weather was turning distinctly colder now and a thin easterly wind was blowing round the street corners and chasing the first of the falling leaves from the plane trees. Morwenna drew up her coat collar and decided it was time to look out some warmer clothes. Maybe I'll get something today, she thought.

'Penny for them!' she called out as she reached the bench where Chrissie was sitting, hunched into a corner. Then as her friend turned and looked over her shoulder at the sound of her voice, Morwenna gave a gasp of shock and her hand flew to her mouth in concern. Something must be badly wrong.

She sat down beside her and grasped her hand. 'Chrissie, what is it?' she whispered, looking into the other girl's pale and haggard face. She had obviously been weeping recently and looked as if she hadn't slept for a week.

Chrissie's raised dull eyes to her own, and Morwenna noticed that she was clutching an envelope in one hand. 'I had this telegram from Ma,' she said tonelessly, thrusting it towards her. 'It came yesterday. I'm on my way to the station now – I'm going down there, but I had to meet you like we planned so I could tell you first.'

Only then did Morwenna notice the suitcase at her friend's feet. With a sinking feeling in the pit of her stomach she snatched the telegram from her and opened it up.

'Prepare yourself for a shock,' Chrissie said hoarsely. Morwenna's glance flickered from her friend's face to the paper, and her hand was shaking before she even looked at it.

Tom missing believed dead. Please come. Mother.

Morwenna's wail of anguish sent a couple of pigeons to flight and earned some curious looks from passers-by, which soon turned to sympathy as they noticed the tell-tale yellow envelope lying in her lap. The blood sang in her ears as everything began to spin around her, and if she had not been sitting down already she would have passed out. Chrissie thrust her friend's head down into her lap, and gradually the sensation eased. And when she sat up again at last, the two girls collapsed sobbing into each other's arms.

'So I've got compassionate leave,' said Chrissie eventually, when they were both slightly recovered. 'For as long as they need me down home.'

Morwenna pictured Maria's brave, defeated little figure and squeezed her friend the harder. Her generous heart went out to Chrissie even in the desolation of her own grief, for her friend had lost not only her young man but now her brother as well.

'When's the train?' she asked, as they stared numbly and unseeingly at the hurrying crowds streaming down towards Piccadilly.

'In half an hour,' Chrissie replied. 'Time I was moving,' she added, getting up as the chimes of Big Ben boomed out over the city.

'I'll come and see you off,' said Morwenna distantly.

Since the devastation of the awful news, she seemed to be seeing everything from behind a wall of glass, which had come down and shut her off from the rest of the world. It was a strange sensation – she could hear herself talking to Chrissie, knew that she was walking down the street beside her quite normally, yet was aware that her real self was far away in some other place. The place she would visit when she was alone, when she could bear to face the desolation that was to be the rest of her life.

A few days later, Morwenna sat listlessly in her room gazing at nothing. Chrissie would be back in Cornwall long ago – she had waved her off on the train until the pinched, white face had disappeared from view – and now she was alone.

She could not shake off the waking nightmare no matter how hard she tried. She was throwing herself into her work at the hospital as if it were a lifeline, because to keep going until she was almost dropping with exhaustion kept her from thinking. And she was able to snatch at least a few hours of restless sleep before she awoke to the anguish which never really went away.

But one day Matron had called Morwenna into her private room and kindly but firmly told her not to come back to the hospital until she had had a few days' rest. As the woman pointed out, they had enough to do without her collapsing on the ward from exhaustion.

Although Morwenna tried to convince herself that 'believed dead' might not actually mean the worst, the casualty figures did nothing to raise her spirits. She felt as if she were living beneath a dull, grey blanket of fog, despite the brief and unexpected sunshine which was brightening the early November day.

Too upset to eat, unable to think straight, Morwenna dragged herself out of her lethargy at last and decided to go and see Kieran. She needed to talk, and he had said he'd always be there for her. If he was not at home she would be no worse off, and it would pass the empty hours that stretched before her. So in a short while she was walking up through Greenwich Park on her way to Blackheath and the address that he had given her.

The last drifts of dead leaves were floating down from the trees with every gust of wind that blew. Squirrels were running about busily gathering in their winter supplies and the grass was looking pale and sere. Morwenna followed the rising ground up past the observatory towards the gates, giving a passing glance at General Wolfe on his plinth looking out over her head, with his eyes forever fixed on the distant view of the river. Then leaving the park she crossed the road and began to walk over the heath towards the village, checking the address once more on the piece of paper that she fished out of a pocket as she went.

The house, when she found it, was a large two-storeyed building and Kieran had said that his flat was on the top floor. Morwenna entered through the imposing front door, which was standing open, and began to climb the stairs. On the landing she hesitated, for she could hear men's voices coming from behind the closed door of one of the rooms towards the end of the corridor. Her heart sank: Kieran must have visitors then.

As she was standing there wondering whether to knock or if instead she should just slip away again unnoticed, Morwenna heard somebody say 'Messines Ridge' and then the word 'tanks'. She sighed. Did no one ever talk about anything else but the war?

She had just made up her mind to turn around and go away when the door opened abruptly and a figure came striding out. 'Toodle-pip, then, old boy,' the man called over his shoulder to someone inside as he walked towards her.

At the sight of Morwenna he paused and raised his hat and she realized that it was Graham Leigh-Hunter. 'Miss Morwenna!' he said, his eyes boring into hers. 'What a pleasant surprise.'

'Hello, Gray,' she replied without warmth. Too downcast to be more than barely polite, she edged past him towards the open door, where she could see Kieran in the distance, and could feel the man's gaze still on her back as she went.

'*Morwenna!*' Kieran's expression of total shock at seeing her surprised Morwenna at first, then she realized how awful she must be looking. She had avoided seeing herself in the mirror lately because she knew that the sight of her pinched face, lank hair and hollow eyes would depress her more than ever. 'What are you doing here? What's the matter? Something's happened, hasn't it?' The expression on his face was not what

Morwenna had expected. He seemed ill at ease and not entirely delighted to see her.

'Oh, Kieran, I had to see you . . . to tell you . . . and to talk. . . .'

He looked distracted as he pulled open a door to an adjoining room, jerked his head and said, 'Come in here and sit down. I'll be with you in just a minute, to be sure – I've got someone with me but he's just going, so he is.'

He disappeared and, slightly taken aback, Morwenna – too much on edge to relax and sit down – paced across to the window and stared out. From her viewpoint she saw Kieran's visitor depart a few minutes later, and was surprised to see that it was none other than John Miller. How odd, she thought, a little hurt that Kieran had excluded her so, especially as they had been talking about him not long ago.

'Sure and I'm sorry about that,' Kieran said, running a hand through his hair as Morwenna turned to face him with the question on her lips. 'But what's up?' he asked with concern, before she could speak, as he moved closer and looked into her face. 'Come and sit down and tell me all about it.' He guided her to the settee and placed an arm around her shoulders.

'Oh, Kieran, I can hardly believe it.' Morwenna's voice was no more than a whisper. 'I saw Chrissie a few days ago and they've had word that . . . that . . .' She could not prevent the tears from falling now. She swallowed hard. 'It's Tom . . . he's missing, believed dead.' She turned to him and Kieran put both arms around her in a gentle embrace, and rested his cheek lightly on the top of her head. 'Oh, my darling girl,' he whispered. And Morwenna, sunk in her grief, did not notice his failure to say how sorry he was.

Kieran was wearing a tweed jacket of soft heather colours and he smelled of bay rum and peppermint. Morwenna looked up into his familiar face, and the dark, gentle eyes met her own with concern. He was the brother she had never had, the father she could not remember, and the warmth of his arms was reminiscent of Gramp's comforting hugs when she had been a child and hurt. Morwenna laid her head on his shoulder and sobbed her heart out.

And as her head drooped, it seemed to Kieran that the slim and delicate neck was like a flower stalk carrying a bloom too heavy for it to support. He tightened his clasp and stroked her damp hair, as a small smile lifted the corners of his mouth at the thought that one day, maybe, she could be his after all.

The tender moment came to an end when Morwenna abruptly realized where she was, and made a move to straighten up as she dried her eyes. 'Oh, Kieran, I'm so sorry. I didn't mean to weep all over you,' she said with a sniff, and gave him a watery smile. 'I really did just want to talk.'

'Sure and it's done you a power of good to have a good cry,' he replied. 'What are friends for at all, if not to support each other,' he added. Then he grinned and said, 'You can do the same for me one day, so you can.'

Morwenna's smile widened at the quip and Kieran nodded approval. 'That's better now,' he said. 'Sure and I'll be after putting the kettle on – don't go away now.'

He left the room and shortly afterwards returned with two steaming cups and a plate of biscuits. He pulled his chair up close to Morwenna's and said, as they sipped their tea, 'Now I've been thinking, so I have, that you and me are both of us in a good position to find out any information about your Tom.'

Morwenna raised an eyebrow. 'How do you mean?' she asked, holding on to her cup and clasping her cold hands around its comforting warmth.

'I mean, what with you working in the hospital, where you get wounded men coming in all the time – you can be after asking questions, so you can.' He looked her straight in the eyes. 'Think about it. There might even be men from Tom's regiment.' He pointed a finger for emphasis. 'Men who might know what action he was involved in.' Warming to his theme he went on, 'Even some who were with him in the same advance and would know where he was before he went missing, to be sure. That sort of thing, do you see?'

Morwenna was on the edge of her seat now, her eyes bright and fixed on Kieran's face, her tea forgotten as she nodded and replied with excitement, 'And so can you too, that's what you meant, isn't it? You could question the men coming off the hospital trains – keep an eye open for the uniform.' She drew in a breath and let it out on a long sigh. 'Oh, you have cheered me. I've been trying to convince myself that "missing" might mean exactly what it says – and that he may still be alive, and now you've given me real hope. Oh, Kieran, you might even come across Tom himself!' Her hands were clasped very tightly together in her lap and her face was radiant.

Kieran let her cling to that thread of hope and did not disillusion her with the practicalities. He would not point out how unlikely it was that out of all the hundreds of men who went through his hands, their faces muffled with bandages and dressings, in uniforms so stained and filthy that they were almost unrecognizable, he would be able to spot a man he had seen only once, and that fleetingly from a railway carriage after dark.

A small silence had fallen while Morwenna, deep in her own thoughts, gazed at the blue glow of the gas fire which was quietly sputtering away to itself beside them. Then as she stirred and looked up at him she said, 'Kieran, I'm sorry I interrupted you and your visitors just now – if I knew you were busy I would have gone away and come back another time.'

Kieran's eyes were gentle as they met hers and he said softly, 'Sure and it's glad I am that you didn't. You're always welcome, and don't you be after forgetting it.'

Morwenna smiled, then said, 'I almost bumped into Gray on the way out. I was wondering about him – what does he do for a living, Kieran?'

He shrugged. 'I don't think he has to do anything at all. He comes from a landed family, backbone of rural England, you know? Local squire – big place somewhere in Surrey, pedigree going back to the Normans and all that. He's got a dodgy heart so he couldn't join up, but I believe he mentioned that the other night, didn't he?'

Morwenna nodded. 'So how did you two become friends, then? You don't seem to have much in common on the face of things.'

Kieran leaned back and took a mouthful of tea. Picking up the plate of biscuits he offered it to Morwenna, who took one and nibbled it absently as he replied, 'I met him at the Epsom racecourse originally. One of the horses from Da's place was running and I had a little flutter on it. Gray was standing next to me and we got talking and he placed a bet on it as well. Sure, the horse won, he was grateful, and now we meet every now and again for a drink when he comes up to his club. We look through the papers and discuss form, that sort of thing.'

'Oh, I see.' Morwenna gave him a long look. 'I didn't know you were a betting man,' she said.

Kieran reddened. 'Oh – I'm not – not seriously,' he replied. 'Like I said, I'm just after having a little flutter now and then.'

She smiled at his embarrassment. 'It's nothing to be ashamed of,' she said. 'And I saw Doctor Miller too, didn't I? So it *was* him I glimpsed at the hospital that day.'

'Ah yes – I asked him about that and he swears that he didn't notice you and would I give you his apologies.' Kieran gave her a disarming smile and Morwenna shrugged.

'I see,' she replied. 'And is he a betting man as well? Are you some sort of syndicate or what?'

'Ah, yes,' said Kieran briefly, 'you could say so, to be sure.'

So *that* must be where his money comes from, Morwenna was thinking privately. They are obviously doing much better on the horses than Kieran lets on. I always did wonder how he could afford that brand new car of his.

Chapter Eleven

WHEN Tom came to, he was lying in the bottom of a crater in a daze. His body was a mass of minor lacerations and bruises, his face was stiff and he could only see out of one eye. His head was throbbing, and cautiously feeling around in his hair he discovered a sticky patch of blood and an area which was swelling up into an enormous lump. He looked down at himself. Strips of clothing hung about him like rags on a scarecrow, torn to shreds by the blast. He had lost everything. His rifle, most of his uniform, his tin hat and his pack. And, of course, Morwenna's letter. With a superhuman effort he scrambled dizzily out of the hole and crawled a few yards across the freezing mud, before a shooting pain in his head made him lose consciousness again, roll over sideways and sprawl flat on his back in a pool of noxious water.

He was roused by voices talking above him and the light from a powerful torch beam on his face.

'*Ach, was haben wie hier?*' came a gruff male voice, as a field boot nudged him in the ribs and a beefy hand clutched at his shoulder to lever him upright.

Tom groaned as a second hand took his other shoulder, between them forcing him into a sitting position. He struggled to open his eyes, and to keep them open. Squinting as if through a fog, his gaze alighted on a pair of legs clad in trousers of field grey, then travelled up to the waist where they were fastened with a metal belt-buckle. This was glinting where the torchlight caught it, and was engraved with the words '*Gott mit uns.*' God is with us. Tom's heart sank and he slumped back into the arms of his captors.

Morwenna went back to her work at the hospital as soon as she possibly could. She had found the time hanging heavily on her hands during the period of her enforced rest, and was glad to be back in the hustle and bustle for two reasons. One, because her days were now so fully occupied that they gave her no opportunity for brooding, and two, she was eager to question the incoming wounded about Tom, as Kieran had suggested.

Days passed into weeks, however, and weeks into months, with no word of him. Christmas came and went, hardly noticed, as Morwenna spent it at the hospital. She was glad to stay, and others who wanted to get away for the break and spend it with their families were grateful that she did. Soon the old year had given way to the new one of 1917 with still no let-up in the fighting or the number of casualties in the field.

'Sooner or later, me girl, you're going to have to face up to the facts, so you are. Surely you must realize that your Tom isn't coming back after all this time,' Kieran said. He must have noticed Morwenna's downcast expression, for he gently put an arm around her waist and drew her towards him. She stiffened as she looked up at him with a set face and bravely tilted her chin. 'I'll never give up hope, Kieran,' she replied. 'I would know inside myself, I'm sure I would, if Tom were dead. Because part of me would die with him, you see.' And her voice had a catch in it which she could not prevent.

But lately, deep inside herself, Morwenna had been hearing a small persistent voice that had been whispering the same message. Surely if he were still alive, Tom would have managed to communicate somehow, at least to his family if not to her, by now. And if he loved you enough, went on the voice, nothing would have stopped him, war or not – nothing short of death. So, you have to face up to the unpalatable truth that either he is actually dead or he doesn't love you – it's as simple as that. Maybe he never ever loved you at all – well, not seriously anyway. You can't be sure about that in spite of all that Chrissie said, can you?

So she swallowed hard and curled herself more closely into Kieran's shoulder, putting her own arm around his waist. She needed somebody to hold and to be held by. With a sigh, Morwenna wondered what she would do without this man's friendship and staunch support – he was always there when she needed somebody most, caring and kind. She knew that Kieran loved her in a way she could never return, but there were other kinds of love, surely. And often, she thought, as she looked into the glowing bars of the gas fire, the steady glow lasted longer than the fierce flame of passion.

'Is that so?' he replied softly, and the grip on her shoulders tightened. Morwenna nodded and glanced up into the black eyes, so quick to spark into laughter, sometimes too deep to fathom, and was not surprised when Kieran bent his head towards her and their lips met in a gentle kiss. 'Well,' he said, drawing away, 'when and if that time comes, Mor, remember that I'm here, won't you? Sure and you already know how I feel about you, but I won't play second fiddle at all to anybody else, not even to a ghost. I'm willing to wait until you're certain inside yourself, so I am. And then I would very much like to think that we could have a future together.'

Morwenna straightened and smiled as she squeezed his hand. 'Thank you, Kieran,' she said. 'Your friendship means a lot to me. More than I can tell you, and I will remember what you've just said, I promise.'

Kieran gripped the hand for a moment longer and held her eyes with his own, as he added, 'Sure and I'll give you until the end of the war to make up your mind, so I will. Then I shall ask you again, Mor, and I shall want a definite yes or a definite no – no shilly-shallying, understand? For I love you more than anything in the world but I want things to be fair. And if Tom doesn't come back when all this is over, I think I shall have given you both a fair chance, and I shan't be after feeling guilty at stealing another chap's girl, so I won't.'

A small silence fell as they looked deep into each other's eyes. Eventually Morwenna nodded and broke the contact. 'I understand,' she said simply.

'Right,' said Kieran, getting to his feet and briskly rubbing his hands together. 'Now let's get back to work.'

They were at his flat and had been going through a long list of names and numbers supplied by the Red Cross, who ran a contact agency for families of missing soldiers, searching as always for some clue to Tom's whereabouts.

The papers were spread out all over the floor and Morwenna, sitting back on her heels as she ran a finger down a list of names, remarked, 'Oh, I meant to tell you this—' She raised her head. 'One of the wounded men who came in this morning said that there are rumours of a big push coming up soon – he said it might even be the decider which could bring the war to an end. Imagine that!' Morwenna turned glowing eyes towards Kieran as she rolled up the papers and put them back in the elastic band which had been wrapped around them.

He shrugged and said dismissively, 'Sure and I'll believe that when I see it, so I shall,' but there was flicker of interest in his eyes and he gazed back at her for a long moment.

Then Morwenna, scrambling to her feet, remarked, 'I'll put these in the drawer of your desk, shall I? You might find someone else who could use the information, even though it's no good to us.'

'All right,' said Kieran absently, his back towards her as he bent to turn up the flame of the gas fire, which was sputtering away quietly in the made-over grate. 'Sure and that's better, so it is. It's perishing cold in here – shouldn't be surprised if we have a freeze-up overnight. We'd better get you home soon before it starts.'

When there was no answer from Morwenna he turned his head to see what she was doing, and his face darkened as he noticed her staring into the open desk-drawer. 'Not *that* drawer,' he snapped, and she looked up in surprise. 'I meant the left-hand one,' he added more quietly.

'Oh, sorry. This is interesting, though,' Morwenna remarked, as she absently hooked a strand of hair back from her face. 'This map of France and Belgium that you've got here, stuck to the bottom of the drawer. It's marked with all the battle positions – I didn't know you followed the war so closely, Kieran.' She traced the arrows with a finger. 'Oh, there's Messines Ridge marked in red and Arras over there . . . and look at all these little flags. . . .' She raised her head to look at him and her eyes widened in surprise, for he was brick-red and frowning as he crossed the room, closed the drawer quickly and opened another one.

'Oh . . . er . . . yes. Yes. So I do, to be sure. Now, in here, this is where I meant you to put those papers.' He took them from her, opened the drawer and shoved them inside, then slammed it shut. In a more gentle tone he added, 'Now, come over to the fire, Mor, do – it's cold in this corner. Your hands are like ice, so they are.' He put a hand under her elbow and ushered her across the room as he adroitly changed the subject.

While his brother had been keeping watch over the benighted plains of northern France, deep beneath those plains and several yards into enemy territory, Jack Edwards and a squad of other former miners were burrowing like moles into the sticky clay soil.

They were digging out a narrow tunnel barely larger than three feet wide, in the direction of Messines Ridge. Jack and his mate, a coal miner from the Rhondda Valley, who was inevitably called Taffy, were fully conscious of the fact that not far away was a team of German miners, most likely from the Hartz mountains, doing exactly the same thing in the other direction. Behind Jack and Taffy were a couple of others filling sandbags with the loosened soil and taking it away to dump at the wider workings further back. And behind them came another team who were making safe the sides and roof with timber shoring.

Parallel to them the men could hear quite clearly the tread of enemy feet and the thump of pickaxes not far away. Occasionally small showers of loosened dirt would rain down on Taffy and Jack, but studiously ignoring the peril they were in, they worked steadily on in silence, taking turns at the face, each having to crawl over the other's body in order to change places. Sweat trickled down their faces, into their eyes and loosened the grip on their pick handles. Every so often they would have to stop and catch their breath, though the foetid air in the enclosed space was hardly worthy of the name.

Their orders were to dig out a listening post, but as the thumps at the other side became louder and nearer, they seemed to have achieved it already. Jack eased himself off the wooden frame, which had been supporting the face as he dug, and looked over his shoulder with a finger to his lips for silence, before jerking his head for Taffy to come closer.

Taffy, his eyes and teeth gleaming in his filthy face, nodded, and the lamp on his helmet sent streaks of light dancing over the walls of glistening mud as he crawled closer and put his ear to Jack's mouth. 'They're breaking through!' Jack mouthed. 'Pass the word back and let's get bloody well out of here pronto.'

Taffy nodded and immediately began to shuffle backwards on hands and knees towards the man behind him. So narrow was the tunnel that there was no room for them to turn round, so until the last man was contacted all they could do was wait like sitting ducks for whatever was to come.

Then Jack could only watch in horror, as like a hideous nightmare, the far wall began to crumble, the aperture got wider and eventually became large enough for a man to thrust his head through. The German shouted to his companions behind him and now his shoulder was nudging the hole wider, while other hands were using rifle butts to knock out the remainder of the obstruction. In seconds, half a dozen rifle barrels were pushed through the breech in the wall and the firing started. The noise in the confined space was deafening, while the air soon became thick and clogged with dust and smoke.

Trapped by the narrowness of the tunnel, the team struggled to ready their own rifles, but it was hopeless. Jack, held fast by the press of men behind him, was the first to go, shot at point-blank range by a German Mauser. It was a clean death – one which many a severely wounded man might even have envied. Before the rest of them could crawl out of range they were picked off like the sitting ducks they resembled, and the tunnel floor was soon strewn with the bodies of the dead and dying.

'Oh no!' Morwenna looked over the top of the letter from Chrissie she had been reading and clapped a hand to her mouth.

. . . wanted to tell you right away, but I could not bring myself to put it into words. Because we had another telegram last week. Oh Mor, Jack is dead – killed in action! What this dreadful news has done to us all you can only imagine. Coming on top of all the worry over Tom, it's really done Ma in – since the funeral she has taken to her bed and won't eat, won't do anything – she just lies there staring at nothing.

I was planning to come back until this happened. Now I can't see myself leaving here for a very long time – I'm going to be needed so much. Ma clings to me as if she'll never let me go, and keeps saying that I'm all she has left. I don't think she really believes that Tom is still alive, you see, hasn't believed it for a long time, but she's never actually said so. Now she seems to have just given up.

Pa is going to work as usual but it's like living in a morgue. Although I try to be positive for their sake, it's very difficult, Mor, with all three of the men gone . . .

Oh, poor Chrissie, Morwenna thought, tears streaming down her face, her heart aching for her friend. Just as she was getting over Walter, now she was mourning for her two brothers as well. It was more than one person should be asked to bear. And dear, happy-go-lucky Jack! Another childhood friend gone, this one for ever. Morwenna wondered if she should go down there and be with Chrissie, but decided that the family would probably be better left to do their grieving in private. Later on, perhaps. She wiped her eyes and reached for pen and paper to write a reply.

Tom, along with dozens of other prisoners of war like himself and of varying nationalities, was crammed into a cattle truck travelling by rail across the monotonous plains of Flanders.

His wounds had been patched up in the German field hospital where he had been taken, and considering the force of the blast which had struck him, they were amazingly superficial. No bones were broken, and Tom supposed it was the aftermath of shock and the bump on his head that was making him feel so woolly-minded, and as if it did not belong to the rest of his body.

Rammed into a corner of the truck, with bodies pressing him on all sides, he looked dazedly down at his unfamiliar clothing, which was a hotch-potch of anything that happened to be clean enough and roughly the right size. What remained of his tattered uniform had only been fit for burning, and he was now without any personal belongings whatsoever.

Apart, that is, from a kind of silver pendant which had been clenched so hard in his hand that they had had to prise his fingers away from it in the dressing station, in order to wash off the blood which was oozing out where the metal had bitten into his flesh. It had been on a chain and one of the nurses had hung it round his neck, where it remained, replacing his identity disc which had also disappeared in the blast.

Tom fingered it absently. It meant nothing to him – he had no idea how he had acquired it or when, but it looked a very feminine trinket. He buttoned up the collar of his army-issue shirt, courtesy of some dead kraut like the rest of his clothes, and hid it from view.

The train was slowing now and drawing into a station. Tom was jerked out of his thoughts with a start at the shouting and catcalling of a crowd of jeering women on the platform. His astonishment was total as they pushed forward, raised their fists and spat in the faces of the prisoners. Then they began to thrust their arms through the bars, still hurling insults, while their hands stretched out to scratch and tear like madwomen at any flesh within reach. They ripped at bandages, laughing at the pain they were inflicting, landing punches where they could and generally venting their fury on the hated enemy.

Tom cringed further back into his corner, trying to make himself as small as possible, while their guard, to give him credit, tried to fend of the howling mob with his boots and the butt of his rifle. Soon they were on the move again but it had been a sobering experience to look upon the face of hate, and brought home to Tom as nothing else could what it meant to be a captive in a hostile land.

They were taken eventually to a camp just outside the town of Moers in Westphalia, a region of north-west Germany situated in the country's industrial heartland, which was bisected by the mighty River Rhine, and where they were to be put to work in the coal mines. After climbing down from the train, stiff, weary and hungry, the prisoners were marched to the camp under police guard – which at least kept the angry citizens at bay.

'Here we are, mate, home sweet home,' muttered Alf White, an irrepressibly cheerful cockney who had enlivened their dreary journey with his wisecracking, and nudged Tom in the ribs as they were herded into a compound surrounded by rows of prefabricated huts. A wire fence enclosed the perimeter and there were manned watchtowers placed at strategic intervals along it.

'If it's got a bath house and a decent bed, I shan't complain,' said Tom, glancing longingly across the yard.

'They have to,' Alf said chirpily, 'and a clinic too, and a kitchen. Under the terms of the Geneva Convention, see?' He nodded importantly. 'It's an international agreement that P.O.W.s on both sides have got to be treated with reasonable care.'

'Let's hope that the camp commandant here knows all that.' Tom's expression was sceptical.

'But I don't reckon we'll be seeing our beds for a bit yet, mate,' Alf replied, as they were herded in single file into another building. 'This here's the medical post, look.' He cast an appreciative eye over a young nurse of Asian appearance who was directing the men at the front of the line. Her crisp white uniform emphasised the colour of her dusky skin, and beneath her head-dress her glossy black hair hung down her back in a shining braid. 'Going to give us the once-over first, they are.'

'Cor, what a cracker – she can do me over any time,' came a coarse voice behind them, followed by a cackle of laughter.

At the head of the line an orderly was writing details of each man in a ledger.

'*Wie heissen Sie?*' he barked at Tom as he approached. Tom stared blankly back at him, uncomprehending. '*Seine name.*' He poked a finger at the column of names in front of him.

'Oh,' said Tom. 'My name's . . . that is, I'm called . . . I'm called . . .' He stammered to a halt and his voice died away.

The German's face grew puce with annoyance as he obviously thought that Tom was making fun of him.

'*Schnell!*' he barked, and Tom felt the first flutterings of panic. He put a hand to his head.

'I . . . I . . . can't remember,' he whispered. 'I don't know my own name.' Something in his expression must have convinced the orderly that he was not pretending, for the man jerked a thumb for him to fall out and went on to the next in line.

The pretty nurse ushered Tom into a side room and indicated that he should sit and wait. Soon she returned with a doctor in a white coat with a stethoscope slung round his neck. '*So, was ist?*' He stood over Tom with a clipboard. Tom looked blankly back at him.

'He says, what is the matter with you?' the nurse translated, and Tom's face lit up with relief.

'You speak English! Oh, thank God someone does. I think . . . that is . . . I seem to have lost my memory,' he went on, and placed a hand to his forehead.

She turned to the doctor. '*Er hat sein Gedachtnis verlassen,*' she said. The doctor's face lightened.

'*Ach, so . . . ?* he replied with raised eyebrows, and smiled in Tom's direction. Then he scribbled at length on his notes and made some remark to the nurse.

'Herr Doktor says maybe it is only a temporary state,' she translated, her soft brown eyes full of sympathy as she regarded him. 'Do not worry about it for a while. Give your head time to heal, yes? But for now you are to go into the hospital to be held under observation.' Tom nodded and smiled, then there followed a rapid conversation between the two before he was ushered out.

Tom found that his stay in hospital was boring beyond belief. Not sick enough to be bedridden, nor well enough to be discharged, he found it difficult to pass the days. He couldn't read the German newspapers, which were the only ones available, was not allowed to smoke on the premises, and could not converse with the other patients in anything but sign language, for none of them was British. Tom had picked up a few words of French in the trenches and he and some of the other men did now and again have a hand of cards, the rules being understood without lengthy conversations, but at first Tom felt almost as if he had strayed on to some alien planet, where his past life had been cruelly snatched away, leaving him to exist in a terrible vacuum.

The only brightness in this place of twilight and shadows that could not be called living came with the visits of the nurse, Shuli, for Tom had asked her for her name. On one occasion he persuaded her to sit down beside him in the day room. 'For goodness' sake, come and talk to me,' he said with the desperation of a thirsty traveller in the desert who has spotted an oasis. 'I shall forget my own language next. Do you know that you're the only person in this god-forsaken place who speaks English?'

Shuli smiled. 'Just for a short while,' she replied. 'And if anyone asks, it is therapy, you know? Because I'm not really supposed to consort with the prisoners.' She perched on a stool nearby and folded her hands in her lap, looking up at him with dark, intelligent eyes. 'So, what shall we talk about, Mr Mystery Man?'

'Tell me about yourself,' said Tom. 'First of all, where do you come from and why are you so far away from your own country?'

Shuli smiled. 'This is my country,' she replied. 'But it's rather a long story.' With the air of someone telling a fairy story to a class of children, she clasped her arms around her knees and said, 'It began a long time ago, with my grandfather who was Indian and owned a carpet-making factory in Bombay. The business was very successful, he was making a lot of money, and he wanted to expand.' She spread her hands expressively. 'So he sent my father, his eldest son, to Hamburg and started exporting his carpets to Europe. There Vati met my mother, married her and settled in Moers, where she came from. They had four children and he never went back to India.' She smiled, her eyes far away in the past. 'He was ambitious for his children and we were sent to good schools. We were brought up as German citizens, of course, but we learned English as well as several other languages.

My three brothers followed Vati into the business and now they divide their time between India and other countries, always travelling.' Her hands fluttered as she spoke. 'I seldom see them. But I had no head for business, nor inclination either, so I chose to go in for nursing, as you see.' She looked up at Tom with a smile.

'Where do you live?' he asked, losing himself in the depths of her dark eyes. It had been so long since he had seen a woman, especially one as beautiful as Shuli, and he could not drag his gaze away from her expressive face.

'I still live at home, in the family house at Moers,' she replied. 'Mutti misses the boys so much that I have not the heart to move out, although sometimes I feel I would like to be a little more independent and get a place of my own.' Shuli's eyes were far away and she seemed to be talking more to herself than to her listener. Suddenly she snapped back to the present and smiled at Tom. 'When the war came,' she went on, 'they wanted volunteers to come out here and provide translations for foreign prisoners. The extra money was very welcome, so here I am.'

'That's really interesting,' said Tom, leaning back in his chair. His head came into contact with the wood, which was hard even through the padded leather, and he winced. The lump had gone down now but there was a huge spreading bruise where it had been, and he was subject to a constant headache. 'Have you ever been to India yourself?'

'Oh yes, many times,' Shuli replied. 'We spent holidays with our grandparents when we were children and now I go whenever I can, for they are both of them old and frail. That's why the extra money I get as a translator is so useful. Although of course since this dreadful war, travelling has become difficult.' She shrugged and spread her hands. Then she smiled and gracefully uncurled herself from the stool. 'And now I must go,' she said. 'I have duties to attend to.' She must, however, have seen the hungry look in Tom's eyes, for she patted his shoulder as she added, 'But I'll come again when I'm able. And we must think of a name for you,' she said. 'Until you recall your real one, of course,' she said swiftly as a shadow crossed Tom's face.

151

Still with her hand on his shoulder, Shuli scrutinized him for a long moment with her head on one side. ' "Max," ' she said with sudden decision. 'You look just like someone of that name whom I used to know. And now, goodbye until next time.'

Tom smiled at her. 'Oh, Shuli, thank you so much for coming,' he said, covering her hand with his own for a second. 'I shall really look forward to seeing you again.' And after that, the rest of the day did not seem quite so tedious.

It was during one of Shuli's visits, which had now become a regular occurrence, that Tom noticed her looking intently at the silver pendant which he always wore around his neck, simply because it was the only remnant of his former life he possessed.

'May I see that?' she asked as their eyes met, and Tom slipped it off and handed it to her. 'I was clutching it when I was found,' he said. 'Apparently I had wound the chain so tightly around my fingers that it survived the bomb blast which ripped everything else away.' His face fell and his eyes were full of pain as he added, 'But it means nothing to me, of course.'

Shuli scrutinized it closely and her eyes widened as she looked back at Tom and said, 'Do you know that this is Indian craftsmanship?'

'What? No – no, I told you I don't know anything about it. It doesn't hold any memories for me whatsoever. I only wish to goodness it did,' he said bitterly.

Shuli held it up to the light from the window and went on, 'I've seen silversmiths in the bazaars doing this engraved work. You know it's a locket, of course. How cleverly the hinge is hidden in the scrollwork, isn't it?' She stroked the trinket with a finger. 'Only a master could do it so well.'

'Locket?' Tom's brows rose and he sat up straighter in his chair. 'No – I thought it was only a pendant. Open it up, Shuli,' he said urgently. 'Is there anything inside?' His voice was shaking with excitement: could it hold a clue to his lost identity?

She snapped open the tiny clasp and they looked at it together. 'Two little photographs,' she said in excitement. 'Look – do you recognize these people?' Tom pored over the pictures, willing his stubborn brain to wake up, to tell him who these figures were, and who he was. But nothing happened. His face twisted and he turned away to hide his bitter disappointment from Shuli.

'Your parents maybe?' she persisted. 'They're about the right age group. And he's wearing uniform; it looks as if he was a soldier, like you.'

Tom was incapable of speech at that moment, and if she hadn't been present he would have hurled the locket to the floor and stamped on it, his frustration was so terrible.

Long after Shuli had gone, he lay in bed with the locket in his hand, staring and staring, willing it to ring some bell, to jog some hint of memory, however slight, but there was nothing. Tom turned his face to the wall and wept bitter tears of hopelessness.

Shuli went to see 'Max' most days during his recuperation period and as a diversion, Tom asked her to teach him a few words of German. It would enable him to feel less of an alien if he could understand something of what was going on around him, and it gave him an interest and something to do to pass the time. Physically he had completely recovered his strength, and apart from the appalling handicap of his memory loss, he was as fit as he had ever been.

Inevitably the time came when he was discharged from hospital and removed to one of the prison huts, where he found himself sharing a room with nineteen other men. Although he was now with others from his own battalion and had plenty of opportunity to speak his own language, the iron discipline and the orders, which were always barked as loudly as possible, were a far cry from the relatively peaceful surroundings of the hospital. Tom decided that this new life was going to take a lot of getting used to.

Every morning they were awakened by the cry of '*Heraus! Schnell! Schnell!*' and were herded into trucks which took them under escort to the coal mines where they were put to work. Strangely, the experience of donning a miner's helmet, climbing into the cage and descending into the darkness did not come as the shock Tom had expected. In fact, as he crawled about the underground tunnels and wielded his pick at the pit face, he felt something flicker in his mind. It was like the slightest crack in an opening door, but the more he tried to force it wider, the more it closed up again. It had been like the distant gleam of light at the far end of one of the tunnels that surrounded him, and equally as elusive.

Chapter Twelve

MORWENNA was sitting in the rest room at the hospital with her feet up, scanning a newspaper, when Laura bustled in with a crackle of starched apron and drew up a chair beside her.

'I say, Mor,' she said, 'have you heard the latest?' Her face was flushed and her eyes alight with excitement. 'It's all over the hospital – Camilla just told me. You'd never guess. . . .'

Morwenna swung her feet to the floor and put aside the paper. 'Well, if I'm never going to guess, then you'd better tell me, hadn't you?' she said with a grin.

'It's about Doctor Miller,' Laura went on. 'Didn't you say that you knew him in Cornwall before you came up here?' She fixed wide eyes on Morwenna's face. 'Yes, yes, I did. What about him?' asked Morwenna, all her attention now on what her friend was saying.

'Well . . .' Laura leaned closer and lowered her voice. 'He's only been arrested!'

'*Arrested?*' Morwenna's jaw dropped and her eyes widened. 'On what grounds?'

'Under the Defence of the Realm Act. You know, D.O.R.A. for short. He's in prison, suspected of spying for the Germans.'

Morwenna was oblivious to the rest of Laura's chatter as her head buzzed with this revelation. So Clara had been right all that time ago, when his surgery had been defaced! It was with good reason then that the doctor had fled from Cornwall, obviously thinking to lose himself in the city and carry on his subversive activities undetected. Morwenna nibbled at a thumb nail. So *that* had been why he had pretended not to see her that day on the stairs, she thought. He had been hoping to avoid her because she knew.

As soon as she was off duty, she made for Blackheath and Kieran's flat. She just had to see him, for she was carrying a terrible suspicion in her mind. Something too terrible almost to contemplate. When Morwenna found herself getting out of breath she had to force herself consciously to slow down, not having been aware that she had been running in her eagerness to see Kieran face to face, to have him put his arms around her and tell her that it was all right, to laugh at her fears and tell her that of course they were without foundation.

But nothing could have prepared her for the shock she received when she arrived. The door was opened to her by a uniformed constable and she was ushered into the sitting room where another policeman was sitting at Kieran's desk. All the drawers had been pulled right out and were ranged against the wall. Kieran sat opposite the other man, looking ashen-faced and haggard.

'Ah, Miss Pengelly, isn't it?' The policeman rose. 'We've been expecting you to call here soon.' Morwenna's eyes widened. 'I'm Detective Inspector Rogers.' Tall and lanky with a long nose and large teeth, he waved her to a chair.

Morwenna sank into it, her legs shaking so much she would have collapsed without support. 'What ... what ... ?' She spread her hands in bewilderment and looked to Kieran for an explanation. But inside herself, of course, she already knew. His shoulders slumped, he gave her an agonized look, then shook his head slowly from side to side.

'I'd like to ask you a few questions, miss,' the inspector went on, his eyes boring into hers.

'M-me?' Morwenna stammered, feeling like a butterfly pinned to a board. 'But . .'

'I believe you are an acquaintance of a Doctor John Miller, otherwise known as Jan Muller,' he said.

'Oh, well ... yes. Yes, I know him. We work at the same hospital. At least ... we did. Someone told me he's been arrested.' Her eyes felt huge as he continued to hold her with a basilisk stare, and she felt all the colour drain from her face.

'Ah. You're aware of that, then.' Morwenna nodded. 'Now, I would venture to suggest that you have known John Miller for a great deal longer than the period you have both been at Woolwich. Is this so?'

'Well, yes, it is. I first met him in Cornwall. He had a practice there. And we also worked together in a convalescent hospital when the war started.'

'Quite so. But what I'm really getting at is this. He is in fact related to your family, is he not?'

'You seem to know a great deal,' Morwenna retorted with a touch of asperity, anger suddenly stiffening her spine. 'May I ask why, since you have obviously been researching my connections so thoroughly, you need to ask me so many questions?'

A spasm of annoyance crossed the inspector's face. 'Just answer those questions if you will, miss. Surely I don't need to remind you that you are in no position to argue with me?' He gave her a steely look over the top of his gold-rimmed spectacles and Morwenna quailed as she realized, with a sickening lurch of her stomach, that this was serious stuff. She swallowed hard.

'Only distantly,' she said in a small voice. 'My cousin is married to Doctor Miller's son.'

The man nodded and looked at his notes, apparently satisfied. 'Right. Now, then. How long have you known Mr Doyle here?' Morwenna gulped. 'Since he came to Cornwall, to set up the convalescent home I told you about.'

'And were he and Doctor Miller friendly then?' Morwenna glanced at Kieran, who was gazing at the floor, his hands between his knees.

With another spurt of anger, she said, 'Why don't you ask him? He's sitting right beside you!'

Inside her head, thoughts were hammering at her brain, filling her with fury, hurt and shock. Oh, Kieran, how could you? she wanted to cry. She didn't know what to say to him but she knew she couldn't tell lies. All she could do was tell the truth. She swallowed against the lump in her throat which was threatening to choke her.

Another look of steel from the inspector quelled her pathetic burst of spirit. 'I don't know about being friendly, but he used to mix up a special cough linctus for K– for Mr Doyle.'

A silence fell as the man wrote at some length in his notebook. Then he raised his head, gave a smile which did not reach his eyes, and closed the book with a snap. 'Right, Miss Pengelly. You are free to leave now and continue with your daily life as before. With a few conditions. You will be kept under surveillance, so do not attempt to leave Woolwich. And you are not under any circumstances to contact Mr Doyle until you are notified that you may do so. Do you understand?'

'Oh yes, I understand,' said Morwenna, tilting her chin and meeting his eyes. 'And I hope that you too, Inspector, understand that you have been trying to intimidate a completely innocent person. I have never done anything underhanded in my life, and regardless of how thoroughly you investigate my past life, you will never be able to prove otherwise.'

'Goodbye, Miss Pengelly.' He rose and opened the door for her. Morwenna flashed Kieran a look of agony and swept out with her head held high.

Her legs were shaking so much that it was all she could do to negotiate the stairs. As soon as she had crossed the road and was out of sight of the house, she collapsed on to a park bench and tried to subdue her whirling thoughts.

Kieran, you swine, she thought, how could you *do* this? And I thought we were so close. You said you loved me – you were even ready to marry me! How could you keep all this to yourself? What sort of love is it without trust? The tears came then and she hid her head from passers-by behind the newspaper that she had bought on the way over.

The sobs quietened after a while and Morwenna dabbed at her eyes with a sodden handkerchief and folded up the newspaper. It was only then that she caught sight of a headline to a column which was tucked away on an inside page:

Well-known land owner and pillar of society, Mr Graham Leigh-Hunter of Ashworthy in Surrey, was executed by firing squad this morning, under the terms of the Defence of the Realm Act. It has been proven that he was consorting with the enemy and handing over military secrets which he had gathered from a web of small-time operators, while passing himself off as a typical country gentleman.

It has come to light that over the years Leigh-Hunter had been accumulating enormous debts owing to his fondness for gambling on the horses, and was in dire straits with his creditors. This was believed to be the reason for his dastardly crime, for which he has unfortunately paid the ultimate penalty.

The article then launched into a polemic about the gentry, who should be setting an example to the middle classes, but Morwenna's hands were shaking so much she could hardly hold the fluttering paper, and she let it drop into her lap as she gazed unseeingly across the heath. Gray! *Executed for treason!* She just could not believe it. But that was what they did to traitors. To spies. *To Kieran?* An icy shiver feathered down her spine and she stuffed a fist in her mouth as her whole body went rigid.

'Pardon me, miss, but are you all right?' Morwenna jumped and looked up into the kindly eyes of an elderly man with a bristling white moustache. He was holding a small dog on a lead and tipped his hat to her. 'You were looking so distressed that I thought I must just enquire,' he added.

'Oh yes . . . yes, thank you. You're very kind.' Morwenna rose to her feet in confusion and pointed to the newspaper. 'Just some bad news, that's all – a momentary shock. I'm quite all right now. Thank you so much.'

He tipped his hat again. 'So much tragedy everywhere, each time one opens a paper. Where will it all end?' He sighed. 'Good day to you then, miss.' And he passed on, pulling the dog behind him.

How kind, Morwenna thought. Then something else struck her like a shower of cold water. 'You will be kept under surveillance,' the inspector had said. Supposing it wasn't kindness at all? Morwenna clapped a hand across her mouth to stifle a cry. Was she to be suspicious from now on of every stranger who crossed her path? And what about her friends? She had been badly let down once already; how could she trust anyone ever again?

Several weeks passed in a blur while Morwenna went about her shattered life like some kind of automaton. During this time she realized that she had taken to looking over her shoulder as she came and went, like some kind of fugitive. But I've done nothing wrong! she cried from the depths of her soul, railing at the unfairness of it all.

She heard nothing of Kieran, but had not really expected to. At best, he would be in jail, at worst . . . She would not think of that. Morwenna stiffened her spine and held her head high, betraying to no one the tumult of her inner feelings.

She grew thin and pale. There was no one to talk to, to confide in. No Kieran, no Chrissie. She would not contact Chrissie, for her friend had enough on her plate already without taking on Morwenna's problems as well. And a letter would have been no consolation in any case. She needed a shoulder to cry on, someone to be there for her and just to listen.

Laura and Camilla must have known that something was wrong but although they were as friendly and supportive as they ever had been, they did not know Morwenna that closely, could not do so, as their acquaintance was relatively recent. So she hugged her troubles to herself and pushed them down deep. If it had not been for her orders to stay in Woolwich, she would have thrown it all up, the job and everything, and gone back to Cornwall. But that was forbidden to her, so Morwenna immersed herself in her work as always, and waited.

Months dragged by, until one Sunday morning Morwenna answered a knock on her door, and there he was. Kieran Doyle, thinner, older-looking, his eyes guarded and wary as he stood turning his hat nervously in his hands.

'*You!*' she said, and her voice was icy. 'After everything that's happened, you have the nerve to come calling *here*?' Her throat was dry and the hand holding the door was shaking.

'I know, I know, but I have to talk to you, Morwenna. May I come in?

Please?' He jerked his head towards the stairwell. 'Your landlady . . .'

'Oh, all right. I suppose so. But I can't imagine that we have anything to say to each other.' Morwenna stepped back and closed the door behind him.

'Just be after giving me a chance to explain, will you?' he said as they both sat rigidly opposite each other in two armchairs. 'That's all I ask.'

Morwenna stared at him. 'Go on, then, explain if you can,' she said bitterly.

Kieran began to speak and his eyes were blazing with anger in his pale face as he pointed a finger at her for emphasis. 'Mor, I'm not ashamed of what I did. Don't think for one moment that I am. Sure and it was for a just cause. My country has suffered outrageously from the English. I've seen my brother injured, so I have, and boys that I grew up with have been killed, mown down in cold blood on the streets.' Thin-lipped, he finished, 'So of course I have no loyalty to Britain at all, I have not.' He paused and looked down at his lap, twisting his hat between his hands, then said more quietly, 'What I *am* deeply sorry for, Morwenna, is the fact that I never told you about it. Sure and I thought that you need never find out, and God knows, I didn't want to jeopardize your feelings for me. I loved you so much – as I love you still.' He raised his eyes to hers but Morwenna tossed her head and looked away. 'Believe me, I would have faced the firing squad along with Gray rather than have you dragged into this mess, so I would.'

Curious in spite of herself, Morwenna said, 'So why didn't you? How did you manage to get let off? And where have you been all these months?' She fired the questions at him sharply one after the other like pistol shots.

Kieran hung his head again. 'I've been in prison, to be sure, so I have,' he said dully. Morwenna gasped and put a hand to her mouth. 'While they went through all Gray's papers and interviewed the rest of his contacts. In the end they decided that I was such small fry that I'd been punished enough. They released me yesterday. Sure and you'll hear from them soon too, to say that you're no longer being watched. Oh, Mor,' he pleaded, and spread his hands, 'can you ever find it in your heart to forgive me at all?'

'Kieran Doyle, you are a devious, conniving, hot-headed *fool*.' Morwenna sprang from her seat and her voice would have cut glass. 'And if you think you can come crawling back here with an apology and an explanation, and expect us to pick up where we left off, I can assure you that you're very much mistaken.' She knew she was sounding like a fish-wife and consciously lowered her voice at the thought of the no doubt hovering Mrs Pope.

A sob was rising to her throat and impatiently Morwenna willed it away. 'You *betrayed* me, Kieran,' she said as she whirled on him and pointed an accusing finger, 'as positively as if you had put the law on to me yourself.' She paced a few steps up and down the room in fury. 'I can see it all now. And worse than that, you *used* me, deliberately used me, didn't you? Because all those snippets of information that I picked up from the wounded men, things that I just mentioned to you in idle conversation, you passed on to your master. And you *lied* to me with all that drivel about horse racing – and I was fool enough to believe you! You are *despicable*. Lower than the lowest crawling creature on God's earth.'

'That part of it was true!' Kieran was on his feet too now, protesting as he seized her roughly by the wrists, forcing her to face him.

'Let me *go*!' Morwenna wriggled and squirmed but he held her in a grip of steel. She tried to kick him on the shins but he neatly side-stepped, not for one moment relaxing his hold.

'Sure and now you'll listen to *me* for a change, so you will,' Kieran said with fury sparking in his eyes. 'Can you imagine for one moment what it cost me to come here today with my tail between my legs – or "crawling", as you so nicely put it, *to apologize* to you? And don't you imagine either, that during six months in jail I haven't had plenty of time to think, so I have, and to regret the way I treated you, Mor?' His expression changed as all the anger left his face, leaving only sadness there, and Kieran dropped her hands. He turned away to pace up and down the carpet, his head bent as he said, 'I vowed that the first thing I would do when they let me out was to come and find you and try to make it up to you.' His voice lowered to a whisper, he added, 'And this is the reception you give me. What more do you want? Blood?' He shrugged and spread his hands in defeat.

They faced each other across the room. 'There was a time, Kieran,' Morwenna said as their eyes locked, 'when I looked upon you as my dearest friend. I confided in you. I trusted you.' She opened her own hands in a gesture of hopelessness and slowly shook her head. 'You chose to break that trust.' Tension crackled in the air between them during the pause which followed, while each regarded the other, unmoving. 'Now get out of this house,' Morwenna said through gritted teeth, turning on her heel away from him. 'I never want to see or hear from you again.'

Kieran went without another word, moving towards the door. On the threshold he looked back, hat in hand, and their eyes met. He gave Morwenna a long look, then as she remained silent, he placed the hat on his curly head, gave it a tap and walked away. Morwenna closed the door behind him, leaned her back against it and let the scalding tears run down her cheeks unchecked.

It took Morwenna only a few days to decide to take, with Matron's blessing, the backlog of leave that was owing to her, to pack her bags and to flee home to Cornwall and the sanctuary of Cove Cottage.

It was December now and the bleakness of winter covered the familiar landscape in a blanket of unrelieved grey. The sea was grey, as was the sky. The granite rocks of the cove were grey and the slate-roofed houses the same. And on the day that Morwenna stepped out of the bus and looked about her, a fine, grey drizzle was drifting in from the sea, making the place appear as insubstantial as a ghost town. But she didn't mind the weather – it echoed her own mood. She felt grey herself: weary, washed out and despondent.

The cottage, however, was warm and snug, the fire in the range already lit. Morwenna had sent advance notice to Maria that she was coming and had asked her to open up the house and air it. Now the interior of the cottage tugged at her heart in the old way as she opened the fire door and held out her hands to its welcoming glow.

An inspection of the larder revealed enough supplies for a day or two, so Morwenna made herself a cup of tea, put her feet up on a stool in front of the stove and truly relaxed for the first time in weeks. As the firelight flickered on the beams of the low ceiling and moisture ran down the window-pane, she thought that weather or not, the decision to come home had definitely been the right one.

As she lay in bed that night listening to the pounding of the surf below the cottage, Morwenna's mind was going over and over the events of the past months. In particular, Kieran's defection and his betrayal of her innocent trust. That wound would be very slow to heal, if it ever did; she had thought him such a steady and reliable friend.

Morwenna's eyelids were beginning to droop, but in the dreamy state between wakefulness and slumber a revelation suddenly struck her, so compelling that it banished any hope of sleep and made her shoot bolt upright in the bed.

What if the information she had blithely passed to Kieran had led to the enemy action in which Jack had been killed? She would have been responsible for his death! Oh no! Morwenna stuffed a fist into her mouth to keep herself from crying out as her thoughts raced ahead of her. What about Tom? Could her careless chatter have contributed to his disappearance, or worse, as well? 'Oh, what have I done?' she wailed aloud in the depths of the night, and there was no one to comfort her.

And she would have to go to see Maria and Chrissie in the morning. How was she ever going to face them now that she realized all this? How could she tell them? But on the other hand, how could she not? For there was no way she could act naturally with them unless she did unburden herself. Morwenna tossed and turned in fitful sleep for the rest of the night and awoke sluggish and unrefreshed.

She stumbled down to the cove hoping that the fresh air might revive her. It was a mild day with little wind, but a pervading dampness hung in the air. The sky was the colour of pewter, and sullen waves were slapping half-heartedly at the rocky shore. Morwenna picked her way over the damp boulders, slippery with wrack, and perched on a craggy outcrop beneath the cliff. She pulled her knees up to her chin and wrapped her arms around them as she gazed unseeingly out beyond the Brisons to the farthest horizon, which was just visible as a darker shadow against the sky.

Morwenna sat there for a long time, immersed in her own thoughts, as the burden of guilt which she felt she would carry for the rest of her life pinned her down with its weight. Loneliness came down with the cloud of fine mist drifting in from the sea and settled like a shroud about her, until its accumulated moisture began to penetrate her clothes and drip from her hair. Then she rose as stiffly as an old woman and slowly climbed up the slip, past the boats which had been pulled well up from the water and upturned for the winter months, back to the cottage.

There, having dried herself out, Morwenna forced her weary brain into action. There was no getting away from the fact that she had to go and see the Edwards family sooner or later, so it might as well be now. Therefore she locked the door behind her once more and trudged up the hill to Praze Cottages.

'Morwenna! My handsome, come in, come in. Oh, I'm some glad to see you.' Morwenna smothered the gasp which rose to her lips, for although Maria had obviously regained some of her former spirit, her head of springy black hair had turned almost white since she had last been here. As she dropped a kiss on the little woman's cheek, Morwenna noticed that her welcoming smile was lack-lustre too, and the dark eyes had lost their inner sparkle. Oh yes, Maria's pain and suffering were written on her face for all to see. 'Hello, Maria,' she said gently, 'it's good to be here.'

At that moment the back door opened and Chrissie came bustling up the passage. 'Mor!' she said as her face broke into a smile. 'How lovely to see you!' She dropped the basket she had been carrying and the two wrapped their arms around each other in a long hug. 'Oh, Chrissie, I've missed you so – you can't imagine how much. . . .' Tears were not far from

Morwenna's eyes, both at the warmth of this unconditional welcome she had received and the thought that in a short while she was going to ruin it all. 'I've got so *much* to tell you,' she whispered.

'Come on down here,' said Maria, 'and we'll all have a cup of tea, shall us?' The two girls followed her stout little figure and they were soon gathered on chairs pulled up around the kitchen range, with steaming mugs in their hands.

Then, before she could lose her nerve, Morwenna launched into her story. Once started she couldn't stop, and out it all poured – about the scraps of information which she had so light-heartedly passed on to Kieran, his involvement with the other two enemy agents, his betrayal of her trust. And last of all, the part which she had been dreading most.

Morwenna's voice sank to a whisper as she finished. 'So you see I could have been, however innocently, responsible for J-Jack's death, and perhaps even Tom. . . .' She sank her face in her hands and let the tears flow freely.

A long silence followed, broken only by her sobs, until at last Morwenna dried her eyes and rose to her feet. 'So I'll go now,' she said, not looking at either of them. 'You won't want to know me any more and I don't blame you.' She stuffed her sodden handkerchief into a pocket and scraped back her chair. 'I quite understand and I'll try to keep out of your way from now on. . . .'

'Mor, you idiot, for goodness' sake, sit down!' Chrissie reached out a hand and tugged her round to face her. 'I've never heard such a load of rubbish. Do you really think that the little snippets you heard from a few wounded men would have been detailed enough or even important enough, to have any influence on the might of the German army?' Morwenna looked down at her friend's upturned face – the wide indignant look in her eyes, the bobbing curls and the determined chin – and a spark of hope lifted her despondency. Could it possibly be all right after all? she thought, and slid back into her chair again as Chrissie forcefully pulled her down beside her. 'Of course not,' her friend went on. 'It was stale news when you heard it – by the time you'd seen Kieran and passed it on to him it would have been even more out of date. Surely you can see that, can't you?' She snorted as if it beggared belief that anyone could be so dense.

Morwenna's haunted expression lifted a little as the faint gleam of hope strengthened. 'Do you really think so?' Her eyes held Chrissie's gaze as if it were a lifeline.

'Of course I do,' said practical Chrissie. What do you say, Ma?' She looked towards Maria, who had been listening open-mouthed to Morwenna's story, while a range of different expressions flickered over her face.

'My dear life, I should think so too. Don't you go worriting yourself like that, maid, over something that wasn't never your fault. They men deserved all they got, if you ask me. They was the traitors, not you – and as for that Dr Miller, or whatever his rightful name is, didn't I tell you ages ago there was something funny about him?' She nodded with satisfaction at having been proved right. 'I knew it, see.' She rounded on Morwenna and wagged a finger at her. 'And we don't want to hear nothing about all that never no more. Hear me, do you? Good.'

Morwenna nodded and smiled with relief, too full of churning emotions to speak. It was going to be all right. All her worries had been for nothing. Oh, how lucky she was to have such staunch friends – friends whom she could really rely on, through thick and thin.

'Now, Morwenna,' said Maria with determination, 'I want you to do me a favour, my handsome, if you will.' She met the girl's eyes as Morwenna raised her own and waited expectantly.

'Of course I will,' she replied. 'You know I'll do anything.'

'You mean anything?' There was something of the old sparkle on Maria's face as Morwenna nodded. 'Right then, maid. I want you to come and spend Christmas here along of we.'

Morwenna's jaw dropped in astonishment and she clutched at the arm of her chair to steady herself. 'Oh, Maria, th-thank you,' she stammered. 'But are you really sure you want me to after what I've done?'

'I told you – that nonsense is all over and done with,' Maria scolded, and broke off as Chrissie interrupted her.

'Honestly, Mor, please come.' Her face was serious as she glanced towards her mother. Maria had reached for the poker now and was stirring the fire with much banging and rattling of coals. Chrissie lowered her voice. 'It'll take Ma's mind off— Well, you know,' she said. 'And I can't tell you what your company would mean to me.'

'In that case I'd love to,' Morwenna said and squeezed the other girl's hand. 'I was thinking I'd have to spend it with the Rayle family.' She wrinkled her nose. 'Or on my own. Bless you,' she said to Maria, who beamed as she wiped her dusty hands down her pinafore and nodded vigorously.

'Good job we do live where we're to,' she said. 'Up London, it said in the paper, the poor souls are queuing all hours for ordinary stuff like bread and margarine and milk and all. That true, is it, maid?' She glanced at Morwenna, who could only incline her head in acknowledgement as

164

Maria went rattling on, giving her no time to reply to the question. 'Well, we shall be all right for a chicken from up the farm, and vegetables. And Willie do always have plenty of milk too, so I can make a bit of cream. . . .' She went on with the catalogue of provisions that had completely taken over her attention, while Chrissie and Morwenna looked at each other and grinned.

The next visit Morwenna made was to Rayle House. Nothing seemed to have changed here. Young men with the faces of old ones still sat about in the lounge, some huddled around the fire, sitting as close to it as they could get as if they would never be warm again, and her entrance was greeted by the same blank stares. The only difference was in their names.

'Hello, Sophie.' Morwenna went to meet her cousin as she walked into the room with a pile of magazines in her arms. 'Oh, Morwenna, it's lovely to see you,' she said, giving her a peck on the cheek. 'It's been a long time.'

Morwenna sensed the hidden meaning behind the remark and replied, 'Yes, I know, but there just wasn't the time to come round here when I was home last time. I just had to see about the repairs to the cottage and go straight back, you see.' She took some of the load of magazines from Sophie and placed them on the circular table. 'We were just so busy at the hospital,' she said over her shoulder, then straightened and swept a hand around the room as she added, 'It never stops, does it? Not here, not anywhere. But I did tell you that in my letter, didn't I?'

'Of course you did. I wasn't upset about it. So how long are you staying for this time?' Sophie whisked a duster out of a pocket and ran it over a couple of pictures which hung on the wall behind her. 'Until soon after Christmas,' Morwenna replied.

'You'll be here for Christmas?' Sophie looked over her shoulder and her face lit up. 'Oh, you will come and stay with us, won't you? It's so quiet with just me and the parents,' she added wistfully, and Morwenna felt a twinge of the old guilt. But why should she feel guilty? She was independent now and leading her own life. She could please herself what she did with her time and was under no obligation to anybody. Equally, she had nobody to love or be loved by. An echo of her grandfather's words whispered in her ear and she felt her mouth droop.

'Sorry, Sophie,' she said gently but firmly. 'I've got my own home now, and besides, I've already promised Chrissie and her mother that I would come to them.'

Sophie's face fell. She shrugged her narrow shoulders and sniffed as she rubbed the duster over a couple of shelves and replaced the ornaments on them. 'Oh well, if you'd rather. . . .'

Morwenna laid a hand on her arm. 'Sophie, don't let's fall out, please. I'll come and visit, of course I will, and it's too trivial a thing to come between us.' When at last her cousin nodded and looked at her with a smile hovering on her lips, Morwenna said, 'Now I imagine it's nearly tea-time, which is why I came. I thought you could take a break and tell me all your news. A lot has happened since we last had a chat.'

Her cousin's face brightened and they made their way towards the kitchen together. After the patients had been served, they were free at last and when they were settled, Sophie, with heightened colour in her cheeks, asked, 'Where's Kieran now and what's he doing? Oh, Mor, I read in the paper all about—'

'Yes.' Morwenna's mouth was a tight line. 'He's still in London. I don't suppose you know the full story at all, do you? How he lied to me, let me down. . . .'

'Let you *down*? Kieran?' Sophie leaned forward and took her hand. 'No! I can't believe he would do such a thing. Tell me all about it.'

So Morwenna went through the whole tale again, and when she had finished there was a silence while Sophie digested it all. 'I see,' she said at last and sighed. 'That certainly fills in a few gaps. We knew of course that John Miller had been arrested – it was a nine-day wonder all around Penzance and St Just – but not about Kieran or the other fellow.'

'So how has this affected Donald and Tamsin?' Morwenna asked. Sophie's face fell. 'Well, when the news broke that his father had been arrested and jailed – it was all over the local papers, as you can imagine – Donald was sent home and they investigated him very thoroughly too. But he was cleared, of course, and he's gone back to the front line again. It hit Tamsin pretty hard – you know what she's like about appearances.' Sophie's brows rose. 'But to give local people their due, they did rally round her and she wasn't ostracized as she might have been. She'd been dreading that, for Rachel's sake as well as her own. Fortunately she's not quite old enough yet to go to school, because children can be very cruel.'

Sophie stirred her tea and placed the spoon in the saucer of the thick white china which was used throughout the house. Looking at it with distaste, she remarked, 'I never noticed before the war how much I took nice things for granted – like dainty porcelain teacups and saucers.' She looked across at Morwenna. 'Donald's father is still in prison, you know. I think if they were going to execute him they would have done so by now, don't you?' She quirked an eyebrow. 'Along with the other chap. But otherwise I suppose he'll stay locked up until the end of the war.'

Morwenna nodded. 'How are Aunt Phoebe and Uncle Arthur? I must go over and see them too before I go back.'

'Oh, they're all right,' said Sophie. 'Stuck in a rigid day-to-day routine. I think it's the only way they can cope with all the changes.'

Morwenna was surprised at Sophie's insight. Her formerly scatty cousin had, with maturity, become more sensitive to other people's feelings.

'Father's still teaching,' Sophie went on, 'and of course the only person they can think of is James. Not that he's in any danger – he's doing a cushy job in some government department at the moment. Did you know that he was invalided out of the army after he developed asthma?'

Morwenna shook her head. 'No, I've been a bit out of touch.'

Sophie drained her cup and remarked, 'Trust James to fall on his feet. But the parents are always dreading that he might be sent back to the front.' She rose briskly and smiled. 'It's time that I was getting back to it. Did I tell you that I'm working here full-time now?'

'Oh, really?' Morwenna replied.

Sophie shrugged. 'I might as well,' she said. 'It's either that or stay at home and keep Mother company, and I know which I'd rather do.'

'There isn't ... anybody.... You haven't ... ?' enquired Morwenna, fishing.

'If you mean a man, then no, there isn't.' Sophie's reply held a note of bitterness. 'And even if there were, I couldn't leave the parents. Mother's becoming more and more dependent, and Father's talking about retiring soon.' Her cousin's eyes were bleak. 'So as there's nothing else on the horizon,' she added, 'here I shall stay until this beastly war's over.'

Morwenna felt a twinge of sympathy for her cousin, for she knew that feeling, and shortly afterwards she took her leave.

Chapter Thirteen

IT was a few days after Christmas, and Chrissie and Morwenna were having a bracing walk along the rugged cliffs. Since the wind had veered round to the north-west, the fog had blown away and the day was cold but bright. The sun had brought back colour to the landscape and they looked down upon a shimmering sea of cornflower blue, which was touched with turquoise in the shallower reaches near the cove. From further out, huge breakers were rolling shoreward and shattering themselves on to the rocks in clouds of sparkling foam. The tang of salt and seaweed was in the air, and the fresh wind had whipped their hair from its fastenings and brought a glow to their cheeks.

Chrissie had stopped to lean both elbows on a hoary granite outcrop to look out over the sea, one hand clutching her woolly tam o' shanter which the wind had removed from her head. The rock was dotted with patches of brilliant orange lichen, and made a natural vantage point.

'From here you'd never think there was such a thing as a war going on at all, would you?' She sighed and sat down on a comfortable clump of thrift out of the wind.

Morwenna joined her and leaned her back against the great boulder. In this sheltered nook the sun was shining warmly down on them although it was mid-winter. Tiny plants were taking advantage of the cover as well – she could see the spreading pale green fronds of bladder campion and sprigs of stone-crop, together with more thrift and some minute scarlet fungi which were glistening like jewels among the wind-bitten grasses.

'I know, it's timeless. I could look at it for ever.' Morwenna's expression was sombre. 'And it'll still be here when all this fighting is over, and when we're long gone besides.' Her eyes were bleak as she looked up at her friend perched slightly above her and said, 'Oh, Chris, what do you seriously think about Tom? Do you believe he *will* ever come back?'

Chrissie was hugging her knees, and she rested her chin on them as she gave Morwenna a long look before replying. Then she shook her head slowly from side to side and the wind caught at some loose strands of hair and blew them across her eyes, as she whispered, 'Deep down, common sense is telling me no. Because it's been so long.' She lifted a hand to her hair and tilted her face to the sky as if to find the answer there. 'But I suppose it's human nature never to give up hope.'

Morwenna nodded and a silence fell between them. It was the answer she had expected and it mirrored her own thoughts exactly. She followed Chrissie's gaze, where overhead the sun's rays were streaming down towards them out of a bank of grey cloud, gilding it from within, and said softly, 'You can understand how people believe that God lives up there, can't you?'

They were toasting bread for tea in front of a glowing fire in the parlour. This was a special treat – normally such an activity would have been banished to the kitchen, for Maria kept the parlour strictly for 'best'.

Chrissie turned to Morwenna, who was sitting on the rag rug and holding the long, brass-handled toasting fork as she gazed into the flames with a thoughtful expression on her face. 'So, when are you thinking of going back, Mor?' she said.

'Oh!' She jerked herself back to the present. 'It all depends, Chrissie. I've got a big decision to make first.' Her friend turned enquiring eyes towards her. 'You see, before I left the hospital I had a long chat with Matron and she was really nice – not at all the old dragon that we normally think her.' Chrissie smiled. 'Obviously she had heard all about Dr Miller's disgrace, and I think she must have heard a rumour too about my connection with it all.'

Morwenna shifted her position, removed the prongs of the fork and turned the toast on to its other side. 'Anyway, I'd been working all the hours I could, to keep myself from thinking too much, you know?' She turned over her shoulder and looked Chrissie in the face.

Her friend nodded, then suddenly called, 'Watch out, Mor – the toast's burning!'

Morwenna jumped and withdrew the fork, from which a column of black smoke was rising. 'It's not too bad – I'll have that piece,' she said, unperturbed, and placed it on the plate in the hearth to keep warm.

Chrissie was flapping her hands to disperse the smoke. 'If Ma smells this, we're done for,' she said with a giggle. 'Give me the fork. I'll do the next slice while you butter those.' They changed places. 'Anyway, what were you saying?' Chrissie asked, with her back towards her friend.

'Oh.' Morwenna paused in her buttering and licked a finger. 'Well, Matron took me to one side and said, "Miss Pengelly, you've been working harder lately than is good for you. You're wearing yourself down and I'm ordering you to take some leave, starting immediately. Much as I appreciate how you've done more than your fair share of duty recently, I don't want to see you here again until after Christmas, for your own sake. You'll be no good to yourself or to us if you fall sick from exhaustion." ' Morwenna mimicked the woman's autocratic voice and they burst out laughing.

'She sounded severe but her eyes were really gentle and kind.' Morwenna picked up the butter knife again. 'That's why I've been down here for so long, you see.' She took another piece of toast from the fork that Chrissie was holding out to her. 'Then, and this is what I have to decide about,' she went on, 'Matron said, "I'm wondering whether you would like a change, my dear – one which would get you away from here for a while. You probably know that after a six-month trial period, V.A.D.s are eligible to apply for Overseas Foreign Service?" So I looked at her and just nodded.

'Then she went on, "Well, the government, as you have probably heard, is appealing for V.A.D.s who are willing to go to the western front, and I'm wondering whether this might suit you. Of course, with your length of service and a recommendation that I would personally give you, you would have no trouble in being accepted."

'I just stood there gawping at her, Chris. I was caught so completely by surprise that I didn't know what to say, and when she said, "I would only suggest this to nurses whom I feel would be able to stand up to the strain of being near the front line," and then, "You have shown yourself to be one of these," I wasn't sure whether I was hearing her properly. She's never said anything at all like that before – only criticized.

'But she went on and on. "I very much hope that you'll think about it while you're away," and "I don't want an answer now – it's something that you'll need time to think about. So off you go, and I hope you have as good a Christmas as one can do in these times of austerity." I was in such a dither I only managed to stammer my thanks before she marched out.'

Morwenna's voice trailed away as she gazed into the fire and Chrissie said, 'Wow! She must think really highly of you, Mor, to say all that, mustn't she? Well done.' When her friend did not reply, Chrissie glanced over her shoulder with an enquiring expression.

Morwenna's face was set, and after a moment she said with a sigh,

'Chris, I don't know what to do with myself. I feel as if there's nothing happening for me anywhere at the moment.'

'Oh, I know exactly what you mean. It's the same for me.' Chrissie lowered her voice and looked to see if the door was closed. 'Mor,' she said bleakly, 'I get so frustrated here sometimes that I could scream. Pa and Ma take it for granted that I'm staying on indefinitely. I knew they would cling to me when I came back, because I'm all they've got left, but I sometimes wonder if I shall ever have a life of my own again.' She turned swimming eyes to her friend and Morwenna patted her shoulder with understanding. 'I shall have to get a job soon,' Chrissie went on. 'I need the money. Then it'll be just the same as if I'd never been away.' She spread her hands expressively. 'Oh, I *miss* it all, Mor – the excitement, the danger, the company, and the satisfaction of knowing that I was doing something useful. I feel so *trapped* now.'

Morwenna nodded. They were all three of them in similar positions, she thought. Sophie, with much the same problem as Chrissie, but with at least the feeling that she was doing useful work. And herself. Single women, and likely to remain so with the way that Britain's young men were being slaughtered or, and she stifled a sob, missing without trace in the hell-hole that was Flanders.

Morwenna made up her mind in that moment. 'Well, I've certainly had enough of Woolwich,' she said, as the image of Kieran Doyle flickered behind her eyes, 'and I can't stay in Cornwall doing nothing until the end of the war, either. So,' she finished abruptly, 'I've decided to tell Matron that yes, I'll go.'

Down in the hot and filthy surroundings of a coal mine, emaciated men toiled like dwarfs beneath the soil of northern Germany. Pale and haggard, streaked with sweat and black dust, Tom was shovelling up the stuff into trucks, along with a couple of others, then pushing them along the tracks to the shaft entrance to be emptied. It was gruelling, backbreaking work and he stopped to wipe a forearm across his brow, where the sweat was running down into his eyes.

They were not too badly treated in the prison camp – men who were expected to do a hard day's work in order to make up for those who were away at the war, had to be kept reasonably fit. But the food shortages which were being felt generally across the country were reflected in the sparse and unappetizing food served to the prisoners. There were redletter days occasionally, however, when a parcel from the Red Cross would arrive, its contents relieving the tedium of their diet and also containing basic staples like soap and cigarettes, but Tom and the others were always tired, both from the deficiencies of their diet and from the long hours they spent in the mine.

Tom could still remember nothing before the shell-blast, apart from being in the trenches, although occasionally, as he was travelling down in the cage, he felt that maybe somewhere, sometime, in another life, perhaps, he might have done this before. And as he put his shoulder to the loaded truck and used all his strength to propel it forward, the action had a familiar feel to it.

However, the more he concentrated and tried to force his mind to grasp this tenuous thread which was too nebulous even to be called recollection, the more it slipped tantalizingly away, leaving him frustrated and furious with himself and everyone around him. He had come to be known for his churlishness and bad temper, and the other men tended to leave him to himself, not understanding the real reason behind his unpredictable behaviour.

It was coming up to Christmas, and in their break-time underground, a group of miners had started up an impromptu rendering of 'Silent Night'. The familiar tune echoed around the caverns and tunnels, and as Tom relaxed against the side wall of a passage and took a swig from his water bottle, through his mind flashed a picture of some long-ago Christmas. Not the one in the trenches – he could remember quite well the fraternization between the two sides – but much further back. Childhood? He saw a family, and they were decorating a Christmas tree. Outside in the street a group of carollers had just started singing 'Silent night, holy night'. Eagerly Tom willed his brain to keep this window open – now he could see two little boys, one older than the other, and a girl, and they were arguing, squabbling, over who was to put the fairy on the top of the tree. Their voices came echoing faintly down the years: 'I want to . . .' 'No, let me . . .' 'It's not fair . . .' And an adult voice breaking in: 'No, Chrissie, you're not tall enough. Let Tom do it, he's the oldest. . . .'

Tom! The image faded, but his excitement was such that he hardly noticed. His name was Tom! For he knew that boy had been himself. And he had a sister called Chrissie. And a brother! A grin split his filthy face from ear to ear – maybe his memory was coming back at last.

But his jubilation was short-lived. 'Tom' was about the most common name imaginable. What was his second name? Where did he come from? And who had given him the locket? Did he have a wife, maybe even children of his own? Frustration set in again as Tom rose to his feet to return

172

to work, and he viciously kicked a stone the full length of the dusty passage.

He wanted to share this vision with someone, but he had long ago lost touch with Shuli. Since he had come out of the hospital he had only had the briefest glimpses of her, as of course prisoners were not allowed to fraternize with any of the staff. Tom longed to be able to tell her his real name, and that he was 'Max' no more, but it was impossible.

Time after time during the months that followed, Tom would lie on his bed at night and open the locket to study the faces of the two people in the photograph. They must be part of his family in some way. Each night he willed his mind to open the window again. Did this woman bear any resemblance to his sister, whose child's face he had seen quite clearly in the flash of recall? She had had bubbly curls and big blue eyes. No, this woman had a thin face and the photographer had tinted her hair dark brown. Her eyes were blue, but that was the only resemblance. As for the man, he wore a pith helmet and had a moustache and beard which obscured most of his face. His parents? Tom shook his head, sighed and snapped it shut.

'Not again, mate! Cor blimey, you'll wear out that bit of frippery wiv staring at it, you will.' Alf White's cheery voice roused Tom from his thoughts and he smiled. Alf was the only man who seemed unperturbed by his bouts of foul temper, and the little cockney was the nearest thing he had to a friend in the camp. Always cheerful, his tuneless whistling tended to grate on Tom's nerves, but he was glad of his company.

'Hi, Alf,' he said and slipped the locket back under his shirt. 'It's the only clue to who I am, you see, and I'm always hoping that one day it will mean something to me.' He swung his legs to the floor and said, 'What's new with you, then? Haven't seen you around for a while.'

'Nah, I've been laid up with a bit of gippy tummy. Been in the hospital and all. Isolation, see. I guess they didn't want me spreading it around to you lot.' He grinned.

'Oh,' Tom replied. 'All right now, are you?'

'Yeah. Thanks to Nurse Shuli's tender care. Cor, she's a cracker ain't she, Max? She asked after you and all.'

'Did she really?' Tom's eyes widened. 'I wish I could see her again.'

The cockney chuckled. 'Oi, oi,' he said and winked an eye as Tom reddened and quickly cut in, 'She was very kind to me when we first came in, you know?'

'Sure, sure.' Alf was still laughing to himself as he went to sit on Tom's bed. 'Thought you might like to see this, mate, but keep it to yourself.' He slipped a newspaper surreptitiously towards Tom. 'Had this come in a parcel from the wife. She smuggled it in along with some copies of *Punch* magazine. Tells you what's going on in the real world, like. Give it me back when you've read it and mind the krauts don't catch you.'

'Thanks, Alf,' said Tom as the little man rose to his feet and sidled off.

'See you, mate,' Alf called over his shoulder as he continued on his way back to his own quarters.

With the feeble light of a torch, Tom avidly read the paper under his blanket after lights out. News from outside was so hard to come by, and they were fed so much propaganda about huge German advances, for the prison guards delighted in trying to demoralize them, that no one knew what was true and what was not.

But as he read on, Tom's heart sank, for the krauts had been right after all. He could hardly believe it. He glanced at the date of the paper. *24 March, 1918 . . . the Germans have made the greatest advance on the Western Front since 1914 . . . the British have been driven back to the banks of the Somme . . . the Allied situation is extremely grave. . . .*

Tom snapped off the torch and stuffed the paper under his pillow. He had read enough.

When Morwenna arrived back at her lodgings she was surprised to find a letter in Kieran's handwriting waiting for her. She turned it over and over for a long time while she debated whether to open it or not, for she had told him that she never wanted to see or hear from him again, hadn't she?

Eventually, curiosity won and Morwenna slit the envelope. The letter had been written just after she had left for Cornwall.

Dear Morwenna,

No, I have not forgotten that you said you wanted to sever all contact, but I cannot let us part in such anger, because of all you mean to me. I think about you all the time and cannot get your face out of my mind.

Morwenna, I made a huge mistake when I deceived you so badly, but it was with the best of intentions. You see, I did not want you to be tainted by the sordid affairs that I had got myself into, because I loved – I love – you so much. I would give anything for this not to have happened, and I know that I have been fortunate in not receiving a longer sentence.

Believe me when I say that I was weak-willed enough to be influenced by people stronger than me. Although that doesn't excuse what I did and I'm not trying to justify my actions, I know now that I was only a very small cog in a much bigger machine.

So, I should like to think, now that we have had time to stand back and reflect, that you could find it in your heart to forgive me. Everyone makes mistakes in life, Mor. This was the biggest one I have ever made – not least because of losing you through it.

It would make me the happiest man on earth if you could see your way to taking up our friendship again, but I shall leave it to you to make the first move. You know where I live. Please come; I find life very empty without you.

With all my love,

Kieran.

Morwenna stood with the sheet of paper in her hand, reliving it all. Traitor, liar and deceiver – the sheer cheek of the man. Was he expecting to wipe the slate clean as if it had never happened? Her wounds had gone far too deep for that. Morwenna compressed her lips into a thin line, crumpled up the letter and hurled it into the fire, tears pouring down her face as she watched it shrivel to ashes. Before the end of the week, she was on her way to France.

The women and girls of the V.A.D. had been posted to a place called Etaples, in north-west France, not far from Calais. For some time, Morwenna had been trying to recall where she had heard the name before, but at last she realized that this was where Tom's training camp had been when he had first come out to France. Her heart ached as she remembered the letter he had sent then, full of boyish enthusiasm, and how he had gone off with a spring in his step and his eyes searching for distant horizons.

He had been looking forward so much to seeing some action. Action! She bit her lip. That had been almost four years ago, and how much action there had been since then!

'Oh, Tom,' she sighed, looking around her at the river and the sand dunes which he had described. Just to share this simple thing seemed to bring him a little closer to her, and the heartache which never went away stirred and surfaced again.

Morwenna had been at the hospital for two months and was at last getting used to seeing the consequences of trench warfare at first hand. Back at Woolwich the patients who had arrived had already been attended to, their wounds decently covered and dressed. Here, however, were men straight from the battlefield, their mutilation plain to see, some with wounds so horrific that death would have been preferable.

'Penny for them! Move yourself, dreamer, you're in the way.' Morwenna came back to earth with a jump.

'Sorry, Tessa,' she said with a grin as the girl from the next bed tried to squeeze past with an armful of clothing.

'There's just nowhere to put anything, is there?'

'No, it's terrible.' Morwenna replied. 'I've got all my undies and small stuff shoved in a box under the bed. Those few pegs on the wall don't hold much.'

The girls were billeted in long wooden huts, about twenty to each, in the grounds of the hospital, which was set on a rise with a view over sand dunes towards the river estuary.

'Aren't these beds *hard*?' Tessa was trying to bounce up and down on her mattress, which was as unresponsive as a plank.

'Yes,' said Morwenna, 'they certainly are. And so's the pillow. It took me ages to get used to sleeping with just a blanket on top – it was so scratchy that it brought my skin out in a rash. But now I get so exhausted after a busy shift that I could sleep anywhere.'

Morwenna liked Tessa, who had just arrived to join them. Tall, thin and gangly, with soft brown eyes and hair, she walked with a stoop as if self-conscious of her height. She reminded Morwenna irresistibly of a crane, apart from the wire-framed spectacles that she wore, which were constantly slipping down her nose.

'I've been working at the Hotel Bristol in Boulogne for two months,' Tessa explained later, as they met in the nurses' rest room.

'Oh, H.Q. no less, is it?' Morwenna replied and raised her eyebrows.

'Yes,' Tessa said with a chuckle, 'but if I told you what my first job was, you'd say that you'd rather be on the wards any day.'

'Oh?' Morwenna put down the paper she had been reading and looked at her friend with interest. 'What was it then?'

'Well . . .' Tessa pulled a chair towards her and put her feet up on its seat. 'They put me to work in a huge underground scullery. It was in a sort of basement and there was so much water on the floor that we had to stand on duckboards to keep our feet dry. There were rats down there too.' She made a face and Morwenna's eyes widened. 'My first job was absolutely revolting – you'll hardly believe this – but I had to cut off the slabs of green, rancid fat from the great joints of beef and mutton they gave me.'

'Ugh!' Morwenna's nose wrinkled, and Tessa laughed at the expression of disgust on her face. 'Yes, apparently the grease is used in making munitions.' She picked up Morwenna's discarded paper and glanced over the headlines. 'And after that,' she went on, looking over the top of her glasses,

'I was sent to work in the kitchen of a hotel which had been taken over as a billet for ambulance drivers. That was a bit more pleasant. Not that I knew a lot about cooking, but we muddled through – and there were a couple of cafés nearby that they could go to rather than starve.' Tessa grinned as she swung her legs down and smoothed out her apron. 'And now I'm here.' She shrugged as she added, 'But I don't know much about nursing either.'

'You'll soon learn,' said Morwenna, grim-faced. 'When the ambulances start rolling in, all hell breaks loose, I can tell you. I expect you've heard the shelling in the distance already?'

Tessa nodded. 'That was the first thing that somebody pointed out to me. She also said that this site was constantly under threat of bombardment – especially from the air. That cheered me up no end, I can tell you. It had me wondering whether I'd been better off in the cellar full of rats – at least we were safe from the bombs there!'

No sooner were the words out of her mouth than an urgent voice came booming over the loudspeakers: 'Incoming wounded – convoy approaching – prepare for incoming wounded – vacate wards immediately – all leave cancelled. . . .'

The girls sprang to their feet and joined the crowd of others who were converging on the hospital. Soon they were embroiled in the task of helping those patients who could walk to go to other wards, moving the beds with the patients in them if they were unable to walk, and stripping the empty beds. Then came the job of making them up afresh, bundling up the dirty laundry and disposing of it, all before the ambulances arrived.

'Here they come,' Morwenna announced as she glanced out of the window. 'Look at them all – it's going to be a long night.' Tessa followed her from the room, bundling up dirty bedding as she went, and they ran downstairs to meet the ambulances.

There followed a frantic assessment of the worst cases, which had already been labelled by the ambulance drivers; of trying to get wounds dressed before they festered; noting limbs that no medical care could save, but which would have to be amputated; injecting morphine and preparing for death those men who were obviously beyond help. It took five hours for the doctors to inspect all the patients, while the nurses and volunteers followed behind them doing what was necessary and trying to carry out their orders.

The doctors' faces were drained with exhaustion and their eyes as bloodshot as if they had been infected by the blood all around them. They were wearing white coats spattered with old bloodstains that no washing would ever erase, and their young faces had been prematurely aged with battling against so much disease, so many deaths. The place reeked of antiseptic and of the all-pervading blood, to which was added the nauseous stench of the morphine, which was used to dull the pain of amputation.

None of the ordered behaviour and petty rules of home hospitals applied here – everybody joined in a common effort to save as many lives as possible. Heroes and enemies were treated alike, while men whose wounds were less urgent lay about on stretchers on the floor.

Morwenna moved about the hospital like an automaton, going where she was needed most, obeying orders with an outwardly calm composure and her chin held high. But her soul ached at the sight of so much needless pain and suffering. Faced with her own inadequacy in the face of such tremendous need, it would have been easy to panic, to crumple, to faint clean away with the horror of it all. Morwenna took a deep breath, stilled her heaving stomach and forced herself to concentrate her energies on just one case at a time. She shut her ears and eyes to the groans of agony all around and bent over the man on the stretcher in front of her.

In between, there were periods of time off when Morwenna and Tessa could actually get away from the hospital for a walk over the sand dunes and along the bank of the estuary. The fresh air was so good after the stuffy wards, it tasted like wine. On one of these breaks, Morwenna kicked off her shoes and sat down with her back to a sandy hummock. With her eyes shut and the song of the skylarks which were twittering high above her head in the bluest of blue sky, she could almost imagine herself back in Cornwall.

Month after month passed in tending the patients and in the heart-rending task of burying the dead, punctuated by the spasmodic bursts of activity when the convoys arrived.

It was at this time that the hospital was at its most vulnerable, and completely open to attack from the air. They had all become accustomed to seeing low-flying enemy aircraft observing them, but carried on regardless for there was no alternative. The wounded had to be dealt with and either admitted for as long as they needed to be or patched up and sent home. Those men who had received a 'Blighty one' – slang for an injury that invalided a man out of the army – were sent back to Britain.

German high command were well aware of all these comings and goings, for Etaples was a vast military camp and also had many hospitals and medical facilities. The area had been under more or less constant surveillance ever since Morwenna had arrived, but it was May before the enemy decided to attack. Then a number of air raids were made upon the town in quick succession, and incendiary bombs dropped on it.

One of these attacks happened at the worst possible time, when the ambulances had just arrived and patients were being brought in to the hospital. A bomb landed about half a mile away and exploded harmlessly in a field, but the shrapnel rained down upon the medical staff and their helpless patients, killing several of the wounded who could not move fast enough to get under cover. But far from being satisfied by the hit, the enemy aircraft that had dropped the bomb continued to circle the area and began strafing the innocent and the helpless with machine-gun fire, despite the huge and obvious Red Cross signs on the vehicles.

'Down!' yelled a voice. '*Get down!*' Someone pushed Morwenna off her feet and dragged her underneath an ambulance just as the gunfire came rattling over their heads again. 'But the patients . . . !' she screamed, trying to wriggle backwards out of his grasp.

'They are all under some sort of cover,' came the reply, and she recognized the voice of one of the young doctors. 'This is no time for heroics,' her rescuer added. 'Our skills are needed, do you understand? We have a duty to look after ourselves because we can be of more use alive than dead,' he said grimly, and Morwenna could see the anguish in his eyes as he turned his haggard face towards her. 'You can only do so much before you have to think of your own survival.'

Nevertheless, three of their nurses died that day, shot as they dived for cover. One of them was Tessa.

It took Morwenna a long time to get over the shock of losing her friend, and she continued to grieve for Tessa long after a semblance of normality had returned to the hospital. She coped with it in the only way she knew, by hiding her feelings behind a front of calm serenity and sinking herself totally in the bustling activity which never seemed to ease.

Month after month passed. Spring had turned into summer, then autumn, and still there was no end to the fighting. Maybe there never would be. Children had been born and were now growing up unable to remember a world without war.

Month after month passed. Spring turned into summer, then autumn, but as he spent so much time underground, Tom hardly noticed the passing of the seasons. He had had one or two more little flashes of recall, so fleeting that they were like pictures seen in a magic lantern show. A beach with children playing on the shore. The sea, and waves breaking at the foot of mighty cliffs. Tom had resigned himself to the present, had almost become too dispirited to search for his past, and could only look forward to an uncertain future.

'Psst!' Tom was jerked out of his thoughts one day as they were being marched under guard towards the mine, and half-turned to see that Alf was catching him up. Both keeping their heads strictly facing front, he managed to hiss the message out of the corner of his mouth. 'Good news, mate – the best. The Yanks have come in and we've smashed the German line. Place called Amiens. Pass it on if you can.' Tom swivelled his eyeballs and they managed to exchange a wink before a guard barked an order to halt and they realized they had arrived at the pit-head.

A new wave of cautious optimism was felt throughout the camp in the months that followed, as more rumours filtered in that the allies were well on the way to victory over their captors. The men showed this upsurge in spirits by their more jaunty way of walking; there was cheerful whistling echoing around the compound and the occasional burst of song as they marched off to work in the mornings. By contrast, the Germans were becoming more ill-tempered and abusive by the day.

Then at last came the monumental and historic moment when hostilities ceased, and the men heard that in a railway carriage in the forest of Compiegne, in the bitter cold and darkness just before dawn, Marshal Foch, the Allied commander-in-chief, and the British Admiral Wemyss had received a German delegation, which led to the armistice that was to follow at 11 a.m. on the eleventh day of the eleventh month.

Then the echoes of gunfire which had reverberated around Europe for so long were still at last, and the nightmare, as King George V announced to his people, was over.

Chapter Fourteen

B Y the beginning of November, Morwenna had been at Etaples for almost eleven months, and the gruelling life had begun to take its toll upon her own health. She had become too physically exhausted to eat properly, and was worn down mentally with the sights, sounds and smells of tragedy. She found herself latterly with a persistent, hacking cough which would not go away, however much she took of the soothing syrup that she had obtained from a sympathetic doctor.

Then at last the day came when the commandant took her aside, and as if repeating the scene from Woolwich hospital the year before when Matron had said much the same thing, Morwenna was told that she must leave, go back to England and recover her strength.

'Frankly, my dear, you are no use on the ward in your present state, for two reasons. One being that you are constantly exposing severely ill men to infection through that cough of yours and two, I'm afraid that your own health will break down completely if you don't get away soon and take some rest.' Morwenna could not prevent herself from dissolving into tears of weakness as she looked into the kindly face, and hated herself for it, but the woman was right. She had never felt so low. There followed a few words of glowing praise for all she had done, a sympathetic squeeze of her hand and Morwenna was free to leave.

She made the Channel crossing alone on a day of overcast skies and a biting easterly wind. As she thought back to the outward journey when she had been one of a group of laughing, chattering women bound for a big adventure, this one seemed twice as long in contrast. Similarly, when she had travelled as a girl, the company of her excited school-friends had made the time seem to fly.

Today it was bitterly cold up on deck and stuffy and claustrophobic down below. Morwenna paced restlessly between the two and could not settle for long in either place. She was leaning on the rail watching sea-gulls tossing on the wind like scraps of torn paper, when the Seven Sisters appeared in the distance and she heaved a sigh of relief. She had never looked forward so much to being on terra firma again.

The boat-train from Dover to Victoria was packed with troops, the corridors full of standing passengers and the atmosphere hot and close. By the time Morwenna had crossed London and found bed and break-fast accommodation for the night not far from Paddington, she was exhausted. But still she tossed and turned for most of the night in a fitful sleep punctuated with strange dreams, and arose tired and listless. She had no appetite for the huge fried breakfast which was set in front of her – her stomach rebelled at even the sight of it – and she left for the station as soon as she possibly could to board the train for the West Country.

This service was crowded too, and all the seats in the Ladies Only compartments were taken. Morwenna squeezed herself in between a fat dumpling of a woman clad in many layers of shawls and scarves, whose two small children were sitting on the opposite side, and a naval officer, and thanked her lucky stars that she had a seat at all.

She was feeling terrible. Her head was swollen and aching and the moving scenery rushing past the window did nothing to help it. She closed her eyes and tried to doze, but sitting between other people was not comfortable, and the lively chatter of the children, two little boys of about three and five, made this impossible. Also, she was so afraid that if she dropped off to sleep her head might slide down on to the sailor's shoulder, that she sat bolt upright and just hoped that her travelling companions would get out at stations along the way.

Unfortunately this was not the case, and when the train eventually pulled into Penzance station seven hours later, Morwenna rose on stiff limbs, feeling more ill than ever. She picked up her suitcase, which seemed to be twice as heavy as she remembered, and went to step down on to the platform. But her head was spinning and she was so dizzy she could hardly keep her balance. What was happening to her? She desper-ately reached out for something to clutch at, but there was nothing. Morwenna gave a moan, there was a roaring in her ears louder than the sound of the sea, then everything went black and she fell unconscious to the ground.

There followed a period of terrifying and horrific nightmares and fever-ish, pain-wracked days. Morwenna knew that she was sometimes semi-conscious and tried to speak, to call out, to reach for a comforting hand when she heard soft voices whispering around her. But her limbs were like lead and her own voice no more than a croak. She could feel tears running down her face, but her eyelids were too heavy to lift and she gave up any attempt to open them. Sometimes she felt her skin burning with heat and would toss her way out from under the covers; at other times she would shiver as if with an ague and her restless hands would try to claw them back, but to no avail. Other hands would come and make her comfortable, and she could only thrash about and turn this way and that in sheer frustration at her weakness.

Eventually the time came when Morwenna awoke from an unusually deep and peaceful sleep, feeling calm and cool again, but with no idea how long she had been ill. She tentatively opened one eye, then the other, and discovered that she was propped up on several pillows in a high bed with a rail at its foot, and that a clean, crisp sheet was drawn up to her chin and turned down over the covers. There was a distant murmur of female voices, and the smell of antiseptic. Hospital! She would recognize that smell anywhere. Morwenna raised her head a fraction but the pain which shot through it made her sink back on to the pillows again. However, she had seen that there was a curtain drawn around the bed which sealed her off in a sort of cubicle.

Then came the squeak of rubber soles on polished linoleum and the curtain twitched as a nurse with a round, motherly face and starched cap on her frizzy grey hair peeped in. Her face lit up in a smile as she saw Morwenna looking back at her.

'At last – you're awake, dear!' She came in and sat on the chair beside the bed, putting one hand to Morwenna's forehead and taking her hand in the other to feel her pulse. 'Fine.' She nodded, looking at the watch pinned to her bosom, and slipped a thermometer into her patient's mouth.

'We've been very worried about you over the past three weeks, I can tell you.' Morwenna's eyebrows shot up and she nearly bit through the thermometer with shock. Three weeks! She'd been out of action for all that time.

'Oh yes.' The nurse nodded, sliding the thermometer out from under Morwenna's tongue. 'You were in quite a bad way.'

'Was I? What's been the matter with me?' Morwenna whispered. 'I can remember fainting away on the station platform as I was getting off the train, but after that – nothing.'

'That's right.' The woman busied herself with the bedclothes and plumped up Morwenna's pillows. 'When the first-aid staff couldn't revive you, the station-master called for an ambulance and brought you in to us.' She drew the curtains back and Morwenna could see that she was in a small single room.

'Is this – am I in Penzance hospital?' she asked, craning her neck to look out of the window. The nurse nodded. 'You are, and I'm Nurse Jenkins. As to what's the matter with you,' she went on briskly as she straightened the already impeccable covers, 'you're just one more victim of this awful Spanish influenza.'

Morwenna's brows rose. 'Oh – it was flu, then?'

Their eyes met and the nurse said with emphasis, 'Oh, not just any old flu – *Spanish* flu. You haven't heard about it?' she queried, as she must have noticed Morwenna's blank look. 'Oh, there's a real epidemic of it sweeping through the country and all over the world too. Hundreds of people have died – that's why we were so worried about you. It can lead to fatal pneumonia in some cases, you see.' She turned anxious eyes on her patient as she added, 'You said you were travelling – have you been abroad lately, by any chance?'

'Yes, yes, I've been living in France for several months and working in an army hospital,' Morwenna replied.

'Ah.' The nurse nodded. 'You probably picked it up over there. They call it "Spanish" but actually it started in the Far East. Claimed a lot of lives in China and India, I believe, before heading our way. That's why Matron has had you kept in such strict isolation, you see, with me being the only one to tend you. We couldn't risk the infection spreading through the wards.' She gathered up the equipment she had brought in with her. 'Now, I'm going to have them bring you a nice cup of tea, then you'll probably want to sleep again. You're going to feel very weak for a long time yet,' she said as she swept out in a rustle of starch. She was right. Morwenna could hardly hold the cup when it came, but she drank the tea greedily and was asleep in seconds after she had put it down.

When she awoke again she was feeling much more lucid and her mind had begun working properly again. Next time Nurse Jenkins poked her head round the door, Morwenna was ready with some questions. 'Do you know where my things are?' she asked, glancing down at her hospital nightgown. 'My suitcase? And my handbag?'

'Don't fret, Miss Pengelly, they're all being kept safely under lock and key for you.'

Morwenna frowned. 'How do you know my name?' she asked.

'I'm afraid we had to look through your bag for that, my dear, and to see if there were relations, friends, anyone whom we should notify, you know?' Morwenna nodded, thinking rapidly. 'I see. Yes of course. And . . . ?'

'And we didn't have to bother, because this nice young man called to enquire after you, the same day that you were admitted.'

'Young *man?*' Morwwenna's jaw dropped. 'What young man?'

The nurse bit her lip and frowned. 'Oh . . . er . . . do you know I can't recall his name for the moment. But I will. He was Irish – ever such a nice gentleman, he was. He's been here every day since, to ask about you.'

Kieran! In Cornwall? But why? How? It was too much for Morwenna's weary brain to handle and she slid back beneath the covers and closed her eyes.

When she awoke next time he was there, sitting in the upright chair at her bedside. '*You!*' Morwenna said with a spark of her old defiance. 'What do you think *you're* doing here?'

'And it's lovely to see you too, so it is,' Kieran replied, with the glimmer of a smile. He reached for her hand and before she could pull it away he said, 'I'm so *glad* that you're out of danger, Morwenna. Sure and you don't know how much. I've been so worried about you.'

Morwenna looked up into his face. He did look worried. There were frown lines on his forehead that she couldn't recall seeing before, and he seemed older. Could she have done that to him? she asked herself as she felt a stab of guilt. But of course not, it would have been the result of his term in prison.

'How . . . how . . . did you know I was ill?' Morwenna's mind was wrestling with the question she had been asking herself ever since the nurse had first told her that he had called on the *same day* that she had been taken into hospital.

'Ah, well, that's a long story, so it is, and I don't want to tire you,' Kieran said with concern.

'Tell me,' Morwenna demanded.

'Right, well, this was the way of it, to be sure. I was on my way to Cornwall to wind up things at Rayle House and see to the return of all the government equipment, so I was, and I had no idea that I was on the same train as you. Until we came to Penzance, you see.'

He patted her hand and released it, tucking it under the covers with a tenderness that Morwenna found surprisingly touching, and went on, 'Well, I went into the refreshment rooms there to get something to eat, and when I came out, sure and I saw this ambulance on the forecourt. And there you were, being lifted into it looking like death itself, so you were.' He smiled at her. 'So I took a cab and followed the ambulance to the hospital. You know the rest.'

'That you've been round every day, so the nurse said.' Morwenna looked into his face with a new respect. Kieran nodded. 'Sure and for a long time they wouldn't let me see you at all because of the infection. But now they say that you're in the clear, so you are, and there's no danger of that any more.'

Morwenna nodded and there was a pause while she thought about all that he had just told her. Kieran rose and stretched his legs as he sauntered over to the window and looked out. From where he stood, with his back to her, he said abruptly, 'Morwenna, why didn't you answer my letter?' He turned on his heel and now there was anger on his face.

Morwenna turned her head away, not knowing how to put her feelings into words. Kieran went on, 'I went round to Mrs Pope's after a week or two of waiting, and she said you'd gone to France. That was like a kick in the teeth – to think that you hadn't even bothered to let me know. So I guessed you were still pretty mad with me.'

Then, as Morwenna nodded and would not meet his eyes, his voice rose in pitch. 'What do I have to do to get through to you, woman?' he said through gritted teeth. 'Can you not see that time has moved on, so it has, and we have to move on with it?'

He strode back towards the bed again and must suddenly have remembered where they were, for he lowered his voice. 'Sure and I'm not the hot-headed idealist that I was, Mor. The war changed all that, and I bitterly regret what I did. But now that the war is over, would it be too much to hope at all that we could declare an armistice as well? That there could be a truce between you and me?'

'*What* did you say?' Morwenna sat bolt upright, feeling her mouth drop open with astonishment. 'The – the war – is *over?*'

'Sure and it is. Did you not *know?*' Kieran's face was a picture of amazement. 'But I suppose you've been out of it ... with being ill ... and did no one think to tell you? Oh, Morwenna, YES!' He sat down, seized hold of one of her hands again and squeezed it, and this time she did not pull away. 'Peace was declared over a week ago, so it was. The Germans eventually surrendered to the Allies when they realized it was hopeless. There's been such celebrating all over the country, you'd never believe!'

'And I've missed it all,' Morwenna said wistfully, biting her lip as she attempted to take in the enormity of this news and tried to imagine a life without warfare. For what would she do now? Where would she go? Her head was spinning. She was only twenty-two – what was she going to do with the rest of her life? Far from being relieved at the change in the world situation, Morwenna was feeling as if a mat had suddenly been pulled out from under her feet.

Maybe Kieran read some of this in her face, for he pulled his chair a little closer to the bed and gently squeezed the hand that still lay in his own.

'I didn't mean to bring this up now, Morwenna, it's hardly the time or the place, but you must know how much you mean to me.' He was looking at her with his heart in his eyes as he went on, 'Sure and I have to say this because I can't keep it to myself any longer – it would make me the happiest man in the world if you would agree to marry me, so it would.' He looked down at their clasped hands. 'But hear me now.' Kieran stopped her as Morwenna opened her mouth to speak. 'I'm not going to beg or plead with you for ever. I've done with all that.' He raised his head and regarded her steadily. 'I'm giving you until Easter to make up your mind, Mor. That's almost six months. Sure and if you can't decide in that time, you never will. Then, if you turn me down, I shall go away and never bother you again. But if you accept, I'm willing to live wherever you choose, so I am.' He paused, still looking deeply into her eyes. 'And that's as fair as I can be – as anyone could be, so it is.' Holding her gaze for a fraction longer, he finished, 'Until then we can continue to be friends as before. All right?'

She was weak, she was vulnerable. Morwenna looked into his familiar face and the tears began to flow. Never had she been in greater need of someone to lean on. Kieran was basically a good man, a man who had been led astray by others and had made a dreadful mistake, for which he had paid the price. Set against the enormity of what had happened worldwide, it put their quarrel into perspective. Surely forgiveness was not too much to ask of her, was it? As for marriage, he had given her a generous amount of time to think it over and she was under no pressure to make a hasty decision. She was tired, so tired, and thinking was making her head ache. She could not cope at the moment with anything as important as that.

Morwenna nodded and sniffed. 'All right, Kieran,' she said.

On being at last released from captivity, Tom had found himself along with almost 2,000 other men on the first stage of their repatriation, on board a 9,000-ton vessel out of Cologne.

Lying flat on his back on his berth, arms behind his head, Tom was thinking back to his last days in the camp. Before they had left, he had gone across to the clinic to look for Shuli. The least he could do was to say goodbye to her after she had been such a support to him when he had first arrived. He had seen little of her since then, only on the occasions when he was ordered back to the clinic for a check-up on his condition. This, Tom realized, was not the normal way of things – other prisoners were not so sympathetically treated. But 'Herr Doktor', he had discovered, was a man dedicated to his profession, with a streak of humanity about him that did not take sides, and Tom's case interested him. He had been almost as pleased as his patient when Tom had remembered his name, and had hailed it as a major breakthrough. Since then they had both been waiting and hoping for further developments.

Tom met Shuli in the corridor as she was hurrying through the wards with a sheaf of papers under her arm. Her face lit up as she saw him and Tom's heart gave a lurch. For she was so beautiful, with her expressive eyes and smooth glossy hair, which today was coiled up neatly under her starched cap.

'Max!' she said, then covered with confusion she laughed and put a hand across her mouth. 'No, *Tom*, of course! But to me you will always be Max.'

'Shuli, I've come to say goodbye,' he said as their eyes met.

'Ah, yes.' She bent her head and fiddled with the papers. When she looked up again there was a glint of tears in her eyes. 'I'm so very glad for you that you are going back to your homeland. But for me – I shall miss you very much,' she said simply.

Tom put a finger gently under her chin and tilted it. Shuli took a step nearer, holding his gaze, and the tension between them was almost tangible. If only he knew who he was, and if he were free to do so, Tom thought, he could love this woman, perhaps make a future with her, who could tell? He had sensed from the beginning, without the need for words, that Shuli felt the same way about him.

But he could well have a wife already, even children, he thought with a surge of pain. Tom felt something twist inside him as Shuli raised her face and inevitably their lips met. Then his arms were around her in a close embrace and he laid his cheek against her shining hair. 'Goodbye, my very special friend – I shall never forget you,' he murmured, and wrenched himself away before he should lose control of his feelings.

The ship took the released prisoners down the Rhine to Rotterdam, where they were issued with clean clothes and a parcel each containing all the basic necessities, which had been provided by the British government. Eventually they returned to London and a reception committee, where they were informed: 'Demobilization will be governed by industrial requirements and broad social considerations.'

'So what does all that mean in plain English, mate?' asked Alf White as he and Tom were discussing it after the meeting.

'What it boils down to,' Tom replied, 'is that the first men to be given work will be the ones who have to tell the others what to do – foremen and such-like. Right now we have to report to a "dispersal station" in our home area, where they'll give us some cash for our present needs, and some sort of weekly allowance for twelve months or until we can get a job.'

But where was *his* own area? Tom felt a stab of something like panic: a feeling he had never known in the midst of the most gruelling fighting of the past four years. Up to now he had always had orders to follow; even in the prison camp there had been some structure to the days. But now? Because of his handicap he was homeless, rootless, completely on his own in a strange city where everybody else knew their place and was bustling, full of purpose and intent on taking up the threads of normal life again. What should he do? Where could he go? His brain in turmoil with a pandemonium of thoughts like this, he hardly heard Alf's voice in his ear.

'I *said*, best thing of all is that they're giving us a month off with full pay and rations,' said practical Alf. 'How much did you say the dole money is, Tom? I've forgotten what he told us.'

'Twenty-four shillings a week for us ex-servicemen,' said Tom automatically.

'And what yer going to do with yerself now, eh?' Alf enquired, eerily putting Tom's thoughts into words. He was feeling exactly like a stranger in a strange land – a land where there were no signposts to indicate the way home. He felt for the locket, which he always wore beneath his clothes, and fingered it like a talisman. Maybe one day it would yield up its secrets, one day he would remember.

'Oh, well, Alf.' He forced a smile to his face and shrugged. 'I'm not too sure of the answer to that one. Find somewhere to stay, I suppose, and have a think about the future.' Something in his face must have alerted the little cockney to his friend's dilemma, for he regarded him for a moment with his head on one side and said, 'Well, I've had an idea about that and all. While I bin away, my Annie have been taking in lodgers, see. She've had a spare room ever since our Eddie was killed – at Mons that was, early on.'

'Oh, Alf, I never knew that. I'm so sorry.' Tom was jerked out of his own thoughts by this shock, and felt a sudden compassion for this perky little man who had hidden his own grief so well that his companions had never even known about it. To have kept himself so outwardly cheerful must have taken a lot of courage, and Tom looked at him with new respect.

'Yes, well, it gave Annie something to do – took her mind off things. He was our only one, see. But what I'm saying is, the room's empty at the moment and if you'd like ter take it, you can.'

It was like a lifeline to Tom. It would be a start. He had a good friend in Alf, he realized that now, and he turned to him with a smile of relief. 'Thanks a million, Alf, that would be fine. I'd like nothing better. Whereabouts do you live?'

'Ah well, proper cockneys we are, me and the wife – both of us born within the sound of Bow Bells, see? Still live there too, down the Whitechapel Road. It's only a little place, mind, a flat over a corner shop, but we couldn't settle nowhere else. Oh yes, all my family was cockneys. My father was a Pearly King,' he added with pride.

'A what?' Tom eyes widened.

'A Pearly. He were a costermonger, see, and they got this tradition of decking themselves out in costumes sewn all over with pearl buttons – in patterns, you know? And the gals wear great big feathery hats. Ain'tcha ever seen them?' Tom shook his head. 'Well, yer can't be a Londoner, that's fer sure.' He looked up at Tom with his head on one side. 'I've always thought with the way you talk and that, you sound more like a West Country man – Somerset, Dorset, down that way. Know what I mean?'

Tom shrugged again. 'Your guess is as good as mine, "mate",' he said, and grinned. Then his face fell and his eyes were bleak as he said, 'Alf, I'm going to have to find myself a surname from somewhere, aren't I? I can't go through the rest of my life calling myself just "Tom". I've got to register – to apply even for a ration card. And I must have an identity to do anything official.'

Alf was looking thoughtful. 'How about if we was to call yer "Tommy Atkins",' he said after a moment. 'You was a soldier – we was all called Tommy Atkins – it would do for the time, wouldn't it, eh?'

'That's a brilliant idea, Alf! Thanks a million.' Tom slapped the little man on the back and Alf grinned in return.

'You're welcome, Mr Atkins,' he said, and gave him a mock bow.

'Well,' said Tom, feeling a little less desolate now that he had a plan, if only a temporary one, 'what I'll do is stay at the Union Jack club for a couple of nights until you and Annie settle yourselves and the room is ready, and then I'll come over.' Tom had no wish to be present at the reunion between Alf and his wife, which would be painful for them and embarrassing for him. 'Then I suppose I'll have to try and find a job, start making a life for myself. I might as well stay on in London as anywhere else – until I remember where I do come from, that is.' He forced a laugh. 'What did you do before the war, Alf?'

'I was a builder, mate, worked for a big firm. I reckon there'll be plenty of jobs going in that line now, don't you? Dear old Blighty's going to have to pick up the pieces and start getting back to normal again.'

If Alf reminded Tom of a weasel with his head of sparse ginger hair and narrow face, then Annie White was a robin. As slightly-built as her husband, Annie was brown and birdlike – brown hair, huge brown eyes shadowed with suffering, despite her warm smile of welcome, and little hands like a robin's claws. Tom clasped one of them in his own and felt that if his handshake was too robust, the brittle bones would snap like twigs in his grasp.

'Hello, Annie,' he said, bending over to smile into her face. 'I'm really glad to have a place to stay, and all thanks to Alf's brainwave.'

'It'll be a pleasure to have you here, Mr ... um ... Tom.' She straightened her floral-print overall and turned towards the door saying, 'Your room's down the passage, if you'd like to come through. Here we are, and the bathroom's just along there. This was Edward's room, of course,' she said and the sadness was in her eyes again. 'You'll find all his books in that cupboard still. If you fancy a read, just help yourself.'

Tom nodded and smiled as he put down his suitcase and closed the door thoughtfully behind her. Something had started niggling at the back of his mind when she had mentioned the name 'Edward'. Had he known someone called Edward, perhaps? Maybe that was the name of his brother whom he had seen in his flashback? But try as he might, there was no response from his damaged memory. Tom sighed and crossed the room to the window, where he stood drumming his fingers on the sill with frustration as he looked out.

Whitechapel Road thronged with humanity. It was densely packed with shops; he could see warehouses, breweries and a hostel nearby for the destitute, while off to each side ran cobbled lanes seemingly unchanged for centuries. Traces of the original Georgian and Victorian houses still survived above the tawdry shop-fronts, and the street was lined with costermongers' barrows. It was colourful, raucous, earthy and vividly alive.

'Caw, you should have seen all the celebrations up west when the peace was declared,' said Annie later as they sat over a meal. It had been agreed that Tom was to be treated as one of the family and that Annie would see to his food and wash his clothes for him. 'Dolly and me – that's me sister' – She nodded across the table at Tom, – 'we went up to see what was going on, and my word, you'd have thought the whole world had gone mad. There was people on the roofs of all the big emporiums, shouting and cheering and waving flags, and one of them even had a stuffed figure of the Kaiser wrapped in a shroud hanging by his neck from a rope over the balcony.'

'Bit gruesome that, I should think,' Alf remarked, his loaded fork poised on its way to his mouth.

'No worse than burning Guy Fawkes,' his wife retorted. 'Anyway,' she went on, her eyes on her plate, 'down in the streets there was bands playing "God Save The King" and women were kissing and embracing soldiers and throwing themselves at anyone in uniform. Quite brazen it was.' She pursed her lips primly and glanced up at them as she added, 'Not quite decent, we thought.' Tom and Alf exchanged a grin but said nothing.

Annie was now in full swing, somehow managing to both chat and empty her plate at the same time. 'It went on all night, apparently, so we was told afterwards, with people carrying lanterns and dancing in the streets. Trafalgar Square was packed, and some people even lit a bonfire by Nelson's Column – that must have warmed the old gent's toes a bit, eh?' She looked up and laughed, and Tom had a fleeting glimpse of the lively girl she must once have been. 'Anyway, we was in the Mall,' went on the irrepressible Annie, 'when the King and Queen came out on the balcony and, well, the roars and cheering that went on you'd never believe. The crowds hardly kept quiet long enough to hear what he said.' Then her expression changed and her face became serious. ' 'Course, people had to let off steam somehow. We'd all been so frightened after we'd had the Zepps coming over and all. People used to shelter down the Tube stations, you know? 'Twas quite terrifying at times.'

Alf stretched out a hand and covered hers, and she looked into his face with tenderness. Tom, sitting slightly apart, envied them their closeness, and sighed. For he had nobody of his own, and longed for the simple comfort of a pair of loving arms.

Now Annie was saying, 'It had lasted such a long time, the war, you can understand people going a bit wild. Dolly and me, we did a bit of a dance ourselves when the band came our way. Had a good laugh, we did.' She giggled at the memory, then her expression grew more sober as she said, ' 'Course, there's bomb damage all over the place still. We was lucky here, though, to get away without a hit. You must have a walk round, Alf, and see how it's all changed.'

Tom had been right about there being no shortage of manual work. He soon found himself doing a labouring job on a bomb-site – clearing away rubble and preparing the way for rebuilding. It was mindless, monotonous work, but it filled in the time, it tired him out so that he slept at night, and it left his mind free to wander while he was doing it.

Christmas came and went, during which Annie did her best to provide what festive fare she could under the food-rationing scheme, and the year turned slowly over into 1919. The cold and dismal winter weather made Tom's job the harder, but he worked steadily on like an automaton, digging, shovelling, wheeling his barrow, tipping it out and starting all over again. It was all he knew, this daily grind was all he had to look forward to, and he slogged on with grim determination as he attempted to exorcise his personal demons with physical activity.

From the site where he was working Tom could see the River Thames. Sometimes if there was a gleam of pale sunshine, he would raise his head to see it glittering like a silver ribbon, winding away into the distance, bringing a fleeting brightness and touch of beauty which lightened the dull winter scene.

This light on the water never failed to cheer Tom in a way which seemed to come from deep down inside himself, and the joy it gave him was out of all proportion to what it actually was, no more than a ray of sunshine over a dirty commercial river. It led him to wonder whether this love of water was connected in some way with his past, and he continued to brood over this as he went about his mechanical tasks.

On one of the finer days in early March, he was jerked out of his thoughts by the sudden cry of a flock of seagulls who came screeching overhead and settled on the mudflats to forage along the ebbing tide. Tom leaned on his shovel to watch them and something clicked inside his head. The tide! A picture flashed across his senses and was gone in an instant. As it had done before, the window opened just a crack – and Tom had seen the sea. The *sea* – not a river but the limitless ocean – and a flock of gulls soaring overhead in the purity of a cloudless sky. Not the grey and muddy-looking sea and sky of the English Channel when he had crossed it on his way here, but somewhere beautiful – a Shangri-la of a place still waiting to be discovered.

Chapter Fifteen

Aᴛᴇʀ coming out of hospital, Morwenna had gone to stay with Chrissie and her parents to complete her recuperation. She had spent a second Christmas there and with the benefit of Maria's loving care, had soon fully recovered her former health and strength. Then as soon as she was well enough she had moved back into Cove Cottage.

Now Christmas was but a distant memory and Morwenna was very conscious of how alone she was feeling. And, unless she accepted Kieran's offer, that was the way she would remain, with no one of her own at all. She knew that she could never hope to recapture with someone else the closeness she and Tom had had, for that had been forged from a childhood shared, a growing awareness of each other as adults, and a final realization of the love which had grown between them over many years.

No, she and Tom had been soul-mates, a precious gift that happens only rarely. In each other's company, a joke shared – anything shared – would lift mundane events out of the ordinary and into a higher sphere of warmth and companionship which she could not hope to find again.

So, what should she do? Morwenna paced to and fro like a caged animal as she tried to come to a decision. Then, still unsatisfied, she slammed the door and went out to pace the wild cliffs, seeking an answer there. But she felt closer to Tom than ever in the out-of-doors, and this was of no help to her in her quest. They had walked this way so many countless times in the past. She could hear his voice in the sound of the sea and see his beloved face reflected on the racing clouds. If his spirit was anywhere now, it would surely be here.

The gale caught at her hair and whipped away its pins, tossing the loosened strands seawards, leaving her gasping for breath as she fought her way against it. Down below, great waves the colour of pewter were hurling themselves in fury at the base of the unyielding granite, pitting their strength against the primeval rocks.

Buffeted by the gale, exhilarated by the mighty force of the elements,

Morwenna returned to the cottage with glowing cheeks, but with the fundamental problem still unsolved. However, it was only February, so she still had a little more time before Kieran's deadline.

She decided to go and see Sophie. She owed her a visit. Her cousin had called to see Morwenna in hospital, having heard the news from Kieran, but that had been weeks ago. It would take her mind off her own problems as well. Too restless to settle anywhere for long, Morwenna was soon on her way up to Rayle House.

'My word, you've been busy!' she gasped, as she walked in to find Sophie stacking boxes of equipment just inside the front door and checking the items against a long inventory. 'Hello, Morwenna,' said her cousin. 'I'll be with you in a minute – I've nearly finished here.' Sophie's brow puckered as she counted under her breath, 'Twenty-five ... thirty ... thirty-five ... Phew, that's the lot!'

Morwenna had wandered off through the house and was peering into all the rooms. The long wards were completely empty of furniture now, all the beds having been taken down and removed, the medical equipment presumably all packed in the boxes she had just seen, and the patients long since removed to their homes.

'Yes,' came Sophie's voice behind her. 'It's all looking pretty empty now.' She folded her arms across the clipboard she was still clutching, and added, 'And a bit sad, too, don't you think?'

Morwenna shrugged and looked around with her head on one side. 'No, not sad exactly,' she replied. 'When you think of all the good work that was done here. The house feels to me as if it's just waiting for the next thing that's going to be asked of it. But perhaps that sounds silly,' she said with a laugh, and went on, 'Are your parents going to move back in now?'

Sophie shook her head. 'No, they've been in the cottage for too long to take on a big place again. We've all moved on, Mor, and you can never go back in life. Nothing will ever be the same as it was.' Sophie's face was sober and Morwenna noticed as her cousin turned towards the light that there were dark shadows under her eyes.

'You're looking tired, Sophie,' she remarked. 'Have you been working too hard?'

'It's partly that, I suppose – there has been a lot to do – but since all that business with Donald's father ... You knew he'd been in prison, didn't you?' Morwenna nodded. 'Well, of course, Donald was serving overseas while all that was going on, and Tamsin was alone down here. People used to point fingers at her and whisper behind their hands – you know what it's like in a small place – and she suffered terribly. So I did what I could

196

to support her – and to keep it from Ma and Pa as well. The shame of it, you know – they would never be able to take it.' Sophie sighed and gestured with her hands. 'Anyway, Tamsin used to come round here and let it all out to me – wailing and weeping – and it all became a bit much.'

Sophie put a hand to her forehead and Morwenna could well imagine what she had been through. She patted her cousin's shoulder with sympathy.

'So when Donald came home and heard about all that, he decided that they would leave Cornwall altogether – get right away where no one knew them and not stay down here any longer with all the tittle-tattle. So they're going to pack up and move away.'

'Really?' Morwenna's eyebrows shot up. 'Where are they going?'

'Up to London.' Her eyes widened even more as Sophie went on, 'Yes, his father is up there now, you see, all on his own in a big house in Surrey. So they're going to live with him. Donald's found a new job and they're up there now, actually, looking the place over and deciding how best to adapt it. Rachel's staying with us until they get back. As a matter of fact, Tamsin's asked me to go up to them when I've finished here, to look after Rachel while they do the decorating and settle in properly. So I shall,' she finished. 'Actually, I'm quite looking forward to a change.' She smiled wanly.

'Well, you certainly deserve it,' said Morwenna. 'When are they coming back?'

Sophie passed a hand over her hair and absently tucked a loose strand behind her ear. 'In a couple of weeks,' she replied. 'Then they'll take Rachel up and let me know when they want me to follow.'

Privately Morwenna was thinking that Tamsin was using her younger sister shamefully, both as unpaid childminder and someone on whom to offload her troubles. But it was none of her business. 'Just mind that they don't make you work too hard there, too,' she said gently and took her leave.

Tom was in his room at Alf White's one day in April, getting his things together before going to work, when the big breakthrough came. Edward's room, he was thinking – he always thought of it as Edward's room, not his own, and the phrase was hanging around at the back of his mind. Tom, in Edward's room – Edwards – EDWARDS!

With a flash of blinding clarity Tom understood. Not Edward's but Edwards. Tom Edwards was his name – *that's* why it was always stuck in his head! He reeled into a chair and sat there with a grin on his face like a lunatic. At last, he knew his proper name. What else might follow? His thoughts began to race.

Tom closed his eyes and tried to sit very still, concentrating on the name, repeating it to himself like a mantra. Then he made himself imagine the cottage that he had seen in his first vision back at the prison camp. The children's faces, their voices.

And gradually the cloud that had obscured his mind for so long began to peel away, slowly at first. Alf had said he sounded like a West Country man, hadn't he? He thought about Somerset . . . Apple orchards and cider? That meant nothing to him. Devon . . . Red soil and farming? Tom shook his head. Cornwall . . . Tin and copper mining? The remaining shreds of cloud faded away and in their place came a glorious illumination, like the rising of the sun after a long, dark night.

Yes! Pendeen, Levant, Botallack, Geevor – the names all came flooding back in a rush. ST JUST! Tom leapt up and punched the air, together with a shout of triumph that brought Annie rushing down the passage from the kitchen, wondering what on earth was going on.

As the woman's small, anxious face appeared around the door-frame, Tom grabbed her by the arm and dragged her into the room. 'Annie, oh Annie – my memory's come back!' he cried, half-laughing, half-weeping, as tears welled up in his throat and threatened to choke him.

'Oh, Tom! My dear boy – that's *marvellous*.' Her face lit up and she threw both arms around him in a big hug. Then she gasped in astonishment as Tom seized her around the waist and waltzed her across the room. 'I'm Tom Edwards from St Just in Cornwall. I'm a miner and I have parents, a brother and a sister,' he sang, 'and—'

He stopped dead in the middle of the room as another picture suddenly flashed before his eyes with blinding clarity. A young woman stood on a deserted cliff top, looking out to sea. Her hair, falling loose about her face, was being lifted by the wind and streamed out behind her in a bright cloud as she hugged her arms across her body as if in pain. Her face was turned away but Tom could sense the sadness emanating from the lonely figure, and gasped aloud. *Morwenna!* How could he have forgotten her?

Morwenna, the most important person in his life! And for all this time – it had been *years*. His hand went automatically to the locket at his neck – *she* had given him that. It must have been her most treasured possession; the couple were her long-dead parents. And she had loved him enough to part with it, had pressed it into his hand as the train was pulling away. . . .

'Annie – I've got to go!' Tom released her and pulled down a suitcase from the top of the wardrobe all in one movement. 'I must go home. To

Cornwall. Now. It's been so long, you see.' He spread his hands expressively. 'It might even have been too long,' he muttered to himself, as he began opening drawers and hurling clothes towards the suitcase, where some of them fell on to the bed, although most ended up in a heap on the floor.

Annie, realizing the high state of excitement he was in, for once kept her tongue quiet and concentrated on picking up the scattered clothes, folding them and placing them in some sort of order as she gradually filled the case for him.

'Thanks, Annie, you're a gem.' Tom grinned as he closed the lid and leaned on the case to close it. He seized his raincoat and cap from behind the door and leaned down to plant a kiss on her cheek. 'Tell Alf what's happened . . . I'll write to you both . . . Thanks for everything. . . .' He was clattering down the stairs and out into the street before Annie had caught her breath.

She ran across the room to look out of the window and from there saw Tom hail a bus and jump aboard almost before it had stopped. He looked back once from the platform where he was hanging on to the rail, and waved a hand in farewell as he caught sight of her. Then, as the vehicle gathered speed, turned a corner and disappeared, Annie vigorously blew her nose and wiped away the tears that were streaming down her face. She was going to miss him so much, her surrogate son.

'Chrissie, I've got a problem,' Morwenna confessed to her friend as they perched on a sun-warmed rock on the slopes of Carn Kenidjack one mild day in early April. They had been tempted out by the spring weather to take a walk down through the valley between St Just and the nearby hamlet of Tregeseal, and up on to the slopes of the hill above it.

How peaceful it was here, Morwenna was thinking as she looked down over the bracken and heather and the tumbled boulders. Timeless and elemental. Wars and human strife had left no mark on this place. An ancient circle of tall stones stood at the foot of the hill, where it had been since time immemorial. Former people, too, had recognized the special ambience of this place and had chosen to make it special for them by erecting this mighty monument for their own purposes. Scattered in the heather not far away were other huge worked stones, each pierced with a fist-sized hole, their significance lost in the mists of time. Legend had it that swains would pass their hands through these in order to be officially 'hand-fasted' or betrothed. Morwenna smiled; it seemed too trite an explanation for something so impressive. She preferred to let the mysterious monoliths keep their secrets to themselves for ever.

She took a deep breath and came back to the present. It was easy to believe that spring had arrived. And with it the Easter weekend, only a couple of days away now, when Kieran would be expecting her answer. 'I just don't know what to do,' she went on.

'About Kieran, you mean?' Her friend had wrapped her hands around her knees and tipped her face up to the sun as she looked out over the gorse and heather-covered slope. Morwenna nodded. She was perched on a flat slab with her face in her hands, staring at nothing.

'What I have to think about, Chris, is this. Could I spend the rest of my life with him, when he would be a constant reminder of what I did? Because I know I wouldn't be able to forget what happened if he was around all the time.'

Chrissie jerked round with an exasperated expression to look her in the face. 'Mor, I've told you – you *have* to forget all that business. It was none of it your fault – you were a completely innocent party!' She put a hand on her friend's arm and squeezed it to make her point. 'You must realize that or it'll sit on your shoulder like a black dog and ruin the rest of your life.'

'I know I should, but it's not as easy as all that,' Morwenna muttered.

'Surely the most important thing to decide is whether you love him enough to marry him,' said Chrissie forthrightly. 'That's what really matters.' She held Morwenna's gaze with her round blue eyes, until her friend bit her lip and looked away.

Morwenna wriggled into a more comfortable position and said slowly, 'You know, Chris, most of my young life was spent wondering where I really belonged, where I fitted in and who I really was. Being divided between your family down at the cove, and the Rayles up at the big house, I was torn two ways.' She plucked at a stem of grass and wound it slowly round and round her index finger. 'But when I grew up I knew that I belonged with Tom. There was no question about it. I'd found my place and I thought that our future life would be together.' Morwenna's eyes were bleak as she paused and gazed out across the moor. Then she savagely tore at the piece of grass and hurled it from her.

She turned to Chrissie and looked into her anxious face. 'Now that he's gone I feel cast adrift again, and to be honest, if I agree to marry Kieran it will only ever be as second best. I can't love him in the same way, Chris. And certainly not as much as he loves me. I've been really in love and so have you, and I know the difference. But I'm going to be so alone without anybody of my own.' Her mouth turned down at the corners and her lips trembled.

'Well, so am I,' retorted Chrissie fiercely, 'but it's no good moaning about it and feeling sorry for yourself.' Her lips were compressed in a determined line. 'You've just got to pick up the pieces and make a life for yourself. That's all that anybody can do. I've had to,' she added bitterly, 'and so can you.'

She jumped to her feet and put her hands on her hips as she looked down at the top of Morwenna's head. 'And as for Kieran, you're jolly lucky to have a man who loves you, if you ask me. He's a good man, Mor, in spite of the mistakes he made – and which he's paid for.' She glared at her friend and spread her palms expressively as she added, 'But it was wartime, and you should make allowances for that. People don't – and can't – always think straight when the world is suddenly turned upside-down.'

'I'm sorry, Chris, I know you're right,' said Morwenna humbly. 'I'm a selfish beast. You've had more to bear than I have – but you're a tougher person than me.'

'Rubbish! And there's no need to grovel either,' said her friend, then grinned. 'I know I've been nagging and going on at you, but it's only for your own good. I can't make up your mind for you, Mor, only put the case as I see it.'

'I know, and I'm grateful, really I am.' Morwenna returned the smile and Chrissie held out a hand to draw her to her feet.

'Come on, up,' she said. 'Let's have this walk if we're going to.'

Tom begrudged every minute that kept him away from his goal of Cornwall and Morwenna, but he was forced to spend a night at Plymouth on the way down, simply because there was no through train that day. On arriving at last in Penzance, however, he jumped on to the bus for St Just, and found himself in the town square by the early afternoon. Hefting his suitcase on to his shoulder, he set off at a stride down the lane towards Cape Cornwall and the place where he had seen Morwenna in his vision.

Over the granite stile and Tom took to the field path which led down to the cliffs. In the distance was the sea, sparkling as he had remembered it, and he paused just long enough to take a deep breath and fill his lungs with the clean, salty air. Then, easing the weight off his shoulder, he stowed away the suitcase in a concealed ditch beneath the hedge and ran down the familiar track. He felt almost light-headed as he was overwhelmed with emotions that were too great to handle all at once.

To be home, to be free, to be on his way to his love – and later his family – it was too much. Tears streamed down his face and he brushed them impatiently away in order to look into the distance.

Tom reached the top of the cliff and stopped to look about him at the familiar scene. The Brisons standing proudly off-shore as they had always done. The sea slapping lazily around them, churning up foam of the purest white with each wave that crashed against their hoary shoulders. Coloured fishing boats drawn up on the slip as if they had not moved since he had been away. The cottage perched above the beach where Morwenna had lived when they were children.

Morwenna. As if thinking about her had conjured her up, Tom had to rub his eyes in disbelief when, far away, he caught sight of a slim figure making her way around the curved edge of the cliff-face opposite him. There was no doubt in his mind who it was. She was here, just as she had been in his vision – although he had never really expected it to happen like that. It was uncanny, and Tom felt a cold shiver feather down his spine.

He was too far away to call out to her, but near enough to see her face raised to the sun and her bright hair streaming out behind her, lifting on the balmy breeze. Tom had begun to run, but he soon stopped in his tracks as another figure appeared on the skyline.

A man, who took a few steps towards Morwenna and held out his arms to her. The couple were silhouetted against the light and there was no mistaking the fact that she had melted into his embrace and had lifted her face towards his. Now his mouth had come down on to hers and they were greeting each other with a long kiss.

Morwenna had made her mind up at last and had set off for her rendezvous with Kieran feeling the better for it. Painful though it was going to be, after a great deal of soul-searching, she had decided that in all fairness to them both she was going to have to turn him down. It would mean that she was left with nobody of her own, but she must find the fortitude to cope with that, as would hundreds of other bereaved women like herself. So she lifted her head high, fixed her eyes on the changeless sea and stepped out along the cliff track.

The path led to the place where she and Kieran had arranged to meet, and they had arrived there from different directions but almost at the same time. She had been looking out to sea when she heard his footfall and had half-turned to see him coming over the rise, his arms spread in welcome.

'Morwenna! At last – I've waited a long time for this moment,' he said as he wrapped his arms tenderly around her.

'Hello, Kieran.' Morwenna returned his kiss of welcome. It was rather more drawn out than she wished it to be, and as she tried to draw away, over Kieran's shoulder she saw a man staring at them from the far side of the cove.

For one foolish moment he reminded her of Tom, but of course Tom was always in her mind at this place. She looked away, back at Kieran, and smiled at some remark he had made. Then drawn to the silent watcher, she looked again. It did actually look quite a lot like Tom. That way he had of standing on one foot and resting the other on a rock while he leaned on his knee and stared out to sea. Only this time he was staring at her. But as she watched, the figure straightened up and began to move away.

The way he turned, the way he walked – it couldn't *be* Tom, could it? But no, of course it couldn't possibly be. Tom was dead. Wasn't he? Her stomach lurched and her throat dried up, as suddenly she was sure.

Morwenna tore herself from Kieran's grasp and flew with her feet hardly touching the ground, along the rough track, over the springy turf, calling his name. She was panting for breath, tripping, righting herself again, frantically running after him as he moved further and further away. At last she could run no more. '*Tom!*' she screamed and doubled herself up, winded, with her hands on her hips. He paused and looked over his shoulder, when Morwenna staggered a few more steps and clutched at his arm.

'Oh, Tom, it *is* you – tell me I'm not dreaming! I can't believe it – I thought you were dead! We all did. Where've you *been*? All these *years* and never a word from you!' She had seized his hand and carried it to her face, leaning her cheek against it as she fought to regain her breath. His other hand was round her waist, pulling her to him in a rough embrace. In spite of what he had just seen, he could not believe that she wasn't his. It was too much.

'Morwenna!' Tom put a finger under her chin and raised her face to his. Their eyes met and Morwenna's heart lurched. Oh, how much older he was looking – leaner, tougher and with a harsh look on his face that she had never seen before. There was a sadness behind his eyes too, hinting at hidden suffering.

'I never thought I would see you again.'

Tom clasped her more tightly and rested his chin on her hair. 'We have so much to talk about, but here and now is neither the time nor the place. I haven't even been home yet. I came straight here because . . .' How could he tell her of the headlong flight he had made to get to her, of the vision he had seen in a dream, how he had come to claim her at last? Certainly not of the desolation he had felt when he had found her in another man's arms. 'I'll see you tomorrow, here, at the same time. Now go back to your sweetheart,' he said gruffly, and pulled away from her. So swiftly did he turn and go that he was running up the hill and almost out of sight before Morwenna recovered her senses enough to scream after him, 'Tom, no! Come back! It's not what you think!' But he had rounded a corner and was out of earshot. Then, as she stood with one hand clapped to her mouth in consternation, Morwenna turned at the sound of running feet to find Kieran at her side.

'That was *Edwards*, wasn't it?' he said roughly, grasping her arm and pulling her round to face him. 'After all this time! Where's he been, to be sure, and why didn't he contact you before now?' He glared down at her and Morwenna put both hands to her throbbing head.

'Kieran, I don't know. He – he was so angry because I was with you. I'm seeing him tomorrow to talk.'

She took a deep breath and tried to stop her limbs from shaking. The shock of Tom's appearance when she had given up all hope of ever seeing him again, and the effect of her headlong flight to reach him, was beginning to take its toll. She needed to go away into a quiet corner to think about all this and what it was going to mean. But she still had to give Kieran his answer.

'Kieran,' she said, raising her head to meet his stormy eyes, 'I told you I would give you my answer today.' He nodded slowly, keeping hold of her arm but saying nothing to make it any easier for her. She paused and took another breath.

'Well?' he snapped, and his mouth opened and shut like a trap.

'I'm sorry,' she whispered, slowly shaking her head, 'but it has to be "no".'

Kieran flung away and swore under his breath. 'So, after nearly three *years* without a word or a sign from him, he has only to show his face for an instant and you can pretend it never *happened*? Morwenna, you're a fool, so you are, and I—'

'Kieran, will you *listen* to me!' Morwenna stamped a foot and grabbed at his arm, tugging at it as she willed him to believe her. 'Tom's turning up had *nothing* to do with my decision.' Kieran gave a snort and his mouth curled in derision. 'It's true! I'd made up my mind before I came here today. Kieran, what I feel for you is affection, it's gratitude, it's respect and it's friendship. But it's not love. I can never return the love that you have for me, and you deserve better than that. I . . . I'm sorry, but . . .' She could not contain her overwrought emotions any longer, and as her trembling legs gave way beneath her, she sank down on to a cushion of thrift and dissolved into tears.

Kieran sat down close beside her and put an arm around her heaving shoulders. Morwenna leaned her aching head against him and was grateful for the support as she strove to contain her emotions.

'It's all right, to be sure it is,' Kieran said in a more gentle tone, patting her shoulder as if soothing a stricken child. 'It's what I expected you to say, although I had hoped. . . . But I appreciate your honesty, Mor, indeed I do.' They sat on in silence for a time, while a bee busied itself in the bells of an early-flowering foxglove spire nearby, pushing its stout little body far down inside in search of the hidden sweetness, then backing out dusted with golden pollen.

'What will you do now that the war's over, Kieran?' Morwenna sat up and reached for a handkerchief.

'Sure and I'll be going back to Ireland, so I shall.' His voice was clipped as he added, 'Perhaps I should never have left it in the first place.' She glanced up into his set face and his eyes that were bleak and cold. 'I was only hanging on for your answer, Mor. Now that I have that, there's nothing here for me any more.'

Morwenna bit her lip. There was nothing that she could say. She looked down at her lap and twisted her fingers together. Then, for the sake of something to say in order to break the silence that had fallen between them, she remarked, 'I was up at Rayle House the other day. It looks so strange and empty now that it's been cleared out.'

'It does. And when I was talking to Sophie she said more or less the same thing. Her family are going to put it up for sale soon, so they are.'

'Really?' Morwenna turned to glance in his direction. 'I didn't know that but I'm not surprised. I must go and see them all again,' she added under her breath, almost to herself.

'Well,' Kieran said, rising to his feet and taking her hand to pull her up as well, 'this is goodbye, Morwenna. I'm going back to London after Easter to finish up one or two things and then, to be sure, I'll be going home.' He brushed some shreds of grass from his knees. 'Until then I'm staying in Penzance – at Sea Winds, so I am.' He smiled down at her. 'It's not the same without you and Clara, though. I don't know any of the staff there now at all.'

Morwenna returned the smile as she thought with fondness of her very first job and how kind Clara had been. It seemed such a long time ago now that it was like another lifetime.

'So, I don't think we shall meet again, Morwenna.' Kieran's voice broke in on her reverie. He was gazing into her face with his heart in his eyes and she nearly dissolved into tears again.

She swallowed hard, forced a smile to her lips and held out her hand. 'Goodbye, Kieran.'

He seized it and covered it with his free one. 'I'll never forget you, Mor. Think of me sometimes – with fondness? I'd like to think you could do that.'

'Of course I will,' she said and meant it. 'Good luck for the future, whatever it may hold.'

Kieran nodded, dropped a peck on her cheek and walked rapidly away. He did not look back.

Chapter Sixteen

TOM came knocking on the door of Cove Cottage just as Morwenna was getting ready to go out to meet him. 'Oh! Tom – come in,' she said, flustered at his unexpected appearance. He ducked his head to avoid the low door frame and stepped into the house. 'I was a bit early so I came over. They told me you were living here,' he said awkwardly as he stood in the kitchen, suddenly dwarfing it as his head seemed to be almost touching the beams of the ceiling. Their eyes met as they each searched the other's soul beneath the veneer of polite conversation.

'So you've come home,' Tom remarked, wrenching his gaze away and looking around the cottage with interest. Then, 'Nothing's changed, has it?' he added softly. 'I can still see your gramp sitting on that settle by the range.'

Morwenna nodded. 'Come and sit beside him,' she said with a laugh, and the ice was broken. She plumped up a cushion and went to fill the kettle from the boiler on the range. As she turned the shining brass tap, she remarked, 'I always keep the fire in, for cooking and hot water.' She placed the kettle on the hob and looked over her shoulder. 'Cup of tea?' she asked.

'Thanks.' Tom nodded and sat twisting his cap in his hands until she handed him a steaming mug and sat down in the rocking chair on the opposite side of the range. There was a small pause while the air between them tightened with tension, until at last Morwenna said, looking down into her tea, 'You'll have heard about Jack by now, of course.' She had to bring the subject up; the guilt was still there at the back of her mind, however much she wanted to believe what Chrissie had said. And she would have no peace until she had told Tom her story and seen his reaction.

'Yes,' he said shortly. 'I had no idea, you see, Morwenna.' She raised her eyes to his face. 'We lost touch quite early on in the war.' Tom cleared his throat but his voice remained husky as he went on. 'I came home with stars in my eyes after being in limbo for so long,' he faltered, 'to be met by *that*.'

And to find that the love of my life had taken up with another man, he was thinking, looking at the neat, contained little figure so near to him. The bright hair, which he remembered stroking in happier times, was wound in a glossy coil on the top of her head, and her slim figure was clad in a gown of sea-green poplin. The colour of it was reflected in her beautiful eyes. His sea maiden. Tom scowled. The only visible sign of any emotion on Morwenna's part were her restless fingers, which were wrapped around the mug, aimlessly tapping against its white enamel. So near and yet so far from him.

'Tom,' she said, jerking him out of his thoughts, 'there's something I have to tell you. It's a long story, but first of all, tell me what you mean by being in "limbo".' She raised curious eyes to his face and Tom sighed.

'Oh, there's such a lot that you don't know, Mor, I hardly know where to begin.' He gazed into the steam rising from his mug and swirled the tea round and round as he tried to find the right words.

'First of all,' he began, 'I've been a prisoner of war for over two years.'

Morwenna's eyes widened. 'You were *captured*?' she gasped, then her expression hardened. 'But why – why didn't you write . . . to let us know? Your parents, and Chrissie . . . me . . . we all thought you were dead.' Anger sparked in her eyes as she raised her voice in accusation. 'How could you *do* that to them – to us?' she cried.

Tom held up a hand to still her. 'There's more,' he said bleakly, 'lots more.' Then he put his mug down and his fingers went to the open neck of his shirt. He removed Morwenna's locket. 'But before going into all that, I must give this back to you,' he said gruffly, looking down at the little trinket that seemed so small in his large hand.

'My locket! You still have it – oh, I'm so glad.' Morwenna's face cleared and momentarily lit up with pleasure. For he had kept it, had worn it close to his heart, all this time. 'It's all that I have of my parents, you see.' Morwenna took the locket and hung it round her own neck. It was still warm from his skin and she let her hand linger on its smooth surface. Then she raised her head and their eyes locked. Tom gazed deeply into her face as he said abruptly, 'I lost my memory you see, Mor. It's as simple as that.'

Shocked and horrified, she could only stare at him with compassion. 'Oh, Tom, how terrible.' Involuntarily Morwenna reached out a hand towards him, but Tom's head was bowed now and he was twisting his cap round and round on his knees. 'I wore your locket all the time in the camp,' he said. 'It helped, although I was so frustrated because I couldn't remember anything about the people in the photograph, you see, and I thought they should mean something to me. Anyway, thank you.' He raised his head and Morwenna nodded. 'I thought for a long time after I lost my memory that I should be able to tell from those pictures who I was,' Tom said and added bleakly, 'No wonder I couldn't think who they were.'

'But you're all right now?' Morwenna asked with concern as she looked into his haunted face, and he gave a brusque nod.

'Oh, yes,' he replied, but his expression was unfathomable and she knew that the quick reply was far from the truth.

Silence fell as Morwenna tried to absorb the enormity of what Tom had told her. To have been robbed of two years of his life – of their lives, in fact – time that would never come again. However must he be feeling? Bitter? Angry? Maybe resigned by now – he had had more time to get used to it than she had. She gazed at his averted face but it was impassive and unreadable. Then as Tom suddenly shifted his position and caught her staring at him, she jerked away in embarrassment.

'I don't want to talk about it now, Mor. Maybe not ever. It's over and done and I'm back in one piece, which is more than . . .' His face twisted and Morwenna held out a hand again, this time grasping one of his. He did not, however, return her squeeze of sympathy, but drew away and picked up his tea again. A little hurt, Morwenna withdrew and clasped her hands together in her lap. It would be a long time, she thought, before they regained their former easy way with one another. Tom must have had a terrible time in the prison camp, while she still had to clear her conscience and get rid of that stumbling block between them. And there would never be a better time than now.

'I know,' she said quietly. 'Tom, I'm so *sorry* about Jack. And there's something I have to tell you as well.'

Tom quirked an eyebrow and sipped his tea. 'Oh? Yes?' He looked impassively back at her.

Then Morwenna took a deep breath and plunged right into it. She told Tom everything from the beginning. Her friendship with Kieran, his welcome support when she was so alone during the terrible times, her total innocence of his subversive activities, how she had unwittingly given him information that he could have passed on to the enemy. And how she felt that she could have even been partly responsible for Jack's death. By the time she drew haltingly to a close, tears were streaming down her cheeks and Tom's face was incredulous.

'So I don't suppose you'll want anything to do with me any more, now that you know the truth,' Morwenna whispered, reaching in her cardigan pocket for a handkerchief. There was total silence in the room apart from the ticking of the clock and the crackle of the fire in the range.

Tom rose to his feet and began to pace up and down. 'Oh no, it's too much to take in – too much. . . .' he muttered, as he shook his head and distractedly ran a hand through his hair. 'I need time – time to think it all over. I'll go now. Must go . . . I'll see you around.' Then he turned and blindly made for the door, wrenching it open and leaving it swinging behind him in his hurry to be gone, as Morwenna gazed open-mouthed at his retreating figure.

A few days later Morwenna had another visitor. 'Hello, Sophie!' she said as she answered the door to her cousin. 'It's lovely to see you.'

'Hello, Mor, I thought I'd come down for a chat. It seems ages since we had one, but I've been so busy.' She took off her straw hat and patted her hair into place. 'But I've got some spare time now that things at Rayle are sorted, and before I go up to Tamsin's.'

'I'm glad you did, it's really nice to see you,' Morwenna said and meant it. Since Tom's abrupt departure she had been like a lost soul, unable to settle to anything. She had found herself wandering about the house picking things up and putting them down again, with her thoughts miles away, and a whole morning or afternoon gone with nothing to show for it.

'What a pretty little place this is,' Sophie remarked, looking about her.

'Of course – you've never been inside before, have you?' Morwenna said. 'When we were children your mother wouldn't let you come down here to play – we were too common a lot!'

Sophie laughed. 'How things change,' she said. 'There'll never be so much of that kind of snobbishness any more. The war's changed all that and knocked the old class system out of the window. You can't get servants nowadays for love nor money, so Mother says. The women who have been doing the men's jobs throughout the war aren't content to go meekly home and pick up where they left off four years ago. Ooh, a rocking chair – I've always wanted one of these.' Sophie sat down on the velvet cushioned seat and began to rock to and fro. 'Very relaxing,' she said with a smile.

'You're looking a great deal better than when I saw you the other day, Sophie,' Morwenna remarked, looking at her cousin's glowing cheeks. 'You must have been worn out then.'

'Mm. I do feel quite good at the moment. Everything's settled and I can have a break.' She stopped rocking and looked at Morwenna with wide eyes. 'I must tell you this though, Mor, it's the most amazing coincidence.' She stood up and fluttered her hands as she was talking. 'I bumped into Kieran the other day and we got chatting. I told him I was going up to Surrey to stay with Tamsin and he said that he was driving that way himself and would I like a lift!' Her eyes widened in delight and a smile spread across her cheeks. 'He's taking his car out of storage – it's been down at Penrose's garage since the start of the war, and of course he couldn't get the fuel for it then.' Sophie paused to draw in a breath, then went on, 'He said that he's going up to a big estate near Ascot to arrange transport for some horses he's taking back to Ireland. The chap who's selling them is the son of a friend of his that died, apparently.'

Gray! thought Morwenna as it all clicked while Sophie was still happily rattling away. '. . . so this place is only a few miles from where Tamsin and Donald are living. . . .' Now I know why she's a person transformed, Morwenna thought. She remembered how Sophie had always worn her heart on her sleeve when she was working with Kieran, and hoped she wouldn't get hurt, but then thought how lovely it would be if they did get together.

'There's another piece of news too,' Sophie went on, rising from the rocking chair and wandering across the room. 'And another reason why I'm feeling so much happier. Mor, James is coming home – to settle.' Her cousin turned on her heel and faced her with glowing eyes. 'You know he was eventually posted to the front, don't you? Well, he got through the war without a scratch and he was decorated for bravery. Did I tell you that?' Morwenna shook her head. 'No?' said Sophie as her brows rose. 'Oh yes. And the parents are so thrilled and proud of him, as you can imagine. It's cheered them up no end. I think the war has been the making of James, actually – he used to be a bit of a drifter,' she remarked, smoothing down her skirt of navy-blue cotton. Worn with a crisp white blouse, its pie-frill collar setting off the glow of her skin, Morwenna though how pretty her cousin was looking. She, on the other hand, felt pale and drained, and had not given much thought to her appearance lately, having tended to throw on the first thing that came to hand in the mornings.

'Anyway, he and Cynthia are going to pick up where they left off,' Sophie was saying, 'and buy a house in Penzance. So of course the parents are thrilled to bits to think that he'll be nearby, just as they thought they'd lost Tamsin.' Sophie spread her hands expressively as she added, 'And just as I was getting afraid they would want to cling on to me for ever.' A smile lit up her face and Morwenna thought generously that her cousin certainly deserved a break from the parents whom she had supported so loyally for the last four years.

A small silence fell while Sophie wandered about the room picking up objects and inspecting them, as if to give herself something to do. Morwenna sensed that there was more to come.

'So you turned Kieran down, then?' Sophie remarked at last, with her back to her cousin as she turned a scrimshaw spill holder round and round in her hands. 'Just in time, as it happened, wasn't it? Now that Tom's come home, I mean.'

'Um . . . yes.' Morwenna was about to add that Tom had changed, that she was no longer sure about his feelings for her any more, but she held her tongue. Tom had been through such a lot and had come back to find his brother dead – it would take a while to get over the shock of that alone.

'Kieran will make someone a very good husband,' Morwenna replied. 'And there are plenty of girls who'll jump at the chance of finding an attractive, available male these days.' She glanced at Sophie's back. 'There's going to be a shortage of eligible bachelors for a long time after all the slaughter.' She paused and drew in a breath. 'But for me, I think the time has come to do something which I first thought of many years ago.'

Morwenna stood with her hands resting on the back of a chair with a faraway look in her eyes.

'I don't suppose for a minute you'll remember this, Soph,' she said, 'but when we were growing up, I promised myself that if in the future the opportunity ever came, I would set up an orphanage for needy and abandoned children, and give them all the love and care that every child should have.' She sighed, remembering the rootless, insecure girl she had been then. 'That was just after we left school and I was feeling lost and resentful, as if I'd been robbed of a proper childhood myself.'

Sophie replaced the ornament and wheeled around with a big smile on her face. 'But I *do* remember,' she said. 'I thought then that it was a marvellous idea, and I still do.' Then with a puzzled look she added, 'But what about Tom? I thought he and you . . .'

Morwenna bent down and busied herself with the hearth-brush, sweeping up some minute grains of soot as she replied with her face averted, 'Tom and I haven't had a real talk about the future yet. He needs time to get adjusted after what he's been through, you see.'

'Oh, I see,' Sophie said, giving her a long look. 'So, are you seriously thinking about the orphanage, Mor?'

'I might be – I just might,' her cousin replied.

★

Long after she had closed the door behind Sophie, Morwenna sat with her chin in her hands, thinking about the future. Now that she had at last seen Tom again, she forced herself to realize that all the hopes and dreams which had sustained her throughout the dreary war years had crumbled to dust and ashes. He was a changed man through his dreadful experiences, which was understandable, and she must make allowances for it. It would take time – maybe years – before he could get over all that, if he ever did. To expect him to adapt to normal life and for them both to pick up the threads from where they had left off was too much.

Maybe in his eyes, she too had been changed so much by her own experiences that any vestiges of what he had felt for her had evaporated. She was no longer the fresh young girl he had known four years ago, the unsure and insecure person she had been then had since grown into a mature woman who had found herself at last. Small wonder that he was not interested in her any more; they were different people now.

Morwenna sighed. She would love Tom for the rest of her life and she could live with the changes in him if he would only let her help him. Inwardly, however, she raged against the agonies he had suffered and knew that he was incapable of sharing them with her.

The tears came then, from deep within her, as Morwenna wept for the futility of it all, the wasted years, the wasted lives. She wept for herself, for Tom and even for her long-lost parents, whose living faces she could no longer remember. And when she had cried herself out, Morwenna rose to her feet, wiped her eyes and stiffened her spine with resolve. So, she would remain single. There would never be any other man for her but Tom, and if that way was closed to her then she must forge a new life for herself. And by fulfilling the vow that she had made so many years ago, she would find the way to do so.

The decision taken, Morwenna slept better than she had been doing for several nights. She awoke with a clear head and dressed herself with care, for once giving some thought to what clothes she would wear. She spent the next few days consolidating her plans by writing several business letters, to the bank, to estate agents, and to the Board of Guardians. This done, Morwenna decided to go for a walk and post her letters on the way. She could always think better in the open air, too.

It was a perfect spring day. The bleached grasses of the moor were rapidly being overtaken by new green, and small flowers were beginning to open their eyes in the turf at her feet. Morwenna looked up at the sky of powder blue and caught sight of a buzzard soaring lazily overhead, quartering the land in search of a meal. Riding effortlessly on the thermals, it was master of its kingdom and seemed to survey the world below with steely contempt in its predatory gaze.

She sniffed appreciatively at the fresh salty tang of the air, and was halfway up the lane, deep in her own thoughts now, when the creak of a swinging 'For Sale' notice board caught her attention. When she realized that it was hanging outside the entrance to Rayle House, her brain did a double-take and everything suddenly clicked into place. The orphanage. She needed premises and here was the ideal place, just looking at her!

Morwenna slid her letters into the pillar box and almost skipped back down the lane, her head so full of her new project that she nearly bumped into Chrissie, who was coming the other way, before she saw her.

'Daft, are you?' said her forthright friend, reaching out to grab Morwenna's arm as she almost passed her by. 'Do you know that you're bouncing along like an overgrown child, with a silly great grin spread all over your face?' She peered closely into her friend's eyes as she spoke.

'Chris!' Morwenna exclaimed as she came back to earth with a jolt. 'You're the very person I want to see. Can you spare a minute or two? And come back with me to the cottage?'

'If you're going to explain why you're behaving like a lunatic, then yes, I will,' the other girl replied. 'And slow down a bit!' she said, laughing, as they fell into step and made their way down the hill together.

'So you see, I shall need help.' Morwenna had spent some time explaining her plans to a wide-eyed Chrissie, who had been by turns amazed, encouraging and openly enthusiastic.

'I know it's a huge undertaking,' Morwenna went on, 'and that I'm going to have all sorts of problems. To have someone I know and can trust to help me would be an absolute godsend.' She paused and regarded her friend with affection. 'And you do hate that job at Branwell's now, don't you? I know it was good of them to take you back, but you don't owe them anything, Chris. So, will you think about it?'

A frown creasing her brow, Chrissie moved about the room as she turned over the idea in her mind. 'I would love to, Mor,' she said, 'but, you see, Ma does rely on my wages to help out—'

Morwenna raised a hand and broke in, saying, 'Don't worry about that. I can match what you're getting at the shop and maybe when I know where I stand, even a little more. I want you to be my right hand, Chris. Of course, I shall have to employ other help as well, but I intend that you receive a salary which reflects that.'

'But,' said her friend with concern as she came to stand beside her, 'you'll have so much expense, won't you? What with buying the house and everything. . . . Think of the risk you're taking! Where's all the money coming from? A bank loan, is it?'

Morwenna shook her head and patted her friend's hand as it lay on the back of her chair. 'You don't know this, Chris,' she replied, 'but Gramp, bless him, left me a generous legacy.'

Chrissie's brows rose. 'It's none of my business, I know, but I never thought of him as a wealthy man,' she said.

'Neither did I,' Morwenna replied, 'but he was always careful with money and he never did spend much. Looking back, I remember that he usually managed to make whatever we needed. And we lived simply.' She nodded and said, 'Yes, there's enough to get me started. And after that I'm hoping that what the Board of Guardians give me for the children's upkeep will cover day-to-day expenses.' She glanced up at her friend and smiled. 'I've gone into it pretty thoroughly, you know, Chris – it's not a spur of the moment thing. In fact, it's been at the back of my mind, as I said, since I was a girl.'

'In that case,' said Chrissie, 'I'd love to come in with you. But I'll have to think it over, of course.' She paced the room with her arms crossed in front of her and her head bent in thought. 'It could be just what I need, Mor. A challenge. Something to give me a purpose in life.' She paused to gaze out of the window. 'Since Walter— Well, nothing's the same, is it?' She turned sympathetic eyes on her friend. 'For either of us,' she added quietly. 'In spite of Tom coming back.'

Morwenna nodded and squeezed her hand tightly.

A few days later, Morwenna was on her way to a duty visit to her aunt and uncle. It was only courtesy to tell them that she was going to put in an offer for their house, besides which she had hardly seen either of them during the past four years and her conscience was pricking her. She would have preferred it if Sophie had still been at home, as her presence would have helped to oil the conversation, but as she had already left for Surrey, Morwenna would have to manage as best she could.

She turned in at the side entrance which ran parallel to Rayle House and walked down the lane to the stone-built cottage where they now lived, about half a mile back from the road.

Phoebe opened the door herself, a little greyer, her bony frame slightly more stooped than when Morwenna had last seen her. 'Oh, Morwenna,' she said, greeting her niece with a thin smile, and clasping her hand between both of her own, 'it's you. Sophie told me you were back. Come in.' She led the way into the parlour, where her husband sat peering at a newspaper through a pair of thick, horn-rimmed spectacles.

'Look who's turned up at last, Arthur,' said Phoebe. 'We thought you'd forgotten the way down here,' she added dryly as she extended a hand towards a chair, indicating where Morwenna should sit.

'Well, bless my soul! If it isn't little Morwenna.' Her uncle beamed at her with a smile of welcome that appeared to be genuine, and laid aside his paper as he stood up and crossed the room towards her. More rotund than ever, he had also visibly aged, having lost most of his hair, and his face was more lined than Morwenna remembered. But retirement must suit him, thought his niece, for he seemed to have mellowed with the passage of time.

'Not so little any more,' she replied with a smile. 'Hello, Uncle Arthur, how are you?' she said as she took his outstretched hand and dropped a kiss on the wrinkled cheek.

'Yes,' she replied to her aunt's sharp remark, 'I've been meaning to come and see you both before this, but I've been really busy since I came back. Actually, the reason why I'm here today is because there's something I have to tell you about.' She laid aside her bag and the sheaf of estate agents' papers she had brought with her, and placed them on the cane table beside her chair.

'I'll go and make a cup of tea before we start talking,' said her aunt. 'We always have one about now.' The inference being, Morwenna thought as she smiled to herself, that her aunt was not making any special effort for her young visitor. This was their everyday routine and she just happened to be there. Secretly amused, for with adulthood her aunt's attitudes had long ago ceased to irritate her, Morwenna rose to her feet. 'Can I give you a hand at all, Aunt Phoebe?' she asked politely.

'No, no.' Her aunt waved away the offer. 'I'm not in my dotage yet, young lady. I can still manage to make a cup of tea, thank you very much.'

'Don't take any notice of her,' Arthur said with a chuckle as his wife left the room. 'Her bark is worse than her bite, you know.' And when Phoebe returned a short while later with a plate of chocolate biscuits on the tray, which was laid with a lace cloth and the best china, he gave his niece a conspiratorial wink.

As they ate and drank, Morwenna explained her plans and at last came to the crux of the matter as she said, 'So you see, I'd already been looking for suitable premises when I found that you were putting Rayle on the market. It seems the ideal place, so I came to tell you that I'm going to put in an offer for it.'

'You – buying *property*?' Her aunt's eyebrows disappeared into her hairline. 'What . . . how . . . ?'

'Gramp left me well provided for, Aunt Phoebe, and with my own savings—'

'I don't know what the world's coming to,' grumbled her aunt and compressed her lips into a thin line. 'I've never heard of any such thing. Women setting up on their own, becoming independent, making business deals like the men—'

'The world is moving on, Phoebe, whether we like it or not,' Arthur broke in. 'The war has changed everything and maybe for the better too.' He smiled at Morwenna. 'I admire your courage, my dear, and I sincerely hope that your enterprise will be successful.'

'Why, thank you, Uncle Arthur.' Morwenna flushed at this unexpected support.

'And I'm really pleased that the house is going to remain in the family. So pleased, in fact, that what I suggest we do is this.' He paused and leaned forward with his hands on his knees as he looked closely into his niece's face. 'I'm willing to take it off the estate agent's books and sell it to you as a private transaction, Morwenna, if you're agreeable. I'll let you have it on an interest-free loan, which you can pay back as and when you feel able. How would that be?'

Momentarily dumbstruck, Morwenna could only stare at her uncle in astonishment, touched to the heart by his generosity and the total unexpectedness of his offer. What a lot it would mean to her, she thought, as her mind raced ahead. She would be able to afford to spend money on adapting the house specifically for her needs – and she could buy new furniture instead of second-hand. 'Oh, Uncle Arthur, thank you!' she blurted. 'I – I don't know how I can ever thank you enough—'

'Nonsense, child,' he said gruffly. 'We always had a soft spot for you, girl. Both Phoebe and I.' He glanced at his wife, who sat stiffly upright with her teacup in her hand, her face impassive. 'I know it didn't always seem like that years ago, but things were different when you were all children – there were pressures then and . . .' He shrugged and spread his hands expressively.

'Have another biscuit,' said Phoebe abruptly, passing the plate. Morwenna smiled at her aunt and took one, not that she wanted it, but with adult awareness she realized that her aunt had always found it difficult to express her feelings, which she kept hidden behind a mask of severity and disapproval. The biscuit was being offered as an olive branch, and as such she accepted it with a smile.

Chapter Seventeen

THERE followed a period when Morwenna immersed herself totally in her dream of establishing the orphanage, and spent all her time thinking of nothing else. It was wonderful therapy for a broken heart and she clutched at it like a lifeline, blocking out any thoughts of past or future save for her great undertaking.

A squad of builders and carpenters were soon at work at Rayle House, converting the large upstairs rooms into smaller ones. 'I don't want the children to feel that they're sleeping in a dormitory,' Morwenna said earnestly to the foreman. 'That's little different from the workhouse where some of them will have already been living. I want this to be a *home*, not an institution.'

'Very good, miss.' The man touched his cap and went off whistling to carry out his orders.

To the representative from the plumbing firm she said, 'I need a new boiler installed, one that is reliable and which will supply without failing, enough hot water for the kitchen, the heating pipes and several bathrooms. Warmth at a constant and even temperature is essential for children's well-being.'

'Very good, miss, I'll see that you get exactly what you want.' He bowed and withdrew with a sheaf of notes under his arm.

The painters and decorators took over after that. 'Bright, cheerful colours, please,' said Morwenna, working her way through a wad of shade cards. 'This place is to have a happy atmosphere about it – I want the children to feel that they are welcome here.'

'Very good, miss.' The foreman tipped his hat and took himself off to get the paints mixed to her requirements, and set the apprentices to rubbing down the woodwork.

For weeks the house throbbed with the sound of hammers, saws and the clang of metal pipes. Morwenna called in every day to see how the work was progressing, and could hardly tear herself away to let the workmen get on with it. As soon as the upstairs was finished she was there with a notebook and rule, measuring up the windows for curtain material, and the floor space for beds.

One day she was standing on tip-toe, opening one of the bedroom windows wide to let the fresh summer air blow away the smell of paint, and paused to look out over the great panorama of moor and ocean. It never failed to move her with its beauty, but at that moment she was distracted by a movement below, and who should she see walking up the road but Tom. His shirtsleeves were rolled to the elbow and he wore a cap on his curly dark head. He looked relaxed and already slightly tanned from the wind and sea; a world away from the tense, white-faced man who had come to her on the cliff.

Morwenna's stomach clenched in the old familiar way at the sight of him. However much she tried to put this man behind her, he still had that power to turn her limbs to jelly, and right now she resented this hold he had over her – especially when she felt a hateful flush creeping up her neck as he raised his head and saw her.

'Morwenna!' He gave her a wave, then called through his cupped his hands. 'Come down for a minute, can you? I want to talk to you.'

Feeling like Juliet on her balcony, Morwenna nodded and withdrew from the window. She was still patting some strands of hair into place and smoothing her skirt as she went down the stairs, her feet clattering on the bare treads, and out through the front door.

Tom had not moved from his position in the gateway and when she joined him he jerked his head towards the stile on the other side of the road and said, 'Come for a walk down to the headland, can you?'

'All right.' Morwenna gave him a searching look, wondering what this summons was all about, but Tom's face was turned towards the sea and she could read nothing from it. Suddenly she was pitch-forked back to the past, when she had just returned home after witnessing the assassination at Sarajevo. They had not known it then, but the repercussions of that day were to change their lives for ever.

They had walked this way then, a carefree young couple beneath a cloudless sky, with the dog Bess bounding on ahead and the sun glinting off the sea in bright shards of light, just as it was doing now.

They were walking in single file along the narrow track across the field and a silence had fallen between them. In order to fill it, Morwenna, with the dog still at the forefront of her mind, remarked from behind Tom's back, 'I was so sorry to hear that Bess had died. You must miss her a lot, Tom.'

Tom slowed his pace and looked back over his shoulder. 'I certainly do,' he murmured. 'It seemed somehow like the last straw, you know? Coming on top of everything else.' He pushed back his cap and ran his fingers through his hair. With a sigh he added, 'I can't even bring myself to get another dog to take her place – at least, not yet.'

This time the two of them skirted the cove and strolled out across the headland, scrambling up through the bracken and heather until they paused for breath at a place of piled rocks, stepped and craggy, which formed a natural cave-like formation. In the small dell between the stones a carpet of soft grasses grew, sheltered from the sea breeze and studded with tiny wild flowers, all holding their faces towards the sun. By common consent and without the need for words, Tom and Morwenna sat down on the soft turf and did the same.

They sat in silence for a moment, until at last Tom cleared his throat and said with his eyes on the sea, 'Chrissie told me that you sent Kieran away. That you've finished with him.' He kept his face averted and one hand plucked restlessly at a nearby clump of grass.

Morwenna was leaning her back against a flat rock, its warmth penetrating the light cotton of her blouse. She was too keyed up, however, by Tom's disturbing proximity to relax and enjoy the sunshine, but sat rigidly upright with her hands clasped in her lap. Startled by his blunt remark, she replied, more sharply than she had intended, 'Yes, I have. What about it?'

Tom turned his head and his dark eyes regarded her steadily. He is looking better, Morwenna was thinking. Not quite so haggard and gaunt-looking now. He's lost that drained look, she thought – plenty of sleep and Maria's cooking must be doing him good.

'When I saw you that day on the cliff, when I first came home – you were kissing him and I assumed . . .' He looked away under the force of her gaze.

'You assumed what?' Morwenna's chin lifted. She wasn't going to make this easy for him because a little devil deep down inside her wanted to make him feel just slightly uncomfortable, to make up for all the uncertainty she had suffered, the long, dreary time when she had been left wondering whether he did return her love or not. She would keep him guessing for a minute or two.

'Ah yes, I see,' she said, as she shifted her position and clasped her hands around her knees, her gaze on the shifting sea where the 'white horses' of her childhood were frolicking and riding shorewards on the crest of the waves. 'Kieran and I had known each other for a long time,

220

you know. I shall always be grateful for his support when you were away for so long – and when I thought you were never coming back.'

Tom snorted and rose restlessly to his feet. 'So where's your knight in shining armour now?' he demanded, picking up a pebble and hurling it with force over the edge and into the abyss which lurked below. 'Still hanging about in case you change your mind, is he?' He turned back to Morwenna and glowered down at her.

'As a matter of fact, he's gone back to Ireland and I don't suppose I shall ever see him again,' she replied softly. She looked up into Tom's stormy face. 'Not that it's any of your business,' she added with a touch of asperity. But she couldn't keep it up. All her old feelings for him came flooding to the surface and were threatening to choke her. 'Oh, Tom, it was only a friendly kiss – just a greeting,' Morwenna replied, spreading her palms for emphasis. Tom raised a cynical eyebrow and scuffed at the grass with a toe of one boot. 'Truly,' she said evenly, raising a hand to shield her eyes from the sun's glare as she squinted up at him.

Tom abruptly stopped his pacing and came to sit beside her again. 'Mor, I must tell you this. . . . All that time when you didn't hear from me, I was trying to write a letter and put into words what I wanted to say to you – how I felt. But I couldn't do it. In those horrific surroundings – it was another world – a hell on earth. You can't begin to imagine. . . . In a place like this . . .' His gesture encompassed the sweep of sky above them, the expanse of shining sea at their feet, and came to rest on a small blue butterfly which, like a piece of cut-out sky itself, was hovering above a patch of nearby clover. 'You just can't imagine,' he said again. 'But I felt so disgusted with myself and with what I was being forced to do, that I couldn't find any words that wouldn't, well, defile you too, I suppose.' Then Tom bowed his head and rasped a hand across his face, as his shoulders heaved with the force of his emotions.

Morwenna laid a hand on his shaking back and gently patted it, her heart riven at such genuine anguish. It made her slightly ashamed of her own behaviour a few minutes ago, for in the light of Tom's agony her pettiness seemed merely childish. She bit her lip in remorse.

'Tom, about Kieran,' she said, her eyes on the seabirds wheeling effortlessly over the sheer drop which lay below them. 'Yes, he did want me to marry him.' She felt Tom's shoulder muscles stiffen. 'And I thought about it very carefully over a long period. Sometimes, when my spirits were really low and I'd forced myself to give up all hope that you might still be alive, I was tempted to accept.'

Morwenna paused and watched a herring gull alight on a rock above and survey them with a yellow eye. There was a catch in her voice as she took a breath and went on, 'I was so lonely and depressed, you see. Life was dreary, I'd been ill for several weeks with influenza, and there seemed to be nothing left to look forward to.'

Tom turned his head and was about to speak, but she raised her free hand and said, 'No, let me finish. I'd arranged to meet Kieran that day on the cliff to give him my answer and I had decided then that I would have to turn him down. It was the only honest thing to do, because I knew that I could never love him in the way that he loved me. But before I could explain all that to him, you appeared out of the blue.' She gave a watery smile. 'I thought at first that you were a ghost and that I'd conjured you up because you were in my thoughts. Until you turned and began to walk away. At that moment I realized what you had seen and how it must have looked to you.'

'As it did, of course. And I misunderstood the whole thing, didn't I?' said Tom humbly, his eyes meeting hers. Morwenna nodded. 'Then when you went storming off, and I told Kieran I couldn't marry him – that I'd decided it was better to stay single than accept him for the wrong reasons – he didn't believe me. He thought it was because you had turned up, you see.' Morwenna caught her breath raggedly and finished, 'So then I thought I'd lost you both and I tried to bury my hurt in setting up Rayle House.'

Tom straightened and turned, grasping her hand and covering it with both of his own as he looked deeply into her face, his eyes soft and gentle as he murmured under his breath something that sounded like, 'Oh, my poor darling.' But Morwenna could not be sure, because at that moment the gull gave a raucous cackle and took off from his perch with a great flapping of wings, right over their heads.

But now Tom was saying, and she could hear him clearly without further interruption, 'I didn't finish what I was saying to you just now, Mor. How, eventually, I did manage to get myself together and write you a proper letter – telling you how much I loved you, have always loved you. But then when I was blown up, it was lost along with everything else, including my memory – so it was never sent. I'm sorry – I'm *so* sorry . . . for both of us.' He carried her hand to his face and laid his cheek against it. His skin felt warm and rough, and so achingly familiar that Morwenna gasped at his touch.

Then all at once she was in his arms, and he was holding her so tightly that the breath almost left her body, and Morwenna laughed aloud at the sheer rapture of it. To have found this joy again, which she had thought lost to her for ever, was heady stuff and she was drunk with it. And as the sun reeled above them, and the waves crashed below, the salt wind caressed their heated skin and the cries of the great seabirds echoed her own happy laughter.

When she came back to earth again, it was to hear Tom's voice whispering into her hair, as he said, 'Oh, Mor, my darling girl, what a lot of time we've *lost*. All those wasted years!'

And she replied, her face serious as she tenderly placed one hand in his hair, which was being blown on end by the salt wind off the sea, and smoothed it back from his brow, 'Then we must be sure that we make the very most of the rest of our lives.'

'That's what I came to tell you today.' Tom put her from him in order to look into her face. 'I couldn't ask you this until I was sure that the mine would take me on again. But they have – I've got my old job back, Mor! In fact, they're so short of men now that they almost welcomed me with open arms.' Tom rose to his feet and pulled her up to stand beside him. With linked hands they looked out over the abyss, where far below waves of jade-green water swirled about the foot of the cliff, edged with frills of white lace where they fretted against its granite sides. 'Oh, Tom, I'm so glad,' she replied, looking up at him with her soul in her eyes.

'Oh, Morwenna, my heart,' he said, turning towards her and wrapping her in his arms again, 'I never once stopped loving you and I came to ask if you think we could possibly have a future together, you and me.' His face reddened as he looked down then and kicked one foot against the rocks. 'That is – oh, my love – would you be prepared to marry me so that we can spend the rest of our lives together?'

He must have noticed the consternation on her face as Morwenna struggled with the enormity of this prospect. Of course she wanted to marry him – wanted nothing more – for hadn't she been waiting all her adult life for just this moment? But what a dilemma she was in now, for she had set in motion a train of circumstances to which she was wholly committed – arrangements at Rayle House had gone too far now for her to give up on them, even for Tom. If only he had made his feelings known before when he had first come home.

Morwenna put a hand to her face and the tears were not far away. 'Oh, Tom, of course I want to,' she said brokenly. 'B-but . . . you see . . .' Then she looked up into his face and saw with astonishment that he was grinning broadly and that his eyes were twinkling with merriment. 'Wh-what are you laughing at?' she said, cut to the quick at his reaction to her heartache.

She tried to speak but Tom broke in, saying as he put a finger under her chin and regarded her steadily, 'Don't give me an answer for a minute, until I tell you this. Mor, I want you to know that Chrissie has told me all about the orphanage and it won't make a bit of difference to me – to us, that is. I'll be perfectly happy to help you with your plans in any way I can.'

Tom was looking tenderly down at her as Morwenna stammered, 'You – you *will*?' Her thoughts were racing, for it couldn't be true, could it? It was too good to be true, that she should have both her dreams come together so perfectly. Things like that just didn't happen in real life. But Tom was nodding and smiling and now he was saying as if he really meant it, 'I know how much this undertaking means to you, and I wouldn't dream of making you choose between us. So, how about it, my maid of the sea?'

And out over the ocean, after which she was named, a sky of flame and apricot streamed towards the horizon as the sun began its descent, casting the Brisons into sharp relief, and Morwenna looked steadily into his beloved face. This face she had known all her life, and as she looked, the long dreary years of separation slipped away with the tide as if they had never been. They had both come home and need never be parted again. Then she looked around this glorious place where they both belonged, and when she raised her head to Tom, all her soul was in her eyes as Morwenna whispered her reply.